RAVEN ROCK

ROBERT J POWER

To my perfect wife Jan.
You are my muse, my heart, my one for life.
We fight on.

1

THE HUNT

"Fuk this shit—let's fuken go!"

Fine words. Dejan thought so, and everyone else did, too. Those who were still alive, that is. Fine words, finer orders.

The lash of rain upon his face was stinging, the battering thunder of his mount under his grip was painful, and the drumming of his heart, ready to leap from his chest, made his ribs ache. As far as horse rides through the darkness in the dead of night went, this one had rightly gone to hell.

"I can't see it, not anymore," boomed a man to the right of Dejan's charging mount. On either side of them the blur of the dark evergreen leaves glistened with raindrops from the broken glow of the shattered moon. Despite the shitty light, it was hard to miss the hulking size of the brute, wavering in his saddle as though his mount struggled under his mass. "We left… *it* behind," the colossal bandit cried again, sparing a swift look back into the eternal dark where evil things crept and hunted them, and probably stole their souls while they were at it.

What hunts us?

Dejan had never believed in ungodly things, absent or not. Oh, aye, he enjoyed tales told around the fire at night. Tales so terrifying of demons, and phantoms, and spectres and probably swamp wretches too, but he had never seen any ethereal creature roaming the woods, slaying innocent wanderers, flaying bastard Black Guards—or decapitating hardened bandits, for that matter.

Until tonight, that was.

A cold shiver ran down his back. He shook in the saddle despite himself. The hairs at the back of his head rose like needles. A primal, evil thing was astir. He and his mates were hunted this awful night—and they, the hunters of this forest.

Don't look behind.

"We must have escaped it," his comrade continued desperately. Dejan wouldn't have minded the man shutting his mouth for a while. The sound of thundering hooves carried far, but so too did careless outbursts. Steps and hoofbeats were one thing; panicked voices were something else entirely.

Don't look into dark places.

Dejan knew it couldn't be a human that hunted them. For if it were human, the savagery that it had wrought would be even more terrible.

Gather yourself, fool, he thought as panic swiftly took him.

To most in the little haven of Raven Rock, he was considered a wise thinker. A right shifty bastard, too. Such things mattered when being a bandit. Such things were respected, too.

I will die tonight.

Cursing under his breath, Dejan put those skills of shrewd thinking to work. For a start, despite the terrifying chase, he tried to calm himself. Panic would get him killed. This he knew. Only composure would get him through this nightmare. He knew this also because, really, he'd been in worse situations than this.

Liar, liar—the entire night is on fire.

He convinced himself that this terrible dash through the forest, pursued by some phantom spectre, was simply a tale he would tell to his many comrades over the next few nights in the Festival of the Sash. He could almost hear the hushed melody from the Fighting Mongoose, taste the sine in his mouth and smell the aroma of safety.

"Once upon a time, I was truly fuked."

Many considered him a fine storyteller. He could drag any retelling of any old tale out for an hour if needed. It was all in the details—creating tension, the sly misdirect and the crushing, punching crescendo that would leave his listeners gasping for more and scrambling over themselves to hear it again.

"Shit. Fuk—I hear something," his imposing comrade called, desperately trying to bring his horse through a break in the trees towards the charging cart. Away from creeping, pursuing darkness and the silent evil within. Towards safety in numbers, really. Hood was his name; he was almost a decade older than Dejan. Some called him a simple giant of a man, unsuited for the subtleties of finer work. He could only stride long and boom loudly in all his endeavours.

Like right now.

Hood was a good man in Dejan's eyes. His soft and timid speech held him back as a leader. As a second-in-command, though, he was deceivingly fierce, deceivingly violent and deceivingly loyal. Such things mattered dearly—at least to Dejan. Seeing him this frightened was an unnerving thing. A foot taller than most, Hood was a powerhouse of a brute, with impressive limbs built for devastating trees, loading bricks and leading a life of toil. Also, for smashing heads where needed. Not for crying out in terror at some unknown threat following in their wake.

Possibly following.

Take a look back and see.

Suppressing his panicked curiosity, Dejan kept his eyes on the path. For only a breath did he consider ordering Hood to slow down, clasp his mighty axe and await the following threat while the rest of them took to the road at pace. Dejan suffered less of that cursed affliction called loyalty than Hood did. Another trait recognised and revered by those he called comrades in Raven Rock.

Raven Rock.

Only a few hours away and all. Oh, how he longed to be there now, tucked up in bed. Safe and secure. He held that imagining and imagined a little more while he was at it. It was something to do to calm his nerves. And most certainly not a distraction from impending death.

He thought of the sultry goddess, Kaya. Imagined her safe and secure with him. All sweaty and excitable as they writhed until dawn, his pale skin gleaming faintly against her rich, darker tone.

She does not like you that way, idiot.

"Shut up, fool," Mouse cried. His mount was galloping wildly on the other side of Dejan's. Mouse's nickname suited him just fine. He was the most delicate of waifs in stature but as mighty as any of Dejan's talented Runners. He was any bandit general's dream. He could ride like the wind against the wind, sneak through the darkest corridor in a Samaran tower and emerge unscathed with a pocket of pieces and a wicked grin. Despite his kind features, he was a cutthroat bastard, too, and such a skill was revered, respected and ultimately avoided in any bandit gathering.

But Dejan liked his bloodstained hands just fine.

"We are fine. We left that vile witch behind," Mouse snapped, glaring as though he were ready to shed a little more blood this terrible night. It was whispered that Mouse saw everything with a quicker eye than most. Or, at least, he gave the impression that he did. If Mouse had said they had left their hunter behind, Dejan would have been inclined to believe him.

"What did you see?" Hood called above the gallop. His horse was already weakening, such was the breakneck speed. Though the winds roared in his ears, Dejan could feel the give in his mount, too. He'd never had much time for mounts. He rarely had the time to tend to their needs. Better to rent one for a job and be done with the creature after. He never understood the bond some Runners had to their mounts. Still, if they got the job done, that was good enough for him.

"That foul creature was upon foot, last I saw. She will be left far behind."

On foot, no human could catch them, but still, Dejan's spine was alive with the threat of death.

He's wrong, he's wrong, he's wrong.

Ahead of the scrambling trio was a heavily armoured cart, laboured and shunting on the forest's uneven ground. It was pulled by four draught horses, charging their finest race. Their hooves thundered on the ground, kicking up mud everywhere, for the earth was damp with the driving rain. At the best of times Dejan was no fan of the rain, especially at the turn of the festival. Rain brought tighter gatherings in smaller quarters. Notably, the Fighting Mongoose tavern. And such things, in turn, brought violence among the rabble. Better the weather was warm and clear, so they could spill out into the few streets of Raven Rock and control the mayhem more easily.

Though Dejan lived a free life, he was chained to a town council seat. It was an easy enough seat, but his responsibility was to keep the peace over the two-day festival. Forgetting the terror of this race and the imaginings of a lover that would never be for a few desperate breaths, there was always a moment to fear a rain-soaked festival.

Concentrate, idiot.

He looked to the woman leading the gathering of racing fiends. Her name was Trieste. With her wavy brown hair whipping her face in the wind, he might have thought her to be an ethereal creature, not unlike the hunter behind them.

Hunted.

With her legs clinging tight to the mount, her beautiful dark eyes staring ahead, watching the path in the eternal dark green, she was fearless and skilled. She didn't look back, nor would she. She was the best rider of them all, and her task was too important: her flaming beacon, attached to her saddle and illuminating their way in the dark, waved slightly with the beat of her horse's hooves, casting shadows like ghastly fingers reaching out, clasping, clutching, suffocating. Her light drew in the hunter, no doubt, and a lesser man might have drawn away, leaving her to race the dark alone. Not impossible with skills as fine as hers.

I will not leave them behind.

Unless I have to.

The crack of the whip returned him to his senses. And to the road ahead and behind, the source of all his misery this evening.

The fuken cart.

The mounts pulling the cart answered as though their lives depended on it. Perhaps they did. Perhaps whatever hunted them would turn its claws, fangs, venom or tentacles to each of the shackled beasts when it was finished killing the Runners.

His Runners.

He looked to the suffering cart driver, Sully, who was no Runner. Was not part of his team either, but he was part of the mission. His temper began to rise, but he held himself. Instead, he watched the cart driver's old head bounce sluggishly with every drumming hoof beat.

"These city beasts cannot keep this pace," cried Sully from his perch at the front of the cart. This wasn't true at all. It was Sully who couldn't keep up with this pace. Any fool could see that, from the blood smeared all over his clothes and pooling on his seat, from how his hands shook as they grasped the reins. It was a shame. They needed pace, but Sully's weakening body could not keep up the drive. Even in the shitty light, Dejan could see the paleness of the man's withered face. Never a good thing. It had been a mistake for the old-timer to pull the bolts from his body, but he wouldn't be stopped. Couldn't be stopped.

Couldn't have just taken the pain a little longer, you old bastard?

Dejan had taken a bolt in the chest once before. He had not been stupid enough to pull the barbed piece free, though. Instead, he had taken the pain until a healer put back together what he had let slip free. Every fool in the Four Factions knew the precariousness of freeing an arrow.

In fairness, the man was always going to die regardless. That second bolt had seen to that. A deep shot that had likely taken out a lesser organ, the type of wound Dejan had never seen anyone recover from.

A shrewd-thinking cur would have checked his instincts, would have kept those bolts all snug in his innards, holding him from bleeding all over his hands, cart and clothes. In that moment, Dejan would admit to anyone that he hated the dying old bastard for denying them a few extra miles. Enough to see them through this ill-fated job.

As Sully had failed, Corvas, on the other hand, was flawless and professional. Youthful and unimposing and unperturbed by any horrors occurring around him, he was a young man who had not found himself. Such things were usually precarious on runs, but every youth had to find their feet in the first tasks thrown upon them, Dejan supposed.

Corvas might have been good-looking, but Dejan couldn't tell. Scruffy hair, firm jaw, eyes that never stopped glancing from one thing to the next. A child's set of eyes. Despite the mania of the charge, Corvas had stuck to task, hacking at the roof of the armoured cart with a prying bar as though this was all part of the plan. Which it partly was.

Before the slaughter.

Before the chasing demon thereafter.

Like Sully, Dejan did not know the boy too well. Late to the team, too, after Kaya had forbidden young Aimee from cutting her teeth under Dejan's watchful gaze. It was a good thing Aimee hadn't attended this ruin of an adventure. It had gone to shit rightly quick, and such was the bloodshed it might have soured the life for Aimee. Kaya might humour his drunken attempts at seduction, but she wouldn't ever forgive him for that misstep.

But youth could be surprising, and the youth Corvas was handling himself admirably. He was the only one who had taken no life this dreadful night. Probably a good thing too. A better thing was not letting the sight of needless bloodshed affect his task, which is precisely what he did.

Corvas kept his head firmly down while others around him lost theirs. In more ways than one.

Dejan remembered his own youthful actions when blood

was first spilt around him. He had hidden from it, too—for a shorter time than most.

"I think I have it," the boy cried, cracking open the roof entrance. A shard of metal careened wide of the cart, and swiftly, the boy dropped into the darkness as though it was nothing at all. A careless manoeuvre, should a bitter Black Guard be hidden below, all eager to punish with a blade for the loss of his comrades. Dejan ground his teeth in irritation.

That said—and it wasn't something Dejan would have told many—but should the boy spring a trap inside and pay for it with his life, it was probably better than losing a more experienced Runner. To be precise, one of Dejan's Runners.

Admittedly, it was a cruel thought, but it wasn't on Dejan to protect anyone outside his command, and the boy belonged to another leader.

A dead man now.

For a cold moment, Dejan wondered about either killing the boy outright or hobbling him completely and using him to slow the fiend that might or might not be pursuing them this awful, dreary night. Such things were necessary. Such things were expected. It wasn't like he'd need to answer for it. For who would know beyond his own group of Runners?

Profits split among four sounds rightly sweeter.

Suddenly, Corvas's voice rose high in delight. "All that city bitch's pieces are here!" he cried, appearing from the hatch with a grin. If the death of his comrades affected him, it showed little on the boy's face—clearly, this task trumped the horror he'd witnessed. For a moment, Dejan considered hiring the youth there and then. It could go either way, he supposed.

They could have left the cart behind after it all went wrong, blamed this massacre on a job turned bad and looked to some future runs without the threat of a beastie in the dark hunting them down, but Dejan was glad he hadn't. And now, he couldn't leave all these riches behind. Not after everything they'd endured. Not after everything they'd lost. Not after all the killing they'd done.

Get paid and worry about unsettled dreams in the afterlife.

This was not Dejan's first run. Nor his hundredth. That number had passed long before. He was still a young enough cur, but the road was wet with inexperienced Runners unprepared for such terrors. At the age of twelve, he'd completed his first ever task. This should have been no different to any other.

But it wasn't.

Traditionally, most heists would require just one tried and trusted group of Runners. The thing was, this heist had been more precarious than most. More savage too. He could have endured this run with his usual crew. Those four he spoke for —those four he trusted.

Too many Runners.

But he hadn't been the one to propose this heist. Oh no. It was that psycho Cole who had proposed the job, and Dejan, ever the spender, had liked the thought of a bit of extra wealth in his pocket come the festival.

Fuken Cole.

The cur was a few seasons younger than Dejan but just as fierce and cutthroat. No, that wasn't true at all. He was far worse.

He had it coming.

Dejan had swiftly learned the dirty bastard had a right taste for blood. Sometimes, such skills were necessary. Even welcomed, given the right little act of nastiness. Dejan wasn't above a bit of killing if needed, but Cole hadn't needed to go as far as he did.

When asked about it, come dawn, come survival, and with Dejan sitting pretty in the council chambers, his pockets filthy full of coin and having at last conjured the words that made Kaya open up her legs to him—when all that came about, he would gladly condemn Cole for the foulest of curs that he was. But for now, in this deadly race in the dark, he would keep his words and thoughts to himself.

Without warning, the young Black Guard's pleas rang in his ears again.

Needless savagery.

Barely come of age, he had wept for mercy in the name of a new child. After that, a new bride. Finally, how recent he was to the job as city protector, too.

Lots of new things, apparently.

With the young cub's comrades slain all around him, Cole had listened as he stood over the young lad before suddenly smashing his head in with his mace. It wasn't a killing blow. It hadn't been intended to be a killing blow. At least not immediately. A vile fuk could tell these things. Cole stood grinning, watching the boy with his now misshapen head, as he failed and flailed, crying out for mumbled unknown things, before he had finally put him at peace with a few more strikes. The young boy had been the last of the Black Guards of Spark City to fall.

Needless murder.

Three, four at most, should have died, but Cole and that fiend Ivanova had torn through them heartlessly from the first moments. Dejan remembered her cackling wildly as she did, and it was a terrible melody of abhorrent, echoed madness. Perhaps this outcry had drawn the hooded monster upon them in the first place.

Despite the outrage and disgust, Dejan had killed with them because that's what Runners did; regardless of revulsion or merciful desire, they stuck together. They killed together, they slaughtered together and most importantly, they got paid together.

Dejan glanced to the cart and wondered about the fortune within.

It'll be worth it.

Ten guards had taken to protecting this bulging cart, full of a season's taxes, to the city. Ten guards were enough to deter most groups of Runners, but not stupid, barbaric Cole and his compelling argument of wealth.

It had been Cole who died first, and that was justice. Relishing their victory, Cole had slipped into the dark to relieve himself "of a mighty burden." It was no surprise, for battle did unusual things to the body. Dejan was not without his own needs before or after a savage skirmish.

It was there that the monster had come for him, no doubt drawn forth from the darkness by his own evil nature or by the scent of blood. Whatever the reason, a flicker of movement had taken the hapless Cole, cutting him down in a flash, severing and tearing, and his wet screams had drawn Ivanova after him—all of them, in truth—swords raised into the dark, seeking prey.

It was then that Dejan had seen the torn-apart figure of Cole, strung limply over a low-hanging tree bough, already disembowelled and seeping blood upon a creature that appeared to gorge itself upon his innards. It knelt below him, humanlike but for its deeds. Dejan knew that if he gazed into the hooded face, he would see madness staring right back. Stories of his youth had filled his mind, and terror had held his step while Ivanova had charged recklessly towards her doom.

Instinct served him well these hundred and more missions, and he trusted it still. He retreated towards the dark as Ivanova screamed her hate and anguish upon the hooded creature. Drawing her blade, she charged towards the kneeling beast. A killing blow she offered, or at least it should have been. The hooded creature from another dominion had spun away impossibly fast. Faster than Dejan's eyes could follow in that light. It turned and crouched low, with a blade of its own or jagged claws of bone and flesh, deflected the strike and immediately turned upon the heavyset woman, squealing maniacally as it did. Dejan's stomach had turned, for he knew this ethereal beast was death, as he knew the shattered moon was touched by the absent gods.

He had barked orders to the remaining Runners as the hooded creature tore Ivanova apart, cutting, slicing, relishing. Only Sully had hesitated, and he paid for it. As they took to their mounts, seeking an escape, the creature had given chase, uttering piercing, guttural howls that might have been a language of the dead. And, curses upon them, it came upon them impossibly swiftly.

From its cruel, unnatural hands erupted two fierce projectiles. They couldn't have been crossbows from this realm, for the creature did not load. They merely took flight and struck true—a clever strike, too. As the creature charged them all Dejan screamed his terror, spurred his mount to run like the wind and dared not look back. Instead, he trusted fate to keep him alive. Trusted his mount just as much.

"Sully?" the boy suddenly cried as the cart shunted wildly, and Dejan was returned from monsters to the moment. To the all-important now. Dejan could see the old driver was succumbing to his wounds even quicker than they'd hoped. Gasping aloud, he slumped in his seat, dragging the reins harshly, drawing the thundering beasts from the path into the treeline over uneven ground. "Sully," the boy cried again from atop the cart as it thundered along, dangerously out of control.

"Get to the reins," Trieste cried, riding up behind the runaway cart as it bounced high, swaying to either side as the mounts dragged it onwards. Spurred on by Trieste's urgings, Corvas climbed towards the front of the cart. The boy was careless, though, and unskilled for this pace. He edged down far too slowly, and the mounts, sensing freedom, broke quicker, perhaps hoping to escape the weight they carried.

Oh, no.

With a thunderous crash, the cart went skywards for a moment, long enough that Dejan forgot all about the nasty monster hunting them, the silky skin of a lover and the horrors of a massacre still ringing in his mind. He could only imagine all the pieces about to spill out all over the land. Miraculously, the cart righted itself and thundered on.

Without Corvas atop its armoured crown.

Seeing the young boy fly through the air, screaming in his puzzled terror, was an awful sight.

At least it isn't Aimee.

Dejan wondered if the boy caught sight of Sully as he passed by. Did Sully catch sight of him as he flapped wildly, grasping at any hold he could find? There was no grip, no nook, no hope.

Despite the rush of wind and rain, gallop and tremor, they all heard the sound of bone crunching and the swift, wet silence as an iron wheel crushed the boy and the cart went on its merry way.

More pieces for us.

"That poor boy," Trieste hissed, finally looking back at the ruined mush of Corvas on the path. For a breath, neither bandit said anything more, such was the awfulness. It wasn't the first time such a fate had befallen a comrade. It was a terrible end, but was there ever a good end?

They galloped on after the cart for a time, attempting to climb aboard, until, as it careened along a crevice in a clearing thick with fallen logs and ancient brambles, the mounts pulled the cart too wide. Its wheels caught the crevice's edge and began to slow and waver. And things got so much worse.

"Not the money," Dejan cried out as the cart skidded to a stop and immediately began to teeter out over a drop into a deep, damp ravine below—a fatal fall for any man, woman, horse or cart.

Convinced the beast was still in pursuit, Hood took to the rear, watching behind, watching alongside for signs of an unnatural cloaked monster.

"Grab that beast," Dejan cried, and Mouse, ever willing to step where the boy couldn't, leapt from his horse and slid up beside the fallen Sully before taking the reins and calming the mounts against their struggles.

"Be quick and all," the diminutive bandit murmured, grabbing tightly and battling the mounts' renewed pull on the reins.

Eventually, with the mounts settled, Dejan began to relax. They all did. And why not? They had rushed for quite a time, but now his gut was settling. Whatever monster had attacked them was long behind.

After a time, they gathered their breaths. Settled their terror. Listened to the night and heard no approaching monstrous fiend. Trieste dropped from her mount.

"Is there something still out there?" she asked, rubbing madly at her eyes, no doubt singed by the torch's light. "I can't see a fuken thing; I'm rightly blinded now. I need a fuken puddle to wash my eyes in," she muttered, wandering into the treeline.

Dejan grinned. Nothing like a little gentle misfortune to distract from the true horrors. He heard her muffled curse from within the trees where her night blindness likely hindered her steps. His grin turned to a chuckle. Whatever the creature was, they'd outrun it. At least for now. Might be the entire night if their luck held.

A cautioned, careless fiend might control the cart, get it back on the road and trundle the rest of the night away. Dejan, however, thought it better to rid themselves of the cursed thing altogether, lest they come upon a monster hunting, or a pack of Spark City Guards out on a ramble. Best to rip free the riches here and make haste upon their mounts all the way to Raven Rock, where no hooded creature would dare set foot.

The absent gods might have disagreed with this, but what did they know?

"I hear nothing at all," Dejan offered, leaving Trieste to her stumbling and listening to the noise of the forest, just in case. With the spatter of rain upon them, it was hard to hear anything, but even the most skilled hunter approaching would eventually slip up and give himself away. "I think we are fine."

We are ice. We are relaxed.

His collected calm must have carried, for the others relaxed —enough to tend to task, at least. All were eager, he knew, to lock away the horrors they'd seen and go about doing the good work of the crushed Corvas who lay somewhere far back along the road.

Probably getting chewed upon by the monster.

"If we can't save the wealth, at least save the horses," muttered Hood, coming up alongside. Dropping from his mount, he climbed upon the far side of the cart to counterbalance it lest it lose the will to remain upon the path. "We need to lose some of that weight, rightly swiftly."

Mouse, tending to Sully with gentleness, wiped the blood-matted hair from the old man's eyes. "He's almost gone," he said, easing Sully free of the reins. The old man groaned pitifully and bled on the diminutive saviour. "He's fuked," he added, wiping some blood away. He eyed Dejan for permission, which was given without word, and then eased the old man up and shoved him gently from the cart over the ravine.

It was a good push, for he cleared any low-hanging debris on his way down. He managed a pathetic moan before reaching the rocks below in a heavy, echoing thud, and so ended Sully.

And then there were four.

More spoils for all.

"Did you have to?" Hood asked, heaving for breath on the cart, earning a little reprieve.

"Ah, he was weighing it down," countered Mouse.

"Fair enough," agreed Hood, thinking of the ratio of payments and preferring the "mercy" given. "Can someone shine the light on me here? I have this bitch set and balanced. As long as these horses don't spook, we'll be fine." He struggled in the dark for a few breaths. "Anyone?"

The smarter move was easing the mounts forward and hoping they held the cart if it tilted over, but at this late hour, in this weather, moving them forward might cause the entire cart to slip further down, taking the beasts with them. Manoeuvring carts over a slippery, muddy slope was no easy task for even the keenest outcast wanderers. Young boys crushed during a mission was one thing, but the deaths of innocent beasts were something else entirely to someone like Hood.

A fortune falling away into a ravine was no end for this mission, thought Dejan, strapping the mounts' reins to a nearby tree to keep them secure while they emptied the cart of its wealth. It was a plan, not a great one, but simple enough.

"Where's Trieste gotten to? That slag should be back by now," Mouse said.

"She's gone to wash the sting of the torch from her eyes," Dejan countered.

"She's taking her time. And don't call her that," muttered Hood, watching the darkness and the lack of light.

"She couldn't have gone far, just enough to tend to her needs," said Dejan, pulling at the cart while Mouse scrambled atop the roof and dove in to discover the treasures his former comrade had come upon. For a time, the only sounds in the night were the rummages of grubby hands on trinkets, jewels, taxes and shiny things. Dejan licked his lips.

"The boy wasn't wrong," Mouse called from within, and the cart heaved a little as they heard the sound of a heavy chest sliding across the floor.

"Trieste?" Hood called out, louder than necessary, and Dejan saw the concern in the brute's haggard features. Protective and adoring, too, worrying like a lover. Only then did Dejan understand the relationship both bandits had, right beneath his nose. It irked him less than he would have expected. "Trieste, where are you?"

"How long?" Dejan demanded, steadying the horses against his cry.

"How long?" Hood asked warily. Knowing he'd slipped up ever so. Just a little. Enough.

"There's plenty here," cried Mouse. "Can someone climb up and help me with it?"

"You know what I ask, brother; I wish no ill upon either of you—I ask only the truth," Dejan said, a little more coldly than he would have liked.

"I thought you had a thing for her," Hood said.

"I have my eyes on Kaya, and once our dear friend Devitt is done with her…" He suddenly thought of Kaya in Devitt's arms, and he fumed. It was no betrayal; it was merely cruelty on his best friend's part. Hood should have asked Dejan for his blessing. He wouldn't have gotten it, but that wasn't the point.

Distantly, there was a muffled thump, and a cold finger of fear crept up Dejan's back.

Hood released his hold on the cart. "I heard something." The cart held, and Dejan followed him. "Mouse, get out of there," he called. "We'll get the plunder after; we're going to find Trieste."

"Wait, what? I thought we were free and clear?" Mouse called miserably, slipping free of the cart, staring every which way into the darkness. "We were swift. Nobody could have followed this quickly. Right?"

"It's probably nothing; stay by the cart," Dejan ordered.

"Oh, fuk off. You stay by the cart; I'm going with Hood."

"We're going into the dark."

"Fine, I'll stay by the cart. Fuken don't die on me."

They followed her stumbling tracks in the low light, choosing the likeliest path through the trees where a half-blind girl could have a little privacy. Though terror took Dejan, he wouldn't leave Hood to go alone. Strength in numbers and all that. They came upon broken bushes and signs of a struggle, and Hood, relinquishing care, fled into the dark, calling for her. Dejan followed behind, wary of the noise they made. Wary of drawing a hooded figure down upon them. He played the moment in his mind and argued there was little chance any creature could have kept up with their pace, let alone waited for the opportune moment to take Trieste. He convinced himself that if it had come upon her, relieving herself in a bush, there would have been only awkward, uneasy hilarity. He began to relax for an entire breath before the screaming started.

"Oh, please no," begged Hood, charging ahead to where Trieste rested on her knees. The hooded creature wrapped itself around her, blade to her throat. Behind them both stood a loose horse that looked pushed near to death from exhaustion.

It rides a mount swifter than the wind.

"Please, don't kill her, don't kill her, I beg you. You can have the cart, all the coin pieces, fuken everything." It was not his place to offer such a thing, but Dejan would allow him to make this pledge.

"I don't want to die," begged Trieste, and her voice cut through him. Dejan had never heard fear in her voice throughout their years running together. It was a pathetic, awful thing. "Please, not like this."

Hood stepped a few feet closer, and the creature hissed and pointed a finger at the brute, ordering him to halt. It pointed to Hood's blade. "Alright, alright, I'll lose it," Trieste's lover wailed, undoing his scabbard and tossing it to the wraith hidden beneath the cloak of grey.

"We can just go on our way," Dejan whispered to the creature, casting his eyes furtively about, searching for any route out of this. He knew Hood was devastating with his fists, so he was hardly unarmed at all. "You can have it all," he conceded to the human-like creature holding their companion.

The moment held, and suddenly, Dejan had an idea. He eyed the tree behind the creature. It was perfect. Loosening his blade, he dared to recover three little pebbles from his back pocket. Three lucky pebbles for such a task would be enough.

He didn't want to lose Trieste; he wouldn't lose Trieste.

He also wanted to keep the takings. He gripped those pebbles real tight and waited for the moment. Just the right gust of wind. A moment of distraction from the beast. He was terrified, but there was a way out of this.

And then the creature slit Trieste's throat.

It wasn't slow, but it was lazy. The bandit screamed in the smaller creature's iron grip. She fought the hold, but the knife slid free, and gasping, she fell to the ground. Soon, her screams fell still, replaced by Hood's wailing anguish. He didn't reach for his blade; he simply charged the beast, and Dejan might have followed after.

Instead, he forgot his plan altogether, left the pebbles where they lay and reached for his sword.

And Hood was already dead.

Though he was felled, he kept fighting, and for a moment, he even took hold of that creature's hood and pulled it free. Dejan saw only a flash of long black hair in the low light before turning on his heel, fleeing the high-pitched screams of manic victory.

He had never feared the forest more as he retreated, fully expecting to feel the sting of a talon in his back. Smashing his face on every low-hanging branch, he charged towards the distant light. And somehow, he reached it and the waiting Mouse, crouched atop the cart with sword raised.

"Did you find her? Where's Hood? Why are you screaming?"

"We're going—leave the cart. Grab the mounts."

"Where are they?" howled Mouse. "What happened?... Ouch, what the fuk was that?"

Dejan turned to see the boy slow mid-step and simply sit down atop the cart. His legs quivered, and he grasped a projectile protruding from his chest. To be more accurate, from his heart. "Little one," Dejan moaned, and the boy wavered.

"I'm not supposed to pull this out, am I?"

"It's alright. You can pull that one out if it hurts," Dejan whispered. He wanted to run to the young man, to ease him from the world. Mouse had little time left, no matter what he did with the bolt.

"Who is that?" Mouse asked, falling from the cart, dead.

Weeping aloud and unashamed for whoever was left to observe, Dejan, the second-wealthiest bandit in Raven Rock, turned around to face the creature.

"What are you?" he whispered, and terror near took his breath.

"Born in blood is what I am," came a serene feminine voice. "Come cover me in your warmth," it demanded, pointing to his blade and gesturing invitingly before revealing her sword.

"I can't beat you, monster."

"No one can but a god." Her tone was both seductive and terrifying, as though her voice alone could tear out his soul.

"Fuk this," Dejan cried, charging the beast. Half-blinded by tears, he fell upon her and was fierce. He threw everything into every strike, but she was incredible, godly and unbeatable. She cackled in shrill delight as he missed with every lunge, slash and thrust, instead parrying, blocking, slipping away from every attack.

And then she began to counter.

Each hit was returned with a slash across a limb. As blood took flight, she screeched in delight. He heard her count as she swung, and he was terrified. His death took longer than mercy would allow. She cut into him, drawing out his agony and revelling in it.

"What do you want?" he yelled, weeping, stumbling from her onslaught against the cart where his comrade lay dead.

"I want to kill you."

"Why do this?"

"Because I was bored."

"Are you one of the Primary's whores? Are you from the city?" he demanded, and she plunged her weapon deep into him, knocking his sword free. He tried to recover it, but the creature had pinned him with her blade through the stomach. He could feel himself die, could feel his bladder release, could feel the darkness call, and he struggled against it all, scrabbling at her hood to see the beast within, and she allowed him. The cloak's hood fell free, and he gazed into godly eyes; she was beautiful, and he thought her a vile last sight before the darkness took him.

———

The vile creature felt his pulse weaken, felt his blood spill all over her and warm her against the bitter night. She leaned into his face to watch death steal upon him, and she thought it a most beautiful thing. She licked his cheek and tasted his sweat, tears and some blood, too. After a moment, she smelled and heard further things leaving his vanquished body, and she knew to leave him where he lay.

"I could have asked you questions that you would not have liked," she told the dead man as he collapsed in the mud in the middle of the forest. Time would take hold of him. His comrades, too. Time would rot them away to mulch and litter the ground with goodness. Better things could grow in these parts, and it would be beautiful. "And you would have given me the answers, too. Then how terrible would your death have been?" she asked of the man whose blood covered and warmed her.

She stretched magnificently and savoured the taste in her mouth and the scent in the air. She reloaded her wristbows and glided alongside the cart, caring little for what remained within.

"I enjoyed that, my friends," she whispered, kneeling to look at the boy. She looked around in the dark for a breath and giggled at her own carelessness. She couldn't rightly remember where she'd left her exhausted mount.

"Crimson," she called out to the beast, knowing full well it was a fitting name, for in the end, all her mounts died or fled her ferocious charge. "Where are you, my beauty?" She listened to the air and cared little for the creature. She had a hundred more to call upon were it needed. "Gone off for a snooze, haven't you?"

She looked to the sky and tasted the dry dawn to come. She could always tell when the sun would shine. Her god would disapprove of her craving warmth and sunshine, but she was far from him now. Marching in his name. Killing in his name as well. Mostly. Not tonight, though. Tonight had been a lovely release from the mundane. Tonight had been a delicate taste of blood, and it was beautiful. Her army waited no more than a few hours' march away. Concealed and awaiting the moment of the hunt.

Hunt.

She wrapped her cloak tightly around her perfect frame and savoured the respite from the chill and the rain. With her hood up and the cloak sweeping round her, few would notice her graceful stride, and that was fine. Sometimes, it was important to remain concealed. Sometimes, it was important to play the humble, meek waif. Other times, it was suitable to present herself in all her divinity—human, but a step from godliness.

His goddess, to be precise.

His chosen lover.

His chosen killer.

His perfect match.

His chosen fist for the taking of a precarious sanctuary.

And she would not let him down.

Her name was Aurora, and she liked to kill.

2

MEET THE ACTUAL GANG

Kaya sighed in the night as the children gathered around her. The rain pelted down upon her braided hair and ran down her back. She might have fought the cold as it crept upon her, but there was little point; even at this late hour, the night was still young. Usually was for any self-respecting bandits. Kaya did her best hunting at night. She figured it was time this season's children learned to do as much.

"Get them in line, Aimee," she murmured to the eldest child. Not a child at all. She was on the cusp of womanhood. Of greatness, too. Of all Kaya's little bandit cadets over the past few years, Aimee was the shiniest little piece in the pouch. The girl had her reasons. A tough life had been dealt to her, but she'd made a fine crack of what she was given. She was Kaya's favourite, too; she loved the girl like a younger sister. Kaya had never had a sister. And Aimee? Well, she had no family at all.

"Oh, come on. The little shits are wild," Aimee countered, wrapping her flapping cloak tight around her skinny form.

"You said the bad words."

Beside this standing sentry giggled two young children. Young and easily entertained by naughty words. Not even that naughty. Kaya could offer a few more choice ones to delight them, but Aimee's were so much better. Really though, all children learned naughty words regardless of where they lived, but in Raven Rock, they learned them quicker than anywhere else.

Whisper and Jak were their names. They were wholly unremarkable children, as most were at that age. That wasn't to say Kaya didn't care for them or desire greatness for them. She was their master, a fine title and far from any she'd ever expected. Kaya was no native of this beautifully savage town but had earned her place among them—a difficult thing for any outsider and worthy of praise. Kaya brought skills from other lands, welcome in this place, and in return, they gave little thought to her heavier accent, strange values and skin colour. They took what they could from her, and she from them. It was the bandit way. She wasn't born into this life, but she was born to live it. Moreover, she was born to teach those who came after. There were worse things than respect in this place, and she commanded it with a tightly clenched fist. Mostly, though, her children followed in her footsteps even if they were not her kin, her blood or her shade of beauty.

From the darkness, the last apprentice appeared. Like a wraith in the night and just as silent, he appeared from nowhere, grinning with his chiselled chin in the dark, his eyes alive with youthful exuberance. Gliding up beside Aimee, the tall young man shoved at her gently. All play, but a little message in the move too.

"Aimee, just calm them down. I could hear you all from three houses back," Ettien mocked. He was as old or as young as Aimee and just as close to adulthood and recklessness. They were two young lovers in waiting. Friendship could only last so long. It was inevitable in a place like this with pickings so slim. But Ettien was a charming young cur, and he could do worse than to have Aimee by his side.

Fine Runners they will be.

Whisper and Jak followed Aimee's gentle shoving down to where Kaya waited. For a breath, Kaya wondered if they would take the same path as so many bandits. Friends their entire life until strange feelings disrupted everything after that. Fine groups of Runners were broken up over lesser things. Greater Runner groups flourished because of it. Where trust was involved, fortune followed.

Kaya was from the Deep North, a thousand miles from Raven Rock; her appearance alluded to her unique heritage. She had lived in this region, this stronghold, for nearly twenty seasons. She was not old, but she was positively ancient to those she cared for and instructed. That was fine; that was the way with youth until they fuked up a lot and got a little old themselves. That's when they became interesting people, she mused.

She peered into the night and saw the guard watching from the wooden tower above the daunting gates, and she swallowed hard.

"So will we just get this fuken done, or what?" Aimee muttered, leaving Ettien to the rear to march the little ones towards the walls. She fell in beside Kaya, her eyes wide and searching in the night. All jests were lost, swiftly replaced by an appetite for the hunt.

Good girl.

"Watch the language, Aimee—fuk's sake," Kaya countered, and smiled at the youngsters' delight. They were quickly learning they were no longer in the safety of their parents' embrace. Beyond the walls, there was threat, adventure, bad language and really, nothing else at all. Kaya was confident that at least one naughty curse would escape their innocent lips come dawn. That was the beauty of the gutter-mouth slide and something Kaya could be proud of. She'd never trusted a soul who didn't curse when they needed to.

"This is so annoying," Ettien muttered as they neared the gate.

"This is necessary," Aimee countered curtly.

"This is tradition," offered Kaya, slipping up beside them and ushering them towards the gate. Once they were past that, it was but a couple of miles through the unforgiving Wastes in the driving rain until they came upon the hunting grounds. Not to hunt, for they few would be no match for frenzied beasts. No, this was but a taste of the hunt, a fine tradition for the youngsters of Raven Rock, all in honour of the Festival of the Sash.

The sound of their footsteps was lost in the deluge. Perfect—but not smooth enough to let them sneak past the watching guard.

"Um… hello, Kaya," the guard called from above.

Don't say something stupid.

"Oh, hello, Devitt… Can you open the gates?"

"Aye… that I can," Devitt said swiftly and began cranking the metal wheel. The screech was piercing, and Kaya ground her teeth. The guard hadn't looked away. He was staring down at her, eager to say something that would probably make them both uncomfortable. He shone his most charming smile and all. She really liked that smile. "So… going hunting, are we?"

The children cheered passionately. Talking over one another, they began to regale the guard with tales of tradition in their holiest of days, the Festival of the Sash. They gushed on about hunting and boars, and Kaya could only smile.

Devitt knew the traditions well but nodded as though learning them for the first time. There was a charm to the man.

Don't think of him like that.

He's an asshole.

Not nearly swiftly enough, the gates opened and the group slipped out into the darkness.

"Good hunting," Devitt called, and Kaya offered a weak wave and disappeared, thankful to be spared more awkward conversation.

———

"Good hunting," Devitt muttered again to himself. "Good hunting… Kaya." He sighed deeply. "Fuk it. Should have said 'Good hunting, Kaya.'" He cursed under his breath and dared a look back over the edge, watching Kaya and her little troop heading off into the distance. "I sounded nice, didn't I?" he called to his comrade, huddled against the flaming barrel of burning wood.

I did.

I definitely did.

"What are you blathering on about, young lad?" Silas asked. It wasn't a question. It was an invitation to stop talking. Subtly so.

Nevertheless, Devitt continued. "She sounded fine, didn't she?" Devitt watched for a time as the little hunting pack entered the forest. Off to scout for the hunt, a grand tradition before the festival's first day. A few boar would be a fine start to the festivities. His mouth watered at such a prospect. Boar had been scarcer than usual recently. But the feeding grounds were always flush at this time of the season.

"Wait. So you also have a thing for her?" Silas asked, leaning out over the edge of the wall and spitting into the night. "Thought it was Dejan who fancied her." The spittle caught the wind and travelled a while, too. Overall, a good spit. "I'm probably the last person to ask about such things," he added. It was a fair point.

Gazing to the forest beyond, looming dark and ominous, Devitt shivered. He hated the night shift, but it was probably a good thing for him to be seen participating in such mundane acts over the next few months. Show his face a bit more and earn a little credibility as a man of the people. He was new to the council; new to needing to impress, too. It was the burgeoning politician in him. A disgusting thing, really. But someone had to look to the future. They spoke more and more of dealings with Samara. With the redheaded princess, to be exact, who pushed for peace talks a little more than the Primary did. Things were on the up for Raven Rock, and Devitt had every intention of being part of it over the next few years. Aye, he was a talented bandit, but he was tired of the road and the threat; if Samara was open to gentrifying this little sanctuary, all the better.

"Aye, perhaps you aren't the best person to talk to," Devitt muttered to the older man. Whispers spread in these few streets easily enough, and most people knew about the problems of Silas and his young wife.

Daisy was only a handful of seasons younger than Silas, but it might have been ten to any casual viewer. Devitt liked Silas; he liked Daisy too, but not in the same room. Their arguing had echoed loudly through the listening streets of Raven Rock these last few nights. Tightly packed as the dwellings were, it was hard to have any privacy during a rousing gathering of words. The two had been married only a few years, and without children to dull the daggers, they were volatile. Devitt wondered if they would make it through this season.

Silas had seen the road and was lesser for it. The years showed in his worn features and scruffy, greying hair. He drank from a little tankard and shoved it back into his breast pocket. "To take away the chill," he'd offer when asked, but really, there wasn't a time Devitt didn't see the man swig from the sine. There was always a bitter aroma from his breath; a sluggishness to his movements, too. He'd been like that a year or so now. *No way to go about fixing any marriage,* Devitt thought.

Devitt had never been one to muddle in the murky world of love and commitment. This wasn't exactly by his design. Though he was no awful beast to gaze upon, he was simply unimpressive. He knew this because his first love had told him so, again and again, until she'd found a finer cad, one more suited to the road.

Unimpressive, for certain, but he knew he had a good smile. A man could get away with a lot with a good smile as an ally.

Kaya certainly thought so the other night.

"Oh, you didn't go and bed that beauty, did you?" Silas asked suddenly. "In the council less than a month, and you're already tallying up votes with your manhood," he added, reaching for the canister again but thinking better of it. The wind wasn't thoroughly cutting just yet, although it would blow harshly after midnight. Devitt could always tell. Most decent bandits could smell the change of weather. "Is there any woman you haven't chased in this little town?"

"Well, I haven't bedded your wife. At least not yet," Devitt countered before he could catch himself. A well-meaning jest between friends was all, but the colour rose in his companion's face.

"Watch your fuken mouth, boy," Silas growled, like a threatening hound before a snap, and Devitt felt an icy coldness run through him like a blade. That was a killer's tone.

"Ah, whisht, young fella. Sure you know I'm only jesting," Devitt mocked, shoving his comrade lightly by the shoulder—a fine political manoeuvre. Silas took the jest after a moment and returned to looking out into the forest.

For a time, they said nothing in their little guard tower, merely casting a few logs into the fire now and then to stave off the cold until Silas suddenly drew up, stretched, eyed the night once more and drank from his tankard again.

"Ah, fuk this. I'm done here for the night."

"I suppose you are," Devitt agreed. It was a fierce night. There was little need to have two guards keeping watch.

"Enjoy the wind," the older man muttered, gripping a rope and sliding down to the ground fifteen feet below. It wasn't the highest of walls. It was undoubtedly minuscule compared to Spark City's, but it did the job. A brute leaping from a mount might struggle to scale the top. As long as a defender stood with pole waiting, that is. It was a small barricade, but effective for any bandit defence nonetheless. Saying that, with no obstructions and a decent run-up, a truly agile fiend might scramble over. Or at least earn a grip and be pulled up over the top. Devitt had done it thrice in his life and stumbled a hundred times more.

Devitt doubted there would be anyone out in this weather to attack the walls at this late hour, but watching Silas disappear through the streets, sudden paranoia got the better of him. Despite the rain, the wind and his less-than-effective coat, he stepped out from the wooden shelter and began to walk the wall's perimeter. With the new line of glowing orbs illuminating his path, it was a far less treacherous wander than usual. The illuminations were set to the lowest light for this late hour, just enough to light his way and prevent him falling off, but not bright enough to alert the world of their location.

Or, more likely, rub it in the face of the cursed city.

The key was to avoid the few wires that stretched unevenly across his path. Each wire was heavy with those golden burning orbs. And each orb was a right mystery to him.

"Are there any nasties out here?" he called out into the wind, and his words were lost. Only the leaves' lonely rustle, the rain's unforgiving hiss, and the wind's eerie whistle responded. Certainly, there were no creeping brutes foolish enough to try the walls of this remarkable bandit fortress.

In no time, he completed his patrol and dipped back into the guard tower cover to warm his damp body by the fire. Rubbing his hands against the icy sting and lost in his thoughts of a warm bed, he caught sight of movement from the forest near the gate.

They've returned too soon.

Something has happened.

A figure emerged from the forest. Head dipped, hidden behind a dark, rain-sodden cloak. Devitt immediately climbed to his feet and, drawing a flaming torch, waved it above his head.

"Who marches at this unreasonable hour?" he called out menacingly. He was not scared, merely intrigued. There came no reply, not even a gesture; the figure merely continued to march towards the gates, the light, and Devitt.

He regretted Silas's absence for just a breath—strength in numbers, decisions, and all that. The figure glided as though it moved upon a thin sheet of ice. It wore a heavy pack upon its back, and Devitt frowned in puzzlement; it was strange that any wanderer would bother to march in this weather.

Too early for the festival.

"I said, who goes there, damn you?"

At this, the figure slowed and waved up to him. There was something ethereal about this interloper. Some unsettling confidence. As though the gate was no obstacle at all. Tossing his torch back by the fire, Devitt drew his bow and notched an arrow. Aye, a lone Runner of the Wastes might have arrived a little early for the festivities, no doubt hoping to find a suitable camp ahead of the masses, but such a thing did seem unlikely. Devitt immediately did not like this hooded figure at all.

"Greetings," the figure called upon seeing the weapon drawn. It whipped back its hood to reveal long, flowing blond hair beneath. "I'm just a soaked-through wanderer seeking shelter," it called out. There was an unusual sharpness to the features—pronounced and chiselled like a sculptor's grandest masterpiece. The stranger was beautiful, and Devitt took another immediate dislike for the man—especially his grin at the weapon drawn his way.

"I see no sash, friend," Devitt demanded, and the figure shrugged as though this was a ridiculous notion.

"I see you have one, though," the figure replied.

"I do."

"Well, I'm glad we discussed this. Can you open the gate so I may step inside?"

"If you have no sash, you are not welcome," Devitt warned, nodding to the black sash strapped tightly to his arm. He liked to tie it tight for nights like this when the rain threatened to work it loose. The problem was, when he flexed his muscles, it stung ever so. Holding a drawn bow caused quite the pain, but he didn't relax his pose, pain be damned.

"Where can I get such a fashionable thing?"

Devitt didn't like his tone, not one bit. It was far too reasonable, with just a faint undertone of mockery.

Fuk off with that tone.

"You must be one of us to have such a thing." Devitt's arm was really hurting now.

"Ah. Perhaps I've come to this place so I might become one of you. And then get myself a nice sash… just like yours."

"Are you here for the festival?" Devitt asked.

"No."

Devitt didn't like this wanderer's attitude. Not one little bit.

"I don't like your attitude… friend. Not one little bit."

The interloper thought about this for a moment. He folded his arms as though suddenly realising he was cold and the correct manoeuvre was to play at being cold. He tilted his head ever so sideways, as though he gazed upon prey. Every movement was a threat. Devitt could tell. He could also tell he would not allow this fiend through the gates until dawn. Rules were rules, and such rules suited him this miserable night.

"You know, friend, I could just slip away and return with a sash slashed from my cloak. Would you stop me then?" the wanderer asked. He was enjoying this battle of wits, and Devitt had a terrible, sinking feeling. Dejan, his best friend, always told him to rely on his gut, and there was something terribly unsettling stirring in his belly.

"That would be a terrible waste of a cloak."

"Aye, that's true, I suppose." The stranger's face lit up. "I have pieces, loads of pieces to offer. Can I buy my way in tonight?" He looked around conspiratorially. "I mean, who would know?"

"There's no shelter to be had in this place tonight. Everything is shut. You'd find better cover beneath those trees over there. You can come in at dawn, friend."

"They are wonderful trees," the figure replied. He didn't look back at the trees. He merely looked along the walls. He was a tall enough brute that he might have a chance at scaling the wall. "Perhaps I could shuffle along the outskirts and find better cover."

"And I'll walk alongside you with every step, watching you."

Devitt wondered if this unusual man wasn't an Alphaline from Spark City, sent here to spy upon them or commit sabotage most vile. "And who would watch the wall in all that time?" the wanderer asked thoughtfully. "What if I have a thousand comrades hiding in the dark, sniggering in glee, listening to our banter?"

Devitt pointed to a little bell on the far edge of the wooden guard shack.

My bell is far more impressive than your thousand hidden fiends.

Devitt then pointed to the treeline behind the cur. "They are nice trees; just wait a little while longer."

"You, friend, are no fun at all," the stranger muttered, finally showing frustration. It was reassuring.

He turned, wandered back to the treeline and began to put up a pitiful tent. For one so smooth in his actions, he was clumsy in erecting cover, and Devitt struggled to hide his glee. He might have been prettier and smoother than Devitt, but he was rightly shit at basic survival. No doubt he'd had little experience in the Wastes.

The wind took the sheeting, and it flapped around loosely. The ropes were far from tight, and Devitt imagined the stranger suffering quite a chill as dawn pushed in. Looking at his handiwork, the stranger must have thought so, too. He set about a fire, leaving the tent to bob pathetically in the wind. His technique could have been better, and the sparks he attempted to catch in the kindling drew little success. For a time, Devitt watched his failures in wonder until eventually, pulling the torch from its place, he called out to the fiend.

"Wanderer, for the love of everything lost, will you use this torch to catch a flame?" He cast the torch into the night, and swiftly, the wanderer slipped free of his "shelter" to clasp the fire from the damp ground and held it aloft as though it were a weapon.

"You, sir, are a gentleman," the wanderer cried, offering a deep bow before turning and setting alight his campfire. "Do you want this back?" he asked, holding the torch aloft. "If you open the gate, I can return it."

"No… no, friend. Take it as a gift," Devitt assured him, returning the bow to its place and sitting back down by the fire to stare across at the figure doing the exact same thing.

"So tell me your name, friend," Devitt called out.

This pleased the wanderer. "I thought you'd never ask."

———

Silas wrapped his cloak around himself as he walked, but it did little against the biting cold, the searing rain and the misery of the fuken night. Popping his neck as he walked through the dark, empty streets, he felt alone and infinitely older than he was.

"Real fuken old," he muttered to the absent gods, himself, and whoever. Come two nights from now, and even at this late hour, the streets would be teeming with life and wretched good times. He'd probably be among the revellers, too. Cutting in from the driving wind and its wet load, he dared another mouthful of sine from his tankard and, grimacing, swallowed the bitter stuff. Simeon's newest brew was particularly potent. Shaking the tankard and feeling its near emptiness, he wondered how much any fiend would need to drink to die of alcohol poisoning. Probably another mouthful or two more, he imagined, drinking deep and swallowing before his throat recognised the cruel assault.

"Fuk ya, Simeon," he muttered of his dealer. His sine merchant. His comrade in arms and council companion. They weren't friends. In fact, the little shit annoyed him no end. But he was a wondrous disaster at providing the shadier things in this life.

"And fuk me, too. I am bested by life."

Though he felt it, looked it, Silas was not old. Yet, here he was, pondering in the rain, doing all he could to slip home before the night was done, but also not early enough that Daisy would hear him, challenge his behaviour, make him feel a right prick for the state he was in. He could feel it, though. Feel the argument in the air. He wouldn't help himself at all. And then she wouldn't help herself either. He formed a fist and cursed himself. He was getting better at begging her to stop and warning her, too. Mostly, though, he was getting rightly skilled at explaining that he didn't mean to lash out as hard as he did.

"My woman has too much fire," he explained to the absent gods, who were unsurprisingly ignorant of such explanations. Wasn't that the way with such deities?

"And that fire is why I love her," he muttered to himself alone. The absent gods didn't need to know that either.

His wanderings back home took him through the streets of Raven Rock, few that they were. Really, the most impressive thing about this wretched town was the wall, and even then, an army could slip over easily enough, given the impetus. Truly, he was no master of tactics, but some things appeared obvious.

Yet here you are, living and hiding behind them.

The ancient structures of Raven Rock were battered and rickety and taken by every bandit playing at civility. It was no life, playing and acting as though in the city or one of the numerous settlements in her light. To Silas, this type of civilised life was one for the crows. He stayed here for her, and even then, most days, he wondered why he bothered.

He paused beneath one of the more significant buildings and looked high at the dim lights behind the curtains. Most families, lovers and companions with such quarters were likely happy with mediocrity. Silas, however, wanted the road, adventure and freedom. He still cursed himself for not going on that run with that wild fuk Cole while he had the chance. A few extra pieces in his pocket, not from Daisy's wealth, might have earned him favour, and a little pride, too.

Sighing and looking to the tallest building of all at the far end of the town, he eyed the solitary light glistening in the night and muttered a curse under his breath. This peaceful town, all snug and warm, was about to erupt in vitriol most vile—most predictable, too.

Dropping his head, he unlocked the door of their home and began the terrible march towards doom.

"Is that you, Silas?" a voice cried in panic as he stumbled through the front door. It wasn't his fault; some concealed obstacles waylaid him in the gloom. Catching himself before he made a mess of it all, he stood still, held his breath and cleared his throat, trying to sound sober.

"Aye."

He looked to the kitchen. It was a straight route. Twenty steps or so, and within, a feast of meats and bread, sandwiched upon themselves with the right amount of mustard to camouflage the stench of alcohol.

"You're home early," Daisy called from above. She didn't sound panicked anymore—just wary, like she was wondering if he was drunk. He was very drunk. He went for the kitchen, forsaking the stew on the stove, seeking meat, bread, mustard, and perhaps some butter, too.

"Aye," he shrewdly replied.

Going to task with desperate, drunken hands, he fought to slap the foodstuffs together and conceal the alcohol. Above, there came barely a shuffle. Barely the sound of her climbing out of bed, and probably coming down and… shouting at him.

"Was it too fierce out there?" she called.

"Very fierce."

The bread was already sliced. A wise move on his part earlier that evening. He went for the butter. A thin spread on both sides. All corners, too. No part would be dry. That was the first sign of a dreadful sandwich. Fuk that. He nearly considered lettuce and a little tomato but thought better of it. There wasn't time. She'd smell the aroma soon; she'd know his plan.

"Boil the stew on the stove, rightly hot, and don't you dare bring it to bed with you."

"Of course I won't." He needed to be hasty. Slapping the meat onto the bread, he poured a dollop of mustard onto its surface. And to his horror, he almost forgot the pepper. Great sandwiches were lost over lesser things. A quick sprinkle later, he found the cheese. Breaking a bit off to chew, he slathered a second slice with a little more mustard before squashing the bread tight around the meat and dropping it onto the stove.

Above him, he heard movement. It sounded heavier than hers, and he froze for a breath.

"Who's up there?"

There was silence but for the sizzle of deliciousness.

"What?"

The stove was hot, but he was swift. Sliding the knife under his sandwich, he eased it from the burning surface to reveal a light golden brown, smooth and crusty. Slipping it back down and pressing hard, he listened to the sizzle again.

"Not this jealousy shit again," she hissed, and he cringed at that tone. That starting-a-fight type of tone. "There's no one here. Would you like to come up and see if they're hiding under the bed?"

He heard no further steps, so he turned and waited for the bread to cook. On instinct, he'd accused her of having another lover. It wasn't the first time he had done it, and truthfully, she had done little to give him reason to believe her unfaithful. He was but a jealous man, holding onto his marriage by a thread. And a sandwich by even less.

"I'm sorry. I thought I heard heavy steps," he called out, sliding the knife under and freeing the golden bread, which was grilled to a perfect finish. He held it up in the light, and a drip of pale molten cheese threatened to escape.

"You know, I can smell that," she called, a little less crossly, and he shrugged, biting into his meal. Immediately, he felt better about himself and the sickly burn in his stomach. She'd caught him, but it was worth the fight, he supposed.

Completely worth it.

"I'm sorry," he said, biting once more into the gooey wonderfulness, swallowing, chewing like a hound with a meal that was three hours late. He would not share, either. "I'm on my way up."

"I should hope so, too," she said dreamily, her tone changing. He recognised that tone and immediately doubted his better senses. He hadn't heard that tone in quite a while.

His feet creaked on the ancient steps as he walked and he truly hated this house, even if it was the grandest, and he the rich husband. He hadn't married her wealth; that had merely been a bonus.

Finishing the last morsel and enjoying the serenity of stillness before the thunder, he slipped into the bedroom and felt something awry.

She was on the bed, sitting up on her knees with no clothing, and she was beautiful. Blonde and beautiful, to be precise, with firmly crafted curves, alluring to any who would gaze upon her. She smiled a dazzling smile, and as usual, it charmed him from his senses. It was that smile that won him over—kind and good and enthralling; all his, nobody else's.

"My darling," she whispered in that tone, and reached for him. His eyes were drawn to a bottle of cheap red and two glasses sitting by the bed. Both were full and calling to him. He wasn't a heavy red drinker, but he appreciated the gesture. "I wanted to surprise you," she whispered. She sounded ravenous, and it had been so long.

So fuken long.

"Are you sure it's me you were waiting on?" he said harshly. A little too harshly in truth, for her face flashed hurt, and then rage, and then sorrow, and it stung that he could cut her most with his tongue. He drew a fist and released it immediately.

He marched to the locked front window beyond their shared bed and looked from her beauty to the night beyond. It was a gut feeling. He almost expected to see a naked fiend racing away in the night. Truth was, though, they were too high up. Higher than the walls. A fiend could see for miles from this high up.

"Of course, it's you, my foolish oaf," she said warmly.

He peered further into the night and imagined no fool would dare climb out into the dark or drop to the path below. Sure way to break a neck. He could hear no whimpering. He could only hear her cover herself up. "Fine, then. Never mind my attempts, oh charming husband," she muttered from behind, and he looked at her again. And then to the silken scarf at the foot of the bed. An expensive thing, no doubt, and he felt that sudden rage come upon him.

Whore.

He wanted to scream. To strike out. To punish and to fall apart. They had grown apart these last few months, but surely she would take no other to her bed. Not yet.

"What is that?" he demanded, and she did not blink; she merely smiled that defeated smile that could break any cur's heart, and it cut through his rage.

"Oh, that? Do you like it?"

He didn't like it. He hated it.

She continued sliding over, stretching her long figure for all to gaze upon. Only him, apparently. "It is a gift from a wife to a husband. An offering of peace for the suffering we've inflicted upon each other." She held it out like a prize at a fair, with her delicious body as the Runner-up's treasure. "I bought it a week ago. Don't you like it? I hope you like it. I thought it would suit you. That it would bring out your eyes."

He looked at the silken scarf and wanted to believe it. "But I have brown eyes."

"Aye, the blue will bring them out," she insisted. As he neared her suspiciously, she leapt upon him, pulling the blue scarf around his neck and, pulling herself closer to him, whispered, "It's been so long. At least a month, my love."

It had been three months since they had furrowed. A man remembered these things. He would have thought a woman would, too.

He could smell the aroma of wine on her breath, and it was tantalising. He wanted to believe her. He looked at her stunning features and saw little deceit behind them. He imagined her discovering this lavish gift, pouring a glass for herself and him, waiting for him to return, welcoming her to him.

It had been so long.

"It is too cold, my love; I can feel you quake," he said after a time. He looked at the massive fireplace, unlit and breathing a breeze. "I might set a fire in here; we might share a glass and spend ourselves in each other's embrace.

"Oh no, my love," she cried deliriously, pulling him to her and kissing him passionately, drawing him away from the fire, towards their bed, to make their own heat. "I only want you to calm my shake," she insisted, reaching for his trousers, pulling them away swiftly before reaching for his undergarments.

"As you wish," he bellowed and fell among the bedding with her. But not before masterfully sliding low so he might discover a foul bastard beneath the bed just waiting to devastate his wife's virtue should he leave. All he found were a few discarded garments of hers and nothing else, and he finally relaxed. Finally, he allowed himself to believe things were improving between them.

For while there was desire and virtue, there was always hope.

She stripped him free of his garments but for the silken scarf. She kissed and enticed him in many artful ways, and he tended to her, and then they fell into tangles of sweat and skin and passion and fervent desires. She moaned as she set herself upon him and he upon her. Their cries echoed loudly, and to many listeners beyond, no doubt, it was incredible.

Only later, when he lay spent with nothing but the light patter of rain upon the roof and she had slipped into a satisfied sleep, did he thank the absent gods that he had slipped away from the watch a few hours early. As sleep took him, he was reassured that there would be no repercussions for such a thing. It was a stormy, awful night. Who'd come a-knocking anyway? And really, what was the worst that could happen?

———

Simeon liked his scarf. Not his scarf. Not anymore. Thanks to the quick-wittedness of Daisy the stunning, he was now without his favourite scarf, and all was rightly shit in the world.

Truth was, his mother had given him that scarf. He rarely wore it, really. Only on special occasions. Tonight was meant to be a special occasion. Daisy was supposed to say "yes" to eloping with him. If not eloping, then to admitting their love to the world. And to Silas too.

Problem was that fuker had returned early, with Simeon balls-deep inside the bastard's wife. And now, here he lay, not ten feet from the two of them, listening as they drew their bodies closer, and it was a cutting thing.

Though he loved his scarf dearly and his lover a little more than that, what he possibly loved most, at least for now, while still hiding in the shadows, was his scarfless neck.

"Oh, that's it, Daisy—keep doing that! Oh… oh… oh!"

Ugh.

Simeon shivered despite himself, despite the chill in the air, despite its nasty draft, despite the real fuken tight space he hid in. He could taste the soot of the chimney and feel its four cracked walls around him. Mostly against his fists and knees where he held himself a foot up inside the wide fireplace. Already, he was tiring, but he wasn't sure the drunken lout was. Daisy certainly wasn't.

His groin ached from being brought so near to eruption

and then abruptly denied it and brought swiftly dormant, where he painfully remained—a cruel thing. Crueller was listening to the woman he loved getting furrowed with such venomous power that he wasn't sure he'd ever be able to feel confident in their bed again. And also, the pain in his groin was something else.

And then he needed to cough.

Oh, by the absent gods, he needed to cough as he imagined the soot forming in his chest, tickling him to madness. He hated Silas even more than usual for not sweeping this monstrous thing sooner. He looked far above to the dripping night. There was a dimness above, and somewhere beyond that was freedom. Somewhere that he could cough aloud and the noise would be lost in the wind.

"Oh, my love, Silas, oh, my love—right there. Please, more, faster, harder—yes, now, now…"

He felt his stomach lurch. Felt worse for the act she played—but indeed, this was no act. She'd hinted long before that her Silas was a beast in bed. He'd laughed at such a notion, hating him even more. Now, though, it was sorrow and anguish. Married, aye, but she belonged to Simeon. He knew it in his bones. His aching, tragic bones.

He fought that cough but lost the battle. He timed it with an explosive eruption of male thrusting, and the moment passed, and he hated himself.

Simeon had always thought himself handsome enough. He sported a fine, charming goatee that hid a devastating sharp chin, and eyes that peered into any woman's soul were he inclined to charm. He was a wisp of a thing. Thin and muscly. A fine Runner, really, swift and adept at breaking into hovels in any manner of settlement he came upon. Breaking out when needed, too. That's what he believed. He was also a fool to some and a joker to most, but he had a poet's heart for any he fell for, and Daisy, sitting on the council with him, had fallen for his charms.

They began to moan in unison, and the bed began to rock harder. He loved his bride-to-be, but he could no longer listen to her tend to wifely duties, or whatever else they could be called.

Timing his moves with the grunts of devastating passion, he stepped down into the fireplace, hoping Daisy had the good sense to manoeuvre Silas's gaze away from it. A skilled thief might have crawled free, slid along the floor and reached for the door, but Simeon was so much better than that, and besides, were he to have an engaging tale to tell, he needed to be special. Turning silently back to the chimney, he began to climb, pulling himself back up in a perfect rhythm, timed to each punishing thrust from the love nest below. Upwards he rose, breathing short breaths lest he choke again on a chest-full of soot and plummet to disaster into the room below.

What she had said of Silas was vile—the thought of the punishment the bastard would inflict upon her, and Simeon too, were he to discover their secret, was truly terrifying.

I do it for love, he thought as he moved up and away from the carnal carnage below.

He did not know how long he climbed, for it was a torment twisting his body around the curve of the chimney to the night sky above. Eventually, he pulled himself free and, with feet dangling and his head a few feet from safety, he sat breathing in the night air. He could barely hear the lovers, but loving they still were, and he cursed Silas's stamina.

"Time for a little break," he muttered. He drew out his pipe, plucked a few pinches of tobacco weed from his pocket and stuffed it into the pipe. Lighting it with a few swift strikes of flint on steel, he inhaled deeply.

Lovely.

After a few moments of peaceful puffing, and enjoying the dizziness, he rose and began climbing the last leg of the journey. Within a breath, he crested the rooftop to the melody of a victorious brute who had finally spent himself.

What if he's just gotten her pregnant?

Ignoring his gnawing thoughts, Simeon sat astride the top of the roof as the echo of her quietening, satisfied moans fell silent too, and truly, it was a terrible thing. Seated upon the roof, steeling himself for the precarious slide down to the next roof while somehow avoiding breaking his neck, he smoked his tobacco weed and tried desperately to calm his raging heart. He was not used to such anger, such sorrow.

Between inhales, he thought on the many decisions that had led him to this very place in this very moment.

"What the fuk are you doing with your life?" he asked the wind, the rain, the drawing dawn, and the absent gods too. He received no answer.

Such a thing didn't bother him at all.

3

HONOURING THE GODS

"Oh, come along. You are far too slow," Kaya jeered to her diminutive companions, who grumbled and argued as they increased their pace, tripping and stumbling along. It was a pleasing night for such exertions. With little light, however, such a trek took that little bit longer. Better to face difficult things at a younger age and learn the skill of resilience rather than drift safely through life and be crushed to nothing by the first boulder ever faced, mused Kaya.

"This is stupid," argued Ettien, stumbling past her, barely keeping to the path, and Kaya sighed. No Runner lasted long in the world without a bit of grit and experience. She knew Ettien to be balanced precariously between skill and incompetence. She could push him, but sometimes a master was not nearly enough. Sometimes, the core was shaped by the hands of wiser parents. Despite their best intentions, some protected their young a little too well. Children bounced back better than any adult, albeit with scars. Sometimes scars weren't necessarily a bad thing, though, were they? She grinned, thinking how hard it was to explain such things to any loving parent, and Ettien's parents were perfectly kind and protective. In the boy's defence, he had done this march numerous times before. There wasn't a great deal he could learn. Moreover, he was a step from offering his services to a passing group of Runners soon enough.

"You know the way; trust your instincts," Kaya countered without a blink. "And lead the little ones who don't yet know the path," she added, hoping he understood the weight of leadership. It was all about testing the dark, trusting one's instincts and relying on a little luck.

"Ouch," cried one of the children, and Kaya grinned again, marching on. No one would stop to help the child. Theirs was to take the stumble and climb to their feet alone. This they did, swiftly enough, but not before muttering a few naughty words under their breath.

Only Aimee managed this route without difficulty. She moved quicker than the rest, showing her grace, listening to the night and using her keen eye to keep ahead of the pack. Pride warmed Kaya ever so. Her parents had been lost these last few years in the Deep North. On an unspectacular run, if Kaya remembered. It was a terrible fate to be without answers.

Aimee lived alone in a small room at the far end of town. Kaya did all she could to care for her, but there was only so much Aimee would allow before she resisted. Wasn't that the way of things?

"Hurry up, idiots," Aimee called out, sprinting towards the river, where, without breaking stride, she skipped halfway across using moss-covered stones as a path and never looked likely to trip. Perhaps it was the extra lessons Kaya had placed on her these last three years that served her well, for, nimbly, she spun on a toe as though in a dance and came to a stop in the centre of the river just as a gust of wind took a stubborn cloud from the shattered moon's glare and lit her up beautifully.

Ettien sighed loudly and followed down after the girl. Such stunning sights could make a hot-blooded young man feel rather taken with her.

The rest of the group stepped carefully across the river stones to the far bank, where Kaya put them to the task of cleaning their apples.

"Not a single smudge of mud upon them," Kaya insisted as they went to task, preparing for the little ritual. It was archaic practice, passed down from those who worshipped the greater of ancient gods. Few bandits did as she did, and that was fine. Kaya wasn't entirely sure of what she believed in, but it didn't hurt to take precautions should there be ethereal things at work beyond her understanding. Also, it was a nice idea to honour the land. Good for the soul and all that. Whatever the fuk that meant.

With the apples cool, crisp and clean, they journeyed deeper into the forest for the next part of the ritual. The tradition of the hunt was one of the few customs many bandits visiting Raven Rock tended to. Filling their bellies was probably the reason. Aye, there would be the grand skirmish and the drinking of ale and sine until blurry, but the grand feast was most loved by all who attended. Such a feast required boar. Plenty of boar.

Eventually, a few miles east of Raven Rock, they came upon the hunting grounds, and with them, the purest horror.

"Fuk me—that isn't right at all," Aimee cried, grabbing the little ones as they watched and pushing them to their knees. "Get down. Get quiet," she hissed.

"What happened here?" Jak whispered.

It was a fine question. After a time, when she was satisfied there were no ambushing bastards lying in wait,

Kaya rose and walked out into the hunting grounds, absently counting the slaughtered beasts by the dozen.

So much for the hunt.

The open plains stretching out before them were drenched in dark crimson. Every beast for miles had been rounded up and slaughtered. She'd never seen so many carcasses in one place before, and the spectacle was dreadful. It wasn't just the male beasts that had been slaughtered, but sows and piglets too, all brutally slain and butchered. A dreadful uneasiness came upon Kaya. Not just at the thought of the blow to the festival, for the feast would suffer terribly, but also at the decimation of the boar population in this region. There were greater things at play, and Kaya began to shake.

Spark fuken City.

Worse, this was no fresh massacre: now, the stench of rotting flesh struck her. No one in their right mind left meat like this behind—gods, the fuken waste of it all. Fumbling, she removed her apple from her pocket.

"They stink terribly," Jak said from beside her. At his feet lay a dead piglet and he did what any young child would do when not understanding terrible things. He kicked gently at it.

"They do," she agreed.

"Are all of them dead?"

"It looks as though," she replied, trying to compose herself. There was allowing children to endure horror, of course, but they would learn nothing if they looked down upon her for inflicting the lesson.

"That's too many."

"Aye, it is, little one," she offered.

Unsure of what to do, Kaya began to dig in the earth. A distasteful thing, for the ground was soft and rotten with blood.

"What are you doing?" Aimee asked warily. In the

moonlight, Kaya could see her shaking as much as she herself was.

"Do as I do," Kaya insisted, playing the master as she must.

Aye, they were alone out here this miserable night, but the Wastes were vast, and there was danger in the wind.

"It is an omen," muttered Ettien.

"This is savagery most brutal," Aimee cried. "What type of vile brutes would cause such horror?" She spoke what they all felt. It was savage, cruel and needless—a blight upon the land. If the gods watched, they would be displeased with such unnecessary cruelty.

This is no mere sign but a declaration of war, thought Kaya. Only an army could have done such a thing. Only a gathering of fiends intent on starving the inhabitants of Raven Rock. From what she'd heard, only Alphalines were vicious enough to think like that. Truthfully, though, Kaya had never met an Alphaline, nor did she want to.

"It is what it is," she declared, sounding stronger. She thought of the grandness they'd all felt on the day the electric lights had illuminated their sanctuary for the very first time. They should have known it to be too easy a task when they came upon the generator, and the cargo of lights just waiting to be pilfered. More than that, as Raven Rock glimmered with the technology of the ancients, they should have known it was only a matter of time before the city sent a message of its distaste. Sent some brutes soon after, too.

The city has come to crush us.

"We do not need to do this archaic act," Aimee hissed, but Kaya shook her head. The children were uneasy; they had come for tradition, and she would insist upon tradition.

"Whisht, Aimee. Enough of that talk around the little ones, and tend to the fruit," Kaya insisted, eyeing the uneasy children. "Same with you two little shits. Get to work. Find a patch in the dark, dig a hole, place the apple within." Sometimes, playing a part allowed the part to become real. She was Kaya the unmoveable when instructing. Shaken or no, she would behave as herself and get them swiftly back home, lest there be hidden nasties out in the dark.

Whisper and Jak went about digging as Kaya did, quietly breaking the ground, offering a gift of the crop in hopes of a better bounty—all in silence, all in quiet reverence. Perhaps the older gods watched and were grateful. Perhaps the fruit simply added nourishment to the ground.

"To the fires with this," Aimee snapped, casting her apple far into the night. A fine, petulant act; Kaya approved of defiance at the best of times. Even now.

"What a waste," Ettien mocked, biting loudly into his apple. This petulance, though, was directed at Kaya. This was an open rebellion from a young man believing himself more interesting and daring than he was. Kaya wondered if he merely showed off for Aimee. There were better ways to go about it, she mused—better ways without insulting the gods, too.

When the children finished their holes, Ettien had only a core. "Can I place this in with yours, Whisper?" he asked nastily, and Kaya hushed him to silence. Shrugging, he chewed the rest of the core in a final act of defiance that he alone thought was impressive. It was something to do, she supposed.

In the time it took them to honour the land by returning the bounty, there had been no sign of life or movement in the trees beyond, and Kaya began to relax. Aimee, less so, paced back and forth until it was time to gather up the children in preparation for returning them to 'the rock.'

"None of you shall speak of this," Kaya warned, knowing

it was a futile request. Nevertheless, her apprentices agreed, and with the cover of dark as their comrade, they marched back home, eager to be free of this place.

They were swifter than before, and quieter, too. They spent little time complaining of the cold, the wind and the late hour. Instead, they drove through the night in single file, with Aimee leading and Kaya at the rear, listening for threats.

In the last mile, beyond the river, Kaya began to count her steps, seeking the glow of their home in the night until, eventually, they came upon the tall gates of Raven Rock. Only then did she discover how relieved she was.

"Kaya?" a voice called out as she led her entourage forward.

"Aye, it's me. Open the gate, Devitt. I have some tired comrades," she hissed.

"Greetings," came a voice from behind them, and as swift as the wind, Kaya drew her sword and fell upon the creature crouching in the shadows. She held the blade to his throat, but he merely raised his hands in delicate submission. "Oh—I did not mean to alarm you."

He pulled back his hood, revealing his face, and Kaya was immediately taken with his blond locks, and his piercing, depthless eyes that suggested wisdom and kindness. A little bit of a threat as well. Not to mention a chiselled jaw that could cut stone. She kept that blade focused on him, but really, she wanted to hear him speak a little more. She did not know why.

"Who are you?" Aimee asked, skipping away behind Kaya. Cautious, but not overly scared. Beside her, it took Ettien a moment to draw his dagger.

The gates began to open and out stepped Devitt, bow drawn, eagerness in his face. "He's some wanderer. Been sitting there all night."

"Kaya, is it?" the wanderer asked, then turned and watched as the children fled through the gates, no doubt straight home, where they would tell their parents of all the dreadful occurrences this night. "What a beautiful name. It suits you."

She stared at him silently. He was male and therefore a threat. But still, something was enchanting in his face.

"I fuken told you not to try anything," Devitt warned.

"Head on in," Kaya ordered of Aimee and Ettien. They would no doubt disappear into the night and perhaps share a kiss or three. It was usually events like this that spurned such daring.

"He smells of the city," Aimee muttered, taking Ettien by the hand as she did.

"Nice to meet you all," the stranger called after them. He offered a wave, and Aimee waved back. It didn't appear as though she knew why.

"That's a shiny-looking blade," Kaya said of the stunningly decorated sword along his side.

"Oh, this old thing? A family heirloom, barely more than a souvenir." He pulled it from its scabbard and offered it to her by the grip. She accepted, testing its weight. The sword was heavy, with intricate shapes smelted into its handle's finish. Importantly, its long blade was flawless and oiled. She dared the edge and slit her skin ever so.

"Sharp souvenir," Kaya said, returning the blade and sheathing her own.

"It's not entirely ineffectual that way," he offered.

"What's your name, stranger? You're a little early for the festival."

"I'm here for no festival, but it sounds delightful. I am a mere wanderer of the road and no more. My friends call me Gray."

Devitt stepped up to him. Though just as tall, Devitt appeared lesser in this man's raw energy. She hated herself for being drawn to such things, but that was the way of it.

"Not much grey on his head at all," her lover of three nights ago suggested.

"You aren't much of a fire maker, are you?" she asked, jerking her chin towards where his feeble campfire smouldered on the damp ground, and he shrugged. He had the look of a man skilled in other things. "Come on," she said. "Let's get you inside these gates."

"Rules are rules, Kaya," Devitt countered, grabbing her arm and immediately releasing her when she glared.

"I will vouch for this young man," she snapped, and with only a few muted curses Devitt allowed them through the gates.

Gray made little noise as they walked, and she again thought him human, but not of this world. She suspected Alphalines moved as he did.

"Thank you for that," he said, looking around the small town in bemusement. He wasn't shocked by the glowing lights either, and her suspicions ran deeper. "I was chilled to the bone." There was a warmth in his tone, and for a breath, a wave of sorrow flashed across his face. "I didn't expect any kindness," he said, and she thought this strange.

For a time, they walked through the narrow streets without a word until they came upon her quarters at the far end of town. Were it the middle of the day, she would have seen him renting a tent or a room in the Fighting Mongoose, but as it was, she led him through her small domain and up some stairs. Then, drawing a key, she bade him enter the spare bedroom in her quarters.

"You understand I can't have you running around all night," she said.

"I will not forget this generosity, Kaya," he offered, looking around the room. He wore the gaze of a simple man who'd never seen the inside of a house before—like a hound allowed to sleep on a master's bed, to be precise.

"At least you'll have something nice to say about us when you return to the Primary bitch and share our secrets."

At this, he laughed loudly, and then, to her astonishment, he began to strip in front of her. First, his chest. It was a nice chest. As far as chests went, it was rather ideal. She slipped out of the doorway as he went for his trousers, allowing herself only a solitary exhale for what he revealed before locking the door.

Climbing into bed to sleep a few hours of the night away, she knew the risk she took in taking him in. As was the risk in locking him up, for were he an Alphaline as she suspected, no door would hold him for long. At least she would hear him coming, she supposed, closing her eyes and trying not to think of the terrible things she felt were coming in the wind.

4

THAT SINKING FEELING

"Well, this whole festival will be a right fuken disaster," Rook muttered. The old tracker was sitting at the table with the rest of the council members, but he did not face either bandit. He never did. It wasn't personal; it was a simple desire to leave these cramped quarters. Or so he said. Sighing, Rook stared longingly at the brightness of the day coming from the solitary window in this murky room. Kaya didn't know why they needed to sit and discuss the town's events in such low light, for it always gave the impression that they were planning deeds most nasty. Perhaps, as council members, they were inclined to do that at some point. Perhaps this room was a reminder that they dwelled among murkier things.

"Ah, less of the theatrics," argued Rua, pushing lightly at him. Like Kaya, Rua also did not come from this town but hailed from the Savage Isles and was disinclined to lose any of her accent. She wore her savagery openly, and took great pride in the metal she forged. Skilled and intelligent, she brought sharp wit to the table. Good humour, too. A few years younger than Kaya, though no less attractive, she had earned her place at this table with as many impressive deeds as anyone else. When she laughed, the town was lifted. When she chose to blink her stunning eyes seductively, many flushed at her gaze, sometimes finding a greater reason to order some metal works. Though they should have been rivals, Kaya called her a dear friend. And on the rare occasion, they sat and drank together, no better comrade, really.

"There are more than enough stocks to keep us going; we'll simply need to venture further east in search of game after the festival," Rua suggested, grinning at Rook's dull nod of agreement. "Go on, you fuken know you'd love a fine hunt," she added, speaking Rook's language. His tracking skills would be put to the test, and such a thing was welcomed by the older man. It had probably been a time since he'd gone a-running, hunting down a convoy out on the road. Any decent hunt was good to get the juices flowing.

"Something to do after the crowds disappear," he admitted, and set aside his worry over the slaughtered boars for entirely the wrong reasons.

"All the theatrics in here," Devitt muttered, playing with his steaming cup of cofe. Today, he had taken his seat as far away from Kaya as possible. Of course, he had. Usually, he sat directly across from her to gaze, challenge, charm and flirt. All innocent-like. Beside him, Dejan would play a similar game. And she loved them both as friends and little more when sober.

Fuken sine.

It was Devitt who had finally, drunkenly, and rather awkwardly bedded her. More importantly, it was Devitt and not his best friend, Dejan. And truly, she was glad of it.

Problem was, Devitt was too wary to gaze her way now, and Dejan was nowhere to be found. Likely heard the rumours in the wind and couldn't take losing the girl. Fool wasn't to know she'd only ever taken to Devitt.

Better you are taking a few days from here, Dejan.

It was typical for a group of Runners to head out on a mission and not return for at least a season or two, usually returning as though nothing had happened, as well. It was rarer for a council member to disappear without a trace, though. She looked to the empty seat where he might have sat at the old mahogany table. His was but one of two empty seats today.

"It is not ideal, but everyone will be so fuken drunk, it will hardly matter that we forgo the butchering," Andreas suggested, and the matter of the hunt felt settled immediately. Though everyone's voice was equal at the council table, Andreas's voice was more equal than others. When the council needed to speak, he spoke loudest, and few Rock inhabitants had anything bad to say about him. It was likely down to his build, which matched those of the legendary Wrek and Ulrik of Adawan. Though his fierce appearance suggested anything but, he was a kind and generous giant. Such things were rare among the bandits. As was his generous approach to the betterment of this town, exemplified by the electricity he had "stolen" from Samara.

Some said it was more about exchanging pieces disguised as banditry, so the city and sanctuary could keep face. Some also said financing such an endeavour had taken much of his wealth. All whispered that he was now a pauper marching in the finest silks.

Kaya had her thoughts on the matter. Mostly, she thought, it would only be a season or two before he'd wrangled himself a fine retirement in pieces and salt once again.

Bandits like Andreas were never poor for long. She admired him greatly; she called him a friend and a mentor. Was it not he who had welcomed her into the fold in those first few months? Was it not he who had branded her as a council member?

Aye, Andreas was impressive, and the council approved of that type of leadership. When elections to the council came, his was the first name voted in—and had been for two decades now. If he said the festival wouldn't be ruined, that was enough for her—probably for the rest of the town, too.

"We still haven't spoken on what army killed the beasties," Simeon said quietly. This charming fiend had been on the council for nearly as long as Kaya. He brought little to the table beyond a poet's silver tongue, and few bothered to respect his word. Apart from young Daisy, that was. She hung on his every syllable. And he on hers. For months now, they'd sat together in the chambers, growing closer and enjoying their little jests, not for interlopers. Afterwards, they met and talked outside these miserably hallowed walls, sharing suggestions. Both brought little to the table apart from their conjoined voting. In truth, they were a potent source to win over, for not once had they voted on opposite sides of any argument. If Kaya had liked to bet, she would have wagered there was an affair brewing between the two young members—if they hadn't writhed in secret already. A girl could tell these things.

As ever-present as the burgeoning lovers were, the opposite could be said of Daisy's husband Silas. Once, he had been passionate and outspoken, argumentative and extremely intelligent. But time and captivity take any brute's claws eventually. Lately, he had less and less time for council matters and made no effort to disguise it. Every fool, up and down the small streets of Raven Rock, knew he and Daisy were having marital issues, and Silas merely counted the days until he could be voted out of the seat and his responsibilities curtailed. Kaya wondered if their behaviour would be so open were Silas to sit among them.

"Surely, it was not the city who did such deeds?" wondered Daisy. Kaya scowled; it was what she herself would have done to send a message. She had said as much. Perhaps the girl needed to listen.

"Well, they have sent a spy. Why not a little message, too?" argued Devitt. This time, he stared at Kaya. Typical man. Wanted little to do with her after the act, but as soon as she showed interest in another male, the pettiness reared its head.

There was laughter at the table. Not entirely at her expense, but enough to make her grin. She had taken a mysterious man into her house. Just for the festivities, she promised.

"Oh, aye, how's the pretty boy?" Rua asked, and Kaya felt her face flush.

Gray, her house guest, was indeed a pleasure to gaze upon. Pleasurable to talk to as well. And curses upon him, but he was charming. Coming downstairs to discover the lock picked and a sizzling egg breakfast waiting for her had been disarming at best. It didn't matter that the food was hers; his charm eased the last of the apprehension away. He was no fine chef, but his scrambled eggs and toast were a delicious surprise. Sitting to eat with him was a finer way to spend the dawn than facing him in a battle to the death.

The following night, she hadn't bothered to lock the door. Moreover, she hadn't rushed him out the door to find shelter, either. His presence was intoxicating. And she, with nerves of steel, was unused to attraction as vibrant as this. He made no mention of his lineage, and neither did she. It was a small matter. As was the matter of his allegiances. Better an enemy closer, she mused. And if she crept into his room and charmed herself a little company one of these nights, well, that was a fine way to overcome Devitt's awkwardness.

A goddess scorned.

She looked at Devitt's pretty eyes and caught herself rightly quickly. Best to keep her mind on a greater prize and all that.

"Gray knows nothing of the slaughter; he is merely staying for the festival," Kaya argued firmly. She eyed the others, silently daring them to counter.

"He didn't even know about the festival when I met him," Devitt argued. She didn't like his tone, and Kaya gazed out the window as Rook did. Below, among the assembling masses, Gray waited for her to finish this tedious gathering—no doubt to learn what he could of the festivities, or at least to sample its finer things, with her as his guide and companion. Love and mating occurred over lesser things.

"Ah, hush, Devitt. Stop playing the part of a jealous husband," Rua hissed.

Andreas sat forward. "I don't believe in coincidences, but he could just as likely be any of a thousand wanderers we will welcome on this fine day. He might be an Alpha prick; he might be a harmless fool. Regardless, it's probably a good thing you're keeping an eye on him. And do keep an eye on him," Andreas warned.

Devitt looked as though he'd much to say on the matter but fell silent, and Kaya was grateful for the reprieve. Besides, if Devitt had any issue with a handsome, marriageable man staying with her, he would have been more than welcome to talk to her himself. He'd had plenty to say to her the night they fell into bed together. No slow build-up, just a long-awaited release of passion. She thought about the nervous writhing with Devitt, remembering the sweet everythings he'd whispered in her ear as he cupped her breast, stroked her leg and gave himself to her ultimately. And it was beautiful. Memorable. Perfect.

Come on, girl.

Don't think of him like that.

"Are we finished, then?" asked Simeon hopefully.

Andreas wasn't. His eyes lit up, he beamed a devastating smile, and the room felt less dreary. "Is the prize ready, Rua?" he asked, and here it came Rua's turn to light the place up with a devastating smile of her own.

"Of course, the pieces are ready. Shimmering and shined. Perfect, really," she said of the new suit of armour she had created for the tournament. Many a year, it was a blade embossed in jewels and gold. Other times, it was a shield or a fine axe. This year, in honour of the town's unveiling of the electric lights, Andreas had provided her with the finest steel ingots to create a stunning piece of full armour.

"Will it fit him?" Rook asked, and Andreas laughed. The table soon followed. Every day, he had been known to venture down to Rua's smithing yard simply to gaze at the pieces as she smelted them together. Kaya had seen the new armour herself. It would fit Andreas rather snugly.

"You'd never catch me entering such a tournament," Simeon suggested, and Daisy giggled. His face was far too pretty for such a thing. Of course, Daisy thought that. Kaya envisioned Gray entering such a tournament and wondered if the combat would bring forth the savage warrior in his bloodline. An Alphaline fighting in the battle would be an interesting thing indeed. But an incredible sight too.

"It is classless, altogether," Andreas agreed of the savage battering he would deal out. And possibly endure. There was no dignity in a council member entering the fray, but Andreas was happy to dig in deep with the muddy and the wretched. Perhaps that ability was another reason he stood out in public opinion. He was the type of leader you wanted to stand on a wall with, and you'd feel assured as long as he stood with you. "But I think wearing such a piece would add a little grandeur to me, so I will do what I must," he said, thumping his fist upon the table. "Come on, my friends, let's be away from this place and out to enjoy the day for what it is," he bellowed, and all the others struck their fists upon the table in agreement. No vote needed; no argument either.

"I'm heading down to the Mongoose for a drink. Does anyone want to come along?" Daisy asked, standing up and waiting for Simeon.

"I have to check things at the gate a little while," muttered Devitt, clearly unhappy at having been drafted to this task.

"Some of us have to tend to Andreas's new armour," Rua declared. "Perhaps after the presentation," she added.

"Well, I'm off to meet Smit and Fitz. They only got in last night," Rook muttered, referring to his old comrades from the early days of Adawan. Kaya liked neither man, in truth. There was a nastiness to them that she could never put her finger on.

Andreas hesitated for a breath. "That leather-wearing fuker owes me a fuken fortune. You can tell them both I aim to collect today and all," he growled, and for just a moment, he dropped that easy appearance. In its place was the fierceness of the brute he could be, should it be needed. For only a moment, Kaya felt sorry for both men, owing him whatever they did. She'd heard tales of the retribution he took when dealing with borrowed riches.

"I might join you in the pub, Daisy. Eh… will Silas be coming out?" Simeon asked innocently.

They began to leave the room, all determined to enjoy the day as best they could in their own little way.

"Have a lovely day, my friends, and be safe, too," Kaya said. She was off to accompany her new friend around the town, but they didn't need to know that.

Nor did they need to know that everything was about to change forever.

5
____

THE VISITOR

Her name was Aurora, and she liked to kill. She hadn't always wanted to kill. She knew that. But she had been born in blood, and she was made to kill. Every kill was sacred. Every kill was memorable. From a king to a lover to a friend to an enemy. It didn't matter. What mattered was the taking.

"It's alright. Everything is alright. You are doing well," Aurora whispered in the girl's ear. The girl could hear her, but she didn't reply, and that was alright, too. "That's it, just relax. It'll all be well." She inhaled deeply the scent of the brunette. She smelled of fragrant flowers, crude soap and just a taste of the road. Perhaps that was the sweat. They had walked long together, these last few hours, these two companions, but all roads ended. Like any good journey, really.

Aurora held that black sash tightly, and still, the girl wouldn't answer. She'd already forgotten the girl's name. It would matter little now; she'd have little use for it.

"There we go. Aye, keep doing that," Aurora said

approvingly as the girl squirmed in her grasp. The girl had long given up trying to pry the twisted black sash from her neck; instead, she grasped at anything around her. A few leaves, perhaps a tiny twig or so. Might be she could get a hold of a few grimy pebbles. Possibly, if Aneesa (that sounded like her name) could grip those pebbles hard and strike Aurora, she might have the strength to knock her away. Take a tooth out as well. That would be glorious, thought Aurora, and adjusting her knees in the girl's sweat-laden back, pulled harder. "Come on, fight for your life. It's the only one you have."

Finally, the girl replied, gasping and wailing as her struggling became frenzied and beautiful. She weakened, though, and Aurora loved this. As the girl faded, she suddenly released her grip.

I love this part.

As a sliver of air returned the girl to momentary life and feeble struggle, Aurora spun her around on the ground, shoving Aneesa down hard, face up now, before resuming her grip just as violently. The girl fought through tears, striking wildly, though with barely any strength.

"I needed to see your face," Aurora assured her, forcing her knees down upon the flailing, fighting arms. The girl was bigger than her and was a few years younger, too. She was nowhere near the beauty her killer was, but that was also alright. "I wanted to see your face. You have a beautiful face. I like you," she whispered as the girl wriggled, gave a fine last shake and died in her hold.

"Are you just playing?" Aurora asked coyly, but the girl's lifeless grin of horror offered no reply. "I bet you are," her killer whispered gleefully, drawing her blade and plunging it into Aneesa's throat. To her dismay and delight, the blade sank deep into the flesh without a stir. And Aurora, licking a little bead of sweat from her upper lip, sat back in the canopy of shade upon the dead girl's waist and cleaned her blade with her victim's hair. "I lose the bet so," she said to the dead girl and held aloft her stolen black sash.

Carefully wrapping it around her arm and tying it tight, she dragged the girl as far from the path as she could. It didn't need to be far. Wanderers ended up getting murdered on the road out in the Wastes every day. Her little family had slain any number of unlucky wanderers careless enough to march through their territory these last few days.

Aneesa had been no such wanderer. She'd had her route all set out. As far from Aurora's clan as possible, in fact. That hadn't saved her, though. Every step she'd taken nearer to the bandit sanctuary had brought her nearer to death. In fact, with Raven Rock no more than a mile away and its low hum already perverting the Wastes' peace, Aurora had been forced to take care of things.

She looked at the body for a time, committing the girl's death stare to memory. For reassurance on cold nights. Aurora liked to count many things, but the number of her victims was not something that took her attention. Aneesa might have been her hundredth kill or more, but there could never be enough. And counting them all would drive her to further madness.

Further madness.

Aurora thought about this and smiled. She *was* quite mad. A girl knew these things as well. She was mad, and madly in love with a god who demanded her blood. She liked this madness—always had, ever since his first godly touch. Brutal, crushing, horrific as it was.

"I did not ask, but were you with child?" Aurora Borealis

of the South asked. She touched the girl's belly and wondered again. "Probably just fat," she mused, playing with the fleshy ruin below Aneesa's chin. The girl had been well fed.

Fat and chatty, really, from the moment Aurora had come upon her—well, stalked her, to be more precise. She'd played the humble wanderer, and Aneesa had played the unassuming bandit all too well.

"Oh, are you going to Raven Rock as well?" she had asked, and Aurora had played along, emerging from the trees with the offer of companionship for the road and a little freshly salted boar. Fat girls liked gifts like that. Pregnant girls, too. For a brutal moment, Aurora considered cutting right into her belly. Just to see.

Don't fuken do that.

She held her own stomach for a time, and a gnawing agony deep in her crusted, broken soul where a modicum of sanity reigned swayed the dagger.

I have done enough.

"Perhaps I have," she decided, and climbing to her feet, she bowed to the dead girl and began to venture back into the forest, seeking the hum of her enemy. "Thank you for everything you told me," she said, as though the corpse listened. As though it cared. She thought it a fine corpse. A helpful one too. She now knew of the tournament, the numbers and, most importantly, when it would end. Such things were important to know before killing everyone. How foolish would she have felt, announcing herself and her clan in the middle of the festivities, and the bandits all rightly drunk and brave. It would have been a glorious bloodbath. She always fantasised about soaking in a bath of blood. All warm and sticky.

Divine.

Still, better to be cautious. Her god would be displeased if she lost more of her clan than needed just to satisfy her salacious appetites. It was better Aneesa had told her how swiftly this festival would end. She could be patient. More than that, she could lose herself in their world a little. Before she killed them all.

"My name is Ealis," she said aloud, practising her bandit accent ever so. Losing the Southern turn and replacing it with a gruffer tone was easy enough, as though it were an accent she'd once owned for herself. Her head spun for a breath, and she cursed and spat away the spell.

"My name is Ealis," she repeated, and was happier with the melody of her tongue. Though not completely uncommon, Southerners were rarely in the North. Too warm, too disciplined, too fuken civilised.

Where am I really from?

She might have considered this a little more, but immediately, her god's seductive tones were in her mind: *"It is a small matter."*

"As you wish, my love," she told her imaginings, and her god and lover fell quiet. This was good. She did not want him gazing upon her, for she had a terrible itch that day.

Her steps eventually led her to the outskirts of Raven Rock, and truly, she was let down at its size. She'd expected something to rival the tales of Samara itself. Great towering walls that touched the sky, a vast boundary a mile in length. Perhaps more. She had prayed for a killing zone and barricades surrounding this immoral place. To die taking or holding this bastard bandit bastion would be a beautiful fate. It should have been perfect and indomitable. Instead, she came upon little more than a settlement hidden behind a brick veneer.

She eyed these walls curiously from her place along the path and wondered might little old she scale them if given the right run-up and the right cleft in its stone surface. If not her, then at least a few of her boys might scale it easily enough. She stored that little thought away in the depths of her mind to retrieve later should the need arise. She swallowed her disappointment and wondered again why this little sanctuary was such a threat to her god's grand march.

She looked upon the walls and the gates anew, this time with a little more kindness. Closed and tight, they would hold sturdy, and a stirring of fire grew in her belly. It was the gates that she would need to tend to first. Or last. It depended on the day. The defence. How she fuken felt.

I can love this place for a time.

Playing the part of a tranquil bandit, drunk on the day's excitement, she glided down the last stretch of the way, over some old tracks, through a break in the trees, to the gathering outside. Tents were pitched along the town's border, and she counted each pointed cover as she wandered through.

She could hear the hum of people laughing, roaring, talking and challenging, and she found it reassuringly familiar. Music flittered into the air from unseen and unskilled musicians within. And she wanted to hum along, dance and announce herself as their vanquisher. She wanted them to see her in all her glowing glory, in her tranquillity, before her blades were drawn, her tongue sated with blood. She wanted to warn them of her coming but also needed to know them first. In the same way, killing Aneesa upon first meeting would have been less satisfying.

"I love it here," she whispered in her tongue before coughing away the last of her Southern drawl.

"I love it here," she repeated in her own bandit inflexion.

Perfect.

The just-about-large-enough gates remained wide open, and many bandits travelled back and forth between festival and camp and forest. She glided amongst them, taking everything in with her goddess's eyes, memorising what she could of this little stronghold and savouring it all. Being this close to the fire was enthralling, intoxicating, perfect. This was as much fun as drawing blood. Though she was sure Uden was absent from her mind, she still hid such thoughts from her god. He would not be best pleased at such liberating thoughts. Not one little bit.

"Excuse me, girl. What are you doing?" a voice called, and she snapped out of her near delirium and followed the voice to a pretty young boy a half-decade younger than she. He stood at one side of the gates, his armour tight and pristine, his glare both welcoming and challenging.

"Who, me?" she asked, flashing her most devastating smile his way. She merely had to blink a few times and lick her upper lip once as he approached to know his preference for a girl like her. There was nothing worse than charming a boy without interest.

"You didn't come through. You didn't register," he said, watching her.

"Wait, have we met?" she challenged. She smiled again, wiped the sweat from her brow and tugged at her neckline a little bit.

"Sorry, what?"

"You look so very familiar; I think we've met." They hadn't met. But sometimes, throwing back a little query was the perfect way to put them off. In truth, she did not know the rules of this festival, nor the protocol for entering this town. Aneesa had insisted the sash guaranteed entry, but that dead bitch could have been lying.

But why would she lie?

Because she hated you.

What did I ever do to her?

Well, you killed her and her baby.

I don't think she was with child.

Just fat.

"I would have remembered you, my dear," the guard said smoothly, and she smiled perfectly. The type of smile that asked what time his watch along the gate would end. She was a girl with many a smile for many occasions.

"Wait, did you watch the gate last year?" she gushed and stepped up to him, unblinking. This was easy. It always was.

"I did."

"I think I saw you there. But you weren't there the whole night, were you?"

"No, I… um… had the evening off."

She dipped her head a little to the side. "That's right. I saw you on the wall. I thought you had a nice smile. I went back to perhaps speak with you. You know, share an ale, but you were gone." It was a tragic, beautiful lie, and the smile on his face was more than just lust. It was delicate pride at hearing such a compliment. She immediately decided this boy had little confidence. Little love, too. Tormenting and tantalising a boy was as good as killing him. Easier to get her way, too. And if it made him feel a little better about himself, well, that didn't hurt, which couldn't be helped.

"Oh, that would have been wonderful," he said, beaming.

"What's your name, friend?"

"It's Devitt. Hello."

"That's right. I fuken knew it was something like that. I might have asked a few people after you," she said, and he blushed.

So fuken easy.

"So, Devitt, I'm glad we've finally met. My name is Aurora Borealis, but my friends just call me Ealis. Now, do you need me to register?"

"Aye, Ealis, and the entrance fees are… Never mind. Just let me." From his pocket, he drew out a charcoal piece, delicately took her hand, and scribed a little symbol on her wrist. "This ensures freedom of movement to any part of the festival."

"Oh, no, dear Devitt, I can pay whatever fees are needed."

She couldn't pay at all. She hadn't a piece to her name.

"This one is on me. Sure, the council has made enough money as it is."

"So, will you be on watch the whole day?" she asked and stepped close to him, resting her arms along both of his undefended ones. He froze.

"I'll be done soon enough."

"Here's hoping we'll meet up soon enough," she whispered and kissed him delicately across the lips, then drew in and offered a full-bodied hug. Before he could react, she slipped away with a wink and a final smile, walking backwards into hostile territory.

"Take care, Aurora Borealis; I hope to see you soon enough," he called, and she bowed, thinking what pretty, anxious eyes he had. She'd love to remove them with her wristbows.

"Hello, Raven Rock," she whispered in her Southern tongue, stepping through the crowd, eager to take everything in. "I'm going to tear your fuken heart out."

Aurora fell in love with this doomed place immediately. The bright colours against the dreariness of the Wastes were intoxicating, and standing below the arch of the front gate, she drank it in deeply. Around her, she felt the energy of movement and vibrancy, all too familiar—a dangerous, messy energy, as though enjoyment was soon to spill over into violence—and she licked her lips.

Her first few steps reassured her of the mayhem a-coming. Among the gathered masses, as though drawn to violence, she focused upon three bandits arguing passionately. She listened to their tones, and her mouth watered. There was murder in their eyes, passion and frenzy. Wonderful, really. A killer could tell these things. She nearly expected a knife to be drawn. And were it not for a heavyset brute, clothed in deep bronze armour, stepping between a regal man in shimmering silks and a wretched rat of a cur in leather armour, there would have been blood. A tragedy, really.

She wasn't the only spectator to this thundering argument, for around them, countless dishevelled bandits were jeering, cajoling and egging on the potential melee. It was as potent as the sine they carried in their grubby mitts, and Aurora felt right at home.

She focused on the shrewd leather-clad fuk most of all. There was something in his sly tones and his darting eyes that unsettled her wonderfully. He looked ready to strike out with a concealed dagger. He had that sneaky, hidden dagger look to him. Aurora knew this because she was also one of those sneaky concealed dagger fuks. She didn't wear her murder as openly, though, did she?

"Pay him no heed, Andreas. Come on, let's just calm down," the bronze peacemaker said, dragging his leather comrade away. It calmed the masses, but Aurora's disappointment almost overtook her mood. Thankfully, a second brawl broke out a few buildings down near the main square, where many more whooping lunatics were gathered. Mugs and fists went flying, followed by blood and cursing and outrage. It was enthralling. Aurora swayed with the crowd as though in a trance as punches were thrown and caught, claimed and countered. Some bodies triumphed, while others collapsed. And along with the crowd's collective bray, Aurora cheered names she did not know, and then, delightfully, the battle was forgotten as swiftly as it occurred. The aggrieved parties were escorted to opposite sides of the street and given ale or sine to calm the fighting fever.

I want this place for my own.

The centre of town was more deserted, but that was only because it was taken up by an arena marked out with lines drawn in crude charcoal. She did not know why this was, but it intrigued her. It didn't take long for her to realise that here was where the grand battle was about to occur, and her heart thumped in excitement. There was violence in the air, and there would be a champion. She wanted to play, too. To step in among them and display her skill for all to see. Or else be trampled by a behemoth far too robust for her. She began to pant, imagining a large-footed man beating the life from her, seeing that fuken foot stamp down upon her dazed face again and again until her skull broke in half, until she pissed herself in a last act of release.

Possibly he won't stop there.

She stumbled ever so at the thought of such an extraordinary death. She could hear her head being crushed in. Could hear her screams, and she wanted it. She needed it. She wanted to die, wanted to be done and wanted to be nothing more than a pool of mushed remains. She felt her heart quicken again, felt herself step away from the makeshift arena, and in truth, it was a difficult step.

Lifting little pouches of pieces in this place was a trickier task than usual. On several occasions, her victims turned suddenly, only to meet the eyes of a stumbling goddess, grateful for their quick reflexes that saved her a nasty fall.

The drunkards, however, were easy enough, and around the Fighting Mongoose tavern, she found much success in less than the time it took her victims to notice. She did not steal enough to cause a stir either. Just a few pieces here and there. Just enough to buy a cheese wedge at one of the many stalls lined up at every corner. It was something to do while taking in the strengths—or lack thereof—of this town's feeble defences.

There were many ladders propped at regular intervals along the wall and at every corner, leading up to the top. Climbing one of these ladders, Aurora, with cheese wedge in hand and jingling coin pieces in her pockets, balanced atop the wall and then walked its entire length with barely anyone noticing. Most certainly, few guards were patrolling up there. Their concentration was upon the wonderful masses a handful of feet below, growing in number, in drunkenness, in rowdiness.

She counted her steps all along the top. Four hundred and seventy-three steps in depth and a little less in width; the town was certainly less impressive than she had expected. She would have preferred an even number on all sides, but such things were beyond her control. It didn't really help, though.

She enjoyed watching her victims from here. Savoured the movement of life as well. In that moment, upon the wall, she felt a softness in her husk of a heart, and she wanted them all to feel her love. Wanted to take a knife to every one of them and slit them from their chins to their navels and spill everything out as well. Were she blessed with all the time in the world, she would merely have befriended an unsuspecting consort for a few days and accomplished her task from within. However, taking this sanctuary in the heat of battle would be a far more impressive thing.

"Take this place," Uden hissed in her mind, and shivers went down her spine, through her not-crushed skull as well.

"I'll do it as you say I should," she whispered to the wind. She heard her god's great pleasure once more, and she suddenly wanted to sing to him. She also wanted to put him back to sleep so she might tend to her duties without his watchful eyes upon her, beautiful as they were.

Then, thoughts of her lover disappeared as a spectre in the crowd suddenly took her attention. She watched the boy and thought him beautiful. But more than that, she saw the danger in him. She'd killed more than enough of his kind these last few years to spot an Alphaline anywhere. Even in a crowd like this. His features were too sharp, chiselled and perfect to be those of a lowly bandit. His blood was divine. As close to her god's as could be. Or rather, their blood was as close to her god's. Close, but not the same. Not at all.

Perhaps it was the way they walked, she mused: head drooped ever so to avoid unwanted attention. But if they were challenged, the aggressor would meet a bloody end. She had seen them fight up close and all personal-like. She had stories to tell and scars to remember. She had a tally of their dead, and it was impressive. More than that, her grand tally of Alphalines was uneven. She took delight at the prospect of evening it out.

"What are you doing here, rat?" she asked the wind and the Alphaline, too. Her mouth flooded in anticipation, and she needed to release her bladder. She felt a creature step over her grave, and usually, such thoughts were comforting, but looking upon this boy filled her with worry. If an Alphaline from the city had a sniff of some war, things would become very precarious. Her slaughter was to be done in secrecy. They insisted upon it with enough force that even Aurora knew better than to defy orders.

She watched the cur glide through the crowd, dodging effortlessly those he passed. Born and bred as the greatest warriors the world had ever known, Alphalines were incredible. Vile and tainted, but incredible, nonetheless. They were human—just a little better at it. And she? Well, she was something else entirely.

"Why don't you just fuk right off," she said with a sneer as a guard wandered past her, hesitating at her threat. She offered her most disarming batting of eyelids and allowed him to go on his way. Besides, she had her sash and that charcoal symbol on her wrist. She could be up here as long as she wanted.

"There's no battle coming, Alphaline," she said under her breath, hoping the fiend would depart the town by the festival's end. "There's nothing here for you at all. Not even that goddess."

Who is that?

The goddess distracted her. She loved this goddess immediately. Loved her exotic skin. Its dusky hue was as far from the dull pink of everyone else she gazed upon. She wanted to make a belt from that skin. Or a satchel bag.

She looked at her own satchel bag critically. It could be so much nicer if it were made from a fine, godly hide. For just a breath, she lost her concentration, and it was enough for her to lose track of her enemy. She scanned the crowd, but the two—the goddess and the Alphaline—were gone as swiftly as she had spotted them. "Ah, to the fires with you," she hissed at the defenceless satchel before giving up, marching to the nearest ladder, and dropping gracefully from the wall to the ground below. "Typical Alphalines," she muttered as she did, then turned and prepared to lose herself among the many bandits, still blissfully unaware of her threat.

She became settled again as she wandered through the

streets. She searched in her mind for her god to guide her, but all she heard were the piercing screams of her many potential victims. So she stopped searching and lost herself a little more in the crowd.

"I love that piece," she said serenely, stopping outside a smithy's forge. Lanced upon a pike hung a coat of arms. Heavy and steel. Shimmering and seductive.

She spoke to herself, but a stunning woman with a beaming smile replied. "Why, thank you. It is one of my finer creations." Her arms were as thick as Aurora's thighs and just as smooth. She spoke with a beautiful, unfamiliar twang, and Aurora wanted to know this woman. Slit her throat, leave her to bleed, but know her too.

"You forged this? You are skilled," Aurora purred, daring a touch of the armour.

"Don't smudge it now, my beautiful young friend; that's the grand prize this evening."

"Is it now?" Aurora liked that piece even more now. She imagined an honourable warrior out upon the battlefield, tearing dozens apart in that coat of arms and turning the tide of war. She also imagined that same warrior slipping from his horse into a pond, unable to climb out, and drowning under its weight. She really liked that, so she thought on it a little more. More than a pond. A river, in fact. Deep and cool and unexpected. She licked her lips and matched the smile of the smith who took great pride in her work.

"My money is on Andreas," the woman said conspiratorially, adding a wink.

"Oh, aye. Mine too; I had heard he was a dark horse for the tournament," Aurora said in agreement. She had yet to learn who Andreas was, of course, but the name sounded familiar. It didn't matter, though. She wanted to meet this Andreas, size him up, see how long it would take her to gut him. If Andreas had been the Alphaline, that would have been interesting. "By the way, I really love your dress," Aurora added, and strangely enough, it was the truth. It was dark leather, thick and sturdy but cut with a skilled master's flair for style.

The smith was positively delighted with the pretty girl admiring her leather outfit. She even allowed Aurora to inspect the cut as though they were close friends trading fashion secrets. Aurora nearly offered her a business proposition until a drunkard proclaiming to be the future grand champion stumbled and fell against the shimmering steel armour, eliciting the crudest, most savage outburst from the smith.

For a breath, Aurora watched the woman tear shards of pride from the wretch, and it was terrific entertainment. The drunkard had no hope of defending himself either, such was the vitriol in her cutting tone. If Aurora had ever had a mother, she would have liked that tone to be used on her now and then.

Without warning, a great chorus erupted, signalling the start of the competition, and crowds began to rush towards the grand arena. Aurora was dragged along with them, leaving behind the charming smithy with her exceptional outfit that looked likely to fit Aurora to a tee. She moved among the crowd like a cork bobbing on a current and could only embrace the day's mayhem. Her clan would wait for her. They would not dare move without her. Even if she stayed for a night with a delightful young guard. She told herself this and fought that gnawing worry in favour of this energy.

"Well, hello again, Aurora Borealis," the boy from the gate said, drawing her from her imaginings. She could only smile as he took her arm and led her through the crowd, and she felt fuken fierce.

With the howling of competition reverberating in her ears, Aurora enjoyed the madness, watching like a gleeful child as fifty combatants took to the arena, waving to the crowd, challenging their opponents, rising to the occasion. Indeed, Aurora Borealis couldn't have been happier.

Especially when the blood began to flow.

6

AT EASE WITH THE DAMNED

"So the lights come alive as darkness draws in?" Gray asked Kaya, no more than a breath after she returned to him. Questions. He wasted no time with the questions. His queries were endless now that they were more comfortable around each other. And that was fine. Questions were perfectly reasonable, even from a city spy. She thought it better she be asked the questions. She knew exactly what and what not to reveal.

"Aye, they are beautiful. You only saw them at half-light the other night. The place will shimmer and glow for miles tonight," Kaya said. "Though you are probably well used to such sights."

"I don't know at all what you mean," he countered playfully.

"Of course you don't. Sure, why would any wanderer have never seen the lights of the Spark?"

"I might not have seen Samara?" he said, admitting to nothing, and she, in turn, pushed for him to make a little slip. This was flirtation in her mind, as well as a precarious conversation. He pried and she allowed him. But not before

86

snapping back ever so. Just to remind him of his place. Just to remind him she suspected his intentions. Besides, she had intentions of her own. "Plenty of wanderers have never seen the Spark." He continued. "Perhaps the lights in Raven Rock are all the spectacle I would ever want to see."

Keep your enemies close.

"So, have you seen these infamous lights of Samara?" he questioned, unperturbed by her frown. Or perhaps reassured by it.

"Most bandits have seen Spark City up close," she said, stretching and taking in the rush of the crowd. She adored the festival. Felt alive in the rush of movement. There were many familiar faces and even more strangers, but all of them were part of an event—a break from the perfectly reasonable monotony of Raven Rock the rest of the seasons.

However, he had more questions—a glint in his eye, too. "So tell me, dear Kaya, would you let me see these grand machines of electricity that rival the great Spark?" There was little chance any brazen wanderer would see the mechanisms of such an impressive thing, especially a spy from Samara, ready to fuk the festival with some nasty espionage.

"Absolutely. I'm sure I could arrange that easily enough," she said, and he nodded, accepting this for the lie it was.

"And I take it that you wouldn't even show me the room they are in?" he said thoughtfully.

"The machines are a dozen miles away from here, wired to run from beneath the ground. You could search and never find them. Perhaps I could give you a map and leave you to it," she said and he grinned.

Holding that grin, he masterfully changed the subject. "So, what did the grand Raven Rock council think of the boars getting slaughtered?" It was a fine change of tactic and yet another attempt at gathering information. She could only offer a smile in reply. She enjoyed Gray's company. Just as much as Devitt's. Her smile faltered ever so.

"They weren't too worried about it," she lied, dragging his arm suddenly and leading him through the crowd. "Though the feast will be lesser without the beasts, there will be more than enough fine foods to gorge upon." She studied his features for signs of disappointment that the city's ruse to starve them out had fallen flat.

"And in the seasons after? Will there be no shortages?" More fuken questions. He wasn't even attempting to conceal his intentions now. A lesser fool might have reported him to the council. Kaya, however, played her part just fine.

More than that, she enjoyed it. Why? Because she wanted to leap upon him and furrow his fuken soul from him. Spy be damned. She understood attraction and the power of charm. This fuk didn't attempt to charm her, and it drove her fuken wild. Nevertheless, "Raven Rock would be no bastion if we relied on meat alone to sustain us. We have enough," she replied curtly.

"Really? What other foods do you rely upon?" he asked without pausing for breath, then stopped suddenly, standing a little closer to her than mere comrades ever should. She could feel his warmth, smell his aroma and taste the yearning he felt for her.

She did not blink first. She enjoyed this game of chase and desire. The first to crack their visage, to reveal their greater intentions and all. He might want her or want to know too much about the Rock. Regardless, Kaya knew the art of war and the brutal majesty of conquest. It paid to send an emissary before the bloodshed—one with keen eyes for defences, too. Perhaps common folk might be wary of luring in the potential enemy as she did, but Kaya was a bandit through and through. Sometimes, the thrill was in the threat.

Neither said anything for a breath. Instead, they returned to passing through the crowd. His steps were assured and smooth. He did not walk; he fuken glided, and she was with him. She wanted to keep walking. Away from it all. Away from dreariness, towards the vibrancy of the day. And they did, and for a moment, it felt less like a battle of wits and more like a preamble to love. Or just a rightly nasty roll in the hay. Whichever, really; it was all about the fun and pleasure.

The town was awash with bright colour, from the makeshift, transient stalls mostly, filled with the road traders' finest wares. Shimmering wooden, metallic and beaded goods, all calling to eager eyes. In truth, most were cheap trinkets or overly sugared delicacies designed to draw in those taken with the energy of the day. Those like Kaya, to be precise. However, she had little interest in paying a gross fortune for anything today. That wasn't to say she wasn't keen to add some jewellery to her collection of ill-gotten gains.

"You ask so many questions, pretty man," she chided Gray playfully, stopping at a stall and perusing its wares with an artificial gaze of surprise. The stall vendor, scruffy and as old as the hills, and likely as hardened from a life out in the Wastes, stared back, and she could see the greed in his eyes. His coffers had likely been full since this morning. By day's end, when he tore down his stall, he'd have enough pieces to wander for a few months more in relative wealth. She had never liked traders but hardly wished them ill.

"I have all the pretty things a goddess might need," the old vendor offered, delivering a smile as genuine as hers.

Gray shrugged and muttered a little nothing under his breath that might have been an explanation. Or else a crack in his veneer. She still knew little of her house guest even after two days, save that he rarely smiled. But she believed him to be a kind and decent man. No act could hide that; kind and decent was good enough for Kaya.

"Oh, that's rather nice," Gray said, pointing to a few shards of amethyst hanging from thin leather strips, and she could barely hide her irritation. She had her eye on them, too. Instead, she leaned in and took in her right hand a dull bracelet of brown balls that looked far too cheap to have any value. Her left hand went to task.

"The amethyst is a fine cure for a hangover, and the bracelet of agate, well, that'll match your…eyes," the vendor offered, and she held the dull piece in the light. "It protects you, as well," he offered, suggesting he'd rather do anything in this world than sell her this glorious bracelet he was attached to. She shook her head. Not for her. Not even with his tactics.

"I might be back before you close this evening," she countered. "Perhaps at a more reasonable price." She tossed the bracelet to the vendor and spun away into the crowd, disappearing immediately from the vendor's mind as he tended to a young child who'd fallen for a silken scarf of black and crimson.

Gray swayed with her as she walked through the crowd. He glided past all the many bodies as though leisurely through a field of straw. She fuken loved his walk.

"I wish I could have bought you the bracelet for the generosity you have shown me," he offered, attempting weakly to distract her from his curiosity.

"It was the necklace of amethyst that I liked," she countered, stopping by another stall as far from the last as she could. This stall provided glassware made with genuine skill and craft. The vendor looked uninterested in pushing hard for any sale, and it was no surprise. Such was the value of every piece of glass hanging safely from strings behind her, she needed to complete only a handful of sales to make this excursion to the bandit town worth it. First thing this morning, Kaya had imagined Andreas losing a little more of his fortune on a set of eight thin goblets of burning red or sapphire, just to subtly show his worth to visiting dignitaries. His home was full of ostentations, and she couldn't blame him. Collecting shiny things was any successful bandit's habit.

The sun's rays caught a few glass pieces as they swayed gently in their bindings, sending rainbows and shimmering speckles into the gathering. This was a finer attraction than any sales approach.

"Well, were I able to afford that, I would have offered such a thing," Gray muttered, and strangely, he appeared a little embarrassed at his pauper's ways.

"Your conversation is payment enough, dear Gray," she countered, dragging him away from the glass stand—from any suspicious glances, too. "Besides," she said, pulling two necklaces of amethyst from her pocket, "I got us each one." She slid one piece into his hand and donned her own.

"Fuk me, that was smooth," he gasped, amazed at her thievery. And why wouldn't he be impressed? He'd probably never stolen a thing in his Alphaline life, and certainly not from the city. It was a perfectly decent lift, especially with Gray unwittingly directing the vendor towards the pieces she had wanted, but what type of teacher would she be if she were caught in such a way?

They walked through the last of the stalls back towards the arena. There was a glorious energy in the air, and though Kaya beamed in excitement, Gray looked little more than amused by the whole affair.

"You are a serious man, aren't you?" she wondered aloud, and he shrugged.

"I suppose I am. Is that a bad thing?"

"I've heard you laugh several times, a wonderful thing, really, but I'm not sure I've seen you smile very much," she said, then caught herself before she said any more. She had never been one to be careful with words, particularly when attempting to charm, but there was a subtleness she knew she should have adhered to. Sometimes, a man only needed to know that a woman wanted him to sleep with her. Sometimes, on rare occasions, too much familiarity sent them bolting. She would very much have liked to break him in long before that. And she wouldn't mind him breaking her in a little while he was at it.

He smiled, and she could see the ruse behind it—the sorrow, too. "I can smile just fine, Kaya, especially in such good company."

Charming fuk.

The two of them looked up suddenly as a crier shouted that the fighting was about to start, and Kaya's heart beat in excitement. Grabbing Gray's hand, she hurried along with the surging crowd towards the arena. As she passed the box reserved for council members and their closest comrades, she caught sight of Devitt scurrying up towards the seating and her heart skipped a beat. He was not alone, and Kaya's stomach clenched ever so before she shook her jealousy away. Gray was intoxicating. A more potent man than Devitt. Anyone could see it. It appeared the glorious goddess by his side didn't, though, did she? She had an impressive walk, and Kaya hated her immediately.

"Devitt is his name, isn't it?" Gray asked, drawing her from her stupor.

"What?"

"The boy you are staring at? A lover? A former lover?"

She squirmed. Especially when the attractive young

woman gladly accepted the seat offered. Then she began to seethe. She did not know why.

Gray continued, "Because of the way he looked at you at the gate the other night. And the speed at which he appeared. I didn't think he'd come down from that wall for any other reason."

"Oh, aye? You could tell that in the brief time that you spoke?"

How does he know?

"If I misspoke, I am sorry," he said. "I was just wary of the boy lest he come after me for taking up so much of your time."

Do you think?

"My time is my own," she retorted. "Are you afraid he might attack you? I'm not sure he would have the ability to take you in a fight."

Gray's face darkened ever so. "You seem to believe me to be something I am not."

At this, he forced a smile again, and still, she saw the sadness behind his beautiful dark eyes. For a cold moment, she wondered if this mysterious sorrow he displayed was all an act. She thought it interesting. "Continue to play this game, dear Gray. I will show nothing but surprise when you declare your lineage and bloodline."

"I'm not that special; I'm a mere—"

"Wanderer from the road," she interrupted. "Aye, if you say so. Come on, Alphaline, let's go watch the fights."

He gripped her arm suddenly. His strength was fierce, and his tone was cold and dangerous. "Don't call me that, not ever."

"Very well, friend," she countered and pulled her arm, but he would not loosen his grip.

"I am no Alpha, nor do I wish people to think of me as

such," he urged. He only then lessened his grip, and she was intrigued further, though she thought less of herself for being impressed with his brute strength.

Definitely a hot-blooded Alpha.

"Get your hand off me, cur," she warned, and shame-facedly, he released her.

"Shit, Kaya. I'm sorry… I…um… didn't mean to grip you as I did."

She was no damsel. Nor was she intimidated. She held his shame for a breath and beamed a smile of her own. No sadness behind it at all. "Come on, you gorgeous young brute," she teased, grabbing him before he could argue or offer further apology. She inhaled him again. The scent of a long time upon the road. Something a few days of bathing couldn't entirely remove. An irresistible flavour, if truth be told, and inhaling deeply once more, she dragged him through the parting crowd as trumpets blared, roars erupted and fifty fierce warriors stepped forward to declare themselves for battle.

"I am… I… um… shouldn't have…" he started.

"Whisht, I over-spoke is all. I'm no delicate waif," she countered swiftly, hauling him towards the temporary wooden balcony overlooking the arena where their seats awaited alongside Devitt and his annoyingly alluring companion.

When they were seated among the roaring crowd, she finally released Gray's hand.

"So this is a battle of the fists alone?" he asked, studying the brutes stripping their shirts free. Fifty shirtless men of all shapes and sizes. Some posed brazenly; others shrank under the crowd's gaze. Most stretched their fine fighting frames nervously, and Kaya began to rap a beat upon her legs in excitement.

"Aye, just fists."

"It looks a little savage," Gray said, but his eyes danced excitedly. Violence, bruising and wild entertainment were in the air. Energy pulsed through the crowd like the beat of a drum or the hammering of blood. Upon a large board of slate below them, a slithering rat of an old man stood scraping the latest odds with the favoured names as a few hundred voices cried out their wagers, and Kaya could barely contain her excitement; her few pieces seemed to burn holes in her pocket. Pieces were flowing, but it was a dead bet for most. Andreas's name was scribed uppermost upon the slate with measly odds, and why wouldn't they be? The slithering betting man was no stranger to this tournament or its esteemed council member.

"Oh, it will be quite the show, dear Gray. It isn't too late for you to throw your name into the fray," she mocked. Though she knew little of Alphalines, she knew how they were drawn to violence and conflict. More than that, they desired a fine challenge. Gray's hands were clenched in fists. She could see the temptation, and this excited her. Devitt would never think about entering. Nor Dejan, either. "If you won, you could sell that fine piece of armour to pay your way." It was a half-joke, and he shrugged.

"I'm better with the blade than the fist," he said after a time, and rested his hands on his fidgeting knees. "Though you have probably realised as much," he added, and she smiled. Their game showed no slowing at all.

She gazed down at the gathered men, sizing each one up. Many she knew, and once more, the temptation to place her feeble wealth on Andreas tugged at her. He'd won thrice in a row and a handful of times in the years before. In the earlier tournaments when he'd been a little younger, he'd claimed the drunkenness of the festivals had cost him the titles. A fair excuse; many times, quite a few combatants were barely conscious, let alone fit and ready to fight. This was the first time Andreas truly needed a win. She'd not seen him touch a beverage in weeks, but she had seen his dawn routines involving sacks of sand and weighted barrels. These training regimes had left him fighting fit and fierce, and such was his muscular physique, she doubted any man would dethrone him today.

"So, can there only be male entrants to this most prestigious event," Gray asked.

"Asking after the females, are we?" Kaya mocked as though he had inadvertently given away his lineage with a few ill-chosen words.

"I'm just a hot-blooded man asking a few questions. That's all."

"Of course you are. I wonder, would Dia, the esteemed Primary, have the ability to stand with these bruisers in a fair fight?"

"She might," he countered wryly.

"To answer your question, of course, anyone can enter."

"I see no women today."

"Some have entered throughout the years; there are no rules against it, nor are any advantages given."

"Has a woman ever won?"

"No."

"Has a woman ever come close to winning?"

"Why would it matter how close she came if she didn't win?"

"I just thought…"

"Unlike the city, most of us in the Rock don't give a fuk about what lies between the legs; we care about victory and the spoils."

"You are an interesting people," Gray said after a

thoughtful moment. It was a fine choice of words. If nothing else, they might entice her to educate him on her people. An understanding of their ways would certainly do no harm, anyway, when he reported back to Dia. *If* he reported back to Dia. It might even give the Alphaline something to think on, beyond the belief they were little more than savages. "I see some fire in that one," he added, pointing to a hulking brute kneeling in the sands at the arena's edge. Each breath he took was slow and careful. A fighter's breath, no doubt. He looked at Kaya, but she did not seem to recognise him. "Aye, he would be my choice. He looks a right killer."

"If you have a piece to spare, you might place a wager."

"He's not Andreas, is he?" Gray asked. She'd made no secret of her admiration for the hulking behemoth. Nor of her belief that he would win this battle outright.

"No, no, that whippet isn't my man. Now *that's* my man," she said, pointing to Andreas, who remained still and composed in the midst of the growing excitement. His muscles appeared to glisten in the sun. He stretched each powerful limb, his eyes cold and scrutinising, wary of any fiend who neared, lest they take a chance at dethroning the champion in the first few breaths of violence.

"He's a big fuker, but that doesn't always help in a fight," Gray said. "Now, my man over there is like a caged bull, just rearing to thunder into any and all."

At this, Kaya laughed heartily. As did Devitt, who leaned towards his potential rival. "Andreas is no mere mountain with tree trunks for arms, swinging lazily, easily felled," Devitt growled before returning to charm the alluring girl whose eyes looked stolen from the stars above.

"We will see," Gray countered, leaning back in his chair.

A hush fell over the crowd as Rua, looking impressive in her savage fighter's attire, took to the centre of the arena and began to recite the honour of the fist. There would be no boar this festival, but no fool dared postpone such a prestigious tournament, and Rua declared as much before reeling off the rules of the battle.

Kaya and most others barely listened, instead murmuring of the day's entertainment, arguing over their bets or speculating about whose round it would be, come evening drinks.

Gray, however, listened intently.

"… until unable to rise, or unwilling to…" Rua barked out.

"I see," Gray murmured.

"… no killing blows either…"

"Probably a good thing, too," Gray agreed to himself.

"Before my time, that was a problem," Kaya noted.

Suddenly, Aimee appeared beside the couple. Her eyes were bright and excited, no doubt due to a stolen beverage or three, and from the smoky aroma emanating from her clothes, a few twigs of tobacco weed smoked down a back alley.

"Hello," she slurred, and carefully fell between Kaya and Gray. She appeared perfectly happy with her chosen seating. "Who are you, again?" she said, turning to Gray. "You are gorgeous."

"Oh, for fuk's sake, pay this ruin no attention," Kaya said, pulling Aimee's wandering hands away from Gray, who smiled politely.

"Oh, now I remember, this is the spy?" she cried in delight. Behind them, Kaya heard Devitt laugh.

"It's very nice to meet you, little one," Gray said.

"Aimee, thank you very much," the drunken cub countered. She yawned widely and laid her head on Kaya's knee.

"Ah, so you are Kaya's star pupil," Gray said, clearly

delighting the young girl, who immediately hid her pride behind another exaggerated yawn.

"Of course I am."

Rua rattled off further rules, including no gouging of eyes, which, too, was a problem years before. Hair pulling was allowed, but it was frowned upon, Kaya told Gray, and his enthusiasm grew as the fight neared its commencement. Enemy to the town or no, he was looking forward to the great entertainment to come. Violence was universal. Good times, too.

"So what's to stop a group of lads charging Andreas in the first moments?" Gray asked.

"Aye, a fair question. It's amazing how best-laid plans fall to pieces once the madness of violence erupts," Kaya said.

"Everyone has a plan until first contact with a fist," Aimee added.

Below, there was a round of applause as Rua announced that her handiwork had been set aside as the tournament's first and only prize. That done, she raised her arm and the crowd fell still in anticipation. The warriors dashed out across the sandy arena to take their places. Some flexed their muscles; others looked ready to spew their belly's contents and a careful few took shallow, controlled breaths in preparation for the coming violence.

"Your boy looks ready to shit himself," Kaya said, and Devitt again laughed from behind them. Kaya didn't look back. Wouldn't give the cur the satisfaction of acknowledging him. He sat with a goddess? She was enamoured with a god.

Gray smiled, though, and that was enough. "Do you know his name?" he said, looking down at the hulking brute he'd noticed before. "No? Fuk it, I will call him Emir. He looks like an Emir," he declared.

"I've never met an Emir, but I'll take your word for it."

"Emir" charged first as Rua dropped her arms. He swiftly became a blur amidst the movement around him, and Kaya, unable to contain herself, screamed in excitement. So did Aimee, who had sat bolt upright, no longer languishing in her childish, drunken haze.

"Fuk me," cried Gray in awe, and it was Kaya's turn to feel pride.

The fifty warriors tore into each other as though this were war. Fists were thrown, and the air came alive with the crack of bone and the slap of spilling blood. Howls of anguish and ecstasy soon followed as the arena erupted with devastation.

Less impressive was Andreas, who immediately retreated beneath a hail of blows from three fierce fighters, all keen to dethrone the king.

"Your boy is in trouble, as I suggested," Gray offered.

"No, they are," Aimee said coldly as Andreas blocked the combinations, ducking well wide of those he couldn't block.

"They say he was a master pugilist many years ago," Kaya explained, and as though to prove her point, Andreas, gliding around the arena and matching the timing of his assailants, began to counter each attack. His strikes were unlike those of any other fighter in the arena. He did not swing his body, loudly pronouncing his attack. Instead, he eased his shoulders ever so. As he did, his fists shot out effortlessly, driving home devastating strikes into the faces and sternums of his competitors. Snapping cracks echoed loudly, and blood began to stream from those foolish three who had, only moments ago, believed their numbers were enough to take on one so skilled.

"I've seen nothing like it," Gray offered, leaning forward and marvelling as Andreas knocked one fiend unconscious to the ground, glided away, and then, with a swift hooking blow, shattered the nose of the second man, leaving him wailing and beaten in the sand, before calmly moving on to the third. This poor fiend he took his time with, not to be cruel but instead to pace himself. As his victim floundered and gasped, Andreas kept his back to the edge of the arena, ensuring that no other fiend could slip up behind him and deal a deathly blow.

Should have placed a bet.

In a desperate attempt to turn the inevitable tide, his opponent swung fiercely with combinations worthy of any skilled fighter. For ten blows he held out, but Andreas, without shifting his stance, leaping for cover or blocking each hammer as it neared his serene face, merely weaved, ducked and slipped wide as though dancing to a melody of his own hearing.

Gasping, his opponent soon fell in the dust, suffering a few swift strikes to his chin, where he lay defeated, and Andreas, as fresh as the morning after a rainy night, stepped towards the next combatant, breathing as calmly as though he were out in the Wastes with nothing but the wind for company.

"Well, I still think my boy Emir will take him," Gray offered weakly.

"Whoever this Emir is, I'll take that bet," Aimee said, drawing three pieces from her pocket.

Gray hesitated for only a breath before holding out the amethyst necklace. "All I have is this, little one," he said, and Kaya's stomach dropped ever so. Despite her pride in having snatched it, she knew it was worth less than three pieces—but that wasn't the fuken point, was it?

Down below, the combatants continued to wage war upon each other, and roars of appreciation swept through the crowd as strikes were thrown and bodies collapsed to the dust, unable to rise again.

And there were many. In no time, the lesser fighters were threshed like wheat, and as bodies fell away, the roars grew louder and the contest intensified. Plans were thrown asunder as alliances were born and betrayed by brothers and enemies, all in the name of glory. It was fantastic entertainment, though perhaps not for those who had bet a large sum on a long shot.

Soon enough, there were less than a dozen remaining. A breath after that, less than ten, Andreas most impressive among them. Each of his manoeuvres was met with gasps and the loudest cheers. He didn't appear to notice the attention, or perhaps he just ignored it, for his face was calm and composed. Despite never catching his breath, he eased himself across the arena, all the while outstriking and outthinking every opponent careless enough to attempt to dethrone him. He was awe-inspiring, and Kaya cheered with the crowd.

"Your boy is struggling," Devitt cried down to Gray.

"I'm not worried at all," lied Gray, laughing as two slithering thugs ambushed Emir.

"Oh, I know those two," Aimee cried out deliriously. "That's Fitz and Smit attacking him, isn't it?"

Kaya knew well these two foul bastards. One burly and charmless, the other slithering and unsettling. Once allied to Wrek and Ulrik, each with a fine, gruesome legacy to his name, it was unusual to see them this far from Adawan. Moreover, it was downright strange to see them bothering to compete at all. Stepping into an arena after having fallen out with the champion over a tiny fortune was foolish. Only then did she realise that Andreas was here not just for victory itself but for a crack at these fools, all nice and legal. As Andreas destroyed yet another opponent, his sixth of the day at least, she could see him edging further towards those greasy fiends, and she giggled at the battering they would both receive at his hands.

But it seemed the fiends had other plans.

Andreas was swift, but not swift enough to save Emir from their assault.

Emir must have fancied his chances against Smit, for though he was a little smaller, his fists had been rather impressive throughout. In truth, Gray had not chosen poorly at all. But alas, although Emir was a fighter, he was inexperienced at this type of melee. He fell upon Smit, pummelling the cur as though he owed him money. As the larger man tucked his hands against his head, protecting himself from the blows, Emir went to task breaking through his defence and never saw the driving strike to the back of the head from the wretched Fitz.

"Oh, fuk me, will you watch out," Grey cried, but it was already over. Dazed, Emir fell to his knees, allowing Smit to counterattack with heavy, pounding blows that never seemed to stop. Having dazed Emir, Fitz stepped back and stood guard as his larger companion destroyed Gray's wager.

"Well, looks like your boy just fell," Aimee cried in delight as Smit left Emir unconscious in the dust.

As Gray handed over the necklace, Kaya ground her teeth but let little emotion show on her face. Before Aimee could take the jewellery, however, she caught sight of the matching piece around Kaya's neck.

"On second thoughts, keep your treasure, city boy," she said, turning back to the horror to come.

"I lost all fair, like," Gray said.

"You can be sure I'd not have paid were the tables turned," she said, sniffing, and Kaya loved the girl that little more. She had little reason to suspect what Kaya felt for this charming brute, but she knew something. More than that, she recognised the necklace was worth far more than pieces alone.

"It seems people are conspiring," muttered Gray, and Kaya did not understand. Nor did it matter, because Andreas, for the first time in the entire battle, charged forward, seeking a victim. His last two victims, to be precise, and Kaya, left the hurtful gesture from Gray in its place and focused on greater things, like a little comeuppance for that leather-wearing weasel Fitz, who immediately retreated behind his larger comrade, bravely allowing his friend to take the beating for him.

It was a fine beating, too.

Using controlled aggression and swift footwork, Andreas danced around the slightly smaller bandit, striking freely. Smit could only block every second or third strike as his head rocked back violently with each controlled jab. It was art, it was menacing and it was inevitable.

Gray was certainly impressed. His head twitched with every manoeuvre. "It appears you were right about Andreas. I've never seen a giant move as swiftly as him in battle, nor any man or woman, really." He held the amethyst necklace for a breath, then kissed the rock and placed it back around his neck. It was a peculiar act, thought Kaya.

"Andreas has this," Aimee said, and most others agreed. Below them, some early payments had already been dished out as the bookie attempted to earn the last few pieces should there be a sudden twist in the outcome.

Dazing Smit and leaving him gasping upon his knees, Andreas sought out Fitz, who attempted to skulk away from the battering he deserved, only to be caught by the swift hunter who, pinning him at the far corner of the arena, dished out brutality tenfold that he'd administered to anyone else.

To the leather-wearing cur's credit, he was quicker with

his fists than Smit and, like the rat he was, put up a fight once cornered—for a time at least. The two combatants roared abuse at each other as they struck out, but such was the din of the crowd, Kaya could tell little of their words, although she doubted their sportsmanship.

All too swiftly, the strikes overcame Fitz's defence and the fight became one-sided. More than that, it became obvious that the warriors were mismatched. Andreas sought humiliation for the smaller man and soon enough had it: he suddenly turned his attention to Fitz's lower abdomen. His meaty fists became blurs. His victim was unable to counter or parry, and each punishing blow winded Fitz agonisingly, evidenced by the desperate yelps he let out until he could barely stand. Perhaps, were Andreas not leaning in so close, supporting his weight, Fitz might have fallen to the ground and given in altogether, suffering the humiliation of no knockout blow. As it was, growing laughter and cries of wonder rang out around the arena, and the pitiful cur kept attempting to strike. But without any wind in his lungs or strength in his knees, each blow landed weakly, and Andreas made a mockery of each strike by refusing to block, instead allowing the fiend to take open shots at him.

A foolish thing, thought Kaya as, from nowhere, in one last-ditch effort, Fitz threw an illegal blow toward his vanquisher—a nasty uppercut, attempting to break Andreas's nose and send the bones deep into his brain.

The world slowed, and Kaya held her breath.

But Andreas saw it coming a mile off and merely slipped wide. He immediately knew the cur's intention, though, and punished him. Gripping Fitz tightly and locking his arm like a tavern bouncer, he drove his free hand down again and again upon his competitor before leaving him to fall to the dirt in shame—

—just in time to meet the cracking right strike of Smit, who had recovered just enough to attempt one final assault. Andreas's lip was split open, but he took the blow like any grand champion. Licking the blood away, he met the cur one last time, quickly recovering his composure and discipline, and pummelled Smit to the ground.

He stepped away to ensure it was all nice and legal, and the crowd erupted in triumph. Smit struggled in the dust, and Andreas's mocking tones could be heard around the arena, daring him to rise and avenge himself.

And then a strange glint of silver caught in the sun. *A peculiar thing*, thought Kaya, for who among the battered fiends would carry steel upon them? It glimmered a little more for a breath, dancing upon Smit's quaking body as he struggled to rise.

Andreas must have seen it, too, for he spun around and met the blade through the belly.

"Oh, fuk me," cried Gray, standing up in horror.

The blade didn't remain in his belly for long. Fitz drew it out and plunged it in again a dozen more times, through his heart, his neck, his groin, his face. Fitz stabbed and stabbed, and this time, it was Andreas who leaned upon his vanquisher, unable to fall, escape or survive.

The crowd screamed and, almost as one, they rushed towards the centre of the arena, but the world had stopped its turning, and there was no hope.

A cluster of onlookers fell upon Fitz, dragging the blade from his bloody hand. Only then was Andreas allowed the dignity of collapsing in the wet sand, where much of his innards already rested. The would-be rescuers beat and contained Fitz in moments, and he roared in triumph for his crimes even as they shackled him and tore him from the arena, leaving devastation behind, along with the slurred cries of Smit, demanding his prize for victory.

"Take the child from this," Gray demanded, shoving Kaya toward Aimee, who was screaming in horror.

"Let her see this so she might learn," Kaya hissed, standing behind Aimee, who fell silent, stunned by the terrible spectacle. Around them, people fled for the exits or flocked to the gruesome sight in the centre of the ring. It was mayhem, but Kaya was serene. Though she quivered slightly, she could not look away, though it ached seeing her friend die so terribly. A king of a man who deserved a finer end than this.

"Can you see how swift blows from such a small dagger took out a behemoth?" Kaya whispered in the girl's ear, and Aimee nodded, taking instruction. Even in her lowest moment, when there was nothing else, Kaya would teach what she could.

7

BOLD LITTLE BEAST WITH BILLIONS OF BACKS

She thought his sweaty grip was firm and reassuring, and she allowed him to pull her gently through the crowds of people. The hour was late, and the stench of the drunken, messy festival rose from the streets into the sky. There were a thousand better places she would have rather been, but as he led her, she settled into her fate. More than that, her body was covered in little goosebumps from anticipation: that, or the chill in the night wind as it carried the season's rain inwards. Probably a good thing for the town's morale, she imagined, thinking of the blood smearing the ground where the body had bled dry—nothing like a bit of rain to wash away the horror, to clear the streets as the hour grew late.

Unsurprisingly, he knew the way and, unlocking the door, eased her through the doorway, daring a kiss as he did. She liked his kiss. It was a kiss of delicate nervousness, and such things were alluring. He tasted her as she did him, and then, pulling away, she bit her lower lip and guided his hand to her, already aflame with desire. Aye, he didn't need to ask; she was rightly desperate to be ravaged, and he was her choice for the night. So she dragged him to her, grinding against him as though there was nothing between their bodies. That would soon change, and she was excited and desperate. It had been a time, and his delicate awkwardness drove her fuken wild.

"I, um, would like to bathe…" he whispered, breaking her kiss, and she wanted to bathe with him. Pull his clothing free, scrub whatever he needed scrubbing. Easy, even strokes in the warm water, and then easy strokes beneath the sheets right after. Suddenly, he was away from her, leading her to their bedding where he would take his fill of her, and she would give everything to him. This was what spies did, was it not? Learn what they could, even if they had to furrow some of that information out of their quarry.

"You are so beautiful," she whispered, and he bent down by the fireplace, setting a flame to stave off the chill of the night. He did so with more skill than she ever did, and immediately, the bedroom lit up, and she could gaze upon him now.

"Really?" he asked in surprise. "I'll… be just a few breaths," he pledged.

"Perhaps you would like me to bathe too," she asked shyly. She dared not sniff her underarms in his presence, but it had been a day, an evening, too. With her chosen lover, she was always made to bathe; perhaps all men desired as much. She, on the other hand, desired the taste of natural things. Though possibly not too natural, in truth. If he felt the need to clean himself, that was fine by her.

"Aye, perhaps you go first," he said after a moment's thought. In the far room, she could see the large basin of water.

Let's just fuken furrow, boy.

"Oh, alright. I suppose I am the guest," she offered,

taking little offence. Playing the meek part he desired. That was fine. That was natural. She slipped past him and stripped her garments free, allowing him to gaze at her perfect body for a breath before dousing herself in chilled water that shook her wonderfully.

"I didn't expect this," he called out, and she grinned. Of course, he didn't. He had far less confidence than he deserved. She liked his naïve charm and dry wit; indeed, beneath those eyes, she saw strength. And that taste of his was wonderful.

She was skilled and swift in many things, and scrubbing was no different. Afterwards, she slathered herself in a few choice oils to tantalise before presenting herself to him, all shiny and pretty like he desired. She would play her part and get what she desired, too. Her hand grazed his groin as she slipped beneath the sheets. Clean and smelling of flowers, she rolled around in them for a time, enjoying their freshness; she wondered if he was not entirely unlike her. Afflicted with thoughts that crippled.

"I'm sorry for asking you to bathe," he said, eventually reappearing from the dark room, displaying himself in less than glory. It was alright; it was a cold room. It was much better under the covers.

"I spent a day walking in the Wastes; it is nice to smell of purer things," she whispered, whipping the bedsheets back, revealing her spread legs and her full womanly glory. "You are beautiful," she repeated as he climbed over her. He did not touch her, though. Instead, he gazed with lust at her, so she played along.

"It is you who are most beautiful," he said after arousal at last took him. And kneeling to meet him face to face, she reached and took his arousal in her hand, and he hesitated. It was a perfectly fine manhood. Like all manhoods, really. She'd gorged herself upon far smaller and left herself sated. She liked being sated. She had also climbed upon larger beasts that had frightened her. She enjoyed being frightened, too. He was perfectly delightful, and she could see his anticipation as he gazed down at her actions. His excitement. His fears. All men were the same. And wonderfully different, too.

They kissed for a wonderful time, and she enjoyed his caressing of her nakedness. Nervous touches that perhaps were not entirely unfamiliar with her heavenly form, but still grateful for the allowing.

With a sudden grip, he pulled her to him, and she giggled in his grasp. She felt him protruding against her, and she wrapped her arms around his waist, and he laid her in the bedding of sweet, fresh cleanliness, and she gasped as he edged into her.

Almost.

"Oh, that's it, Devitt… um… just a little lower," she whispered as he struggled upon her ever so. She took his weight and moved herself with his gentle attempts. "Oh, I want it… just a little lower, nearly there. Oh… um… oh… I can almost…"

She could feel his body tense, and she reached to kiss him. All men were wonderful, and sometimes all men could struggle. Her name was Aurora Borealis, and she was a godly lover, even to mere mortals who needed a little coaxing.

"I'm… trying… I'm sorry… I'll get it…"

"You are so beautiful. I want you in me, I want all of you, oh, nearly… Oh… this is so nice… nearly."

"I'm sorry," he said again, this time urgently. He thought he had struck gold. He hadn't. He thrust against her. His manhood, ever close, slid upwards and wide, and she ground against him, seeking a joining, seeking pleasure. "I can't… get into you."

She kissed him again, and he was frustrated. He tasted her, less urgently this time, and she wrapped her legs around him. "I'm having a wonderful time."

"I'm glad someone is," he cried, gripping for purchase among the lovely sheets. Linen, they were. Fresh, expensive and ever so smooth. Fantastic for rolling in. Most of the time. "Ah, fuk sake," he gasped, trying to stay over her and slipping as though upon a steep, wet mountain track. She could only smile, playing the part her god would disapprove of. She felt it before he did. And then he did. "Oh no. Give me a breath," he said, wilting, and what vigour he'd had fell limply upon her most sensitive area.

Perhaps if you just placed it in there all delicately and waited a while…

She could have offered advice, but she could see his embarrassment in the light from the fire. Such unfamiliar emotions were intriguing. She licked his shoulder; a bead of sweat was trickling down it. She bit his neck right after, kissing him as she did.

"We'll try again," she whispered, pushing him off her, and he offered no struggle. He lay back in the sheets in dismay.

"I'm sorry, I don't know what happened."

"Am I your first?"

"No, that's not it at all."

"Does this happen all the time?" she asked, stroking his chest and then below. He shook ever so. She slipped across his chest, pushing herself against him, awaiting his arousal. She would have him this night regardless of this moment. Sometimes, furrowing was perfect and excellent. Sometimes, furrowing was as awkward as fuk and tenfold the perfection.

Sometimes, though, a cur could place his hands upon her throat and bring her to unconsciousness, and those times were divine and perfect. It was all perfect. If she could have convinced him of such things he might have relaxed a little more, might have begun to enjoy himself too. Manhoods were all well and fine, but a true lover, regardless of ability, brought every fuken limb to the battle and made it purest wonderment. She wished all men knew this.

"It has happened… before…" He started to weep. And she was upon him counting the tears as they streamed from his eyes.

"I… I can't believe what happened to my friend."

"He was a good friend," she agreed. It felt like the thing to say. She took his hand and placed it where she liked it best: above her most godly. He immediately went to touch her where flaccid members couldn't enter, and gently, she held him in place.

Just here is perfect.

She rubbed his fingers where she adored, and after a slow breath, he began to follow.

"It shouldn't have occurred like that; I can't stop thinking of it," Devitt offered and continued to pleasure her.

"Tomorrow, he will still be dead, will still be remembered, but tonight, my pretty boy, think only of me." He was mastering her now, and Aurora moved with him, moaning gently.

"And Kaya… Kaya and that man," he gasped. He was forceful now, and she loved it.

"You love this, Kaya?"

"Perhaps."

"Would you prefer her right here?" Aurora gasped, reaching back, taking hold and pleased at his turning. She could manoeuvre him the rest of the way.

"You are so beautiful, Aurora."

"Tomorrow, you can attempt to win her heart, but tonight, I want your soul," she demanded and eased herself closer to his face, away from his wonderful hands. "Will you give me your soul?"

"I will give what I must," he cried, and she slid across his face and thought how foolish Kaya was to ignore a man with such fine jaw, lips and tongue.

He weakened ever so as she ground gently against him, allowing his hands to hold her and dominate her. For a time, they remained so, locked in rapture until, half-sated, she spun away from him, and he gasped for breath. "That was the most pleasurable thing a man has ever done to me," she half-lied, and he grinned. Then he smiled as she spun around and delivered upon him what pleasures her mouth could.

She went to task, for she was a goddess of such things, and he took her for what he could. Long before he spent himself in her mouth, she drew away and gazed at him with godly eyes that could command every moment. "You are beautiful, every part of you," she whispered, and he groaned again as she sat above him, easing herself down until they became as connected as any lovers could.

Wrapping themselves in each other's flailing limbs, they ruined those sheets wonderfully and thought less of gods and lights and murder and lovers. They screamed and climaxed and kissed and caressed, and they did so awkwardly and without finesse, and it was wonderful until eventually, when her knees could take no more, and her jaw ached wonderfully, they collapsed in sweaty unison and lay there for a time.

"Will I see you tomorrow?" he asked, mid-gasp.

"No, my dear, I will leave this wonderful town by dawn."

"If I had any more, I would try and claim you again," he said, and she smiled, for he was a dead man. She knew this because every man in this town was. Women too. She would see to it.

"I'm sure we will meet again, Devitt. Keep an eye upon the watch, and I will look out for you," she pledged, and it was a right fuken shit pledge.

They talked about simple things for a while, but her feet were itching to flee from this place. She feigned sleep for a time until he fell deep, and then, kissing his manhood once goodbye and then his lips, she slipped from the warm covers, dressed swiftly and produced her favoured dagger.

Gazing at him and his manhood as it reared itself ever so in sleep, she considered keeping herself a little treasure. He was a nice enough boy and certain to be forgotten in the days ahead, she reassured herself, sliding the knife along the sheets and stopping beneath the rising beast. He sighed in contentment, and for a breath, she imagined the rage in her god's face for such an act. Perhaps the severed sliver would have erased the sins, she mused, and almost cut.

"Goodbye, pretty Devitt," she whispered, leaving him where he lay. Instead of savage, beautiful acts, she threw two logs upon the fire to keep out the chill and let him sleep longer. Gliding through the rest of the house, she counted her steps as she did. Twenty to the door, and four more back out into the streets. It was long before dawn, but a burning energy was in the air. Distantly ahead, she thought she heard the screams of some drunkards, and she wondered if there was more murder occurring this night. She might have sought it out but instead marched onwards.

Devitt had claimed that in no more than two days, this town would be as quiet as ever, with most visitors disappearing back into the Wastes to find their way home. This was the finest piece of information she'd gathered from her lover.

Taking three hundred more steps and discovering no trouble from the guard at the main gate, she slipped out into the morning, never looking back. She had taken what she could from the town for now. Come a couple of days, she would take the rest of it.

8

SESH BEHIND BARS

S mit caught a flash of himself in a building window as he concluded the deal and thought himself rather splendid. And why wouldn't he? Admittedly, the new suit was a deep breath too large for his impressive frame, but such things mattered little when dealing with treasures like this. And it was a treasure.

"You are picking my pockets," he growled, slipping his fingers through the pouch of pieces in a fine show of bravado before pocketing them. "Still, what am I to do with two fine suits of armour?" he added, concluding the trade with the bandit, a young cur with barely a beard to cover his chin. Smit couldn't help but feel elated. If the young man had taken time inspecting his older bronze uniform, he might have seen the fraying in the seams between each shard of heavy bronze. Smit had worn that hefty beast to the point of rusting, and he had worn it well. So well, in fact, it was easy to find a foolish mark to take the suit off his hands at quadruple the cost. Replacing the shoulder piece and seams would cost a second fortune for the young man, but Smit couldn't care less about robbing the young lad. It was a harsh lesson in bartering, and Smit was happy to instruct.

"Don't forget to keep her shiny," Smit added, leaving the boy to carry the cumbersome armour suit out into the dark streets. Spinning in the reflection of the glass, Smit smiled again at his fortune and his treasure, too.

Absolutely worth it.

There had been a near riot in the aftermath of the tournament; bodies abound, panicking, arguing, weeping and screaming. His voice, demanding victory, had been loudest. He'd never been knocked unconscious, never given up either. With Andreas dead and Fitz disqualified and duly arrested, there remained only one fiend. Smit had endured cheerier funerals while standing on the stage, enjoying the subdued audience's applause, but he didn't care.

He could still see the tears streaming from Rua's eyes, but he didn't bother offering condolences as she presented the armour. If asked, he would have admitted being rather fond of Andreas. A decent man, generous too, especially with loans. All in all, a fine leader of the Rock. If he had shown just a bit of patience with Fitz's debt, such distasteful actions wouldn't have been needed. It was a small matter now, though. All debts were quenched, and Smit was a happier man for it, if not a little unnerved at losing his comrade to the manacle.

This year's festival had been a lesser experience than usual. Fewer traders offered bargains, and the disaster of the boars just added to the disappointment. It was Andreas's murder that had ended the festivities. The visitors in the taverns, and those stumbling through the streets, still drank for a little longer, speaking of the battle and the bloodshed too, but indeed, the mood was low. The people had come as guests and killed one of their hosts. There was less cheering, singing and dancing, and while the festival usually spread to a second day, this one petered out as the hours drew on. Even now, after midnight, groups of bandits were still slipping out of the town. Done with their distaste. Marching at night was no rarity to any self-respecting thug.

More than that, Fitz would be charged after dawn, and he would hang for the murder, and rightly so. It would be a spectacle, but there would be ramifications, for Fitz, like Smit, was a privileged guest. They both were royalty in Adawan. Regardless of justice, Ulrik, the wild fuker, would take umbrage when Fitz hung. Smit knew this because if it came to it, he would be the whispering demon in the behemoth's ear. Raven Rock was a fine bastion, but the true bandit strength lay in Adawan. Always had, always would.

No bandit wanted to be part of that drama. No bandit wished to be seen standing in silence, allowing Fitz to hang, either. Bandits were hunted down and killed for lesser things. So yes, the few visitors slipped free of Raven Rock right swiftly, and Smit intended to be one of them, too.

"It's a right fuken mess," Smit muttered to the wind, marching off through the emptying streets seeking out his best friend.

It didn't take long to find him, such was the size of the town. With the dull drone of festivities coming to an anticlimactic end, he came upon the shack any self-respecting bandit was keen to avoid during the Festival of the Sash. Tapping lightly on the door, he pushed it open and stepped from the cool night into the smoky, transient cell within.

Though the rest of the town suffered the horror, there was less misery in this tiny shack. Grinning manically, holding an ace of queens for all to see before slamming it down upon the card table, was the murderer Fitz. And truly, he looked quite at home in shackles.

"I can do this all night," he cried, pulling his ill-gotten

gains back into a large stack of winnings and carefully placing the pieces on top of each other, counting obnoxiously as he did.

"Fine evening to you, Smit. Have you come to break this fuker out?" Rook muttered, looking up at Smit and throwing down his cards in disgust. Smit didn't know the two young guards playing at the table with them, but such was the laughter that he suspected they were fine curs altogether.

"I have come to ensure his safety this night and also to ensure the slippery little fuk doesn't break himself out," said Smit, watching eagerly as a guard shuffled fresh cards.

"Well, look at you, all shimmering and shit in that new outfit," Fitz said, clapping his hands in mock applause and sending the tower of pieces all over the table. "Oh, spit on me," he muttered, recovering his wealth. He might face death at dawn but wanted to be as rich as possible while swinging in the breeze. Smit liked that in him. He always had. Wonderful greed that spotted an opportunity in the least of places. There were worse things in a Runner partner, and Fitz was the best Runner he'd ever seen. Even better than Ulrik, even better than Wrek and all.

"Don't splash the pot," warned the dealer to the prisoner, and dealt four cards before gesturing to Smit and a spare seat.

Why not?

The small wooden shack barely stood upright, and Smit imagined a hefty breeze sending it down upon their heads. It was heavy with the cracking coats of a thousand different paint jobs, and it was impossible not to feel utterly anxious within. Its walls were so compact and claustrophobic that Smit imagined there would be less than enough air to breathe. Those within must have thought so too, for in a small ashtray burned two lazily wrapped sticks of tobacco weed. Who needed air when one could be eternally drunk by breathing in this haze? Two cots and the card table in the middle were all this prison could hold, and Smit couldn't help but feel bad for the two poor fiends who were probably evicted from their beds just to keep this prisoner away from the masses. Saying that, there were better places Smit wanted to be this night, too. Fitz looked right at home, though, waiting for dawn, waiting for death, and waiting for Smit.

"Fuk it," Smit said, dropping a few pieces into the pot, weighing up the few left in his pockets. The card players went to battle. Time moved differently when battling wits for chance, and the five rowdy players fell more and more silent with every changing hand. Sometimes they bluffed, sometimes they fled and sometimes that fuken ace of queens ruined a carefully laid hand. Tobacco weed was inhaled and shared, fresh sine, still sizzling, was poured out, and Smit found himself enjoying this wait for his friend's inevitable death more than he'd expected.

Rook was a master cheat at cards, and Smit always paid closer attention to his dealing, and Rook noticed. It was a fine battle of wits. They were friends and had been for years. They had done several successful runs together, but he'd chosen the green of the Rock over the sands of Adawan, and Smit didn't challenge his choices. While Smit and Fitz were privileged in Adawan, Rook shared the same status in the Rock.

"This is the place to be, this dreary night," Rook said, yawning, after he'd lost his third hand in a row. One of which he'd even dealt.

"A fine place to rest before the gallows," muttered one of the guards, and Fitz laughed maniacally at his gruesome fate.

"I'll get some fine rest then," Fitz added, pouring a fresh glass for himself. His seventh of the night. It may as well have been his second, so steady was his hand. Smit knew he'd drink as long as he could. He thought it would be a terrible thing to be strung up with a nasty hangover. That said, there was probably no better cure than a little dying.

Rook's face darkened. "Did you have to kill the man?" he asked. "He was a popular one." It was a fine question, and the other guard held his shuffle. That type of tone was likely to start a fight.

Fitz grinned, wiped his nose, peered at what remained on his finger and shrugged. "Ah, it was defence; I had to."

Nobody said a word for a moment.

And then Fitz continued. "He had it coming, the bastard."

"The council will decide on that," Rook mumbled.

"Aye, whatever's left of them," Fitz countered coldly. Neither guard appeared thrilled with these words, and Smit could feel his hair standing on the back of his neck. He always felt like this before a fight. Before murder, too. He wasn't as accomplished or careless as Fitz, but some fuks needed killing. Regardless of friendship, he didn't think Rook needed a killing. Nor Andreas, either. That was the problem of marching with a wild fuk like Fitz. It made it fun, though.

"Brother, I will stay on your side, but I'll probably be the only one," Rook said, stretching to leave. "Don't think your connections to Ulrik will help you either." Pocketing what measly winnings he still had, he roughly grasped Fitz's hand and drew him to his feet. "I have enjoyed this last night with you, friend," he said, embracing Fitz as a brother before embracing Smit, offering a bow and disappearing into the night.

"When a brute like Rook has lost all faith, there is no hope," Fitz said after Rook's echoing footsteps were lost to the growing settled sounds of the night.

They played for a time longer, though not too long that an entire hand could be played. Smit voiced aloud thoughts any desperate man might have had. "Perhaps," he whispered, leaning close to the remaining guards, "you could just let this rat fuk go, and we'll pay you kindly."

Both guards laughed for the jest it was.

And Smit was suddenly upon the nearest with fierce violence. Maru was his name, and he was a boy of two decades or less. Smit smashed his fists against the young man's unsuspecting face, and Maru reeled from his chair, hitting his head on the stone floor with a sickening thud.

The other, a man called Leeder who was just as young and just as unprepared, was taken from behind by Fitz. Wrapping his chains around the gasping brute, Fitz strangled him, silencing his call for alarm. Smit did the rest. Hammering him thrice in the stomach, he watched as the boy collapsed to his knees, whimpering.

"Whisht, or we'll kill ya," snarled Fitz, waiting for the snivelling guard to gift him the keys.

"Play along, and we'll bind you; it will be a fine tale and all," Smit hissed, and the beaten guard nodded his head, offering the keys. "Oh, fuk, what is he doing?"

Maru, lying upon his back, began to shake uncontrollably; blood spilled freely from beneath him where his head had struck the ground, and Smit's stomach dropped.

"Oh, no, he looks rightly fuked," hissed Fitz, freeing himself of the shackles. He knelt over the boy as he struggled towards his last. "How hard did you hit him?"

"It was an accident," argued Smit. Maru's arms waved wildly, and with a gargle, his breath released and he fell silent.

Leeder, still kneeling, began to panic, and rightly so. "Oh, please, fuk, Maru, oh no."

"Whist, will ya?"

"Please don't kill me."

"We won't kill ya. It was an accident."

"Oh, fuk, oh fuk," the boy whimpered. He'd drawn the short straw, guarding the killer this night. Short straws were a fuk at the best of times.

Fitz thought so, too. He drove his boot down upon the boy's head, sending him to the floor.

"Ah, there's no need for that," Smit argued.

"We can't leave him to escape," argued Fitz, stamping again and again. "If you hadn't killed the other, we could have paid them to shut their holes." It was a fine argument, and Fitz continued to stamp, and the boy began to thrash like his comrade had. And then he fell still like his comrade did, too, and the room fell silent but for Fitz's muted cursing for the wet and bony matter upon his boots.

"I'll never get this shit out."

"You'll walk it off in the Wastes."

"Do you think?"

"I do."

"So, what's the plan?"

"Get the fuk out of here, get hunting, get back to Ulrik."

"Sounds like a simple plan."

"The best ones usually are."

Gathering their belongings, they slipped out into the cold night as though on a bandit run and quickly fell into routine. Stepping swiftly and softly, ducking through alleys and side streets, they avoided the glow of the lights until they were below the city gates, where Smit stood out in his shimmering suit of steel. Still, Fitz, with his leather suit, could easily remain unnoticed.

"Couldn't rightly wait for the fun tomorrow?" called the guard, winding the levers and easing the gates open just enough for two seemingly innocent bandits to slip through.

"We're heading to the Deep North; nothing like a night

march with a beer in our bellies and the wind at our back to get some miles done," Smit called out.

"Besides, we have no interest in watching a snivelling rat be hanged for murder," Fitz added, keeping his head low, suppressing a snigger.

"Aye, there will be high drama once Ulrik learns of that fuker's fate," agreed the guard, releasing the lever and returning to his idle watch, and both fiends slipped from the town, eager to get some miles towards the village of Nioe before all fuken hell broke loose at dawn.

9

______

THE ARMY

It felt good to march.

To return home. She missed her home. Her home was where her boys were. Mostly boys. But some girls as well. She had never been good with girls. A strange thing really, considering she was the same breed. It was a small matter. Aurora loved coming back home to her army. Hers. Nobody else's.

Dawn was breaking, and Aurora was very tired. She had exhausted herself in the arms of the boy, having had to earn his pleasure, and really, she might better have spent the rest of the night sleeping. She might even have purchased a mount for the return trip. However, this trek would have been near impossible for a solitary mount; it was a difficult enough trek for a goddess on foot. As the dawn erupted around her, she felt the gnawing grumbles of hunger in her belly. Soon, sleep, rest and death would come; she only needed to finish her wander first.

"Good morning, world," she whispered in the wind, ducking below some heavy green branches. Even as the sun rose, she could already sense the murky day ahead. Shadows loomed, and there was a bite to the air, a far cry from the warmer season it was becoming. Despite the chill, some of the sun's warmth was breaking through, and Aurora imagined the clouds parting in honour of her. She imagined the day's greyness giving way to blue and beauty, and it was a calming thought. As was seeing the first sign of her comrades appearing on the horizon. A few light puffs of smoke, a few deep cart tracks here and there. Not to mention the effect of a hundred beasts of swine and milk upon the local foliage. A casual wanderer might not notice such things, but a keener bandit would. Their camp was well chosen, sheltered in a valley deep in heavy green, miles from any path. It was no surprise they'd ventured this far north without arousing suspicion. Few would ever know they were there until she allowed everyone to know.

She knew Uden's orders, and she almost swayed as though drunk, knowing she was but a few steps away from pleasing him. Uden's insistence that she take out Raven Rock and his demands for blood were ambrosia to her.

It is almost time to gather.

Resting by a tree log with a sharp edge and a decade of moss-cover, she embraced the silence. Out here, where she didn't count her steps or dream of blood, she could find a peacefulness. Such things were necessary before the horrors of war took her mind, before the call of her god took her waking thoughts. She sniffed the air and felt as young as she was.

Just a child, new to this world.

Suddenly, a glimmer in the eternal green caught her attention. A bright flash of sunlight reflecting on glass, high up in a tree quite a distance away. *No glimmer of glass belongs that high in a tree,* she thought, frowning. She gazed fixedly at the glimmer, and it did not waver. Instead, it played its secret game, following her every move, and terrible anger took her. A spyglass was a precarious thing in unskilled hands. A spyglass was the type of thing that was made for curious visitors. Were they not doing all in their power to remain concealed while marching these last few months? Was there no irony in a watcher giving away their whereabouts to any wanderer with a keener eye? Probably. But she didn't like to think of things like that.

Her watcher followed her every movement, and she considered gesturing her distaste. Her mouth watered, for usually, upon her return to her boys, she needed to send a message to those who followed her—a quick reminder of her severity. Such things mattered.

"Hello, little spyglass bearer. I might kill you," she whispered, dipping her head and gazing at that glimmering shard. As though realising her thoughts, the spyglass's shine disappeared, leaving nothing but the flow of green in the gentle wind. "That's it—hide away from little old wanderer me," she mocked, slipping her pack onto her other shoulder and marching back into the seemingly abandoned woodland.

Unlike a spyglass, a few wisps of smoke were unavoidable. Like any fine wanderer, she followed a thin line of smoke and the clefts left behind by the grazing beasts until, eventually, she heard the unmistakable drone of her comrades as they prepared themselves for the day.

She began to giggle to herself as the signs of life appeared among the trees. "Right where I left you," she whispered to the wind, with only a faint trace of disappointment. They had followed her far these last many months, but there was nothing like a delay in movement to draw frustrations. She might have liked a little disobedience on the part of one of her boys, at least. Just a little dissent. Just a little show of manhood. Fewer things were more enjoyable than teaching manners to one of her boys. In the beginning, when there was nothing but the proclamation of a god to establish her leadership, she had needed to stretch her muscles, slit a few dissenting throats and earn her place, as it was. They were good times. She led by love as long as they knew their place.

She emerged from the forest, and her gathered comrades immediately stood to attention as she appeared. No doubt her watcher had spread the word of her arrival, for she saw preparations for a march to war in the camp, but that was fine. Let them wonder and hope. She would not be rushed.

Home.

Hidden near a river of rushing water, the beasts were paddocked in the lushest areas. She inhaled deeply; theirs was quite the fragrant area of the camp. Beyond them, she reached a hundred before she ceased counting the number of tents she passed. A hundred was a fine, even number, and she didn't have time to walk past each of them. A girl could go mad doing such things, especially as her comrades began to disassemble them upon her approach. They were as excited as a bandit at a festival. All eager for action and war and fine times. They were her army, and she loved them all.

No, not mine at all.

Uden referred to each wandering army as one of his fingers, for they spread out like the digits of a masterful hand across the land. Her finger numbered a few thousand in strength—a fine number altogether, rivalling the largest finger of her people. Most were fit to march with a blade and might have to do so in the months beyond Raven Rock. However, it was the two hundred Riders that were most impressive—and undesired. For they had been foisted upon her against her will.

She gazed at them as she passed, busy among the crude stalls, tending to their beasts with brush, feed and good cheer.

Theirs was a position higher than most others, and why wouldn't it be? Keeping those beasts fed, fresh and fearless was no small skill. Nor was thundering down upon settlements in a flash of violence, crushing and killing and warring perfectly in Uden's name. She'd seen them, and knew that to command them was an extension of her god's wrath. If Uden's godly fingers were a creeping threat, these Riders were a fuken fist to dash upon their enemy. Aurora, however, liked to do her killing a little more intimately.

The Riders continued their duties as she walked, but an unease spread through them as she ventured through the camp. Words of war were soon to be upon her tongue, as she had said they would. More and more Riders emerged from their bedding, their eyes upon the shapely goddess. This pleased her greatly, and for a breath, she considered not taking the life of the careless watch guard. Considered.

It wasn't just the Riders who felt the coming of beautiful things. The further in she marched, the more she watched her kin begin to move as one. Keepers tended to swine beasts; a few hundred fires were swiftly lit to cook a hasty hot meal, lest this be the last for a day and a night.

Soldiers staging mock battles in crude training arenas eased their thrashing of each other to tend to their blades with oil and whetstone or else to prepare armour and shield. Seeing such things around her was mesmerising, and she suppressed another giggle. Instead, she continued ahead, eager to take the weight from her feet.

Her tent was separate from all others—the largest in the entire camp. Of course, it was. A goddess needed these things. Sometimes, her followers needed reminding, too. Head bobbing as though listening to a melody of severing limbs and the ripping of skin, she spun through the open flap, announced herself to the nothing within and smiled at the steaming bath that awaited. They'd likely begun boiling the water when she appeared on the horizon—or at the end of a spyglass. It was good to be queen and respected, too.

Wasting little time gazing around at the rest of the decorations, for there were scarcely any, she began to strip her grubby clothing from her perfect body. As she did, she glanced around this uninviting room and missed her god anew. There sat merely her bed, her bath, a mirror and her crate of vileness. Within were her most precious weapons. There was little else. Unlike others, she had little need of books, reports or decorations. This room was for bathing, furrowing and sleeping. Not usually in that order.

Sliding into the bath, she stifled a scream of pain. It was a good pain. When away from her army, she usually bathed in cold water. Uden liked it so. Hers was not to argue or challenge. Out on the march, though, she allowed herself this one additional painful pleasure.

Sitting in the steaming water and taking the stinging ache for the pleasure it was, she began to scrub the boy from her body. A difficult task, such had been their writhing and her march after. A careless girl might have taken a chance of becoming with child, but Aurora understood the natural cycle of things. She was also good at counting days. Uden would never forgive her if another laid his seed in her.

And what a glorious death that would be.

She suddenly imagined Uden's fingers upon her body, fantastic imaginings with wondrous agony, and, spreading her legs, she began to tend to mightier things, and oh, she imagined his fury. She imagined those fingers gripping her eyes and pushing ever so deep, lovingly, and cruelly.

I want to die like that.

She pulsed in the water and vaguely heard voices approaching from outside. She thrashed against Uden's grip as he took her sight, cursing her shame, and she loved his hate, loved his touch, loved his murder.

"May we speak with you, General?" one of her boys called, but she didn't want to open her eyes, for how could she? Her god was squashing them to mulch, entering her as he punished her sins.

Furrow me to death, my love.

Eyes might not be enough, Aurora thought, in near ecstasy. She splashed steaming water over the edge as she thrashed and dove deep with his might, and oh, it was perfect, as every act with him was.

"You may," Aurora whispered, and whimpered as Uden took her further into the abyss and finished her with his love and hate and godliness. Her body weakened and pushed for more, and she was no longer in a tent watched patiently by her favourite general, all eager to attack for her. Oh, no, she was back in that frozen prison, being murdered and furrowed. And it was perfect.

Kill me, Uden. Fuken kill me.

Gasping, as Uden dashed her against the bath and she could only cry out in death and desire, she moaned her last and died. And floated in the tub. She imagined the blood streaming down her face. Such beautiful eyes, all gone to waste.

"I am glad you have returned," Ferat whispered. He was beside her, kneeling, watching, and she sighed as the blood ceased its flowing, and she was very much alive and sated for the first time in an entire day.

"I do love these moments," she whispered, finally opening her eyes. He smiled with adoration at her. He was her most trusted servant in this army, a fierce young cur destined to rise high in the ranks, and she had all the time in the world for him.

"Who doesn't, my queen," he offered. In his hand was a bar of soap. A fine gift, really, and she took it gladly. He allowed himself to gaze at her form for an entire breath before remembering his place and the punishment for such an act, and she couldn't help but picture him in his cot this night, imagining her body next to his doing delicious things. She felt little embarrassment for whatever actions she played in his mind. A warrior's thoughts were their own. She wondered if she might take his hand and drag it to salacious places to test his resolve more thoroughly, but thought better of it. A look was enough. A touch was something else entirely.

Scrubbing the last of Devitt and Raven Rock from her perfect form, as Ferat sat upon the ground in her shadow, she listened as he read aloud the dealings and goings-on of the camp these last few days. She found such things tiresome and considered tending to matters once more but thought better of it. Though she had been ruling this finger less than a year, she wasn't disinclined to learn what she could of monotonous things. Ferat was adamant such things mattered, and so she listened.

"Food stocks went up, what with the taking of the beasts," he offered, and she nodded along as though it meant anything.

"That's good."

"We sent off the birds yesterday, as you asked."

"Very good."

"Three hundred or more sightings, but only… ah… um… fourteen wanderers came upon the perimeter in the last two days."

"I see. And they are taken care of?"

"They are."

"Oh, good." She wondered absently about the many bandits she'd seen come and go from the festival. She wondered had she spoken to any of the now dead fiends and decided she didn't care. At least it was an even number. "Any more you come upon, keep in chains, for now."

"It will be done."

"Anything else, my dearest friend?"

"The camp is fit, fighting and… ready to march." He was subtle. Prying for her decision.

"I see."

She lay in the bath a little longer and felt the first tinges of a draft. From outside the tent, she could hear a stillness as her comrades waited for word. For no reason whatsoever, she felt terrible exhaustion come upon her. She imagined freezing cold water, heavy chains, plenty of fire and torment, followed by the divinity of blood. She licked her lips and drew herself from the bath.

He tossed her a gown for sleep, but she merely used it to dry herself. She allowed him to watch, and strangely, she enjoyed the act.

"Is there anything else?" she asked, standing beside him and staring into his eyes. Pretty eyes. Not as pretty as hers, but young and beautiful. They matched his jawline—a strong jawline without blemish or gristle. Perfect, really.

He only needed to reach out and kiss her navel, and all would be lost.

Do it and be beautifully doomed, my dear friend.

Truthfully, he was her dearest friend. Although she needed no friends, only war and death and a god tearing her throat out.

"Do we march upon the town… as Uden demands?"

She fought the flash of anger as it took her. And thought better of lashing out. He attempted to separate himself from her. He did nothing more than obey and serve, and here she was, tormenting and tickling his very nature with her perfect body. He was allowed a little snide retort now and then as long as it was between them. What occurred beyond these thin fabric walls was for the world. Within, well, that's where the fine times could occur.

With the speed of a snake, she reached out a hand and stroked his cheek gently. It was a fine cheek, and he blinked in reply.

"I trust you, my lovely Ferat. Never forget this," she whispered, and swiftly, he snatched her hand in his and delicately kissed it. She had not expected that tenderness.

"I live to serve you, my dear Aurora," he said.

"You will do all I wish?"

"As you wish," he said, releasing her.

"Very well. For now, gather those who need to know my word," she ordered, and swiftly, he was away from her, and she was left alone in the chill, naked as well.

Taking but a few moments to slather her garments in sweet-smelling oils, she dressed, and then drew every blade and weapon she would ever need from her wooden chest.

Catching a glimpse of herself in the mirror, she was disappointed. "It is time…" she whispered to the wind, donning her leather armour, "… for a better outfit."

Wrapping her cloak around her, she felt better. More alive and better prepared for death. As a comrade and as an enemy. Whichever, really.

She might have lain back in her bed for a few hours, perhaps thought a little of Ferat and his desire, but her heart raced as she fed off the silence from beyond. There was a thrill to delivering fine news, and this day, she aimed to please.

Stepping through the tent flap, she was pleased to see her word had spread. They waited as they might have waited for a god, and perhaps this is exactly what they saw: a vessel for his wrath upon the entire Four Factions. Some people desired to live. Others desired to hate, and truly, she would welcome those upon this march.

She stood out among the many hundreds now lined up side by side, Rider beside keeper, beside chef, beside general, beside soldier, beside child, beside mother, father, brother, sister, and everyone after that who served the Hunt. They were her comrades, they were her family, they were her objects of conquest. She promised them the world, and she would deliver.

The silence drew in, and the world became nothing but a collective, careful breath, the swish and groan of beasts, and the thumping of her heart.

The few, the many, the beautiful killers eager to please waited in silence and desire, and she smiled as only a goddess of war could. They came for word, and she would deliver the gospel.

Her name was Aurora, and she liked to kill.

"We march," she said, and the roar shook the land.

10

AFTERMATH

"We can't keep talking about the same thing repeatedly; we must move on," Kaya declared weakly. She was making perfect sense, but nobody at the esteemed table appeared to care. Simeon certainly didn't. All he cared about was that festering, burning hatred growing deep in his gut. What had started as a spark to overcome his grief now became a furnace, that threatened to become an inferno. He was near ready to explode. He wanted to explode. He was also quite terrified he would explode because all would be lost if he did.

The council room felt heavier today. Somehow, the gloom stuck to the walls like lacquer. The warm air felt thinner despite the fewer deeply taken breaths. Perhaps that was the smoke. "It's no easy thing to move matters along," Rua said quietly. She sat staring at Andreas's empty seat. Though she spoke measuredly, Simeon could hear the break in her. She had fallen to desolation—a strange thing for a woman as sturdy as she. Andreas's passing had taken much from them all these last three days. After three fuken days of misery and mourning, the world had turned tragically, the town had emptied and lives were now somehow supposed to move on. "But perhaps it's what the big eejit would have wanted." Her fingers shook, and she caught them in a fist.

Beside her, Daisy started to weep again, and Simeon wanted to take her in his arms and comfort her. Fuk those watching. Instead, he stewed in his seat and fanned that fire. And he inhaled deeply from the tobacco weed once more before leaving it in an ashtray. Simeon liked to think Andreas would have disapproved of him consuming the herb. Would have shouted at him, no doubt. It would have been nice to hear his disapproving tones once more. Holding the smoke in his lungs so it might go to work, rightly fuking up his senses, he released and leaned back in his chair. It was a fine weapon against the rage. Perhaps they might make better decisions if more at the table smoked as he did. Or else get nothing done at all. Regardless, it would be a better experience.

"He would want to be remembered, but there are also interesting whispers we must speak of," said Kaya. Simeon knew her agony was almost as depthless as Rua's, but she hid it like any master. Perhaps she'd smoked a little before the meeting.

"Oh, for fuk's sake. The wandering convoy? Mutterings and little more," Rook hissed. He cracked his fingers loudly. He looked around the table as though seeking a fight. Then he stared at his feet.

"It's not far from our borders," countered Kaya, and Simeon could only look to the sky in frustration. Aye, there were whispers of a grand gathering of fiends a day or so from here. There was always a buzz when dinner came to you, mused Simeon, deciding a quick dismissive shake of the head was a fine show of disagreement.

"You take the word of drunken oafs about some fine hunting, and still no sign of any of our trackers," Rook spat.

He leaned towards Kaya, attempting to intimidate her. He had taken the jailbreak worse than anyone else. He was friends with the curs that had killed not just Andreas, but two innocent guards. A disgusting act without provocation. There had been quite the arguments that following morning from the many who desired to seek out the bastards. Those close to Andreas, those closest to the guards. It was the master hunter, Rook, who had demanded loudest that he lead the hunting party and had been voted down by the rest of the council—a wise move at the time. The problem was that no cur had returned with those foul fuks' heads upon pikes in the days since. "I've had it with waiting. I will track them myself," he growled, stealing Simeon's tobacco weed and inhaling deeply.

Share and share alike, my friend.

"With Dejan absent and Andreas lost, we can't afford to lose another voice," Devitt countered. It was a fine argument. If nothing else, stability ruled in a place like Raven Rock. It might turn into a wild place like Adawan without it. Besides, Andreas wasn't getting any deader. Surely the shrewder task was paying attention to the large gathering of wanderers approaching their gates. It would take only a few dozen Runners to scatter them and gather their spoils. An opportunistic council might consider how much wealth such a gathering could amass. The furnace festered a little more, and a delicate bloodlust came upon Simeon at the prospect of sacking some wealth and releasing his wrath and angst over his loss.

"Ah, spit on that," Rook said coldly. "I will leave, and none of you will stop me."

"That is not how things are done in Raven Rock," Kaya warned with equal coolness. Rook could intimidate most, but not that fiery bitch. Simeon had been on the receiving end of her wicked tongue on more than one occasion. A friend, aye, but not one to back down.

"Let the man go; if anyone can pick up and catch up with those two bastards, it's Rook," Silas growled, and Simeon immediately felt his temper rise. Since Andreas's death, the fuker had been to three council meetings in a row. He sat directly across from Simeon, exactly where Simeon had sat this past year, as though he had any fuken right to that seat—and other things.

Simeon could feel the tempest within rising, and he allowed it. He could still hear that bastard's grunt as he thrust into Daisy. Simeon began to count to ten in his head. As he did, he heard less of her satisfied moaning. After a second inhale of his herbs, he heard only his beating heart.

"I'm not altogether sure it's a wandering pack of easy prey," Kaya said, ignoring the pressing issue. "I heard it was a travelling band of warriors."

"Ha, that's some fine shit," roared Rook, slapping his knee as though it was an excellent jest altogether. "Who told you that? Some drunkard in the tavern, that's who! Or else the boy you've been sleeping with?" He was getting angrier again. Had been for the past few days. "Whispering city lies in your ear after he's furrowed you sideways all night." He faced Kaya as he spoke, but his eyes were on Devitt. Simeon wondered why. "You think Spark City has amassed an army? Or that Magnus and his Rangers have crossed the east to come hunt us down?" He spat on the floor in disgust at that name, and Kaya was silent for a breath.

"There are no armies in the Factions," Rua suggested, and this was partly true. It was no secret that Dia had outlawed the gathering of armies over the last couple of decades. A narrow-minded view on keeping the peace, yet peace had reigned to this day. No armies, except for Magnus's, of course. But that was only because he had won the Faction Wars. Those who remembered his marches declared he had earned the right to do whatever the fuk he wanted.

Simeon didn't know how he felt about an old relic like Magnus. Whatever he did, he did it quietly. That was something, at least. And as for Rua's lunatic race? The savages who answered to no Primary but themselves? Well, they were less inclined to sail to these shores anytime soon. And to get here, they'd have to travel through Magnus's territory anyway. The world would hear of that disagreement, no doubt. No armies were at march, and Magnus would never impose his warmongering ways. Simeon was confident of this, yet, for no reason whatsoever, he felt a chill run down his spine. So he took another hit of the weed and felt better about himself. And then he looked at Silas and felt worse.

"We vote," Silas declared, rapping his knuckles on the table. "Daisy and I vote to allow Rook to hunt those bastards. That's three votes and enough."

Simeon wanted to hit the cur. Reach across the table and strike him right across that smug chin.

"I didn't wish to vote that way," Daisy said suddenly.

It was only a flicker of movement, but Silas's hand rapped the back of her head like a master silencing a pupil in the most demeaning way. It wasn't the first time he had struck her. It was just the first time he did it among comrades. She shuddered at his touch, and Simeon stood up over them both. His heart ached like a poet's, all tragic and romantic, and desperate to win her love with sonnets alone, as though the world worked that way.

It wasn't this dismissive strike that earned Simeon's ire, nor was it even the loss of his friend. It was the older swelling of Daisy's beautiful eye which drew this anger forth. Anyone could see the tale without it needing to be spoken. Silas himself suffered a mild redness across the cheeks. No doubt she had gotten a solitary strike in as he beat her, and Simeon was proud. He tried not to look on with awe and love and horror as Daisy, pulling up the front of her high-cut vest, attempted and failed to conceal the bruising around her throat. The eye didn't lie, though, did it? No matter what paint she applied to the blemish, nothing stopped swelling. It was the restraint of a man in love that held Simeon's fist and held his tongue as well. Here, they argued of lesser things upon the council, and for all eyes to see, there was purest evil at the table. Simeon was sickened with it all. Better to ignore it, he imagined. Truthfully, he would have said something if he had not been bedding this goddess.

What type of coward sees these acts and says nothing? Does nothing.

FUKEN SAY SOMETHING!

SAVE HER!

Unlike the others, it wasn't fear or embarrassment that held him silent. Instead, it was love even as that foul bastard struck her in his presence.

"Have we a problem?" Silas asked, eyeing Simeon and eyeing his fists. Silas's fists were miscoloured and split where he'd beaten her. Oh, aye, Daisy might argue that it was just Silas's way. Andreas's death had affected him, too. She might even say that she'd run her mouth a little carelessly. That it was partly her fault. That there had been too much alcohol consumed. That she hadn't had his dinner prepared to his liking. That she should have known better. That it would never happen again. That everything was fine.

Save her.

Do nothing.

Simeon looked at his love and saw the panic on her face. She wanted to be saved, but she wanted to be safe. Suffering

Silas's wrath was no way to live. Simeon could see the terror in her eyes. Pleading him to sit, to restrain himself. To realise that were fists to be raised, Silas would pummel the life out of Simeon. And then realise Simeon's motives.

Save her.

Do nothing.

He looked back to Silas and fought that anger. He focused on the blue silken scarf around that cur's neck and fought the anger bravely. He did it for Daisy. He did it for himself. For all his faults, Silas had more to offer than Simeon. What were words and emotions when his abode was barely large enough for himself? Let alone a goddess like her? Daisy was used to the finer things in life. Perhaps, in another few years and after a few more significant scores, he might be able to afford the silks, jewels and triple-roomed houses. She might love him regardless, but after the life that had been dealt to her, Simeon wanted to treat her right.

Save her.

Do nothing.

"Sit the fuk down, boy," Silas snarled.

He probably should have. If asked about it later, he would claim the tobacco weed had eroded his better judgement. Perhaps, though, it urged him to do precisely what he needed to do. He envisioned her weeping and bleeding as Silas stood over her. Grinning. Undoing his belt. And his trouser buttons after. It was too fuken much, and Simeon was an idiot in love. There were fewer things more potent in this shitty world.

Save her, fool.

Fuk it.

"I want my scarf back," Simeon mumbled, and Daisy recoiled as though she'd been struck, as though she should have known better.

"What are you talking about?" Silas spluttered.

Simeon went and saved her.

"I want my fuken scarf back, you foul bastard," he screeched, leaping across the council table like he was diving into a pool of water. He slid the last foot or so, but his arms reached Silas's throat just fine and kept going. A good leap, in truth. He fell upon the cur, and they tumbled to the floor. And then there were more screams, some curses too.

"You vile piece of shit," roared Simeon, driving the man's head down upon the ground and wrapping his hands around his throat. He felt arms upon him, but he didn't care. And then he felt Silas's fist upon his cheek, and the room flashed a shade darker for a breath.

"Oh, no, oh no, oh no," wailed Daisy beside him, and he struck Silas fiercely, and then again and again, and it was terrible and wonderful, and Silas was a cur, and Simeon was a hero, and he wanted that scarf back. But he'd give it up for her.

"I'll fuken knife ya! You are dead!" boomed Silas, meeting the strikes better than Simeon would have liked. And why wouldn't he take them? Simeon was closer in weight to Daisy than to Silas. The odds were hardly fair, but in that moment, a hero in love would do what was needed.

It wasn't enough.

With a heave and at the expense of a few open strikes, Silas shoved his attacker back with powerful arms. The arms of their comrades did the rest, pulling him away altogether, and for a breath, it felt like a victory as he was dragged across the room while the council got in the way of both fighters. Simeon could see Daisy attempting to pull Silas away from the melee, and he loved her more. At her own expense, she protected him.

And then Silas grabbed at her throat once more, and Simeon leapt again through the council members and struck the fiend again as he struggled with Daisy, who fought his hold.

Eventually, it was Rook who pulled Simeon away before Silas recovered and killed him outright. That wasn't to say Simeon went quietly. Kicking and punching at the smoky air, the larger man pulled him down the stairs, through the gloom, away from the council, out into the morning's light. The last he saw of Silas was him being pinned to the far wall by Devitt, Rua and Kaya, all attempting and failing to calm his outburst.

"Come on, boy, cool your cap a while," Rook growled, pulling him through the streets, away from violence and danger. Away from his murderer.

"He's a bastard—you all saw," cried Simeon, wiping tears of fright, hate and shock from his eyes. The worst type of tears. "You all fuken saw what he did."

"It was always going to happen," Rook said, dragging him less now and sensing the calm and the regret for his actions. Only then could he see the betrayal on his part, and a terrible sadness took him. "You two eejits, off like young lovers, without a care in the world." He spun on Simeon. "Did you think you could avoid this?"

And then she was beside him, matching his step, taking his hand in hers, and he loved her.

"You were so brave, my love," Daisy whimpered, gripping hard as though letting go would reveal the right fuken mess he'd just made of her life. His own, too.

"Oh, for fuk's sake," growled Rook, though there was a softness ever so. He'd seen the damage the brute had inflicted upon his wife. His lesser wife now. "You two are like children." He was smiling, though. As was she, beneath the tears, the bruising and the shock. When Rook released his hold, she leapt upon him, weeping. "Just don't aggravate Silas until I get back," Rook muttered.

"So you are going to go out hunting regardless?" Daisy asked.

"No vote was going to stop me. I believe I know where the fiends are marching. I can wait no longer."

"Thank you," Daisy said. She refused to let Simeon go.

"Look, you two. I know Silas, and he'll have an eye out for the pair of you. Lock your door, keep your distance, but eventually, with time, this will pass over…" He looked down at the dirt and shuffled his feet. "Silas will see it is better this way," he offered, then spun on his heels, leaving the two young bandits to themselves.

———

"I hope it's alright, at least for now," Simeon said. She'd seen the room plenty of times before, usually with desire blinding her sight. For now, though, it appeared less cosy and more cramped. She hadn't stopped weeping until they reached his hovel on the top floor of the old building at the far end of town. Not even after he'd bolted the door in two places. The room was small enough, but it cost him little to maintain, and the rent he paid to the council was even less. A far cry from the home she lived in, and he was ever so ashamed at its humbleness. Had he known she was coming, he might have made a better effort to clean the place. Light a few candles, burn some sweet-smelling oil or pick a few flowers and leave them on the modest table, fit for only one person.

"It is perfect," she said softly, standing in the centre of the room, shaking ever so. There was a chill, admittedly, but she'd have to get used to that.

But not today.

As he tended to the fire in the small fireplace, with its narrow chimney that no cur could creep in or out of, he replayed the fight in his mind, relived his pride and terror. It was something to do while trying to make sense of his choices. It was love, it was commitment, and it was terrifying. He could see she was in shock and had no words to draw her from it. He had sine, though, and plenty of tobacco weed. He even had a batch of honey cakes in the larder. That was a start, at least.

"A few more runs is all I need to do, and we can afford a little more," he offered as the fire took light. "Perhaps even that fabled large gathering of wanderers," he offered. Anything to give her hope of something more. Anything to ease her pain.

"It is perfect."

"I… I am sorry," he whispered. It was pathetic and necessary. For all his fears, she faced tenfold the turmoil—all because he couldn't stop himself.

She pulled him to the bed, removing her clothes as she did, and he gasped at the bruising.

"The fuken bastard," Simeon cried, losing any guilt or terror he felt. She lay before him naked and ruined and in need. He'd never loved anyone more. "I'll kill him for you; I pledge it."

He considered it a good pledge.

"Whisht, my darling, our revenge is already cast." She pulled him to her softly. "He is cursed to live without the love that I can give. I give it all to you willingly if you will have me."

"I've loved you from the moment we spoke. I'll always love you," he whispered, and amazingly, this was the truth. Deep down, if he had admitted it, he might once have believed he was little more than a dalliance from her unhappy marriage. But now the fears slipped away, and the anger, too. If this was all she needed, this was all he needed. There were worse lives to be lived.

They writhed gently, and the hours passed in a haze of lust, passion and deepest love. Eventually, spent and ruined and blissfully happy, they rose from the bed and he led her to his most prized view in the entire settlement. Climbing carefully out the side window and onto a platform, they edged up the old slates, where, sitting upon a large open roof, they nestled in together to watch a water-coloured sky darken in burning amber and pink. Passing the tobacco weed back and forth with the wind seducing them into blissful peace, they waited for the new settlement lights to glow to life and light up the world.

Simeon could only think of Rook out in the Wastes, hunting down those vile bastards, and truly, he suspected the older bandit would hunt down his prey successfully enough. He would owe the man a drink when he returned.

Around them, the lights suddenly came to life, glowing faintly at first and then burning brighter than ever. He did not understand their ancient mechanics, but from here, upon this high perch, there were few better sights to impress a new lover with.

"They are beautiful," Daisy said dreamily, leaning her head upon his shoulder. And for the first time in his life, Simeon felt relaxed and satisfied with his life. "They must draw all living things for miles," she added and sat upright suddenly. "Are those fireflies off in the distance?" she gasped, pointing deep into the night where the forests were at their deepest and darkest.

Simeon followed her gaze. They might have looked like fireflies, but there was something else. *Torches*, he thought, and suddenly, the serenity left him.

"There are so many," she whispered, and Simeon inhaled the last of his herb and blew it out swiftly. Were it to be a marching convoy of bandits, they would be welcomed in. There would be blood and wealth if it were a marching convoy of wanderers. He feared the thought of a marching army, so instead, he admired the glow of the sanctuary below. Distantly, the hundred flickering torches moved ever closer.

"Aye, my love, so many," he said evenly.

"Darling, are they torches?" she asked as realisation came upon her.

"Whisht. Everything will be alright," he whispered, and knew his words were hollow.

11

ROOK 'N' RUA

"They must be from the city," Caius whispered through gritted teeth. Rua thought so, too. She was lying between the young Runner Caius and the gnarled fiend of Rook. Neither bandit dared move lest they disturb the evening or their good fortune too. Well, terrible fortune to come upon these fiends, but a fine thing that they remained concealed. It was the little things.

"Aye, but I've never seen banners like that around Spark," Rook muttered, shrugging. It was a fair point. The banners, painted in full deathly black with some vibrant red in a crude design that looked like fingers, suggested what Rua could only imagine was meant to mean murder. They hung high in the breeze over the leather- and armour-clad army.

Though close and concealed, they could hear no accents or words. Moreover, they saw no sign of any brutal Alphalines, be they male or female, marching among them. But, saying that, what exactly did an Alpha look like anyway? Some said they were taller than most. Stronger, too, with limbs like tree trunks. And eyes that cast fire if you stared too long. Others believed them to be simply human, just better at it. To her knowledge, Rua had never met one and never been hunted by one, either. This felt like hunting, though.

"Perhaps they are mercenaries, doing Dia's work all nice and tidy like," Rua suggested, swallowing as she did. Rua had been part of roving brigades in her own lands long ago, in a different life. Back when she was fierce, foolish, carefree and cruel. Back when Magnus was just new to the throne and the lands were not entirely at peace. Some said Magnus was the only Alphaline born of the Savage Isles. That would explain his brutal success. She had never cast eyes upon her king, either, and had never wanted to.

This march of conquest was a familiar thing, though, even if her last one had been a decade and a half before. Those had been fine, brutal times. Clenching her jaw until it hurt, she thought of lesser times when she was younger and carefree and without blood upon her hands. Back when she'd been on the other side of a menacing brigade. She absently counted the many as they marched through the Wastes, ever so threatening, ever so leisurely, towards her home.

Rook agreed. "It would be bad to be seen wiping out a town. Bandit infested or not."

"Fuk me," Caius whispered.

"They couldn't possibly think to attack Raven Rock, could they?" Leander, the last of their troop, asked. Unlike the others lying prone on the muddy forest floor, Leander sat casually in the shade of a tree with a strand of grass wedged in his teeth. He was youngest of the four in the hunting party and most eager to follow Rook into the Wastes after the murderers. He had the wildness of youth. A fine thing it would have been indeed, if not for his casualness. These hunters appeared tranquil, but all things changed in a breath. "I'd like to see them try it," he added, spitting some grass-flavoured phlegm into the grass. Rua could see the eagerness and fear in his eyes. He'd probably only killed a fiend for the first time in the last few months. A thing like that could break anyone. Sometimes, though, it gave them a taste for the task. There were worse things.

Looking back, Rook caught sight of the young Runner dug in against the tree. "What the fuk are ye doing? Get low and get hunting, you fool," he snarled. Rua grinned as the boy shrank beneath the criticism and dove to the dirt lest their leader take further umbrage at his casualness.

In truth, the four were no fit fighting group of Runners at all. They were simply the last few remaining comrades willing to hunt Smit and Fitz. Rook, master tracker among them, took leadership duties, and no one was to argue, especially now, with them all happy upon the hunt and all closing in upon a roving army marching towards their home.

Rua felt the agony of her loss as it came upon her anew. Visions of her mighty Andreas flashed in her mind, and once more she fought the blame she carried. The magnificent suit of hardened steel had been fitted perfectly to him. Her finest work. She'd done it out of love. She should have known better. She was superstitious enough. She'd merely been blind to his requests.

Blood everywhere.

She felt no guilt about missing the funeral, though. That shit would have been far too tragic. Far too real as well. There were blissful moments when out hunting; she could forget for a precious moment that he was slain. But seeing him cast into the dirt to serve as food for the land was too much. Not yet. Fuk that.

When Rook took the lead, she'd happily ridden with him out of the lonely gates.

Limbs convulsing.

She swallowed that heartache swiftly, though. Love, loss and horror marched hand in hand with Rua. It always had. She didn't want to die like Andreas either. Watched by countless fiends and friends, unable to intervene. No, she desired a quiet death. Away from prying eyes and horror. In her bed, alone or loved. It didn't matter. Just not with an audience.

The army in itself was a terror. They'd heard it from afar, and though loath to break from their trek towards the little town of Nioe, they followed their curiosity and, through a rightly shitty bit of luck, dug in closer than needed as the army passed by. A shrewder move would have been tearing right back to Raven Rock to give warning. But these things happened. They were surrounded but, in a way, they were used to such things. They simply became the surrounding green. Aye, scouts were marching alongside, but it was unlikely that one of those fiends would stumble upon them, and there was little reason to worry. Instead, they had a plan, a simple one: count those curs as they passed and get running home right after.

Smit and Fitz be damned.

To the burning fires of hell and all.

"Fuken tonnes of soldiers," Caius whispered, and he was not wrong. A few thousand at least, and a real terrifying contingent of cavalry leading the ranks. They were the absolute terror. Soldiers they could outrun: they knew the brush, travelled light and all. Mounts, though, cared little for obstacles and sprinting. They'd charge them down quickly enough.

"That's probably more than anything Raven Rock can handle," Leander added. "They probably took out all our scouts and all. The Rock is ruined, I tell ya."

"Wouldn't be sure of that," Rook said, stiffening as though suddenly realising that a grand assault was occurring under his nose. "The Rock can dig in like a mighty fist, like Andreas's strikes."

That last breath, wet and final.

Again, the sorrow came upon Rua, and she fought it again. She also fought the desolation of Andreas's loss should there be a battle. Such things required strong leaders. Those hunted bastards had struck quite the blow. She could imagine Andreas grinning and challenging as these fiends upon mounts came charging towards the gate. The Rock would hold, and those mounts would become bandit property soon after. She missed Andreas like no one ever before. A tear slid free of her eye, and, horrified, she wiped it away quickly before anyone noticed—Andreas himself would have disapproved of her agony.

You went into the darkness first.

Have a glass of red waiting, you bastard.

Though they were no less than a hundred yards from the roving army, the ground shook as they passed. In the wind, Rua heard a guttural few words that she did not recognise, and for a cold moment, she wondered if the Deep North had finally gathered its thousand and one warring tribes together to come and invade the Four Factions as they so very much desired. Rua wouldn't have minded at all if this was the case. The Deep North were aligned in word with the bandits and their countless Runners. Who else had made the cofe runs these last few years right into the heart of the Factions and, more recently, into the city? Problem was, invasion would be bad for business, particularly an unexpected one. Andreas or

Ulrik of Adawan might have taken umbrage at such behaviours. Regardless of the reason, Rua sensed warring from these wandering soldiers, and war was no good for anyone unless you were part of the winning side.

Countless brutes passed, and the bandits remained still and at ease. Studying the mass and seeking out any apparent leader was no easy task. Each barbaric animal-clothed brute was more daunting and impressive than the next. But no cur atop a mount, appearing pompous and proud like any decent leader, stood out among the crowd. Perhaps the leaders resided within one of the massive carts carrying siege engines of the ancients. All savages knew the potency of those foul things. Anyone who fought in the Faction Wars doubly so.

A dozen large mounts pulled each weapon along, and Rua's stomach turned at the sight of these rolling beasts. She'd never seen one up this close before, but she had felt the devastation they could inflict upon stone walls. Few attempted diplomacy when they could just hurl a few boulders at the enemy.

"Stay low," Rook warned above the rumbling terror, and it was fine advice.

Alas, it didn't matter, for no luck was with them.

They never heard the scouts approach. Perhaps it was the rumbling, or perhaps the beating of their hearts. Perhaps everything might have been different had the two foreign curs simply taken a different path or, better yet, announced their approach and faced a swift slaughtering. As it was, it was Rook they tripped upon, spinning in surprise at finding him beneath the bush they stepped through.

"Oh, fuk me," Rook cried. Fine words too.

They screamed and stumbled, and Rook was upon his feet quicker than the rest, with a weapon in hand, but they were away from him rightly quick.

"Get them," cried Caius, gathering his wits and stepping after them. The two scouts, shouting in their unusual tongue, took off through the heavy brush, no doubt screaming warnings of interlopers. A step behind them sprinted Leander and Caius.

"No, you fools," cried Rook.

Rua might have charged after, but Rook grabbed her roughly before she took a second step. "Those idiots are already caught," he cried, charging from their hiding place back into the forest, seeking escape.

Rua hesitated for a cold breath as Caius and Leander swiftly caught their prey, leaping upon them and grappling. All four figures struggled, and only then did Rua see their mistake. "Leave them," she cried, and unsurprisingly, neither comrade heard her, such was their preoccupation with murdering the scouts. They did this effectively, but not before alerting the Riders of the commotion.

With daggers swiftly stabbing and killing as though it were a skirmish in an arena, they were smooth and efficient, and were the army to have appreciated such skill, they might have hesitated.

They didn't appreciate it at all.

It is no small thing to stare down an entire army, but these two fools liked their odds, and Rua, before turning to flee after the older hunter, watched them give a fight to the charging warriors who surrounded them with shouts of grief, rage and hate. She heard the screams, thought them familiar, and swiftly heard nothing else but the wind, her gasping breath and the thundering mounts at her rear.

Focus on the fools, not on me.

It was a prayer to the gods and an order to their chances.

"Keep running," Rook cried, leading the escape through the trees, ducking beneath a few low-hanging boughs, leaping over a stream and down a sharp incline to where their mounts awaited. A small journey, the longest of her life, and she was a step behind.

Distantly, the roar of rumbling hate and shattering woodland disturbed the silent forest, and it added to her panic. With clumsy hands, she undid the reins all too slowly. Cursing herself for the double knots in her mount's bridle, she struggled and pulled, twice taking a chance and pulling one strap through the knot in hopes of slipping it free. Then, discovering to her horror that the knot had tightened, she cursed a little more. And then took a knife to the stubborn things.

"Come on, come on," she hissed at herself. She noticed Rook gripping his mount, watching her, watching the woods, and watching her again. It wasn't helping as she sawed at the thick leather.

As she worked, he began releasing the other two mounts whose riders were long dead. "Easy, nice and slow," he muttered as though out in a meadow without an entire army trampling through the forest. It might have been calming himself, might just have been an attempt at instructing her. She wanted to scream in his face. Give a reason for her panic beyond the obvious. To wail that her man had been taken from her only a few days before. Instead, she cut at the knots, hating her fate, her luck, her stupidity in tying the reins so tight.

Fuk fuk, fukety fuk fuk.

"I think you should hurry up, girl," Rook said, slapping the other beasts before climbing upon his own. "You have moments left alive." That didn't help either.

"Fuk off away from me, Rook… nearly have it… there… right… I have it, I fuken have it… let's go."

He'd already left. It was a fair move on his part. Still,

though, she'd never felt as alone as she did at that moment, watching him race off through the green without a care in the world, seeking freedom, while all around her, the oncoming thunder of doom was only a tree trunk away from reaching out and plucking her from her mount. She suddenly needed to relieve herself.

Get on the mount, girl.

Climbing up and kicking off, she'd never been so grateful for the mount she chose, not to mention her lighter frame. Thrashing through the green, ducking where she could, gasping in time with her horse's desperate huffs, she clung tight and fled the sound. Only then did she realise the precariousness of this chase. In the moments from their flight, the army spread out, spread the word, and went charging in no time at all. From either side, she could hear the rumbling brutes closing in. Flashes of movement appeared from every side, and she wanted to answer her gut. To draw sword and die not in flight, but in war, taking at least two in her place. That was any savage's duty. She could kill two fiends no bother.

Distantly, she heard the deep, booming drone of war horns, and they took her nerve. Rook must have heard them, too. She could hear his mutterings in the wind as she drew upon him. While her mount was built for flight, Rook had chosen a brute of a mount, built for the slow slog at a leisurely pace through the Wastes. He watched the trees as she rode alongside him and listened to the thunder.

"They've caught our scent—faster beasts than this workhorse." He dared a look back again. "I reckon they could charge us from either side," he cried, and as panicked as she felt, he appeared calm. Within a breath, she was a full length ahead of him. A breath after that, she considered leaving him behind. He must have considered it, too. "You chose a fine horse," he called.

They rode like a weak wind for a time, watching behind them, fearing the growing roar of pursuers. Rua considered dropping from her mount, diving for cover. Any sort of cover. Perhaps a bush or two big enough to conceal her and hoping for the best. A fine plan in a deeper part of the forest on a darker afternoon. The soil here was dry and rocky. Barely suited to anything more than sickly-looking evergreens, thin grasses and a nasty few patches of weeds. Perhaps, after a few miles more, they could find a better place if they made it deeper into the forest. As it was, it wouldn't take more than a casual glance from any of a thousand careless pairs of eyes to spot her best hiding place.

Not even a large rock to hide behind.

Rook stared to the north, seeking a hiding place of his own. She wondered at how well he concealed his terror. And how skilled he was at cards.

"I think we'll be alright," he suddenly exclaimed. "If we can stay ahead of them, there's a bandits' sanctuary not far from here. Stick to the path," he said, kicking his beast forward, and she followed. It was all she could do.

Rua, as instructed, took the lead, not only to entice Rook's mount to charge its best, but also to give herself a better chance of escape should they be discovered. She could leave him in the wind if needed. Rook would be a fine distraction. It was nothing personal.

They charged as far and as fast as their horses could carry them—a terrible chase with no end in sight. The rumble around them grew as an entire army hunted them down. Any moment, she expected to see the flash of a banner followed by a few dozen arrows and a Rider or two—or just a flash of silver dagger as it struck her down. Nothing mattered but the road ahead, and they tried their best.

And they did rather well.

"Here, here—it's fuken here," Rook suddenly cried, dropping from his mount, slapping its rear furiously. The beast took the hint and fled from the path.

She looked for a cave, for a gathering of boulders. She'd even heard of clever fiends hiding an entrance beneath a bush. She saw no bush. What she saw was a tree. It was a very nice tree because it was the largest tree among a cluster of denser evergreen trees.

"Here, here. Over here—come on," Rook demanded as she dropped warily to the ground. There was still time to bolt from this place. Leave him to his delusional fate. The path was just calling, and her horse was fresh and lively.

And then she saw something more. The cluster was more than it appeared. Obviously, if one knew where to look, there were a thousand such clusters either mile along the path, but this one stood out. She slapped her beast and watched it sprint after its comrade while she surrendered herself to Rook's better instincts. Charging after him through the treeline towards the looming cluster of trees, she realised the genius behind such concealment. A casual observer might not know the forest, might never wonder how an evergreen tree was as large or as bulbous as this one, but to Rua, as she drew nearer, it was a monstrosity out of place.

Beneath its roots, Rook scrambled for a hold. Then, from among the dark, long-decayed branches, he pulled out a concealed rope ladder, and, ever the gentleman, he began climbing swiftly up the massive tree ahead of her. "Come on, come on, come on."

Within a breath, he was off to the top. Clambering over himself to seek cover behind a thin break in the thick covering of dried brush that was nailed and secured to a wooden structure, he suddenly disappeared. It was as large and grand as a decent room in Raven Rock and probably just as cramped. She followed after, each step a strain and terrifying—like unknotting a stubborn set of reins. Three steps to go. Thunder closer. Two steps, roars and screaming. Final step, those cursed horns reverberating in her chest.

And in.

"What is this place?" she gasped, sliding free of the rope ladder as he desperately pulled it up and into cover.

"Whisht, my friend," Rook said, kneeling beside her. He was gasping, but his cold eyes stared into the deep forest beyond. "We are safe."

Rua marvelled at what master craftsman had come upon the idea and somehow completed such an improbable thing. They knelt in a dark room of concealment, painted the same colour as the wood outside. Her first thoughts were that it was unnaturally cosy. The carpet on the floor certainly helped, and kneeling upon its soft sheen, she looked through thin slats in the wood, beneath the cover of long-dead branches painstakingly attached to the outer surface, as the first of the mysterious army appeared along the path.

"They are many," Rua whispered.

"Too many," he agreed.

They came charging through the path, ever onwards, no doubt following the prints of their quarry's mounts and the dust kicked up by their beasts.

"Keep on going," Rook whispered.

The absent gods must have heard his prayer, for little changed in the mounts' charge, and the Riders kept galloping on into the distance. Each one that passed was a welcome sight.

For a time.

Then, a group of Riders dressed differently from the previous few hundred came lazily down the path as though out on a warm day's ride. Theirs was a leisurely pursuit, though all of them kept their eyes not on their comrades but upon the path. A solitary Rider halted her mount and steered it to the side of the trail.

"She can't see anything; the hunters will have covered our tracks," Rook whispered.

The girl shook her hair out as she stared at the ground, allowing her mount to drift slowly along the scrub where Rook and Rua had fled only moments before.

Rua tried to remember the land's cut, the depth of soil, and the moisture underfoot, as well as whether they'd left any obvious tracks behind to be found by a keen-eyed tracker.

Oh, no, oh no, oh, no.

"Oh, no," whispered Rook, daring to blink, trying to looking away and failing.

"She sees us, doesn't she?"

She must have. She dropped from her mount smoothly. Her comrades left her to it. As they did, she stepped towards the treeline, keeping her eyes on the ground.

The click of Rook's crossbow made Rua start. He slid a bolt into the notch but rested the weapon by his side. It was panic, but not pure panic, not yet. Soon, though. And she would play, too.

The girl glided through the forest. With the thunder of the Riders distant now, Rua began to play the options and came up with nothing. With her heart in her mouth, she waited for her fate to turn.

The girl wandered towards their hidden camp alone and stopped short as though playing a game of her own devising. For a time, she stayed still as a statue, and Rook drew his crossbow, held it aloft and slid it easily out through the gap beneath the dried dead branches. It was a difficult shot for the best. From what Rua understood of his ability, he wasn't the best.

"Easy, Rook," she mouthed ever so, and he nodded.

The girl looked straight up the tree and rested her eyes upon the darkened gathering of branches.

Fuk, fuk, fuk.

She watched for a time. A long time. At least three breaths worth of time, and all the while, her patient comrades continued to wait, and Rua was desperate for Rook to hold a breath longer. She didn't want to die. Not unless she had a blade in her hand, and it was bloody and swinging. That would be a fine enough death. It was Andreas's round, after all.

Opening her arms wide as though pulled from either side, the girl stood still. With her eyes closing, she began to giggle ever so, a terrible, echoing sound in the afternoon sun. They knew then that she knew their ploy.

"What the fuk?" Rook hissed. It was a fine question. Rua hadn't a clue either.

"You win this game of seek," the girl suddenly cried before spinning around and marching back towards her mount. As she did, she barked orders, and immediately, her comrades appeared on the path, returning from whence they'd gone. Grabbing her mount, the girl placed a kiss on her hand and nodded again to the concealed bandits before riding away with her comrades.

"Who was that?" Rua whispered.

"That's the strangest thing I ever saw," Rook said, sitting back in the long leather couch at the far wall. He stared at the bolt carefully as he unloaded his weapon, and Rua, shaking from fright and the unfulfilled anticipation of battle, sat down at his feet on the warm carpet and stared at the wall.

"Perhaps she didn't realise we were concealed here," Rua offered weakly.

"I wonder, deep in my bones where my better senses reign, should I have taken that shot?"

A cold shudder came upon Rua, and she shook it off as though it were little more than the breeze. "What now?"

"We wait until this shit quietens down, and then we go a-hunting."

12

THE BRINGING OF DEATH

The beauty of the lights never failed to affect Kaya. They stirred feelings of sorrow for a life she could never have imagined, let alone had. Their mysterious glow, concealed within a thin glass sphere, was knowledge beyond her, but she thought them the greatest remnant of a civilisation long forgotten, burned in the fires and everything else after that. They were machines of the ancients and a cold reminder of all that was lost. They burned bright throughout the town, like waves of fire upon a sea of lava, and they were beautiful. These shimmering lights were a reminder of how high they had risen above natural things. But as much as she loved the lights, she hated them with every part of her being. They brought light, hope and reassurance, but they came at a cost. The greatest cost in life. Death.

As the lights took fire, so too did she begin her lonely walk. Lonely in her soul, for she was anything but a lone figure this awful night. Her steps echoed in the street and it was a disheartening, unusual thing. She led the line and she took every step carefully. Out ahead of her, the burning torch warmed her quivering fingers against the chill.

She believed she would have the words by now—deep, meaningful words to make sense of this horror. Instead, the silence unnerved her, took her concentration and quelled her thoughts.

He would have found this so funny.

The bastard.

The wonderful, wonderful bastard.

She imagined she could hear the electric hum in her ears as she walked. Truthfully, she'd never heard the town as quiet as this. Not even at the witching hour in the coldest night, or at dawn on the final day of the hot seasons when hangovers blanketed the town and no soul reared their head at day's first light.

Alone.

Gray was not beside her. In truth, this gathering was for all, but Gray knew better. Knew his place. Saying that, however, she wished he had matched her step at this very moment. She would have felt stronger with him by her side. There was something in his manner that was both challenging and dependable in equal measure, and she couldn't help but feel stronger with the fiend beside her. If only to prove to him her confidence. Especially when she felt anything but.

How should I even begin?

Still, no speech came to mind. She'd agonised all day over the final words she would offer to those gathered. Kind, heartbreaking words to help commit the tragedy to memory, but also words of love. In Gray's absence, perhaps Devitt would have been a welcome tonic. Alas, as a council member, his part in this performance was already at play. Albeit a few steps behind, he marched as one of the bearers of the dead. Carrying such a great man on his final run was quite the honour. Bandits had little in the way of tradition or honour, but putting the dead to rest was a tradition they held deep. She might have looked behind, hoping to catch a glimpse of his charming, grim face, but perhaps that might have been too much.

Hold it in.

The world would watch and cry, and she would let it happen without her. She needed to be above such things. She didn't know why, but it was something to hold on to.

She sped her steps into the abandoned streets away from the healer's bay door. Behind her, the carrying kin followed. All in time, all rightly careful and respectful. She led the procession towards the gates; this trip was the longest one imaginable. Around her, where the cluster of little spheres were brightest, she squinted against their glare. They honoured him, but she might have preferred them dimmed throughout this event. What was wrong with a few burning torches anyway? She had argued against their burning but was voted down swiftly enough, and she didn't desire to challenge any further.

He loved those damned lights.

Images of his murder flashed through her mind, and her torch wavered ever so. Nothing much, just a reminder of the precariousness of fire and the world's unfairness. Andreas had ruined his wealth negotiating, smuggling, and eventually installing these lights, and here they shone for him. These lights were his legacy but also his downfall.

Fuk you, lights.

Walking through the streets, she heard the gentle unlatching of every door she passed. Soon after came the swift steps of the mourners as they fell in line with the walking procession. She wished Rook was walking with her. She wished the cur would take her responsibility while he was at it. Take all the duty of the words as well. Had Rook not known him longest?

Knew the killers as well.

Swallowing the sudden surge of hate, she thought of her dear friend Rua, broken and bereft. She wished she'd had the words at least to offer her. She wished Rua, too, was walking with her. Rua would have had all manner of fine stories to offer the gathering crowd. Did Rua not know Andreas most, above all others?

Kaya wanted to be angry at her comrades but couldn't be. Their grief was tenfold whatever hers was. Though she hated her place in this event, she couldn't be angry with Rook and Rua for choosing to charge out on a manhunt over bringing out the dead to rest.

Turning at the gate, she glanced back and was shocked but not surprised to see the entire town had come to attend the ceremony. Seeing the sullen line of mourners, going two by two, heads hung low, silent as shadows, brought a lump to her throat something awful. And also added to the terror of speaking to so many.

Fuk you, Rook, for leaving me to do this.

Fuk you too, Rua.

I should have gone with you.

Like any decent friend should have.

The only reassuring thing was the figure of Aimee. She was as proud as any girl that age, cursed with beauty and grace. Marching just ahead of the weeping group of six with their long sack of ruined, dead meat upon their shoulders, she was a sight of stillness—a welcome one, too.

As usual, Aimee knew exactly what to do. Gliding up to Kaya, she kissed her hand and then placed it to her heart so Kaya might know she wasn't alone, and Kaya loved the girl anew.

The gates creaked open, and she shuffled through. Her pilgrimage brought her down past the gate, back up along the far wall, out beyond the town's lights, where they came upon a crop field. It was here that Aimee stepped up beside her.

"Kaya, have you written anything yet?" the girl whispered.

"No, not yet."

"That doesn't seem like an excellent idea, Kaya."

"I'll just make it up as I go."

"Oh, dear. I would not like to be you right now."

"Thank you, Aimee. You are a wonderful help."

The girl grinned and immediately set Kaya at ease. Distantly, Kaya thought she saw a flicker of fire in the forest. For a hopeful moment, she wondered if it was Rook and Rua returning with news of bandits captured—or, better, slain and done with, and vengeance had. Also, perhaps they might be armed with the words the entire town needed to help move them.

Alas, it was a trick of the light, and as the townspeople began to fan out in a monstrous pack, she once again considered approaching Silas to do the honours. Unfortunately, the wretched man's wife had left him rather spectacularly earlier that day, so no doubt the drunken bastard had other things on his mind.

She offered one last prayer to the absent gods she'd no faith in, that they remove this burden from her. Then she remembered she didn't believe in the absent gods.

That was fine, though, because they believed in her.

"He would have hated this silence," she whispered to Aimee as the townspeople formed a grand flanking manoeuvre on all sides, as though they had been drilled in such positioning. They gathered and grouped in close, drawn like moths to her fire. She would need to raise her voice, though, for they were many, and she felt as small as a weasel.

"Aye. That's true," agreed the younger girl, who leaned in

close so others wouldn't hear her. "He would have hated being dead, as well."

Kaya sniggered beneath her hand. Better that than weeping. Aimee wasn't done.

"At least he'd rest well, knowing he put you in this position."

"You think?"

"Aye, Kaya, he would have loved the expression on your face right now. It's hilarious."

Kaya smiled warmly. With or without some watchful gods, it felt miraculously healing to smile, and strangely, she thought about Gray. She wondered what a warm smile might look like upon him. It would probably be a rightly charming thing, too. Once again, she wished Gray was in the crowd. For just a suspicious moment, she imagined him desperately seeking out the engines that ran the lights. She imagined him breaking into building after building in the abandoned town, seeking answers for his reports to the Primary. She caught herself sniggering again. Even he wasn't that tactless.

Andreas would have liked the boy. That shit stung rightly.

The bringers of the dead eased Andreas's body to the ground beside the large mound. She wondered what seeds they would bury with the man. She'd never approved of living on as compost, but Andreas was quite the avid supporter of it. More than that, he thought it an amusing fate altogether.

A fine seeping oak tree would have suited Kaya, she mused. Eternal and grand, adding to the beauty of the land. Knowing someday she would be an afternoon's potato soup was a grisly reckoning. Still, dead was dead, she supposed. She hoped she would make some of the nicest potatoes if it came to it. It was the little things.

Distantly, she heard the roll of thunder and looked to the

dark sky above. It was strange to see nothing but the stars and shattered moon. Feeling a little breeze, she imagined the storm would come nowhere near the town this night.

She was wrong.

Hesitating for as long as she possibly could and still without inspiration to carry her thoughts to words, she caught sight of the last two mourners in the smitten forms of Daisy and Simeon, hand in hand and looking the worse for wear. Kaya smiled once more. Andreas had long since whispered that those two would end up together. *Should* end up together. Saying that, it might have been better for them to stay away for now, what with people's wounds so fresh.

She peered through the crowd and spied Silas. He wasn't hard to miss, such was the redness in his face. She could also see murder in those eyes, and were she able, she might have taken him aside and calmed him down. As it was, he kept silent despite the rage, despite the dreadful embarrassment he must have felt, having woken up this morning as a somewhat happily married man.

Perhaps also the shame for beating his wife.

Distantly, she heard a raised voice on the wall's far side. A common thing in a town on any other day, but worse with this hush around her. She couldn't make out the words, and few mourners seemed to notice. Their attention was upon the mound, the hole, the ruined body and the struggling woman before them wondering what the fuk to say.

With a heavy heart, she stepped forward to kneel by the body. Easing the hood over ever so, she gazed upon his still form and fought the rancid aroma of fresh flowers against the rot growing inside him.

Real good potatoes soon.

"It's time to rest, my friend," she whispered, fighting those tears again as she knelt and kissed his forehead.

Freezing.

She'd almost forgotten what it was to kiss a dead body. Her lips felt slapped, and her mind reeled with horror. Nothing living ever felt that cold. She felt herself begin to shake. The ground she knelt upon felt unsteady, as though quaking beneath a thousand-strong charge.

She had no words, but she could deliver her soul, for it was all she had.

The rumble of thunder drew nearer, and it made no sense. Suddenly, the silence around her became a low murmur, and she looked out into the night. She did this because that's exactly what the entire town did.

"What is that?" Aimee asked, spying a spattering of flame through the clustered trees.

Aimee wasn't alone in her queries; the murmurs grew louder around them.

The voice rose from the wall a little more—louder now than before—and turned to screaming. Through the dark, Kaya saw more flame and movement. Then she heard the blare of horns, and a terror came upon her.

Already, some were running back towards the gates. Towards the sound.

And then, from the dark, they came.

Hundreds of Riders upon mounts. For just a breath, she wondered if it was the arrival of Ulrik and his comrades from Adawan, here to honour the fallen leader. To offer his condolences upon the death of his most trusted generals?

Really, though, she knew better. Knew there was no way word could have even reached Ulrik by now.

And then she saw banners of black and red waving.

Then came the swords in their hands, and that's when the true screaming started, and the invasion of Raven Rock began.

13

PRELUDE TO THE END

Simeon recognised the danger long before the first mount appeared from beyond the treeline. A life spent listening to the wind, listening for some sneaky threats or just sniffing out a nasty little trap, had prepared him. It had probably prepared most of the other bandits too, but Simeon's knack for dodging potential doom was well known. This was more than a mere rumble. He felt it like an insect felt the threat of a lazy swipe. Despite the haze from the delicious tobacco weed, or perhaps because of the paranoia it imparted, he followed his feeling, and that feeling suggested, *"Get away right now."*

The world around him slowed but for the beating in his chest and the adrenaline surging through his body. Suddenly, everyone in the crowd was a little close, and this gathering was a too-enticing target.

Slowly, as the wind carried the drumming from a distance, he took hold of his love and began shouldering his way through the crowd.

"What are you doing?" she asked in a hazy voice. The wonderful aroma of the drug wafted off her.

She did not fight his leading; she merely followed, albeit warily, and he thought her rightly beautiful, with that goofy smile and all, even as his instincts rallied.

She's too stoned to notice the threat.

"Everything is alright; we just need to go," he whispered. Nobody noticed them, and that was fine with him.

Even so, progress through the densely packed mourners was slow, and it became frustrating in the low light, with their heads bowed so low. Perhaps, if they looked up, they might see birds rising in the moon's shattered light as they escaped the coming of terrible things.

Move faster, fool.

He wanted to shout out a warning but thought better of it. Why cause a scene if it was all in his head?

"Is that thunder, my love?" she asked dreamily—a fine question. A part of him wanted to protect her from the coming darkness. From whatever sought them all out. Like the foolish parent who protects their child over teaching them the value of experience, he almost told her everything was fine—almost whispered that no matter what, fairness and luck were a thing.

"We should be far from here, my darling."

Dazed and drugged, she followed his lead, and he felt worse for having insisted they share a second pinch of weed before the funeral. It had seemed like a kindness at the time. She'd endured such trauma this awful day, and Simeon, for his foolish sins, believed a little more numbing than normal was no bad thing. Better that than downing a bottle of sine, he imagined. The thing was, she wasn't half the smoker that he was. "On occasion," as she would say. He considered her the sharpest mind in the town. With the drug in her system, less so. Spectacularly.

"Wait! What? Where are we going?" she cried suddenly

as they broke away from the crowd, and he began to jog. The crowd started to notice the thunder now, too.

"Just go," he snapped, dragging her towards the darkness, his step slower, weighed down by her drag. Out away from the masses, he felt both naked and better. In the low light, he dragged her towards the cover of some trees on the edge of the town's eerie electric glow. He began to count his steps, even as the cries in the distance grew—first of alarm and surprise, and then of horror.

He dared a glance back and saw them, riding upon fierce mounts with weapons raised and swinging. He knew this was Adawan's doing; it just had to be. Surely Ulrik, for whatever reason, had finally had enough of Raven Rock's shit and ended their alliance. He wondered if it was because of the lights. Or the soft support of Wrek? Was it a vulgar grasp at power? Revenge for Rock placing a bounty on the heads of Adawan's most golden sons? He wondered, in that terrible moment as the killing began, if Andreas's murder was not just a cleverly contrived assassination and the first step towards taking this bastion. In that moment he hated Ulrik something terrible.

The first bandit to fall was a girl called Arwin. Since he was a boy, Simeon had taken a liking to her. It was probably her walk. It was a good walk. She waved her hips and everything. It certainly wasn't her skills at cards that charmed him, either. In fact, by count, she owed him three drinks after the last night they spent gambling. He'd always appreciated her devilish wit. She was perhaps not as witty as Daisy, but she was sharp, and these things mattered, as did her ability as a Runner.

Agile and swift, she wasted no time now breaking from the procession back towards the gate. Perhaps, on a better day, with a moment's notice more (such as a terrified yelp from a stoned comrade fleeing towards the forest), she might have made it too, but a Rider appeared along the far side of the treeline opposite the gate and charged her directly. The bastard did not even raise his blade. He didn't need to. He charged her down as she tried to reach the open gate. They met upon the arch's shadow, and Simeon couldn't look away. The meeting was soundless but for a dull thump like a fist upon leather. The rider thundered over her shapely form as though she were nothing more than low grass under a careless step. Simeon could only watch on in horror as he realised this attack was truly happening.

Oh fuk, oh fuk, oh fuk.

She died well. Things like this mattered. Rolling from the mount's powerful blow, she cried out just once in shock as a dozen riders followed the first. Her head was mushed to nothing in a breath, and Simeon, realising that shock had left him motionless in the wide open, began to drag Daisy once more away from their companions, who began to separate. Some ran towards the murder with fists raised, while others raced towards the wall. The rest went towards the cover of the forest. They did not scream nor bring attention to themselves either. They followed instinct, and instinct suggested shutting the fuk up—even the children. Born and raised for any threat, they ducked low, seeking instruction, following instinct. All of them separating. All of them potential targets for faster-moving killers. And Simeon thought it better that any of them be hunted down, rather than him and his lover. A cruel and necessary thought. Likely shared by everyone else.

The screams became louder and more agonising as more and more bandits met a terrible fate.

"Oh God, what is happening? Why are they doing this?"

Daisy wailed, and he wanted to protect her, keep her safe, and wake her from her stupor.

He could almost imagine them being hunted down, turning to catch the eyes of a thundering bastard. The rush of hooves behind them, closer and closer… A breath after and that would be that. Their story done, their lives lost to obscurity.

He himself might have turned around. Faced the death as it snuck up on him, all brazen and brutish. He might even have leapt at the Rider, as some bandits were already doing, even as they were crushed and killed.

So close.

So fuken close.

He awaited the moment of death. And then the moment after that. Still, he kept running, and she, now frantically weeping, followed. A desperate marathon that felt like an age was merely moments in the dark. They finally came upon a perfect spot to get in from the rain. To cover their heads and try to survive this storm.

"Down, down," he cried, sliding down into the mud, and she fell with him. They rolled, but still, he held her hand tight lest he lose her in the light, the haze and the bushes. It wasn't the best hiding spot, but it was better than being out in the dark, being herded and slaughtered by faceless, vile brutes.

In every way, she was slower than him. As he lay low, staring at the carnage as it unfolded, she sat upright, wearily watching. Tears were still streaming down her face, but mercifully in silence, as she tried to make sense of the carnage.

"They're killing everyone," she moaned, and he pulled her roughly to him, deeper among the trees, deeper into cover. Still, the rolling rumble continued as more and more Riders appeared from countless breaks in the trees.

Think, you fool.

He looked to the night, to the distant darkened woods, and nearly leapt to his feet with her, nearly began running again, this time never to stop.

He wasn't the first to consider such actions, he realised. Around them, he could see others fleeing into the forest. They passed by without gazing at their cover, without seeking their own, and soon were made to pay for it.

More Riders appeared, and only in that moment did he realise the town would fall this night. They were too many—some charging, and others lying in wait to ambush those fleeing the slaughter.

No one is to live to tell this tale.

It was a cold thought, and he felt his bladder release. He hadn't even needed to relieve himself, either. In a flash, he didn't even think about it again. Instead, he watched in horror as men, women and children were slashed and run down, battered and murdered, and it was too much.

We can't hide; we can't outrun them, either.

"I'm so scared," she whimpered, gripping him tight as though she were a newborn, and perhaps, in a way, she was new to this world. He knew her to be brave and proud, but she quivered terribly now, and his heart broke for the ruin she was.

"We cannot stay here," he whispered as a Rider charged past them, no more than two feet away.

"Let us be free from here," she said, fighting to free herself from his grasp. Her eyes were drunk, and she looked utterly unprepared for decisions so grand and final. He simply had to care for her, had to protect her.

"No, back to the wall," he hissed, and, pulling her to her feet, he darted out into the turmoil, back towards the wall at the furthest end of the town. He did not think lest he lose his nerve. A good thing, too, for they ran into mayhem.

"Please, Simeon," she cried, fighting him ever so. She was built like a goddess, but speed was not her skill. Nevertheless, she sprinted as fast as her shapely legs could take her. Away from the deceivingly safe darkness, out into the glow of the town. Where they could be seen, could be hunted easily, could be killed.

Only moments before, the world had still been peaceful and so sad. Anyone who survived this would likely never remember Andreas, such was the tragedy.

Far down at the front of the town, the remaining townsfolk had gathered to defend the main gate. No horse could clear that wall, no matter how large, and Simeon was overcome by an urge to be with his doomed comrades. He saw them begin to give fight to the Riders, who, less out in the open, could no longer rely on their mounts as barging weapons but only on themselves and their weapons. The odds were hardly fair, but anything was better than being run down from behind.

Deep, guttural cries of war carried in the air, and he turned and ran towards the far wall, as far from heroism as he could get. The wall appeared more swiftly than he expected. Dashing himself against its grey surface, he gathered a breath as Daisy fell against it with him, and he took stock of his surroundings. There were others along this monstrous defence, climbing to safety up and down the length of the wall. They did so silently; they did so below the low haze of the burning lights; they did it as though breaking into a house in the heart of the city. The perfect escape, if only to lock themselves in behind the bastards outside.

Daisy began to wail again, and he felt her anguish. But also, he wanted her to carry herself a little better. She'd always been the most calculating person he'd ever met. A grand thinker despite her choice in men. She wasn't herself now, though, and they might die because of it.

"Whisht, my love," he cooed, holding her close, matching her stare. Dragging her back to him. "They'll close the gate; they'll hold the wall. We only need to climb."

She began to panic. "I could never do it. I never could. I always thought I wouldn't need to," she wailed loudly. Simeon desperately hushed her to silence lest she bring the attention of a nearby Rider who was busily lancing an older woman who, trying to beat the odds, had tried to unseat him from his saddle. "I always fell. I always fuken fell," she wept, and Simeon could only cover her mouth with his hand.

"Be still, little one."

Please, shut up.

Just as Daisy uttered a long, lamenting, stoned wail of melancholy, the woman finally fell to the Rider's third blow, and the horseman spun his mount around, eager to find his next victim.

Truthfully, there were plenty of victims running everywhere, all enticing and shit, but the cur set his eyes upon the two lonely bandits crouched in against the wall.

"It's alright, little one," Simeon insisted, eyeing the wall, eyeing their hunter, eyeing the wall one more time in case it had shrunk in the last moments. It was a daunting beast of great height to any warrior or invader. To any skilled bandit, though, it was merely a challenge to be tested. Any Runner worth their salt attempted to scale this brute, and most defeated it at least once in their life, usually egged on by a watching audience as well. Such was the value of bragging. The fleetest of feet could do it without thinking too hard.

Simeon could scale it just fine.

The Rider turned and began his charge, and fresh terror

took Simeon. However, he had a plan; any plan was a grounding thing when terrified. He put that fear shit away for a breath and calmed the girl. "I will hoist you, and you might use those perfect hands to find a notch and heave yourself up," he whispered and kissed her cheek. That Rider was gaining speed.

"I can't, my love."

"Oh, of course you can."

"I'll fall."

"Not at all. I won't let you."

The Rider began to up his pace, spurring his mount on. The mount looked like it could crush bones if needed.

"I'm so scared; why is this happening?"

"I'll tell you when we climb atop the monster."

"If you think I can do it."

That Rider was real close now.

He smiled and fought the terror, panic and frustration. A bead of sweat rolled down his forehead. That would have given up everything were they at battle in cards.

"Just ease yourself up, and it will be fine."

She stepped upon his waiting, clasped hands and rested gracefully upon his shoulders with a gentle heave. It was here that she hesitated, and Simeon looked directly at the Rider and held his calm despite every instinct screaming at him to do otherwise. Then, at last, she grunted and pulled herself up as though it were nothing at all—as though they could have scaled the wall side by side.

"To the fires with you," Simeon cried to the oncoming Rider as she pulled herself over. The brute was nearly upon him, a few dozen feet away or so—but who bothered counting these things?

Simeon stepped away from the wall. Just enough to get that momentum going.

When it suited, they all claimed the wall stood fifteen feet high. Simeon considered it a little less from specific points— where the land rose, where there was give in the ancient rock. In those places, a clever little rat bandit could scurry up without effort and avoid a sticky, pointy end. Two steps back, and, like the wind, he suddenly rushed forward and leapt. His hands were a blur, his feet slid and slipped but held against the old wall, and he climbed upwards as though upon an evergreen, all the while imagining himself playing at ease and not near the business end of a blade.

Hurry.

Up and over he squirmed. It wasn't even close, either. He counted at least a breath and a half before that blade struck the wall and missed, and the Rider turned away to seek fresh prey in the night. Lying over the top and watching the Rider charge off, completely unmoved that he was denied a kill, Simeon caught sight of the horror at the main gate. Again, he felt an unusual desire to be part of it. To stand proud and hold firm against those who desired to desecrate his home.

He could see that some of these vile invaders had fallen to their town's meagre defences—some blades, a few pikes and stubborn bandit cunning. A terrible anger came upon him when he turned to see Daisy gasping on the ledge. He imagined her cut and bleeding as his comrades were. For a moment, that small dagger at his waist felt a lot larger than it was. He considered going to war for the insult of this invasion. But his anger quickly evaporated, for no more than twenty feet from him, where others sought to climb as he did, he caught sight of Silas struggling up the wall.

Hobbled by advanced age and his love of alcohol, the older man was not as agile as he once was. Despite this, he attempted the impossible, and Simeon couldn't help but extend his arm down the wall, gazing in wonder at the man as he reached out his hand. He was tempted to simply leave him, of course—oh aye, visions of Daisy's bruising clung to his mind, as the day's horrors still did. Despite this, he called out, "Give me your hand, comrade."

In a moment, Daisy was beside him, helping the others who were attempting to climb the wall.

"I can help you," she called out to those who scrambled upwards, nearly standing upon each other in their haste. They had fled from the gates or back from the forest, having seen what Simeon saw and knowing sanctuary remained only within Raven Rock. "Climb up," Daisy cried again desperately, and at the sound of her voice, the Riders slowly turned their attention back to them.

———

It was Silas's battered back that did him in. It was dodgy at the best of times, an affliction no healer had ever been able to rectify. He'd stretched, massaged and cursed it by turns, but had never gone longer than a season without enduring the agony on some particular morning. Many a time, he'd taken to drinking away his woes, and it helped, but the following morning, it would be a toss of the coin as to how healed or ruined he would be. He hadn't had a chance to drink away his sufferings today. He doubted he would ever drink again, for that matter, and it was all down to a shitty back.

It had ached the entire walk as he'd done his part to carry the dead, but he'd taken the pain and the burden, too. While it was one thing to endure the pain, sharing the weight of a dead friend with five others, it was another thing to attempt to scale a massive wall with his lower back in agony.

I did this a hundred times in my youth.

He tried again to gather momentum, but his stiff leg

barely answered his commands, and though he leapt high, he swiftly slid back down the insurmountable obstacle.

This is how I die.

Around him, others, desperate to escape the forest, rushed the wall, making finer attempts than he. He cursed them, cursed his luck, cursed his bitter, bitter life, and, last of all, he hurled his best curse for his death. Oh, to reach into his pocket, drain his flask and numb the pain enough that he could gather his war axe and take the fight to the invaders. Instead, he slid and failed like a child.

I am a lesser man.

"Help us," he heard a dozen voices cry out as they reached for the waiting hands above. Their wails disgusted him. His own need for help disgusted him even more. As was the desire to accept the help of the man who had stolen his wife.

So he rightly forsook any help, consequences be damned.

Silas charged again for the wall and again suffered the same terrible failure. He did manage to slap away Simeon's waiting hand, though. That was bitter progress. That was all he could do.

"Fuk me," he growled, seeing the Riders turning upon them all. Absently, he considered fleeing back into the forest and taking his chances in the treacherous darkness. There was enough of his comrades' blood upon him that he could just crawl through the dimness, playing the dead fiend, were the Riders to approach.

Coward.

A shard of agony shot down his back and on through his leg. The type of agony that took a man's mind. The kind that made him swallow his pride and all. Whatever pride remained after today, that is. He didn't want to die in this much pain. Somehow, that would be worse. As would dying with this anger in his soul. The anger that burned so brightly as he stared at the bastard high above offering his hand.

Kill him.

That'll make dying easier.

He fought that want something fierce. He wanted to leap high, grasp the cur's hand and drag him down to the murkiness. He might kill him here and now if he were gifted the time; more likely, the first thundering Rider would take both their heads off.

He didn't want to die that way either. That would feel like a cheap end. No, it was better to die with a blade in his hand, killing his killer, swinging like a legend. Many decades from now. He leapt again, ignoring the raging fire in his muscles and the dreadful, debilitating distress. He roared defiantly as he rose and by the grace of an absent god, his fingers caught and held, and he rose a little more. And then, cruelly, that hand appeared in front of him once more and, curses on him, he took it gladly, desperately.

"There you go, Silas," Simeon said, pulling him ashore from the tangled storm below. He dragged him along the top until his feet were clear, and that terrible fury retook Silas. He tasted murder on his lips, delicious and bitter all in the same gasping breath, and he hated this bastard anew. Hated him like fire upon dried wood in a warm season.

Kill him.

He imagined reaching for the boy and tearing out his throat and screaming victoriously as he died. Feeling that warm, wet flesh would be a tonic.

Kill him.

Then he thought about simply placing his larger hands upon the boy's neck and squeezing tight. Real fuken tight. That would be a satisfying end to the little shit. He imagined strangling Simeon until he shat himself. Or pissed himself.

Either one, really. As long as Daisy saw the weak fool die, it wouldn't matter.

Kill him now.

He imagined taking the boy's pathetic little dagger from his side and plunging it deep. Just once, to shock and murder him. He would be unnoticed by everyone upon the wall. It was mighty tempting, too, with its fine ivory handle. He could plunge the blade deep and shove him off the side. If anyone asked, and they would ask, it was an accident: an arrow struck him. On this dreadful night, who would care really?

Do it.

Daisy would care, of course, and that was fine. He could batter any truth into her if he wanted. Who was likely to protect her once Simeon was taken care of, anyway?

Kill her, too.

Silas imagined dashing her head against this wall while he was at it. Shove her over the edge after her lover. Leave the two of them to fall eternally under a hail of cold steel. Still, though, glancing at her battered form, his heart twisted and burned, and he loathed how much he still felt for the whore. Loved her, still. Until death.

"Leave me," Silas roared, slipping away from Simeon without fresh murder to his name. He did spit in the cur's face, though. There was that, at least. Like a weak-willed fool, Simeon took the slight without word or argument and went back to grabbing at the next scrambling hand from below.

Resisting a last temptation to kick the cur in the rear and send him right back over the wall, and with a barely stifled scream, Silas dropped down to the inside of the town and immediately went to gather his wits.

It was no surprise the city had suffered an attack. For

many a year, he'd suspected Raven Rock was a blemish in the eyes of Spark City. Unlike Adawan, its people were incapable of keeping out of the watchful eye of the Primary, unable to behave themselves at all. Those grand lights were the catalyst, no doubt. Word of the gaudy, shimmering things had likely spread like wind across the world. It was a fine last act by Andreas. But such things brought growth and wealth, and Spark City would not countenance such a thing. It was just a shame that bitch in the city could allow nothing but her own power to grow in this shitty little world.

Around him, stunned bandits stood ready and bewildered. Silas had never seen such a thing in his life. They stood along the wall, below it, throughout the streets, and more. Most watched the horror at the gates, unsure of what to do. In traditional battles or out on their runs, where murder and cruelty were required, bandits reigned supreme. As a people, they were forever ready and willing to challenge death in a glorious game of risk. But an attack upon their sanctuary had taken their nerve, their instinct. They stood like lost children, or like broken-backed climbers below a monstrous summit. Some had the sense to draw a blade, but this was no skirmish in the Wastes. There were different rules at play here, and they hadn't a clue.

Silas did.

"What are you all doing?" he roared, sprinting in among them as swiftly as his aching body would allow. "Get down there and get to killing," he demanded. His voice, ablaze with leadership, anger and desperation, stirred them to motion as he jogged past, urging them to follow. Though his words were cutting and direct, he didn't charge the gate. Not yet, at least. He sprinted hard towards his house despite the terrible pain. He wanted to relieve himself; he wanted to vomit; he wanted to fall upon his knees and weep in fear and sorrow.

Instead, his hatred infused him. It was a gift. He reached his empty house and stepped inside, fighting the desolation and dread that filled him as he stumbled through the dark building, seeking his wares.

"Fuken come *on*," he roared, strapping on his heaviest armour with clumsy, shaking fingers. "Come on," he demanded again, channelling his hate for his wife, her lover and the brutes attacking their town. Having managed to fasten the needful, he stopped below the grand mantelpiece in his living room and stared at the decoration hanging above it. He'd never liked the weapon. He had no idea why he'd kept it these last few years, why he'd always sharpened the blades yearly on his father's anniversary. He hated the man. The man hadn't been too fond of him either. Perhaps they saw too much of themselves in the other.

"If you are with me, Da, guide this fuken thing like you claimed to," he growled. It might have been a prayer. It felt like a threat.

Suppressing the pain of pulling the massive battle axe from the wall, Silas limped back into the night, determined to die swinging. It wasn't the finest plan, but he had little desire to allow these bastards to enter their territory without delivering a few bruises of his own.

He jogged back down towards the gate, and the pain worsened with the heavy burden of armour and weapon. He could have taken a sword. Or a bow. Or a few shiny, pricking daggers like that bitch Simeon would have chosen. Instead, he chose the battle axe and knew he would unleash some rightly brutal devastation upon those curs who came attacking.

And then he would die swinging, and that was fine.

As he ran, he roared, "On me!" to some stragglers unsure of their feet. Again, he used a tone that inspired motion.

Gathered followers. Around him, bandits, armed and wary, began to jog also. "On me, you cowardly fiends," he demanded, and a few roars of approval grew around him. He became two, then three, and then a dozen after that. Hardened bastard bandits, ready to be as brutal as he imagined and hoped for. Ahead, he could see the open gates and the melee of blood, death and horror beyond, and he charged onwards, eager to face it before some fool finally had the good sense to close the gates.

"On Silas," a female voice cried from behind him. He looked back to see a woman. Dion was her name. She roared as though she were a beast, and he knew her prowling ways. A fine-looking woman she was, with sturdy thighs, in truth. He knew this from the angle he'd seen them from: she was a fine Runner and a finer furrower. Things happened out in the Wastes upon a run. Daisy had never needed to know. It wasn't her place either; it had simply been a necessity. A natural thing, really. Dion had come a-sniffing for more after that dalliance, but he was no fool, and she was no Daisy, not even without her clothing. She'd taken the slight and given him a spit in the face, but they had remained friends. No better fiend to murder and die with, he decided, offering a nod.

"Let's go kill some fools," he bellowed, raising his battle axe magnificently, and they roared with him.

———

Daisy wrapped her arms around herself for a breath. The need to relieve herself came upon her suddenly, and she fought the urge. It was all in her mind, no doubt brought about by the terror of the moment surrounding them all. But also, in Silas's threat.

Don't kill me.

A few years before, he'd never have dared lay a finger upon her. Nor would she have allowed it. Now, though, she could see how close he was to murder. She'd seen it many a night. Many a morning, too. She mourned for her younger, better self. Not this waif who cowered and tasted her stomach's churning. Not this waif who, with numb, tingling fingers, stepped away from her husband as he struggled over the wall and knelt before her, out of neither duty nor honour. She could see murder still vibrant and fresh in his eyes. For more than a breath, she wished Simeon had left him to fall. Instead, her too-good-natured lover pulled the bastard to safety.

She felt numb, even as the hands from below reached for her. Desperate and scraping, bloody and awful. So many hands desperate for a saviour. She couldn't save them, though, for she was frozen in terror, staring at her husband. She thought Silas cruel, and she thought it cruel that he could inflict this terror by his mere presence. Even now. Even with her saviour beside her.

Saviour.

She hadn't expected Simeon to behave as he had. She hadn't expected to leap so willingly from everything she knew.

And for a few hours, she had been free of Silas. But now, at the end of the world, the cur was before her once more, ready to kill. She ignored the hands as they clawed and slapped loudly against the wall before slipping back down. She knew her responsibility was to her comrades, but she couldn't take her eyes off him.

Don't kill us.

She could see his scowl, his fist tightening, and she was helpless to save Simeon—helpless to even warn him. She was a shadow of herself and lesser for it. She wanted to hide away, to save herself, to be anywhere but here.

And within a flash, Silas was away from them, dropping back towards the town. She eyed him again and felt a terrible weight lifted. Only then did her lover's calm voice draw her from her drunken imaginings.

"I have you—grab on," Simeon cried, hauling a heavy woman over the edge and, without pausing to breathe, reaching for the next. With his feet dug in tight against the far side of the inner wall, he could hold quite the weight, and he was heroic.

Inspiring.

She dropped back down beside him, determined to swallow the anguish and terror. Ahead, out where they should have been burying a legend of the town, there lay a few dozen dead or dying bandit brethren. Down at the front gates, though, where the masses were attempting to get in, fight back, and somehow survive, a vile skirmish had broken out between the larger cohort of Riders and the foolhardy, heroic bandits. She wanted to be as far from that terrible place as she could. In between were those who were still hunted. Those who chose flight over war. Those who needed a right helping hand. They seemed to gather up below. Perhaps they believed this part of the wall was most accessible to climb. Perhaps, like birds in flight, they believed in safety in numbers. A wiser move was spreading out along the wall, but humankind craved company even when the fires drew in all around them.

What am I doing here?

She felt fresh panic as her tainted mind betrayed her. "Please, please, calm. One at a time," she cried, wedging her feet precariously against the back edge, just as a young girl leapt high, kicked against the wall and held for a breath. Grabbing her outstretched hand, Daisy nearly slid right over to the ground below, killing them both. Miraculously, as her body stretched out, she somehow took the girl's weight, allowing her the extra moment to pull herself over.

I can't do this. I can't do this.

A solution came to her. "I can only carry the women," she cried, reaching only for feminine hands now. Below, a frenzy came upon the desperate bandits as though seeing a fresh threat bearing down upon them. Perhaps this is precisely what occurred, but Daisy wouldn't dare look out into the night lest she lose her nerve. Twice, she was nearly pulled back over by a heavier-than-expected weight, but she began to remember herself despite this.

"Come on, scramble harder," Simeon cried as the local barkeep, a fiend twice his weight, clambered up and held the younger, lighter bandit for a few exhausting breaths before finally getting his feet to kick hard and edge upward. "Keep going," Simeon gasped as the man gripped his shirt and, puffing himself, finally pulled himself up to sit on the edge.

Watching, Daisy hated that man in that moment for the time it took him to save himself. Hated that Simeon could have pulled three up in that time and hated how he served his drinks in the tavern as well. Without dropping down, the heavy barkeep spun as Simeon had, dug his feet in and reached for the next waiting climber.

"I'll get ya all," he bellowed, wrapping his hands around a scrambling young trader before whipping him over the wall as though he was nothing at all. It was almost a beautiful sight, watching the man save souls. And then all at once, the thunder of some approaching Riders caused fresh panic among the handful of desperate climbers.

"Flee, you fools," cried Simeon, seeing their panic. "Get to the far side," he cried, motioning down towards the far corner, where there were no Riders hunting. "Over there," he cried, seeing what they could not. They were terrified, they were desperate, they were panicked and they were stubborn. They did not flee, and in a flash, they suffered for it as the mounts thundered down upon them.

One young bandit, taller than Daisy and quite a bit heavier, leapt and scrambled, and desperation guided his hands. He might well have bested the damned thing, but instead, reached for her, took hold, gripped real fuken tight, and she was helpless to stop him. The world slowed as she felt herself being pulled over the wall. Digging in and wrenching every bone and muscle, she howled at the weight. The boy slipped and struggled, but kept his hold. Looking back, he saw the Rider a few feet from him. She began to scream.

"Save me," he begged, and through the haze of desperate panic, she truly wanted to. She wanted to whip him over the wall and reach for the next as though she were the bartender, blessed with a full belly and a sturdy grip. Instead, she hung out over the wall, slipping dangerously, becoming easy prey to a fiend with a large blade.

"Let go of me," she murmured, even as the boy realised she had no strength and understood his fate.

"Oh, god, please," he begged as she shook her arms. She freed one hand first, and the curses be upon her, with that free hand, she thrashed at him. First, a few slaps, and then a weighted fist, and by the third strike, she drew blood. A terrible thing to see his nose explode as it did, as hers had under a similar few strikes.

What have I become?

The boy released, fell, and met the blade as his feet touched the ground, and she backed up, away from the threat. She could do nothing but watch the boy die. It was her only way to honour him. After that, though, she was broken. She slunk away from the wall.

Horrified by her actions, she slid back down the inside wall, tripping as she dropped. She tasted dirt in her mouth, and she wanted to lie there. Give up and be done with it. Her hand stung where she'd murdered the boy.

"There was nothing you could do," Simeon told her, though his eyes were upon the far gate and the gathering skirmish.

"I can't do this," she cried, struggling to her shaky feet.

"My love, we need to get to the gate; they are dying there," Simeon called. Gracefully, he dropped down to where she'd fallen. He might have said more, but she could take no more. The terror was simply too much; she was a shadow of herself.

She left him behind and felt little remorse. She sprinted through the chaos as the town fell around her, and she could not look at the gate. Nor, as a council member, could she follow duty and answer the thousand and one wailing questions from all she passed.

"What is happening?"

"Who is attacking?"

"Is it Magnus?"

"Why did the city do this?"

"Have you seen my child?"

She shook her head to all, keeping her eyes on the path. The drug was still coursing through her veins, and she begged for sobriety, for a clearer mind. She begged the absent gods for courage, and they must have been disgusted with her, for they offered nothing.

I killed the boy to save myself.

She ran hard until she came upon the biggest secret in the town. It wasn't a great secret. It was innocently lying out in the open, in the middle of the old road near the town centre, just waiting for anyone curious enough to bother checking. Those honoured few in the know claimed it was a sewer. That nothing but rainwater and roots flowed beneath the town. It was a solid enough lie. Who indeed would question such a thing? But those on the council knew the tunnel well enough and what to do should the need arise.

Daisy dropped to her knees by the heavy metal hatch, a relic from ancient times, and immediately began to dig at it with panicked fingers like a mouse scrabbling at a bottle's cork, believing there was some forbidden delicacy within. A few nearby townspeople glanced at the crazy lady attempting to open the sewer as they ran past, but none took notice. Moments later, a metallic clashing sound drew Daisy's attention, and she looked up to see an old woman dashing towards the gates. She carried at least a dozen swords and scabbards, and for a breath, Daisy was stung with guilt at her own cowardice.

You're leaving everyone behind.

"You have less to live for than me, old woman," she mumbled, but the old woman never heard, nor did Daisy want her to. It was the pathetic thought of a waif, beaten by life and love.

Cracking her nails, scraping her fingers until they bled, and once catching her finger sharply, she finally eased the lid free of the hole and, without delay, slipped below before easing it back over her—far easier than removing it—and found herself in near darkness.

It was a fine tunnel, she was told, stretching far beyond the outskirts of the town, far beyond where the Riders ambushed and surrounded the walls. It was a concealed escape route, constructed for when Spark City came a-calling. For a dim moment, she allowed herself to ponder their attackers. She thought of the Faction Wars brewing slowly and growing to a tempest. The few words she'd heard uttered were in a tongue that was not familiar to her, and she wondered if the South had finally had enough and begun a grand invasion upon the rest of the Factions and the Spark thereafter. It was something to do while giving up in melancholy, she supposed.

With no lights to guide her, she stumbled forward, listening to the dull thumps of everything she'd ever known getting cut down somewhere above.

Do not do this.

She managed another couple of steps before falling to her knees and weeping for all that had befallen her. She did not know how long she wept, only that eventually the tears stirred her mind to life. Feeling the pressure in her bladder, she manoeuvred her dress and her undergarments, relieved herself and wept for a few breaths more as the release offered relief but also the clarity she'd desired.

"What the fuk am I doing?"

Leaving him behind.

Unsurprisingly, she had no true answer. She could only think of Silas and hated him to near murder. No, not that much. Not yet. She turned and, with quivering fingers, she edged herself back towards the dimness, back towards the faint circle of light. The lid was easier to lift from beneath, and despite the horror, the terror, the guilt, she climbed free of the tunnel, back into the glowing light of the night.

She had taken no more than a dozen steps when she came upon a sword lying in the dirt, no doubt dropped by the old woman who, with less reason, displayed far grander class and heroism. Lifting the blade and looking at the carnage behind the closed gate, Daisy began to run towards death, hoping to find herself and perhaps Simeon as well.

———

That is no way to die, thought Kaya, sprinting towards the gate. The unfortunate soul she gazed upon was the first casualty in this battle. A young woman, whose name Kaya couldn't remember. But now, her name didn't matter, nor her screams as they fell silent. She was dead, and it was terrible.

Around her, the manic frenzy of panic continued. In the dark, townspeople sprinted, screaming and terrified, in every direction. Some went to the forest, where they were swiftly set upon by emerging Riders, while others flooded towards the gate, for bandits were brave and dishonourable and unsuitable for mere slaughter when fighting was a choice. Whether they held a weapon or no, they surged, gaining false bravery from their pack, and Kaya was helpless but to run with them; there was safety in numbers and savagery in such a gang of bandits.

"What the fuk is happening?" wailed Aimee, running up beside her. Protecting the girl became her priority, and suddenly, Kaya veered away from the flow, away from the masses charging towards the thundering mounts.

"Stay with me," Kaya cried, dragging the girl towards the wall. The impossibly high wall. Further down, where the Riders hadn't yet attacked, she saw bandits helping themselves up the impossible obstacle. She might have lifted Aimee, but neither was tall enough to help the other over. Aimee was graceful and skilled but wasn't close to contending with the wall.

Perhaps next year, my dear.

They moved more slowly than the panicked masses around them, as Kaya wracked her brains for a solution. It was all she could do. Keeping her head low and motioning to Aimee to do the same, she prayed to the gods that they looked like anything but attractive targets. Behind her, Aimee began to weep. It was a terrible, unfamiliar thing, and Kaya wanted to wrap her in her arms, comfort her and reassure her that this would all pass.

"Hush, little one. Cry after," she hissed in disapproval, daring a glance back into the impromptu battlefield. It wasn't a battle at all. It was a slaughter. A few bandits carried blades to their funerals, and Kaya watched as, one by one, they fell under the thundering horses and their slashing Riders.

"Oh no," screamed Aimee, watching in horror as one such bandit attempted to break a killer's charge. He swung once before the cur on the mount struck him down. Then, suddenly, the Rider turned and faced her down. "You bastard," Aimee screamed. *A fine show of defiance*, Kaya thought, even as the Rider readied his horse to charge her, even as she was about to die.

Kaya never hesitated. Within a breath, she was away from Aimee, sliding low to where the dead bandit stared to nowhere and grinned at nothing. In the dark, she scrabbled on the freshly soaked ground and came upon the sliver of wet steel, marred with its owner's blood. Her blade for now.

"Come on, you cur," Kaya roared, leaping to her feet again and charging the Rider, who met her pathetic offence with casual grace. He blocked her strike, releasing his reins to meet the blade with his two-handed grips, and his strength was extraordinary. Countering her strike, he knocked her away, and she could only parry twice before he disarmed her, taking the wind from her as well as the blade.

This is the end.

It wasn't the end at all. As he swung, Aimee leapt high as though scaling that insurmountable wall. She took hold of the cur's leather-skinned armour and clung tight to it.

"Fuk you, fuk you, fuk you," she screamed in the Rider's

bearded face, then swung around behind him and tried to unhorse him while he struggled to get his sword at her.

He let out a fierce cry and spurred the horse to rear up. Recovering her fallen sword, Kaya struck once and left the blade plunged up to the hilt in the fiend's shoulder, where the leather was weak. The mount knocked Kaya back again as it protected it's Rider, but the damage was already done.

"Fuk you," screamed Aimee and fell upon him even as he attempted to pummel her with a gloved fist.

He might have screamed profanity as she did, for his tongue was unfamiliar and guttural. Or else they were simply his dying cries. Aimee took hold of the blood covered blade and drove it deep through his armour, screaming wildly. Eventually, by the fifth or sixth strike, he struggled his last, and Aimee fell to her knees beside Kaya.

"What have I done?" she moaned, holding the sword like a poison most foul, as Kaya took the dead man's blade. It was larger than any she'd owned and strangely lighter than she expected.

All experienced bandits were forced to take a life at some point in their endeavours. It was a tragic, needful thing, and if this had taken place while they were out on a run, it would have been treated with the profound respect it deserved. Kaya was no fan of taking lives, nor did she believe she'd taken the life of an undeserving bastard, but Aimee was years from such a thing, and she could see, even here, in this moment of stillness in the midst of horror, the terrible effect it had.

"Whisht," little one, she snapped, climbing to her feet, dragging the girl back towards the wall and on towards the gate. "You did the needful; you did it well. You might well need to do it again in the next few moments. So suck up that horror right swiftly." It wasn't the finest advice she'd ever given, but it was all she could muster in these dire moments.

"Aye."

As they sprinted up towards the gates where hundreds of Riders still clustered against poorly armed bandits, Kaya whispered a prayer to gods she had little faith in. She only hoped she could get Aimee through the gates before they were closed for good. They ran like spectres against the night, below the low glow of the town's lights in the walls above their heads. She counted many horrors as they charged, but not once did she delay or deviate. As they neared the melee, she heard the guards of Raven Rock finally begin to counter the impossible charge.

On any given day in the season, with the gates closed and the town locked down, Raven Rock would have protected itself against such an attack. But with Andreas's funeral diverting everyone's interest, there had been fewer guards on watch—a terrible case of shitty luck for the town, and excellent fortune for the Riders.

Above them, a few arrows took to the night. She knew this because, in quick succession, they landed just ahead of her, embedding themselves securely in the scrambling bodies of Riders, who screamed as they fell.

For a breath, she believed she might make it to the gate—until four fiends upon the most terrifying of mounts gathered in a line and charged towards her. She knew it was the end.

"Get in against the wall. And get running after they strike. Don't look back," Kaya screamed, stepping out into the open, raising her blade, and preparing to die. It was a foolish thing to think she had any chance. She would have considered such sacrifice a foolhardy act were she to have instructed her students to do the same thing. She might have condemned her actions as unnecessary valour in the same lesson. Such things were likely to get any bandit killed.

From directly above her head, another hail of arrows

rained down upon the Riders in unnaturally quick succession. All deathly blows, and though some screamed as they fell, others merely slumped in their saddles and charged by without engaging Kaya.

What the fuk?

"Keep going," a voice cried from above, and she finally saw Raven Rock's first line of defence.

It was a man.

Alone.

Human, just a little better at it.

Gray stood upon the wall with a bow in hand. He did not acknowledge her beyond his instruction; he merely went to war like a god. Like an Alphaline. He was ethereal in his movement. Graceful and assured, he never stopped moving along the precarious wall as though in a dance of his own devising. At his waist were two half-emptied quivers. She watched his incredible technique which struck her numb for an entire breath.

He's protecting me.

He moved like a flowing embodiment of war, firing arrows with blinding speed. As he held the bow, he also clutched half a dozen arrows. Every draw of the bow was also a simultaneous reload. It was smooth, effective and impossible, yet here he was.

Within a few moments, he drew back six times, releasing six times, killing six times.

"What are you staring at? Keep going, the both of you," he demanded, moving back up along the wall towards the gate, towards the horror of the kill zone.

Only then did she see he was without armour or even a shirt. He was naked from the waist up, as though inviting a blade or arrow to pierce his chest. Yet none came. Perhaps the Riders saw his technique and cowered before him. Perhaps they could tell he was Alpha and feared that he might, alone, turn the tide of this invasion.

Digging back in against the wall at the corner and gasping for breath, she awaited her moment.

"I'm a killer," Aimee said, shaking. Her eyes were upon her hands.

"Aye, and a good one, too," Kaya countered and offered a weak smile, although the words felt heavy, empty and unsatisfactory for what the girl needed.

"Aye, alright… Aye," Aimee said, releasing her guilt, if not for the future, then for the moments before she died.

Die.

We are all going to die.

None of us will survive.

This is the end.

Give up. Give up. Give up.

As Kaya felt their good run turn to shit, she suddenly felt the fear of the end pricking the back of her neck. She tried to calm her panic and look ahead to their route, but taking a step seemed harder than before. She knew the gate was only a few feet around the corner. She merely had to endure the most precarious steps of the skirmish.

Take that step and be done with it.

So, she did.

Poets might tantalise an audience with tales of grand heroic battles, salivate over descriptions of the delicious art of swordplay or spend themselves in ecstasy recounting a warrior's heroic courage. More likely, though, the silver-tongued fuks had never seen a moment of true horror. Nor were they tainted by the taste of death, nor had they witnessed the actual agony of battle. To see a brave warrior piss and shit himself as the end came made for a terrible rhyme or epic tale. Piercing, deathly screams rose louder than

the mightiest of victorious war cries. But that was a rightly
shitty way to tell a tale of victory.

Kaya had seen such gruesome death, alright; she'd been
in that dreadful mire of confusion and desperation more than
once, yet somehow clung to her sanity. After enduring such
things, one lost the taste for sonnets of war, death and
sacrifice.

This is it.

A small brigade of defenders with pikes stood around the
corner, where the fighting was fiercest. They were at war with
the Riders, and the bloodshed was awful. Pieces of bodies
were strewn about. Riders had been thrown from their mounts
to the ground, to be crushed to liquid beneath trampling feet
and thundering hooves.

"Just follow me through, and do not hesitate," she warned
Aimee, gripping her sword anew. The girl nodded in terror.

They sprinted for the gates, dashing between the mounts
and ducking swinging swords, avoiding the defensive pikes
as they plunged and sent warm, wet spray upon all around.
The air rang with the clanging of swords and the piercing
screech of metal on metal. Kaya ducked low and pulled
Aimee the last few steps as the gate began to swing shut,
sealing the defenders, the attackers and the two young women
out of Raven Rock.

"Oh, fuk," Kaya screamed, hitting the impenetrable gate
with her blade.

"Now what?" Aimee called, falling up beside her.

"We fight until we die," Kaya whispered.

———

The unbearable weight of guilt was a crippling thing. The
type of thing to keep a man's feet rooted to the mud when all

around him was on fire. Devitt felt that guilt something terrible. Instead of hiding from it, he charged headfirst into it. It was all he could do.

By the time the Riders appeared, the first warnings were in the air. He should have known better. It was no small thing to be one of the bearers of the dead for such a man, and Devitt should have known to have someone replace him on his watch at the wall. In truth, he thought it a small matter to miss an hour's watch. The boy Inigo should have been more than capable of covering for him, but truly, the call of the funeral was enough to distract the most disciplined of warriors.

This is on me.

He was running before he saw the mounts, instinct carrying him towards the gates. He wasn't alone, of course, but he was the luckiest. As the first of his comrades and friends fell around him to beast and blade, he remained untouched, as though the absent gods had picked him out for the task. He saw limbs torn and wrenched free with the flash of steel. He saw bodies mangled beneath the charge of rushing mounts. He tripped on corpses and gore, and heard the shuddering gasps of comrades reaching out in their last moments to save themselves or be saved. He might have dropped to the ground among those he considered closest and held their hands if he could. He might have begged forgiveness while down there, saying he had chosen to honour a friend over duty. Instead, he kicked free of their shuddering grips, kept his head high and his eyes focused, and sought redemption or true damnation.

As he raced, he frantically wondered why the Riders were killing only the bandits at the front and at the funeral and not charging through the town's gate, lying all open and inviting. Then, in a cold moment, he realised their mission was not simply conquest but annihilation. Those gates would have been their first entry point if they desired the town for their own. Instead, they butchered all they met, and it was an awful thing indeed.

The world slowed as he leapt over the last few crumpled obstacles, ducking beneath careless swiping strikes from hunters with mounds of prey at their feet. He touched the shadow of the arch and kept going, propelled by his fierce guilt.

Resisting the urge to retch and cower, he charged back into safer territory. Coming upon the ladder, he was certain a blade would take him, yet he never looked back. Instead, Devitt kept focused and determined, telling himself that sealing the breach would alleviate a modicum of his guilt. That doing his job would somehow absolve him of his many sins. He knew it wouldn't, but if he were capable of helping hold the town, he might be able to look at himself in the mirror someday.

For just a breath, he slowed and realised how drenched he had become, and he wondered if the blood was his own. He might have checked for a wound, no doubt delivered from behind by some sneaky fiend. Instead, he ignored the increasing numbness and the cold and climbed up to the gate tower platform, overlooking the misery below.

"What is happening?" cried Inigo, scrambling to load his crossbow as he looked at the mayhem. "Wait, are you injured?"

Devitt could see the boy's fingers slipping carelessly on the weapon as he tried and failed to load it. It was no surprise, what with the weapon shaking in his panicked grip.

"They came from nowhere. I had my eye on the forest, I swear," the boy pledged, but Devitt cared little. The boy had stood watch as he was ordered. It was Devitt who had failed the town.

Failure failure, fuken failure.

"I'm fine," he cried, grabbing the boy's hand and setting the bolt correctly. "Every moment you fuk up, more of us die," he hissed, and the boy settled, though his usually tanned skin had turned white as snow. "Take breaths, trust your body, and get killing."

He wanted to scream at the boy for missing the obvious signs of an attack. He wanted to chastise him for leaving the gates open, even when the Riders appeared. Such foolishness might earn the boy five lashes come dawn, if he survived. If any of them did. He'd take a dozen for himself for his sins while he was at it.

"Aye, sir," the boy said, looking at his loaded crossbow as though for the first time.

"I said, get killing," Devitt demanded, and through the terror and uncertainty, Inigo nodded and leaned back over the edge and sought a target and killed.

"I did it! I actually did it."

"Count them as you kill," Devitt growled, reaching for the gate's chains. As he did, he heard a thump beside him. And then a gasp.

"Help me, Devitt," Inigo cried, falling away from the edge and reaching for the axe sticking from his back.

Devitt's reactions were too slow. A driving kick from behind took his legs out from under him, followed by a thunderous strike to the face that took his senses. Within a breath, the killer had pinned him down and was preparing to stab him.

Still weren't keeping an eye out, were you?

Devitt could imagine the glee on his killer's face as he followed Devitt through the gate and up the ladder to where he and the boy offered themselves up as perfect little targets to be taken out.

Worst guards ever.

"You bastard," Devitt hissed, squirming away from the blade and the punches. He slipped on Inigo's blood as the boy dragged himself slowly towards the corner to pick up his crossbow. The axe remained embedded in his back. He probably knew never to wrench a weapon free until the danger had passed and surgery was an option.

"Get him, Devitt. Fuken get him," the boy croaked, though he sounded like he spoke from beneath a splashing brook. A curious, regretful thing, for Devitt knew that sound, too. There would be no surgery needed.

Regardless, it was a fine suggestion, and Devitt tried his best. He grappled with the larger man, earning a reprieve and the use of his stronger arm, albeit at an angle. He drove his elbow into the bastard's face and found success. "To the fires with you, prick," he screamed and repeated the efforts, earning a little more freedom. He scampered to his feet and his gaze fell upon a dull longsword upon the watchtower's wall.

It wasn't much of a fight. The cur attempted to draw the axe from the boy's back, but not before Devitt struck him fiercely across the arm. The sword clanged loudly against the metal-plated armour.

"Fuk it," Devitt cried and attacked again, his movements slow and awkward and utterly unthreatening to a warrior who was no doubt built for war and swordplay and all that heroic shit.

"Get away from me, you cur," Inigo moaned, keeping his back to the edge, away from the scrambling killer, who, with a broken Southern accent, appeared to curse the fact that the weapon was lodged so deeply.

"Will you ever kill him already?" Inigo called, trying to hold the attacker with shaking hands.

It was enough, and Devitt, throwing all his weight behind his next lunge, broke through leather into the flesh beyond and kept going as he sent the man back over the wall. His body landed on an unsuspecting Rider below and knocked him to the ground, where desperate hands tore him asunder—a fortuitous thing.

"I'm kind of fuked, aren't I?" the boy whispered, dropping to a knee to recover the crossbow. Devitt thought him heroic.

"Aye… um… I reckon you are."

The boy, wiping away tears, exhaled slowly and loaded the crossbow. "You don't need to see me die," he gasped, turning to the fight below and quickly releasing and reloading.

"You fought well."

"I'll continue until I'm gone," he murmured.

For just a moment, Devitt could only stare at the sudden change in Inigo. He had grown up just in time to die. Just in time to know the impressive measure of himself. As the crossbow clunked and released, he reached down with a steady hand, slid a fresh bolt securely into the slot, chose a target and released. Grinning at his success, he mumbled a number and reached for another bolt.

Devitt, stunned by the boy's determination and courage, hobbled towards the gate controls. Set against metal mechanisms and heavy iron counterweights, it was a beast that slowed for no one as it shut.

Around him appeared other warriors eager to hold the defence of the wall. Some were familiar; some were new and exotic and utterly unlikeable. They took what crossbows and bows were waiting and went to war along the top. A pathetic defence, admittedly, but all great fires started as a spark. They all went to war, but Devitt, hoping more bandits would make it through the gates, held the controls in his shaking hands.

Just do it and be done with this life.

It was a cruel thing to condemn those at the front to doom, but from here, it was a better thing to make secure the bastion that Raven Rock could be. Seeing so many bandits skeet over the far wall at the end of town convinced him as much. It was weak persuasion, in truth, especially seeing comrades giving their all just a few feet below. And then he saw her. Radiant and protected by a better man than he. Kaya, brave and beautiful, against the night, tearing through the melee, avoiding death by luck and faith alone.

She was a goddess, perfect, and she would never make it, and he couldn't wait for her, and a thousand curses upon him, because he pulled that lever down and felt the screeching rumble as the gates shuddered and began to close, knocking people back into the relative safety of the town but also locking out those who, just three steps from safety, were abandoned to their doom.

"It needs to be done," he whispered, watching the gates rolling shut. "As does this," he added, gripping his sword and sparing one final glance back at the wounded, dying boy, who went on killing despite the terror and agony and cruel inevitability. He found his own strength in such stubborn bravery. And then he looked for Kaya and her companion and, seeing her, stepped over the edge and dropped down to meet his death, like so many others, this most horrible day in Raven Rock.

14

———————

THE LINE

"Now what?" Aimee called, falling up beside her.

"We fight until we die," Kaya whispered, but she had never felt fear as pure as this. Tears streamed down her cheeks as she struck the gate one last time and then turned and faced the melee for the horror it was.

"We are dead, we are so fuken dead," screamed Aimee from beside her. It was a fine point. An unwanted one, admittedly, but fine indeed.

"It doesn't matter about the gate," Kaya lied, hoping to draw out the warrior survivor in Aimee a few years ahead of its time. The murderer had been brought out too soon, so why stop there? Why stop tonight?

The girl won't survive this.

Aimee raised her blade and looked to the ruin all around them. She knew as Kaya did: there was no surviving this.

"You stick beside me, little one, and we'll try to make a stand right here," Kaya cried, knowing her words were hollow. Too many of their comrades lay slain at their feet. Each one had no doubt believed they could make some similar stand. What chance did any of them have?

"As you wish, Kaya," Aimee moaned, raising her blade, stepping nearer to her, covering her flank. For a breath, Kaya wished Andreas was in front of them, roaring for war, inspiring a counter-charge. He'd have found a way. As for Kaya? Well, Kaya was just an instructor from the Deep North, about to die without having lived a life of significance. There were worse fates; there were far better ones, too.

"Be brave, Aimee," she cried, raising her blade, and suddenly, from nowhere, Devitt appeared, and she'd never loved him more.

He was no master swordsman, but that didn't seem to matter. Charging to her right, he began to swing carelessly at any foolish attacker careless enough to be in range. He missed as many blows as he struck and, unbelievably, unhorsed an even share of Riders before she had the good grace to join his ill-fated stand.

"Kill them all," Kaya screamed, and beside her, Aimee screamed too, driving her blade into seated Riders as though it was a natural thing. Kaya, between both killers, drove forward and killed for herself. It was easier than she remembered. With the enemy up close, all clustered like, it was like stabbing into the dark and striking gold every time.

They swung wildly and struck wonderfully, which was a tonic to the terror she felt. Aye, she knew a blow would come from somewhere to take her from this life, but it felt right to go out swinging. Any thoughts of fleeing for the woods or attempting to climb the wall were lost to the killing. It wasn't just her either. Aimee moved more freely than before and struck with such disturbing efficiency that, for a breath, Kaya suspected just how chilling a Runner the girl might become, having earned her blood this day.

A right tempest of a killer.

"Watch him," Devitt yelled, tearing her from her

imaginings, just as a Rider charged her. Kaya now became the hunter. The Rider roared and boomed and did all manner of intimidating things, but she had little to lose, never mind her nerve. He swung wide with a great longsword just as she dipped to his blind side, avoiding the blow, before spinning her sword high as he passed. She took his hand with her deadly slash. He screamed in horror, dropping his sword and charging away through the mass of bodies, clutching his wrist where just moments ago a perfectly acceptable hand had been. His piercing cries were contagious, for as he fled the field, the other Riders seemed to lose heart.

The bandits, less so.

For this was Raven Rock, home to the nastiest bastards of the Four Factions. This settlement had been built for such an assault. It took only a little time for them all to breathe, gather their wits and follow their instincts. They'd prepared and watched all these years, ready for word of the city's final patience running dry. This awful day had happened today, because of sheer bad luck, but Raven Rock answered as she always would. Around her, in a frozen moment, Kaya saw the battle as it had been, then as it was in that moment, and last, how it could be. Unarmed, overrun and outnumbered, the townspeople still held the line of defence as only rightly skilled, rightly hardened and rightly vicious bandits could. They were not Alphalines, these bastard few; they were something else entirely. In the first few breaths, clustering at the gates, their fists and the will to leap at their killers and drag them from their mounts had earned them a chance. Lives lived at the edge of the blade in search of a few shiny pieces had prepared them for such horror. But that time of wild suicidal defending had passed.

We angry few.

Kaya could now see their blades striking back and cutting deep as the defenders gained ground. More than that, she thanked the gods for the shrewd actions of the cur who had seen the recovery of the anti-cavalry poles long before the gates were locked. For just a breath, she saw the desperation upon the faces of her many comrades. Those same few who felt the betrayal of the gates slamming shut, dooming them all to certain death.

There were few things more dangerous than wild beasts backed into a corner.

Or bandits fighting for their homes with no hope whatsoever.

At first, Kaya believed it was Gray who was responsible for the turning of the tide. As countless Riders stormed around the mass of defending bandits, the Alphaline made a dent in their numbers with his mastery of the bow. He roared defiantly as he went to war from atop the wall, challenging any cur to take him from the battle. Kaya would have sworn she saw him smile as he killed. Just a little glimmer of warmth upon those perfectly kissable lips as he took life after life. He was glorious and beautiful and chiselled and perfect.

I knew it.

Anyone who doubted he was a hardened Alpha male from the city was a fool indeed. His speed and accuracy were a sight to behold; he moved like a leaf in the wind, never slowing, consistently smooth, reloading and releasing in the same stunning motion. The arrows disappeared from his quivers rightly swiftly, and his victims fell just as quick. He never took more than one shot per Rider, and honestly, in that moment, Kaya wondered if, alone with a thousand arrows and perhaps a suit of heavy armour, he wouldn't have held this town alone.

He was inspiring, a leader. Wordlessly, other bandits climbed out along the wall with bows and crossbows to take the fight to the deadly mounted threat. Aye, they weren't as skilled or as effective as Gray, but en masse they were a force, and like a boulder breaking a wave's rush, they began to halt the charge.

Added to Gray's impressiveness was the unexpected arrival of Simeon to further the cause. He was not alone either, and, charging as though he had a point to prove, he inadvertently led the defiance of Raven Rock. Away from Daisy's side, he was an unexpected storm. He charged without fear, and Kaya had never known him to be brave, yet here he was, charging through the Riders as though in a casual contest of the fist. His six-foot-long spear of finest Raven Rock steel was a sight to behold. The town had long since commissioned a few hundred such beasts, and Rua could never have expected to see this particular weapon wielded with anything near the efficiency with which it was designed.

She might well have been proud.

He did not challenge a solitary Rider; he challenged them all. He engaged them all, too. Sprinting at the curs and nimbly dodging their slower strikes, he was a diminutive target. He took them one after the other, with easy lunges, and moved on to the next. Not entirely unlike Gray, he was smooth and constant, bringing much wrath upon his victims. Great oceans of spraying crimson soaked him right through as he moved, as well as those who charged alongside him, screaming their venom, venting their wrath, showing these bastards exactly why they shouldn't have expected a straightforward assault. He, too, inspired beautiful, murderous things.

As effective as Simeon was, however, the axe-wielding

maniac on the other side of the battlefield brought the actual changing of the tide. Kaya might not have recognised the brutal figure of the broken Silas on any other day, but he was a hero now. Wading through the Riders with an impressive battle axe, his comrades found it hard not to charge with him. He carried his own pack of hunters on either side, and they were vicious. They were upon the ground, at a dreadful disadvantage against their elevated opponents, but it didn't seem to matter. They dug in tight like a fighting unit of a thousand and drove forward from the left of the gate.

We can live through this.

Silas howled with every strike as though swinging the axe was agony, adding to his impressiveness. He never stopped, as though he were fuelled by hate alone, and perhaps it was a fine act on Simeon's part stealing his wife from him, for these invaders suffered his wrath. He swung through flesh and steel as though it were nothing, cleaving limbs and bodies, splitting heads open, severing necks, and from all sides, the Riders began to find the battle that little bit more compact, that little bit more precarious. Were it not for the lack of warning, the glorious under-preparedness of the bandits, and at least a hundred souls lost in the first charging wave, Kaya might have believed they could hold this day, and push back and punish their hasty conquerors something fierce.

As it was, they were limited in their attacks.

And were it not for the horns, they would have brought all manner of slaughter upon the Riders but eventually fallen to their relentlessness.

But the horns played a terrible drone, and for a striking moment, the world stilled as though a shard of the shattered moon had landed right in the middle of them all, causing much fright, shock and awe.

"They're retreating horns," Devitt cried as the mounts broke from the melee in disarray.

"That's right, you fiends," Aimee cried, falling to her knees as the Riders, as one, cast their torches to the ground and fled from the fighting.

And nearly all the defending bandits ceased their counterattacks upon seeing them scurry. All but one, that is.

"I'm not done with yiz," Silas bellowed as the mounts thundered through the defenders, sheathing their blades so they might escape more quickly. "Come here," he demanded, breaking through the ranks of bandits, the fallen, the injured, and those who stood proud, cheering in delirious glory despite the horror of their kin dead at their feet.

Silas did none of this.

He screamed wildly, daring any to "finish him," or "face him," or "flee for the cowards" they were. None turned, but perhaps one of them should have. With the last of his energy, Silas gave a mighty heave of his battle axe and sent it skyward. It spun wildly, flew far and true, and embedded itself in the back of one of the Riders.

Those who watched gave a mighty cheer as the Rider fell from her mount with a sickening thump. Her mount followed its companions while the girl, screaming in torment, reached for her fleeing comrades. Perhaps it was the fortuitous strike that caused all eyes to turn to her, but of the many injured and dying upon the battlefield, her screams were loudest, at least for a time.

Silas screamed back at her for a while, saving his most colourful of expletives for when recovering his axe from beside her. She understood nothing of what he said, of course, but she likely understood his meaning at the end.

"Die, you blonde bitch," he roared and, with a final

heave, he sent the heavy piece through her head, killing her instantly.

The attackers disappeared into the night as silently and suddenly as they had appeared.

Surrounding Silas as though he were a hero, his companions chanted his name. They dragged him away from the edge of the green lest he go after the curs himself, and only then did he appear to notice the applause was for his own actions. He did not smile or chant with them. Instead, he looked as the gates were slowly opened and Daisy, with weapon drawn and far too late to the gathering, came rushing out with a dozen other eager warriors ready to kill long after the battle had ended.

They spread out and then halted upon seeing the devastation on this side of the defences. Daisy kept running, however. Dropping her blade, she ran for Simeon and threw herself into his blood-covered arms. Whatever she whispered in his ears was lost. Still, Kaya, beaten and eager to bring Aimee back inside where she belonged, all rightly snug and safe, did hear him utter "Everything is alright" in Daisy's ear; his reassurances were kind yet empty.

Around them, the tears were falling, the shock was setting in and the dead were beginning to be counted.

"You came to save me," Kaya said to Devitt, who hung his head as though ashamed.

"Of course I did."

"Thank you," she whispered, and she might have had more to say, but he was gazing at the forest where a gowned creature upon a mount sat staring out at the landscape of blood and ruin and mulch and tragedy. She was there for only a glimmer before disappearing back into the cover of the dark green.

He was still staring as though he'd seen a ghost. "I thought I saw…" he said, then fell silent, mouth agape.

"Come on, dear friend. There are wounded and the dead to attend to," she whispered, remembering her place among the council. Her hands were shaking, and something about decision-making appeared oddly reassuring at this late hour.

He took a breath and turned to her, his voice cold.

"Aye, this is just the beginning."

15

THE HUSH

In the beginning, there was the shock. Shock most pure and awful. Cutting and cruel and silent. It brought a stillness, and a collective calm came over every survivor as, slowly, the true horror of what had occurred dawned upon them. For a time, Kaya stood mute with them, avoiding looking at the blood on her hands, the torn bodies, the townspeople tragically accepting their fate.

But soon enough, that passed.

Then came the anger, for that was the bandit way. Hatred for the bastards that had taken life, but also for their defences failing as they had. More than that, their wrath fell upon the council members who stood at the gate as grief overtook them all. They accused, condemned and threatened, and Kaya stood facing those awful words. Somehow, the words were deadlier than the horrors endured by those who uttered them.

Anger was easier than melancholy.

Kaya did not cry in the first hour after the attack. Instead, she tended to the comrades around her. Some of them were lost and forlorn, some hate-filled, and some hobbled by unimaginable injuries. In many ways, this aftermath was harder than the savagery of battle.

She felt her soul diminish ever so as she helped to carry the injured and dying down through the gates, on through the town and into the small dwelling of the healer. The few healers within suffered trauma of their own as patients begged, pleaded for mercy and life, or to be eased into the dark. These brave healers, without any grand teachings to their name, without great skills beyond whispers inherited from a bandit master from generations before, suffered and struggled and truly did miracles without the touch of an absent god to guide their hand. Kaya could only watch them desperately seal up wounds, administer syrup to the lost or contain handfuls of innards with grit and determination alone.

The numbers delivered to them were too many, yet still they came, and all too soon; the few beds they had were swiftly filled and crimson-covered. After that, mats and blankets were placed down in the streets, all lined up, bloody and neat, and Kaya was horrified and lost to melancholy. She was a lesser warrior in that sense, for there were willing helpers with courage greater than hers. They enlisted and went to task stitching, cleaning and relieving where they could. They stripped sheets, went to bandaging, and truly earned themselves a fine seat in the afterlife.

As the wounded spluttered and died, the echoes of heartbroken loved ones filled the air and Kaya stayed on, holding their hands and watching them fall still. She remained as though it was penance placed upon her for some cruel deeds of which she was unaware.

She stayed there in a daze, taking in horrors enough that she feared she might lose the run of her mind, until Devitt appeared and pulled her from this place of misery to tend to some rightly shitty dealings. It was a cruel mercy on his part.

He led her to the wall, eased a massive ladder up and over it and quietly slid down and returned to the place where the savagery had occurred first.

Do not weep.

"So many," Devitt whispered, dropping to a knee by a young boy who had nearly, but not quite, made it to the wall before being trampled by a charging mount. Kaya could see the boy was dead. His unblinking stare and demented grin suggested as much, yet Devitt held his fingers to his neck for a pulse. A futile act, for he lay in a pool of blood. As did the body next to him, which had suffered a blade through the heart.

That's right, Devitt. So many.

"It's all my fault," he said, standing suddenly. His eyes were upon the many dozen dead bandits further out in the darkness beyond.

"Whisht," she hissed, watching the treeline, listening for movement beyond. The attackers had appeared from the dark in near silence. What was to say they weren't waiting for a couple of careless fools to step away from the ladder's safety and rightly ruin their night?

"I should have been at the gate," he whimpered. "I should have had another stand watch and not leave it to a child," he added, wiping his nose, leaving a smear of brown as he did. Mud or blood. Both washed off in water.

It was tempting to hate. To wrench free that sliver of horror that stuck in her gut and churned it to bile and sickness. To deliver her purest hate upon him. To blame. Oh, to blame anyone who made that feeling so potent.

"You cannot carry such a weight, you fool," she said softly. She wanted to go to him. To wrap her fingers in his and take his agony. Because that is what people like her did for people like him. "We had ample opportunity to tend to these marching fiends, and we did nothing," she countered. This was no time for a council member to doubt himself. Besides, those who had invaded had known precisely when to charge. One more eye upon the wall wouldn't have changed that at all.

"Fine lies, Kaya," he said though not too unkindly.

"You locked the gate; that redeems you somewhat," Kaya said, taking hold of him. For just a breath, she remembered lying with him and moaning, pleasuring him as he did her. It had been wonderful, exciting, unexpected and wonderfully awkward.

"I climbed a ladder," he said softly. He wrapped his arms around her, and for a breath, she felt warmth, desire, comfort and reassurance.

Love?

"Get off me, you cur," she mocked, pushing him away, but not until she'd squeezed back with all her might. Were they in a room embracing like this, well, it may as well have been furrowing. She shook her head as the devastation took her anew. She knew her thoughts to be childish, closer to those of Aimee than of a woman as wise as she. Still, though, better a little flirtation and a few happy moments over the memories of the screams of the dying or the moans of those left behind. Both would stay with her forever.

"You were amazing," Devitt mumbled. He began to walk, trudging among the dead.

Which time?

Stop it, girl.

"We fought our best. We all did," she said after a time, then dropped down and checked another dead bandit, discovering him to be… well, dead.

"Who committed this act?"

"The city? Magnus? Perhaps Ulrik?" she wondered.

Devitt thought on this for a longer time than she expected. Looking over at him, she saw him bent over as though weeping in silence. She might have asked after him, but instead, with head low, keeping an eye upon the treeline, she crept further away from him, giving him his privacy. She thought of the funeral, of those who had come to honour the dead warrior so many hours ago.

Are they with you now, Andreas?

Being this close to the treeline was terrifying. Squinting and watching for movement beyond, she moved quietly, listening, as though out on a run. She was glad of the lack of wind. More than that, she welcomed the crickets, gaily singing their song. Few things were more reassuring than nature's whispers that nothing lurked in the dark.

She wandered among the ruined bodies, every one of them broken, trampled, hammered or punctured. The curs had left none alive. They had taken their time ensuring the defenceless were put to death.

Every time she bent down to listen for life in those she recognised, it was gut-wrenching. Devitt had the right idea, going off by himself, she realised. Out here, in the dark, Kaya could weep as much as she wanted—were she willing, that is.

But like she had done at Andreas's funeral, she was determined to hold it in, lest she crumble.

And then she very nearly crumbled.

For out at the furthest point, collapsed beneath a fallen log, she caught sight of Whisper's parents. Both had been slain by many a blow, and it was horrifying. From the times she had spoken with them, she had always thought them young and naïve, kind and gentle, and suited for a far better life than banditry. Their true wealth in the world was their lovely young daughter, Whisper. She looked closer, her eyes filling with tears—and there, lying dead in their protective embrace, was Whisper herself.

"Oh, god, no," Kaya wailed upon seeing the dead child. Still, she refused to let her tears fall; her breath caught in her chest, such was the depth of her grief. In the aftermath, she had seen Jak among the living, watching with mouth agape and tears drying upon his cheeks, as he absorbed the horrors around him. She had taken solace in seeing the boy, and aye, the fear of Whisper's absence had struck her for a breath, but such was the trauma around her, she had let go of that rightly swift. Now, though, the grief overcame her as she pulled apart the broken, dead parents and pulled at the child until she was in her arms. "To the fires with you all," she cried, wandering through the night, cradling the child's body, oblivious to the noise and threat. Whisper looked pristine and at peace but for a dull bruise on her forehead and a little blood trickling from her lips. On another night, she might have looked like she'd merely slipped in the mud, knocking her senses away. Kaya did not even know why she had lifted the child either. It was probably better that she be left with her parents.

Ahead, though, Kaya could see Andreas's grave. It was a better place for the child to sleep, she determined.

Andreas be damned.

He would have approved.

"Ah, no, is that Whisper?" Devitt cried, rushing to help Kaya with the tiny burden.

"I'm going to kill every last fuken one of them," Kaya roared, and she held that fury as long as she could, even as it flittered away from her, replaced with grief and agony.

"You said the bad words," whispered a small voice, and the child squirmed in Kaya's arms.

"What the fuk?" cried Devitt.

"Whisper, are you alright?" Kaya said, brushing the child's hair from her forehead.

"I think my mommy and daddy are dead like everyone else," the girl said quietly, then reached for Devitt, who wrapped his arms tightly around the child and fell still.

"Get her to the healer's," Kaya ordered. Devitt nodded and carefully carried her back to the ladder, where he somehow managed to carry her up and over.

Only when she disappeared did Kaya thank the absent gods for the minor miracle that had just occurred. Marvelling at the bravery of the parents, taking the fatal blows while protecting the child beneath them, Kaya went back to the task of tending to the dead, hoping against hope that there might be another similar miracle delivered this awful night.

Time became nothing more than moving from corpse to corpse, checking breath and pulse, cursing and moving on. She did not know how long she had tended to this task before Silas's heavy footfalls shook her back to the world.

He looked bloody and fierce. He had not bothered to bathe the gore from his body, nor had he eased up on his alcohol consumption, either. She wasn't going to call him on it, though. Drunkard or no, he'd been fierce and heroic. As he approached, he still carried his battle axe. His eyes were upon the forest, and, unlike Kaya, he looked desperate for the bastards to emerge.

"We need to talk on some matters," he said, stopping beside her.

It was no small thing to be betrayed or to betray. Each was as painful as the other, though for different reasons, obviously.

"Come along, will you?" Kaya hissed as she marched

back through the town with Gray. She kept her head low; she dared not meet the eyes of the many who attempted to stop her, ask her questions or demand further answers about their attackers. Instead, she betrayed and marched, and it was all she could do.

"There is no time for this. We should be out along the wall with our eyes to the darkness," Gray replied, marching a step behind. Now that the violence had settled, he was less the imposing godly being. Instead, with his shirt removed and spatters of blood on him from assisting the dying and tending to the dead, he simply looked ravishing and a little cold, too. He was not simply a man weeping, carrying a wounded child; he was something else entirely.

"I need you, Gray," she said, turning to him.

"As you wish, dear Kaya," he said carefully after a time. Though Gray had earned approval for his antics on the battlefield, the bandits still looked suspiciously at the man, though with a hint of respect. They stepped aside from the two warriors as they marched through the town, away from the horrors, on towards fruitless conversations with likely dreadful consequences.

She avoided the healer's bay. It was still too much to take. It was cowardly of her, she knew, but she couldn't take another hour standing among those inconsolable wretches. She looked back at Gray and his pleasing chest. There were other things to distract her from the horror. Simpler things. She craved simplicity.

They arrived at the council chambers, and she slipped up the hallowed stairs with the Alphaline in tow. He caught her arm at the door and turned her to face him.

"Do not lie; why am I here?" he asked, and she realised how close they stood together in the dimly lit hallway. A girl could reach out and give him a full-bodied hug, and it would be simple. Problem was, there were issues at hand and betrayals to live by. She caught sight of a chiselled chin, though, and shook distracting thoughts from her mind.

Perhaps, after all of this.

After I'm done charming him.

Within, the remaining council stood watching. Daisy, quivering behind Simeon, stood on one side of the room. Silas stood on the other. The big brute looked through Gray like he was the enemy, and Kaya wondered if he was. He likely was. A bandit should have been able to tell these things.

Between them, in the centre of the room, stood Devitt. His lovely face was frozen in a stare of nervous concentration, likely from maintaining the distance between Simeon, Daisy and Silas. Or else preparing for nasty things to come.

"Raven Rock has never suffered such an attack," Kaya started, and Silas took over, gesturing for Gray to sit at the table. As an equal?

"And we are not best skilled at such things as siege and warfare," Silas said, as Gray, suspecting nothing, took a seat. Daisy sat opposite him.

"Your warriors did quite the job of defending," Gray offered, slumping low as battle fatigue finally struck.

Without warning, Silas and Devitt set upon him, swiftly and smoothly like the fine Runners they were. The rope was around the Alphaline's neck in the blink of an eye. Perhaps, had he been paying attention, he might have smelled the ambush. Might have fought it too.

As it was, he was betrayed, and as Silas wrapped that rope tight and squeezed, Gray could only gasp and struggle, but not before Devitt wrapped his arms in his, trapping them behind the chair and holding him fast.

It was then that Kaya leapt upon his lap and straddled him like a lover before digging her blade into the naked flesh of his chest.

"Who are you really?" she screamed.

16

______

WHO WE ARE

Kaya held the blade steady and allowed a drop of blood to run free. Not a lot, just enough for him to see. She stared at her handiwork for a breath, and Silas twisted the rope tighter. Gray gasped. He met her eyes, and she read the betrayal in them. But this was how it was done in Raven Rock, particularly at the worst times. It felt like the worst of times.

"Answer me, you piece of shit," she cried and drew the blade out, letting it catch in the light. Around her, voices cried out and demanded answers, but Gray said not a word. He simply took this slaying, and Kaya fought the gnawing shame in the back of her mind where terrible things occurred. It mattered little; this was Silas's doing. She was part of this.

"What do you know?" demanded Daisy loudly. Kaya hadn't heard her raise her voice like this in nearly a year. A strange thing that the end of the world brought about nerve. Desperation brought strength, she supposed.

"Are you an Alphaline?" Simeon roared. He kept his distance, staying on the other side of the room. It was

229

probably the smarter move on his part lest Silas sacrifice his hold on the Alphaline to pummel him instead.

"When you came to spy for your city whore, did you know you would have to kill your own people to remain concealed?" This last question was uttered by Silas, who ground his teeth as he tightened the rope yet again.

Gray winced and might even have shaken his head ever so. That was something, at least.

Just answer the fuken questions.

"Are you from the city?" Devitt cried, renewing his hold on the Alphaline's arms, lest Gray suddenly break free using his ungodly powers. Gray's gasps became desperate and weaker as Silas continued to kill him. It was a terrible thing, really, and Kaya, sitting upon him, was to have the finest view of this murder, deserved as it was.

To his stubborn, frustrating detriment, Gray still wouldn't answer, so Kaya returned the blade to his chest. It was a fine enough piece, with a pristine, jagged edge and its handle wrapped in dark leather; it was good in the rain and when blood was spilt upon it. She held it steady lest a sudden jolt send it too deep into his flesh. Taking a breath, hoping he'd relent and prove himself, she twisted the blade and drew it sideways across the wound to form a gruesome X. He probably didn't notice this; he probably just felt the pain. It was a small matter. What mattered was getting to see the measure of him.

Silas loosened the rope just slightly.

"You vile wretches," Gray said at last, through gritted teeth.

"Tell us," Kaya murmured.

"I already gave you my word, Kaya." He winced as she cut. "What you learn here will mean nothing if the words come from the lips of a dying man," he countered, sucking in the miserly amount of air granted by Silas's mercy.

"I'm still not convinced," Silas muttered.

"To the fires with you all," Gray roared, yet still struggled far less than any cur should have in their grip. Perhaps he knew he had no chance, for rope was rope and Devitt's strength was most impressive, even though his slender arms were more suited to embracing and cradling lost children.

Eventually, accepting his fate, Gray yielded slightly. "We faced no Alphalines. If we had, the town might well have fallen."

"Any fool can see that," Simeon hissed.

"In truth, I haven't seen the city in a half-dozen years," he said quietly. "I couldn't tell you if they were Dia's actions or not, but if they were, I want nothing to do with them."

It felt like the truth.

"That's not much of an answer," growled Silas from behind and, ever so slightly, pulled back on Gray's chair, holding him at an angle. For just a moment, he allowed Gray to breathe again, releasing the rope once more with the delicate skill of a man well used to controlling the breath of a lesser fiend. And then, like a master torturer, he tightened that damned rope again, sending the beautiful boy into fresh waves of suffocating agony.

Balancing carefully lest she tip them over, Kaya wrapped her legs tight around Gray's waist and stared into his eyes; they were almost nose to nose. Even now, those eyes were beautiful. Kaya had long believed that, in the end, there was no way to conceal the soul. Everyone was who they were before they stepped into the abyss. It wasn't every day a girl had a chance to gaze upon such interesting things. And, she looked deep into those eyes and saw little staring back. She saw only the purest form of emptiness and, shaken, she held the blade to his face.

"Who are you?"

"I'm Gray, and lesser for it. I have no kin, I have no legacy, I have no ties, I have no allegiance to my kind or my city. I am all that dies before you."

Silas released the rope a little more. If Gray was lying, it was an impressive thing. Besides, there was only so much they could pull from him.

Somehow, Kaya felt his words were truthful as well. As he spoke, he fell still, and for a breath, she wondered if he was about to lash out with such ferocious strength that all three would be knocked aside. Or would fire bolts fly from his eyes? All the things parents told their little ones of the terrifying Alphas of the City of Light. Kaya had long suspected that stories about the Alphas were simply tales calculated to scare. She saw no monstrous brute in him. Only agony. Only betrayal.

"Will you kill me?" he whispered.

"Aye, you will likely die tonight."

"Very well," he said, falling entirely still, accepting his fate with bravery and feebleness, and breathing only when Silas allowed it. He did little, even when Devitt, doubtless satisfied with his admissions, released his hold.

Are you truthful?

Can you be one of us?

Even with his arms no longer bound, he did not try to break Silas's hold; he merely gave in to death as though he'd played a hand and lost it all and left the table—without argument, without outrage, without emotion. A curious, abysmal thing, really.

Delivering one last blow, for that was his way, Silas pulled him from his chair, and Kaya fell with him. They collapsed in a heap, but Kaya remained upon him. Were they alone, she might have enjoyed such a thing. Especially knowing the anguish it would bring to Devitt. As it was, she couldn't help staring into those soulless eyes again, and for a flash, she saw beyond the emptiness to the deep tragedy beneath. She almost reached out and caressed his cheek. But this was not how it was done, and swiftly, as his breath returned, she saw that terrible emptiness come upon him again. He wore it as a concealing thing, like a master thief would don a heavy black cloak while out pilfering in the witching hour.

What have you suffered to lead you to this?

Around them both, there was movement as the event came to its rightful conclusion without a seemingly innocent man dying by their hand. There were low murmurs of agreement amongst them, laced with approval.

Devitt might even have cracked a jest at Kaya's expense.

Kaya and Gray remained on the floor, however. Their desperate game of wits had reached a terrible end, never to be replayed. She'd seen an end to them; she'd betrayed him, even if it was a needful thing.

He did not shift her from his lap, and she recalled that terrible beast upon the wall, roaring his wrath. This gelded creature before her was as far from that beast as it was possible to be. She wanted to embrace him, charm him, draw out the source of such sadness, and reassure him that he had her trust, even if she did not have his.

Instead, she cut him again, and this time, he did react. A tear slid from his eye, all silent and cruel.

"Why should we trust you?" she whispered.

Silas finally eased the rope away from his neck. It might have been the tear that pleased him. Knowing he had a hand in breaking an Alphaline was a potent thing—and a wonderful tale to tell around the campfire.

"Perhaps you can't trust me," countered Gray, and grinned suddenly as though the light behind his eyes had returned. As though he'd remembered his place and wasn't in fact lying like a beaten brute upon the floor with a knife to his chest, allowing a right bitch to cut into him.

"He sounds rightly legitimate to me," Silas muttered, stepping away and sitting at the council table with the rest.

"I think he's earned his place. I think he took it well," admitted Devitt, taking his own place at the table. There were further murmurs of agreement, and why wouldn't there be? It was tradition to test any new council member. It was tradition to have their trust as well. Gray might have earned their favour upon the wall by killing as he did, but his value was more than a mere soldier—desperate times called for rightly desperate decisions. Admittedly, there were about a dozen candidates better suited to sit at this table, but to recruit an Alphaline was a wise move and one of Silas's better suggestions. Whoever had attacked the town would return, and it wouldn't hurt to have a master tactician sitting amongst them when they did. Even if they could do little more than stand upon the wall and beat back whatever tried to climb over.

"Are you with us?" Kaya whispered, holding the blade to his chest once again and continuing to cut. Though nothing held him, he allowed her. He merely stared into her eyes, into her betraying soul, and it stung as much as the mark she placed upon him.

"Until I die," he whispered. It was a fine answer.

"Kaya, I think he's had enough. I think we're good," Simeon suggested. Beside him, Kaya heard Daisy agree, and they were probably right.

"Tell him why we did this," Devitt mumbled.

She wanted to tell him, but also, she had more to say. "Why did you come to Raven Rock?" she asked quietly, for his ears only.

He thought on it for a while. He never blinked or looked away or wiped his tears. "I came here to die." This, too, sounded like the truth.

"Will you join us here?" she asked carefully. He nodded, and she tended to his chest and continued to ruin it. However, this time, he swiftly gripped her wrist.

"I will take no further cuts," he warned, and she did not fight him. She merely slid the neck of her blouse a little lower so he could see the etchings in her own skin of the letters X and V. They were inscribed upon each other, in the skin over her heart, in a careless attempt at decoration. He looked to his own half-completed mark and grudgingly bade her continue, grunting quietly now as she went about her work.

He could not have known that this marking was part of the council's tradition, although he would soon learn. It symbolised dedication, but was also a signal to the elders of other bandit settlements who knew their history. Andreas had inflicted this mark on every person at the table. This was Kaya's first attempt at making the marks; it might also be her last.

"Do you think it's fine if I join this council?" Gray asked when the deed was finished, when she had helped him to his feet and bade him sit in his choice of seat. Her stomach churned when he took Andreas's chair, but there was little she could do about it.

"We need a foreign voice of war," Daisy said quietly. She kept her eyes from Silas, who cracked his fingers as she spoke but did not interrupt or offer his true thoughts. In love and war, things were far from fair. If he could hold his hate for the benefit of the Rock, then Gray could amble into the council as well.

It was all about survival, and bandits would take whatever advantages they could. Bringing the Alphaline in was a calculated bet, and it had taken Silas's rather well-thought-out arguments to entice them to even consider the action.

The boy couldn't merely wander in all entitled, though.

"So you near kill me, just for the sake of it?" Gray spluttered, grabbing his throat.

"Oh, whisht, boy. Anyone who sits at this table will face some sort of initiation. Aye, it was a little crude to punish you as we did, but at this late hour, and considering this threat, we had to… improvise," Silas argued.

"Initiation? What if I'd said no?"

"You didn't, though," Kaya muttered. Her heart felt heavy, but he'd taken their abuse well. She thought it was a fine thing. Only Devitt had taken their initiation better— better than she had taken her own. She had visions of Andreas laughing at her outrage as she nursed the wound, demanded retribution, started a fight with Rook, and all.

"What if I'd broken free and killed you all for your treatment?"

"You didn't, though," countered Kaya, and he glared at her.

Kaya sniggered. "Oh, don't look at me like that, beautiful boy. You can choose to be a right bitch about our manhandling and dwell on it for the rest of your days, or you can suck it up as we all eventually did and help us with this nightmare out in the forest. You are welcome to sit at our table, outsider. A rare thing, but necessary."

At this, Simeon, entrusted with the most critical task of the night, placed down a few glasses and poured each one full to the brim with sine most volatile.

"You fiends are nasty pieces of work," Gray said, watching him do it. Perhaps he needed a drink. Hardly surprising. "Perhaps Dia should bring proper ruin upon this place after all. I'll tell her this when I report back," he mocked weakly, taking the glass, drinking hard and coughing loudly. Such was the fire.

Simeon thought this was fantastic. He poured the man a second glass immediately and, laughing loudly, downed his own. The others followed suit.

That done, the council conferred for a time and bickered far less than usual. Exhaustion plagued them, but so did the echoes of wailing from the healer's shack, the walls, everywhere. After a time, Gray ceased to gaze upon Kaya with revulsion and contempt, and she wondered if he didn't at last understand her actions. Better for her to inflict the cutting and cruelty than anyone else, he might realise. He still would not smile or look her in the eyes, but that was fine.

They formed no plan of defence; they merely discussed their paltry actions—fleeing like cowards through the tunnels or standing firm upon the wall. Regardless, they all agreed it would take the full force of Spark City to crack the little town's defences. It wasn't the bandit way to bring a fight, but losing Raven Rock to fear alone was something no council member was inclined to suggest.

They discussed defences and the strengths they had in reserve. There were quite a few, as it turned out, and with pride, Kaya listed what weapons they held in storage and what plans they had in place should another attack come imminently. Gray listened and agreed that they did, indeed, have an advantage. Outside the walls lay death. Behind them, though, all locked up nice and cosy, there was hope.

There were far worse things than making a stand against an unstoppable force.

As the night wore on and fatigue took most of their shrewder thinking, they mused about who the attackers might have been. Daisy argued that their language was that of a Southern clan of war, but in the end, it really didn't matter. They were an enemy to be defeated.

Gray took it all in, though he protested tactfully that his kind dealt with such matters more civilly. "During the Faction Wars, this town was a fortress. Even under bandit rule, we all know they played their part," he mused, holding a glass of sine in the candlelight like a rare treasure. "Regardless of who defends her walls, were the Factions to go at it again, there are worse places to set a staging point." He drained his glass and sought no refill. Fatigue was one thing, but the bottle was nearly polished off between them. No one wanted to fight with a hangover. At least not yet. "Worse places to take shelter from a marching army."

"So, let's hope war is not coming to the Factions once again," Simeon said, and the room fell ever so quiet. War was simply bad for everyone.

They spoke a bit longer, tossing ideas around, sipping the last of their sine, and were just preparing to retire to their beds when they heard raised voices in the streets and the familiar sound of panic. They were already standing when there came a knock at the door, and a blood-covered young girl in ill-fitting armour barged in.

"I was sent with word from the wall. I think there's movement in the forest—marching," she cried, gasping to catch her breath.

Though she had known it was coming, Kaya felt a coldness run through her. *So soon.*

"To death we go," said Gray evenly.

"No mercy," hissed Silas.

"We will hold strong," Devitt muttered.

"We must do, or we are lost," Daisy whispered.

"Aye, let's kill them all," declared Kaya.

They began to march from the room. Shattered and lost, yet still defiant, they were united, each absorbed in their thoughts of the battle to come. The lives they would take, the friends they might lose.

It was Simeon who spoke last as they left the council chambers. "Hey, perhaps it's reinforcements," he jested.

It wasn't.

17

HELL COMES TO BANDIT TOWN

They made their way swiftly down through the town. As before, Simeon took Daisy's hand as they ran. Each step reverberated through his body. Each step was anxious; his mind was awash with terror. It was an unnatural thing to run this swiftly towards death, yet here he was, leading his love through and all.

Be brave.

Be better.

They followed the sounds of urgency and panic. It was hard to miss, what with the desperate gathering of battered bandits climbing the wall to try to get an eye on the threat. Simeon was wary. It was easy to feign an attack from one side, and then launch an assault from the other.

Imposing wall or not, it would not be too difficult to slip over if left unwatched.

Nevertheless, curiosity and duty got the better of Simeon. There was safety in numbers, too. Below the wall, he took hold of a ladder and took a breath to calm himself before climbing. Bandits were doing the same all along the side wall, up and down the length of the town.

"Over here, Simeon," a voice called. Looking up, he saw a gathering of those he'd stood the gate with. He knew most by name. And a desire for camaraderie took him. It was a strange thing, really. He'd never been one for popularity or attempting to gain it. He was a recluse by nature, if only to be a better Runner and thief.

As he climbed the last rung, hands reached down and grabbed him, hauling him up to the top and setting him on his feet, then shuffling him along the wall. "Is this the right way?" he called to Kaya, who had already climbed the defence.

She shrugged, but her eyes were upon the darkness. It was difficult to see what with the glow of lights all around them.

"Cheers, lads," he said, releasing himself from their hold and edging close to the drop below. Daisy came over beside him and stood watching. She looked calmer than she had during the first attack. Perhaps it was the tobacco weed slipping from her system or the addition of a few drops of sine. Regardless, it was a fine look to her.

"What is that?" she mumbled. Daisy's eyes were focused on the darkness beyond, and the sound of movement, heavy and methodical from somewhere within. All around them, the defenders raised swords and axes, bows and hammers, and a few shields. They were better prepared but terrified.

"There're a lot of us upon one side of the wall," Simeon hissed to Kaya, who nodded in acknowledgement. They all had an equal voice at the council table, but that never worked out in the living world, away from conversation and questions and too much voting. Without Andreas, well, Kaya was as good a leader as anyone. Leadership was sometimes earned in blood or battle, especially in Adawan; other times, it was achieved with the calmer voice of reason. Without Rook present, Kaya was the natural successor.

The thunder of movement arose. This time, though, rather than the boom of thundering hooves, they heard the crunch of breaking trees, a stamping of mud, the thudding of armoured feet. It was no less daunting than a mounted attack. There would need to be a great many soldiers to create such a racket. Distantly, he could see the flames again, flickering against the leaves. They looked less like fireflies now and more like a wave of fire as they bobbed up and down with every step.

"Kaya, should we be moving further up and down the line," he called, and around him, a few voices agreed. Suddenly, Simeon began to fret about the rest of the walls, which were under-protected. It had been bad luck to be caught out by the first attack, but to be tricked for a second time that night would be truly unforgivable. "Perhaps we should send a few bandits down each end to keep an eye on the darkness," he suggested, and again, a few of his comrades around him agreed.

"Do as Simeon orders," Kaya called out, though her eyes were transfixed by the coming fire.

"It will be done, sir," one of the bandits cried out, and he watched in bemusement as his orders carried weight.

Kaya suddenly spun on Simeon. "If needs be, you get running to the far side rightly swift, and take whoever you need," she said, eyeing Daisy. The lights in the trees suggested the assault would come from this side, but Kaya was no fool. Simeon had proven himself as much as she had at the gate. He was positively a hero. Or at least hardened. It wasn't enough to simply send a few bandits down to hold the line. And as for Daisy? Well, she hadn't proved herself at all, had she? Better she did not flee from her spot upon the line.

"This could be the end," Daisy muttered, looking into the

night. She stood beside him, wearing the same terrified stare as she had when she'd fled the battle. She looked pale from exhaustion and horror in the glow of the lights. He dared to grip her hand just once before returning to the awfulness upon the battlefield. Simeon shuddered, imagining how easily they both could have been among the dead upon the wet grass.

"They need to pay," Devitt hissed, stepping in between Simeon and Kaya, and the others made way for him, allowing the three to be together. Simeon thought this an interesting thing.

Nearly two hundred warriors stood upon the wall now, and a quarter of that number were spread throughout the rest of the defences. Simeon knew that there had been double that number before the first costly attack. It was no small thing that there were any of them left to stand upon the wall now, waiting for the end with blade and shield ready. Bastard bandits or not, they would not go without a fight.

Moreover, they had an Alphaline in their ranks. What could possibly go wrong?

That notorious Alpha stood beside Kaya. Every now and then, he glanced at her, but as though possessed by clairvoyance, he managed to look away the moment before she turned to meet his eyes. Simeon suspected there was a thing between them, certainly on Kaya's part. Simeon wondered how Devitt might feel about that.

Simeon thought Gray impressive. Anyone with the balls to fight without armour or a shirt was both suicidal and terrifying. The blood from Kaya's handiwork was already drying, and he looked immense with the council tattoo upon him. It must have hurt her to cut him as she did. It probably hurt Devitt more seeing her gazing at him as she did, too. A few bandits had already commented quietly about his promotion. If they lived through the night, that would be quite the topic in the morning.

Whenever that is.

"Sounds like a lot of footsteps," Gray said of the sound as it reached the treeline, and Simeon looked to the far side. A difficult thing, for his eyesight had never been the strongest. Still, through a break in the buildings, he could just about make out the warriors upon that wall as they took up arms, and he fought the urge to step away.

Suddenly, Silas appeared from one of the ladders. Unlike Simeon, who'd scrubbed some of the grime and ruin from his body before meeting with the council, Silas still looked as though he had walked right off the battlefield at that very moment. He also seemed rightly ready to step right back onto it. His blade clung to his back. His eyes were bright with drink and ready for war. It was annoying how impressive he looked.

Sitting with him in chambers had been a greater challenge than Simeon had expected. But this newborn sense of duty had him hold his tongue and his fists, too. After they survived the invasion, they could share words and fists, and hopefully not blades.

Silas eyed Daisy and Simeon, and while he'd avoided them in council, out here in the dark, as an army drew in, he looked ready for murder once more.

"Prick," he growled as he marched, and Simeon's hand fell to his small dagger. It was a fine dagger. Ivory handle, reasonably sharp. He'd paid a fortune for it one drunken night in the tavern. It was an expensive purchase, admittedly, but it had seemed like quite the bargain at the time.

Silas slowed, nearing Simeon. His fists looked ready, his grin cruel. From nowhere, Daisy stepped forward and planted herself in between the two, as a protective swan upon her eggs.

"Just keep on walking, husband; there's plenty of room along this wall," she hissed in a tone that intrigued Simeon. He recognised it from the days of debate upon the council, long before they ever fell for each other. Back when she was no more than an opinionated, wealthy woman, with ideas above her station and an outstanding rear. And he? Well, he was an opinionated little rat of a Runner. But also with a beautiful rear.

I loved you from the first moment you cut me down with that tongue.

For a terrible breath, Simeon believed Silas might do something anyway. He leaned in as though to whisper a curse in her ear before sniffing her hair once and walking on. "A pox on you both," he growled as he marched past.

That could have gone a lot worse.

Further down the wall, he was greeted by the warriors he'd gone to war with. Most notably, a woman wrapped her arms around his waist as he stood out over the edge, watching the coming of the end. They were brazen, riotous, and they gave the impression that they wanted to go to war. Simeon couldn't help but notice that Silas's comrades hadn't bathed the shit from themselves either. Simeon's comrades, however, had the class to appear as though they had at least tried. Some had even changed their clothes altogether. Simeon shook his head; the people one attracted were a reflection on one's character, he thought snidely.

"Oh, baby, I really needed that," Daisy whispered, and, glancing at Silas one last time as his gathering of warriors flocked around their new master, she kissed Simeon passionately, and indeed, for a breath, he could see the fire in his goddess. He could also see her remove her hand from the grip of her blade. Probably a good thing she didn't murder the newest Raven Rock hero in front of his savage horde and all.

"Everyone be still and use your wits," cried Kaya, and the forest fell to a sudden silence. The flickering flames remained within. From his perch on the wall, Simeon began to count them, and they were in the hundreds, no doubt. They stretched out the breadth of the town, and if he had scampered down to gaze at the front gates or the far wall, he feared he might see similar flames in the darkness beyond.

Flee to the other side.

Still, he didn't. Curiosity kept him upon this edge. Among the majority of warriors. Where perhaps most of the fighting would occur.

"Keep your blades ready," Silas added, and those were fine words, even if they came from a right cur.

For a time, it was all still and awful. The silence took everyone's nerve and Simeon began to count the moments in his mind.

"Will they just come and attack, already," he mocked, and around him, a few of his comrades sniggered. Usually, on any given night at any table, he might share such wit with anyone who listened and meet silence. Again, he wondered if his status upon the council or his feats upon the defence hadn't propelled him to a place of some standing.

If you could only see me now, Dad. I made it.

Nothing happened for a little while longer, and then something did happen.

"Oh, no. I knew it," hissed Devitt and dropped to a knee.

"Hush, Devitt, you fool," Kaya snapped.

It was simply a girl who emerged. A very pretty girl, to be exact, whose silhouette beneath the flaming torch she carried suggested something alluring and delicate. With long black hair and eyes that were perhaps startlingly pretty (though it was hard to see from up here) she stepped away from the cover of the trees as though she knew exactly what she was doing and where she was going. She wore armour as intimidating as that of the mounted warriors, but apart from that, she looked unimposing as she walked out onto the battlefield.

Stopping over a cluster of dead bandits, she bent down and ran her fingers across the wounds of those who had suffered the most savage of blows. It was an intriguing and unsettling thing to gaze upon, and the crowd fell terribly still watching her, lest the first to speak would set off an attack or bring about doom.

"Who are you?" cried out Kaya after a time. Beside her, Gray drew three arrows from his quiver but remained, to the casual watcher, entirely at ease.

"Just give me a moment," the girl countered, as though ordering a beverage during a festival before everything went to hell. She tilted her head and leaned in towards one of the bodies.

What is she doing?

If he were asked, Simeon might have believed this girl was kissing one particular wound or else smelling the fresh meat right before it turned to decay. He'd take no oath on it, though. Regardless, Simeon thought this strange, beautiful girl was far too comfortable around the dead. And that was never a good sign at the best of times.

"Um... alright," Kaya replied, shrugging her shoulders.

Eventually, the girl looked up. "I am Aurora Borealis, and I like to kill."

"Um... alright," Simeon mumbled, and a few of his newly gathered followers sniggered again, despite the growing feeling of terrible things so close.

Aurora Borealis, who liked to kill, wasn't finished.

Standing, she resumed marching forward, waving her torch like a blade. As she came, she looked out across the length of the wall and appeared very impressed. "And tragically, I have come with my kin to kill you all."

"You want war? We'll give you war," Kaya roared with such menace that Simeon gripped his sword and felt his guts clench.

"That's right," he growled, and Daisy drew her sword beside him. A few more beside her did the same.

"War?" Aurora Borealis, who liked to kill, countered. "This is not war. This is merely the taking of the tainted. These are the actions of a god. This is beautiful and predestined, and oh, in his name we rise. In his name, I kill."

"This bitch is crazy," Simeon muttered before he could help himself. Again, his comrades laughed at his bravado. He suddenly wanted to crack a few jokes. Make them all feel a little bit better.

Before everyone died in blood and misery.

Silas could only stay silent for so long. "Listen, you whore," he called, "why don't you come a little closer, and we'll have a little chat." Unsurprisingly, his comrades thought this was as funny as he did. Simeon didn't laugh, though, and neither did his comrades.

Good comrades.

Though it was rather funny.

Aurora appeared to approve. "Oh, I like you, old man; I'll bathe in your blood until my skin is a wondrous shade of rosy. Do me a favour and die with as little blood loss as possible," she said.

Simeon shuddered; her tone was a little too unsettling for his taste, although he liked the 'old man' comment. "You do look like you could do with a wash, you crazy bitch," he called out, and plenty of people found this hilarious. Except for the girl, who looked through the crowd to see who mocked her.

Simeon leaned into Gray. "Tell me, comrade, can you hit that lunatic from here?"

"Aye, that I can," Gray countered without missing a beat. He gripped his bow but did not load or release. They were all still engaged in conversation, after all.

"Best not miss when the time comes. You will look a right Alpha tool," he said gaily.

Kaya stepped forward. "Who are you?"

"Does it matter?" the girl countered.

"Well, can there be peace mediated?" she said, and her comrades gave a collective gasp.

Peace?

Fuk that.

Terrified or not, those bastards had come upon their territory and wiped a hundred of them out. There would be no peace brokered. Not until they had a taste of some vengeance.

"Hush," Kaya hissed to the dissenting voices. She was playing the leader perfectly. She wanted no peace either. Her words at the table had suggested as much. Nevertheless, she desired to learn the extent of their attackers' will.

"Peace?" Aurora said. "Well, that is quite the question," she replied, her tone almost careless. She suddenly began counting aloud. She stepped forward a few paces, held, and took one more step as though landing on an even number was the best move.

Her strange behaviour stung Simeon greatly. He had once counted his steps as a child. His words per sentence, too. It had been rightly annoying—for him as well as his family and playmates. His mother had beaten that out of him quickly enough. A good thing too. Who knew how easily such a thing might have taken over his mind?

"Peace?" continued Aurora, counting a little and thinking about it a little longer. "Why, yes, oh beautiful Kaya. Just run on down there and lift open Raven Rock's gates and let me and my kin get a little step inside. We only want to stay a while," she added.

How does she know her name?

"I think this is the moment," Simeon muttered, but Gray was already firing. Three swift shots released in less than a breath, less than a moment, too, and they were perfect. They sailed high and swift. Aurora must have seen the movement. Must have suspected only an Alphaline was capable of firing and hitting from that distance with any accuracy.

"Wonderful," she cried, spinning with flame outstretched, twirling wide of the first arrow, continuing the pirouette as though upon a stage, and dodging the second before, in that same beautiful smooth motion, catching the third from the sky with her flaming torch.

The crowd gasped at the spectacle, and for a dreadful moment, Simeon felt an icy finger of fear slide up his back as he watched this crazy bitch. Her defence was nothing short of miraculous—and devastating to morale.

"I see you, Alphaline. I fuken see you," she called, cackling unsettlingly but keeping her eye upon the fiend lest he fire again.

"What was that?" Gray gasped.

"She just made you look bad," Simeon said weakly.

Aurora stepped forward once more and flung her torch of fire and arrow high into the sky towards the wall. Immediately, she disappeared into the darkness. Not that anyone saw, for from the trees, there emerged a long line of warriors. Three for every one of the defenders. Each of them lit a torch and passed the flame to the next as they marched forward in one direct, intimidating line of fire.

"I'm going to have nightmares about this sight," mused Simeon, drawing his blade as the defenders spread out along the wall. The others took up positions towards the far end and beyond. They were outnumbered, but they had the wall to cling to.

This was their territory; they were ready.

18

HELL

The long line of defenders fell silent, and it was dreadful. Terror took hold of Kaya with a grip like cold steel. The attackers drove forward like a wave of fire threatening to swallow them all in ruin. They marched down upon the town, and the distance to the walls allowed ample time for fear to creep deep into the defenders' souls. All around her, Kaya could feel terror, similar to her own, brewing among the defenders.

The numb silence carried across the defensive line, which was still but for nervous panting and shaking of weapons. Kaya knew well that panic could quickly surge over them all. Even a bandit line was likely to scatter if given a long enough time to watch approaching death. Running away, finding a place in the dark to wait out the storm suddenly became that little bit more tempting. She imagined Andreas standing on the wall with them. He would have had the words to carry them. As it was, no one looked to lead.

Fuk this.

"Be ready, comrades," she bellowed, her voice firm—a good start. "We have the higher ground and the defences," she added, turning to address all those around her. To Simeon, she leaned in. "Get going to the far side of the wall, and plug any gaps along the way," she hissed.

Without delay, Simeon darted down along the wall, followed by a dozen comrades. For a breath, Daisy remained and then, with an apologetic grin, she followed after. It was no loss, thought Kaya.

"Oh, no, there are so many," a voice tight with dread cried out, and she cursed aloud. Less of that panic was needed.

"I need someone to reinforce the rear," she cried, but few reacted. Their eyes were glued to the charging brutes. "Fine." She looked around. "Hey… you there… you seven… Aye… you fools… Head on back towards the rear, and be ready," she ordered a gathering of younger bandits who looked rightly ready to bolt. There appeared to be few flaming torches appearing at the far end of town. She thought it better to get the greener warriors to a quieter section where they could serve their purpose by simply keeping an eye out for right sneaky snakes in the grass. They took the orders well, sprinting along the edge, no doubt grateful not to face the mass charge. She did not judge them in any way.

"Well, they looked ready to bolt," muttered Devitt. "I should move along there with them," he said quietly. The appearance of the girl he had spent time with had shaken him somewhat, and though Kaya's jealousies played a cruel game on her nerves and control, she could only feel sorry for the guilt the cur must have felt. It wasn't his fault he had bedded a spy. She could not hate him for it. Not really. Well, not much. Another part of her wanted to claw out his heart or his eyes, or other such things.

"Lead them," she said with finality. She might have said more and wished him well, but instead, she focused on how thin their defences were beginning to look. Kaya looked to the far front gate, where a second attack would likely come. She knew that in the skirmish, some curs would get over the wall somehow. Keeping those gates locked nice and tight was a necessity.

There were already a dozen guards at watch, but she needed more. She looked at Silas and knew he wouldn't move. His eyes were upon the coming threat. Probably not the worst type of fiend to stand with her, she supposed.

"Will you and your comrades stand this wall with me, Silas?" she called, and the cur grinned warily. Perhaps he understood her words and their weight. A council meeting was one thing, but a definite leader emerging was entirely another. She had claimed this unwanted crown in this moment.

"You order me to stand the wall?" he called. "It would be a pleasure… General," he said, gripping his axe and turning to the coming warriors. He looked positively ready to leap from the wall and take them all on himself.

Gray glided up beside her, silent except for the gentle clatter of arrows at his waist. "Would you have me tend to the gate?" he asked, and in that moment, she knew her crimes were somewhat forgiven. She placed her hand on his chest.

"I am sorry for what I did."

"When we know victory, we might speak of such things," he said, before bowing and racing towards the gate. For a breath, she felt far more alone than before.

Like a rushing wave, the attackers neared the glow of the town's lights, and Kaya, gripping her sword, awaited the charge as they increased their pace from a march to a jog to a sprint.

They must know the height of the walls, yet here they are, charging towards them.

"Here they come," she warned as though it was needed.

As though the archers weren't already drawing and holding and releasing. Many arrows took flight just as the attackers released their own projectiles. Their torches took flight. High and far they flew, a shower of terrifying beauty.

They struck the wall and the grounds beyond, exploding with showers of sparks as they landed. All around her, Kaya felt their stinging warmth. A few fell short; others cleared the wall completely and landed down behind the defensive line, where they could create all manner of mayhem.

Silas blocked a few as he spun his battle axe. It was no impressive deflecting of arrows, but it was remarkable enough. As fires took light all along the inside wall, Kaya heard screams of panic and fear, but also shouts for water and blankets. It was no small thing to set alight a convoy of travellers; it was another to feel the threat of the ground beneath you going up in smoke.

Nevertheless, these flames were not the real threat at all. It would take a master of the throw to strike any building behind their ramparts, but they were the perfect distraction. For every fiend carrying a torch, another sprang up behind. A line of them moved forward, swinging long chains in near unison.

She looked closer and suddenly understood their game and their terrible threat, too. She wanted to scream a warning, but really, what words would prepare her comrades for what was to come?

A huge grappling hook was attached to the end of each chain. All that remained was to swing each one up, catch it on the wall, and climb.

Here we go.

All along the wall, hundreds of these hooks clanked loudly, each seeking the treasure of a sturdy hold. While Kaya remained untouched, many of her comrades were too slow to step aside, and the air quickly filled with screams as the dreadful barbs found purchase in unwitting flesh. Far below, the attackers pulled on their chains, as though they were securing a fish upon a rod, and Kaya watched in anguish as many bandits were pulled wriggling to their doom.

The luckier ones were only pinned to the wall or to the ground they stood upon.

The invaders did not hesitate. With barely a test of their weight on the chains, they began to climb. Up and up the wall they rose, using their feet to brace themselves against the wall, and soon, the bandits' focus turned to a desperate rush to stop the climbing bastards, while avoiding the next wave of glittering hooks swinging up towards them.

At first, Kaya tried pulling free the nearest hook as the chain stretched tight, vibrating as those below climbed. She pulled with all her strength, but the hook was stuck securely as a limpet. Next, she turned to the chain. It was thin, and she tried desperately to slice down through it where it was most taut, but her blade merely rebounded off the metal and nearly took off her nose.

Cursing her luck, she turned to her comrades and saw that they were suffering similarly. Panic took her, and she suppressed it; she bent low and leaned out over the edge, determined to lead by example.

Stabbing deep with her sword and cursing at the effort, she struck the first attacker's hand as it reached for a hold at the top. It was a fine strike; it cleaved the grasping hand half free of the wrist. Problem was, he didn't fall. With his one remaining hand holding the chain, he spat in her face and wrapped his other arm and its claw-like ruin around her, tight enough to keep an Alpha in place. He screamed in pain and perhaps triumph that he had a victim in his grasp, and the two engaged in a pathetic, mighty struggle.

"Fuk off away from me," Kaya cried and hammered back with the grip of her sword, smashing his nose for good measure before pulling herself from his grasp. She slashed her blade down once upon his shoulder, knocking him free of the wall. It wasn't a kill—she was sure the cur survived—but it was enough to clear her line.

Do better.

Right after the fallen fiend, a second woman began to climb. She was better suited to the task, using agility and determination to reach the top. Kaya thrust down and missed her completely.

Come on.

The girl kicked away from the wall as Kaya struck and then leapt towards the new unspoken leader of Raven Rock. Like her comrade before her, she secured a hold. She screamed incomprehensibly in Kaya's face as she pulled herself over the top. Out of the corner of her eye Kaya could see the similar struggles her companions upon the wall endured.

This is how we fall.

Hammering the girl's freckled face with her forehead, Kaya edged her aside and freed her sword. Stabbing deep, she took the woman's life before kicking her corpse free of the wall. At that moment, Kaya recovered her sharpness and better senses, too. She focused only on the next fiend sprawling up over the top and the large sword he drew before attacking. Somehow, this steadied her as she held her stance, watched his moves and ignored a potential strike from behind her. She chose to trust her comrades in their defences. It was all she could do.

It was enough.

The cur spat out a curse in his guttural language and swung. Balanced and assured, she ducked beneath his struggling defence, drew her dagger and plunged it deep into the side of his armour, where it was weakest. He howled, and she shoved him from her sight.

Facing the next fiend, she was even more composed, believing herself better skilled with the blade. She killed him where he stood before he had time to swing once, reaffirming her confidence.

Kill them all.

The next victim after that was dispatched just as smoothly, and she felt herself a goddess of war. Pushing towards the next foe as though his impending death were little more than a notch upon her belt, she felt all powerful. She even considered counting her kills as she swung, blocked, parried and killed, but really, what type of foul, savage fiend would take any pride in such numbers?

An Alpha, probably.

The world around her became a frenzy of death and defiance, war and bloodshed and much violence. Yet still, the brutes continued to stream over the wall. Their numbers were greatest where there was less resistance, and Kaya discovered this all too late, for as she kicked her umpteenth victim back over the wall, suffering nothing but a bloody nose for her trouble, she was surprised to see no attacker following. She thought she and her bandits were winning for a moment, but then realised the attackers were simply avoiding those with greater sword skills. Instead, they moved along the wall seeking out gaps in the defence, but also less skilled defenders. And when they found them, they surged up and over.

Save them all.

Moving along the wall, Kaya came upon the blood-covered figure of Silas, limping along, seeking out murder most divine. He was without a victim, too, and the brute looked crestfallen for it. His battle axe hung limply by his side as he gasped dreadful, exhausted breaths, yet he never stopped moving.

And then it occurred to her.

As it should have occurred to any strong leader a long time before.

"The chains, Silas—see to them," she cried.

He looked at her doubtfully for a breath until, with a delicate swinging gesture of his axe, he acknowledged her order.

Big axe, giant swing, thin chains.

"I couldn't break them before."

"You will break them now," she assured him.

"Fine… will someone cover my arse?" he cried, but Kaya was already beside him, peering down both lengths of the wall and the hundred struggling warriors on each. "This is going to hurt a bit, my love," he muttered in apology to his weapon before swinging down upon a chain. It did not break, and he howled in fury, perhaps in pain. The axe bounced up at him again as though upon a spring, but she immediately saw the damage it had inflicted.

Just a little more.

"Is that all you have?" she challenged, and, cursing her, he raised it high and brought it down hard, shattering the chain and sending a sprawling attacker back down to the bottom. "That's incredible," she cried, dragging him along the wall towards the next one a few feet away.

Only a hundred or so to go.

As Silas attacked each chain, Kaya moved along on his flank, keeping an eye out, stabbing deep at those who attempted to climb over. They moved as a strange silhouette against the town's eerie lights, like demented dancers, repeating the same manoeuvre for a watching audience. They were not friends; he disgusted her, and Silas himself had never had much time for her, either, but as a unit, and in that moment, they were divine. And they alone turned the tide.

With every attempt, Silas improved his technique. He roared with every blow and severed each chain every time. And she was smooth in her killing and covering.

Behind them, a few of their comrades caught sight of Silas's feats, and those with similar heavy axes went to task upon the marauders' chains as he did. They were hardly as effective, but snap the chains they did, albeit at a much slower pace. After a time, the numbers of surging attackers began to lessen as the defenders moved further down each end, the sound of their axes ringing against the stone. At last, and all too soon, the pendulum started to swing completely.

"We nearly have them," Kaya cried, urging her defenders to one final push. Only when the first shards of light appeared across the horizon did they fully believe they would hold the wall this terrible morning.

She didn't hear the calls for a retreat, but suddenly, as though a signal had been given, the attackers began to recede like the turning of the sea.

"Did we do it?" Silas cried, dropping to a knee. Watching the attackers fall away, leaving the chains where they clung, he fully allowed himself to collapse. Gasping, he leaned over the edge of the wall and threw up on the dead below before lying flat as though taken by a blade himself.

At that moment, Kaya saw the torment he'd put himself through, and she thought him truly heroic, if not the worst bastard she had ever met.

"I just need a moment, is all," he said, and his comrades surrounded him, many dropping in exhaustion as he did.

Emboldened, the defenders began to roar abuse as the attackers fled. Yelling and taunting, they marched along the wall, down towards the gate. Kaya followed, and there, she came upon Gray, still standing firm upon the wall, surrounded by no companions whatsoever. He hadn't needed them. Below him lay a carpet of dead attackers, covered in a sea of at least fifty protruding arrows. Gray was breathing quickly, but his eyes were cold and calculating; they were fixed upon a more significant threat.

Kaya and her comrades turned and stiffened in terror. Below them, through the break in the trees opposite the gate, walked Aurora. She was alone and casual. Her cloak flowed out behind her, displaying the long sword she wore. She kept looking up at the defenders as she walked back along the battlefield, towards the far side of the wall where she'd first appeared.

"Where is the pretty brown-skinned goddess I spoke with?" she said after a time. All eyes fell upon Kaya; apparently Aurora Borealis had decided that Kaya spoke for Raven Rock. "Oh, no—I do hope none of my kin slit her pretty throat already?" she added. "I wanted to cut myself a piece of her," she said and dropped her head as though truly distraught.

"What do you want?" Kaya called, and the crowd around her separated. The cheering now absent, was replaced with tension.

"Oh, brilliant!" Aurora cried and waved. "Hello there."

In a grand act of defiance, Kaya did not reply, so Aurora, who liked to kill, continued. "Apart from killing you all, I wish to offer a game of chance."

Kaya had a rightly shitty feeling about this. She felt a fresh trickle of sweat stream down her back. A little rivulet of terror. She did not know why. They had held firm; they had shown their teeth, but there was something in Aurora's tone, something in the way she seemed utterly unmoved by the defiance shown was unsettling.

"What do you mean?"

"You wonderful fiends did far better than I expected." She looked around at the attackers as they skulked away from the battle. "Far better than any of us thought. You should be proud of yourselves."

She clapped a few times.

Six times, to be exact.

"We stood as any would. Speak your words, or rightly fuk off."

The crowd cheered her words briefly. Perhaps they were not as intimidated by her.

They don't have to talk to her.

Aurora smiled and stepped a little closer. Close enough that Gray might have considered another few shots. As it was, Gray made no effort.

Perhaps he was tired.

Perhaps he was wary of being shown up by her.

He's definitely tired.

"I offer you a chance to earn a little grace."

She didn't want Aurora to go on. She wanted her to leave and never come back, so they could tend to the wounded, mourn the dead or prepare the town for another invasion, some other time, defended by some other leader from some other council. Kaya had always argued that the only truly safe place for a bandit was in Adawan. She wanted to be in Adawan at that moment. On the other hand, Devitt had always said he'd like to see the Deep North.

"Go on, Aurora," Kaya said, letting go of imaginings.

Aurora did go on. "A little game of chance, played in blood. I desire to wet my blade." She held out her sword all shiny and untouched by bandit victims. "I challenge your finest warrior to a duel."

This will not end well.

"Name the terms," Kaya countered, her mind racing. Skilled as Aurora might be, the town had an Alphaline to call upon. The odds would hardly be fair.

"I desire only death and chance as my victory spoils; you name your terms."

"If we kill you, will your supporters retreat and be gone from here?" It was a foolish opening counter, but who knew—perhaps Aurora was crazy enough to listen. Perhaps she was willing to bet a reprieve for the day so they might recoup and recover their wits. And of course, most wars were fought at the whim of a solitary fool. Perhaps this girl's comrades were just desperate to retreat, and the slight matter of their leader being killed would be a good enough reason to give it all up.

"Aye, that sounds fair."

Kaya's heart dropped. Aurora was lying. She'd agreed far too quickly.

"We have your word?"

"Oh aye, as valued as it is."

It's a trap.

It's a trap.

It's an obvious trap.

Immediately, warriors bent on vengeance and glory accepted the duel on behalf of Kaya. Eager voices rang out, and Kaya could only gaze at Gray and Silas. They were the two warriors she would not allow to compete. For as intimidating as Aurora was, and given the slight chance she was genuine in her word, Kaya was loath to lose either warrior. Their value behind the wall was far too great.

"You know this is a trap," Simeon said beside her. He was

covered in a fresh layer of blood—some from his forehead, where a healer would need to save his flawless face from a nasty scar.

"Aye. What do you think?"

"I think we have to try it."

"If it ends now, will we not feel aggrieved at vengeance lost?" she countered, and Simeon chuckled.

"We wanted no peace, but a win is a win. We've kicked the shit out of each other; I think it's a fair deal."

Aurora stood forward. "I want the Alpha; give me the beautiful Alpha so I can mount his manhood upon my mantel to gaze at and mock," she cried deliriously before laughing as though her wit was endearing.

"She's a lunatic," Simeon countered. "Killing her would be a fine thing for the world, even if she's lying."

"I will do it," Silas muttered, hobbling over. His face was red and fierce.

"Aye, let Silas at her," agreed Simeon. "He can wear my scarf as he does it."

"You can barely stand, hero," Kaya countered, and though Silas turned to argue, he nodded his head, dropped to the edge of the wall and, letting his legs hang down over the edge, closed his eyes and began breathing deeply.

"I am not so sure I should walk out from these walls," Gray said when eyes fell upon him. His fingers tapped at the blade at his waist, but he let it remain in his scabbard.

"I agree," Kaya declared. "It is likely death to whoever steps over, and I will command no brave fiend to throw away their life on a game of chance."

Her words lessened the defenders' enthusiasm. All but one, that is.

Lucian was a fine young warrior, if not a difficult man to call upon. Tall, graceful, good-looking and well-built, he was a well-renowned bandit. However, there was cruelty to his soul and several kills to his name. It wasn't necessarily bad, especially at war, but Kaya had never been fond of the boy. After Silas, his ability with the blade was unquestionable. The blade in his hands was ancient and impressive, an heirloom he'd taken from some Black Guard a few seasons back. He'd given the guard no chance to reclaim it either. He was a cold killer with an easy smile. There had been discussions about bringing him into the council at some point in the days after Andreas's murder, but his bloody legend was not something that fit with Raven Rock's council.

Champion for the town, though, was a fine title altogether.

"I cannot ask you to do it," Kaya said as the young man stepped forward, carelessly wiping his blade free of some victim's blood.

"Then I demand a crack at this girl," he declared and looked down upon Aurora, who waited eagerly at the edge of Gray's kill zone.

Kaya was unwilling to lose the opportunity to kill this savage woman who commanded an army. Lucian was a calculated risk. It would be a shame to lose a potent warrior to an arrow from the treeline, but it was an acceptable loss. Besides, few would stop him from climbing down to face her, which is precisely what he did after exchanging a gentle embrace with a woman who might or might not have been his kin.

"If you kill her, you'd best get sprinting rightly quick back up here," Silas called as he slipped down the wall.

"I'll be right back," he said, grinning and displaying the bravado of a conquering master.

Kaya feared such arrogance would work against him.

They had all witnessed Aurora's impressive reflexes. Who knew the complete measure of her swordplay?

Dropping, Lucian stood facing the wall for a breath, and Kaya caught his prayers as he spoke them swiftly. When he opened his eyes, the grinning cur was gone, replaced by the thoroughly professional killer he could be.

Perfect.

Sic 'em, boy.

Neither combatant rushed to the other. If they spoke words, they were lost in the wind. The world fell silent but for the breeze of the morning and the collective held breath of a shaken town, wondering if this act of madness would be their liberation.

Or the damnation of a comrade.

Their blades met, and Lucian's skill was instantly obvious. He dared not rush the attack; he merely moved around her, holding his blade close, countering her swift strikes, for she, like her behaviour indicated, acted the aggressor. To any master gazing upon the fight, it was clear she was evenly matched to him—at least, at the beginning.

"She is talented," Gray murmured, standing beside Kaya.

"He looks in control," Kaya countered.

"Aye, but he's not reckless. He's a killer."

She agreed, for Lucian matched her strikes and held his guard carefully lest she pretend to be less skilled than she was. Instead, he studied her shoulders and countered her every movement as though he were a master pugilist in a dreadful tournament.

They gasped and croaked out curses, threats and mocks, and each warrior countered the other. For a moment, Kaya imagined it similar to two training swordsmen, merely practising without allowing blows to land.

They circled without disengaging, and the pace increased.

"He's seeking a kill. He should move her to her left; it's weaker there," Gray said thoughtfully as the spinning bodies increased their pace. Aurora's moans became a little louder, her curses a little cruder. On more than one occasion, she cried out in her unfamiliar tongue, and still, Lucian could not strike her down. Would not strike her down. He glided around the battlefield, his face a grim portrait of calm and effort. He was sublime, and she was a perfect fit for his style. Especially when she drew first blood after a careless strike from him, and were she quicker, she might have punished him further. As it was, she ducked his blow and slashed him across the chest ever so, and they spun away from each other for a breath.

"Be careful, Lucian," Devitt mumbled. His face was a concentrated grimace of purest hate. Were she to fall, perhaps his guilt would be fully alleviated.

They met again. This time, Aurora was eager, giggling as she struck.

"She thinks she's winning," Gray muttered. Kaya nodded, but honestly, she knew little of proper swordsmanship. She knew to stab and slash wherever the other blade wasn't. How some spoke the language of a skirmish was beyond her. She thought Aurora was quite the threat.

It was luck that changed the battle. Aurora turned awkwardly and stepped into a splash of morning sunshine. She must have felt the warmth at her back, for she parried a lunging strike, kept her left a little too low, and teased to end the fight. Lucian leapt in to send the blade through her heart —and his eyes met the dazzling burn of the sun's rays.

He swung wildly and dipped his head, raising his hand to his eyes for just a breath. In truth, after the night he'd had, it was instinct on his part, and she was upon him.

With terrific, terrible speed, while sliding his blade wide

with hers, she seamlessly pulled a small crossbow bolt from the cuff of her wrist and stabbed his unprotected abdomen. Such was the pull of flesh as she plunged and tore it free that those watching knew the fight was over in a flash.

He wailed as he fell, dropping his sword and grabbing the wound as he emptied himself of blood. A terrible thing, really. It was a bad defeat altogether.

"Stop screaming, boy," Silas cried, but the young killer was lost to the torment as she plunged a second time with the bolt before picking up his impressive sword and studying it. Scrambling pathetically, he reached for the blade, and she pushed it through his open hand and pulled it out before placing it upon a rock and stamping on it thrice until it broke.

"He liked that blade," Simeon said, spitting over the edge in disgust.

The warrior collapsed in the grass, moaning, and Aurora stood over him, quietly speaking to him words only he could hear. As she did, a gathering of mounted Riders appeared from the trees. Bowing to Lucian, she stood aside and left them to their task.

Walking towards the gate and the shaken bandits, she bowed again.

"I really enjoyed that; thank you, dear Kaya."

Behind her, the Riders strapped the man's limbs to chains similar to those that were used in the invasion, securing each with a hook. His screams were louder than any other that day. Especially when the fifth was driven through his groin just as the five mounts were walked apart.

"To the fires with you, whore," Kaya screamed, but she couldn't help but gaze at Lucian's awful ending.

"To the fires with us all, my dear," Aurora cried and spun around as the Riders drove their beasts forward and the chains with them, tearing, severing, killing in a haze of awful horror. Aurora, standing beside him as he was torn, opened her arms to the warm spray as it covered her entirely.

Those with the stomach to honour Lucian's fall dropped to a knee as the last thundering echo of hoofbeats disappeared into the forest.

Kaya could only stare in misery at the ruin the girl left behind, and she knew Aurora wouldn't rest until they all died in a similar way.

"None of us are going to live through this, are we?" someone asked.

"Not a one," Silas said. His head, too, was dropped. He spat over the edge and climbed to his feet. "I need a drink so that I might face my last day drunker than the first."

And the leader of Raven Rock couldn't find any words.

19

HELL HEADS HOME

Her name was Aurora, and she liked to walk alone. It was good that she liked this, as none of her kin bothered to talk to her as she made her way through the undergrowth on the short walk back to the camp. It was their way of showing disapproval, and Aurora respected this. It had been a to-and-fro type of invasion. More costly than any assault before. She'd expected some resistance, but they had been battered back, and it was just a little bit wonderful.

I did my part.

The boy's blood was still warm upon her, clinging to her, reassuring her. She licked her lips, thought of steaming cooked meats and also the slaying of innocents, and her mouth watered.

"*You are doing well, my darling,*" she imagined her lover whispering, and she knew these to be false words. It was irrelevant how well she was doing. Nothing mattered, not even the costs, until the town fell. That's all that mattered, and that's all he desired of her.

With the Riders driving their beasts forward, little old blood-covered Aurora was left far behind. And that was fine.

Though she gave them orders, she had no kinship with these curs. Her army, though, would be arriving at the camp by now, and their reward would be a well-deserved rest after a night's glorious endeavours.

"Two hundred and seventy, two hundred and seventy-one, two hundred and seventy-two," she whispered, counting her steps. Only a few hundred more and she would be home. Back among those who loved her, those who worshipped the Woodin Man as she did. She craved a little silence. The hours had been tough; the respite would be welcomed, and she was ready to bathe that boy from her skin now that she was sated.

She was ready to stretch out, reassure herself and rightly go to killing them all.

She replayed the delicious first assault in her mind and smiled at its extraordinary success. Sleeping with Devitt had been worth that intelligence alone. There was nothing like a little funeral to distract from the signs of the march. Nothing like an unarmed slaughter as well. Even Nika, the Riders' general and ever-so-subtle naysayer of her position, had little to argue about such an assault. At least for a time. A fury came upon her, and she blew a breath into the wind, counted a few more steps and let that matter settle.

It could have been so much better.

As her kin charged down upon the town, she had nearly wept for denying herself the opportunity to kill with them. She was good with climbing walls and all. Alas, this was a grand battle, not hunting an Alphaline clan in the darkest of stormy nights. There were too many risks to war. A stray bolt, arrow or blade could have ended her life upon the charge.

Wouldn't that have been lovely?

She took a deep breath and felt the drive of a blade through her chest, severing, rupturing, gratifying. "I might have pissed myself at the end," she whispered to the wind, and her mouth watered again at such a divine prospect. "Slithering in my waste and dying in it. A fitting end," she added, wiping a tear from her eye. She wept from joy, from need, from loneliness, from regret that her god wasn't walking with her, that he wasn't punishing her for her sins of life and hope, tearing her asunder, loving her, furrowing her, finishing her off and leaving her dead. Or else a ruin, or else sated. Whichever, really.

She wanted none of it but also all of it.

Distantly, away from the breeze and the hiss of morning insects, she could hear the camp in motion. No doubt preparing for the next assault, no doubt dressing the wounds from that second attack.

Failure, failure, fuken failure.

"They were delightful in their defences," she mused aloud, inhaling a wonderful aroma as it drifted in the air and reminded her that she hadn't eaten anything since the morning before. A girl had to look her best when she burned the world, you see.

Kaya.

She loved the goddess. She loved her nerve and shrewd ability upon the wall. Oh, aye, the girl had fought and led, and Aurora had gazed from the treeline with mouth agape, craving her, needing her, just dying to make her dead. She imagined slicing that delicious skin a little to bleed her dry. Bleeding dry those she loved, too.

Like Devitt?

She grinned and continued towards the gathering of her army kin. She could hear their voices now. Foreign, familiar tongues, and she without a nation to call her own.

Not for a decade.

She thought about the defence and wondered about her tactics. Looking back, she had not wanted to flood the town in the first drive. What fun would that have been? But perhaps she had chosen a more cautious assault than needed. It was simply a taste of things to come. It would be over once the great machines of war arrived. Or at least, it would crack their heart, and sometimes that was more appealing than killing.

Breaking through the treeline, she came upon the camp, and unsurprisingly, it was a frenzy of excellent motion. They ran from every corner, all desperate and frantic, at task, fighting a blaze, and it was an enchanting sight.

Three large fires lit the dawn, sending sickening black smoke into the sky. Wondrous things, really, more violent than any pyre her god demanded.

Who's been sneaking around my camp while we were out playing?

She walked through the chaos, passing the Riders' encampment first, and unsurprisingly, they cared little for the labour of putting out the flames. They were subdued, and it was no surprise. This mass of Riders seemed closer to mercenaries than devout followers. Predestined for her uses by a god's right-hand man, placed upon her by Gemmil's will, and a pox upon him, and them as well. She knew General Orin would have found far better uses for them. Not her, though. Aurora liked killing up close and personally. Not upon a war beast from so far away. Saying that, the crunch of a hoof upon the head was a charming-sounding thing.

She looked at Nika's tent, and the slashes of blood on its entrance flap, and fury came upon her again. He was a costly reminder of the threat a casual strike could have upon leadership.

Aurora thought it poetic that Kaya had delivered the blow. She thought it fate, really. And it was the only reason she didn't hang the entire lot of them and their mounts for their behaviour.

In her mind's eye, she saw the girl taking off his hand. It had been cleaved at the wrist, from what she remembered, and oh, such a thing was brutal. It was awful for a Rider as well. Killing him would have been less costly to the war effort. Were he to have fallen, his martyrdom would have served the Hunt well. As it was, he was gelded and useless to her efforts, and she went first to his tent.

Within, he was tended to by a healer and no one else, his mind lost to agony and dream syrup. Aurora gazed upon the severed limb and the healing that had been attempted.

Shush, boy. It'll just grow back. All you need is a little koko's oil.

She looked disapprovingly at the wretch of a warrior, sprawled out and useless. "Healer," she said quietly, "there are more worthy patients. Others with an actual reason to live. Leave us for a time." The healer recovered her tools with a deep nod. Aurora stayed the older woman's hand as it reached for the large bottle of dream syrup by Nika's cot. A girl could have all manner of fun with this little delicacy.

"I will check him later," the healer offered, before slipping free of the tent to tend to the many other broken and battered bodies, no doubt in need of greater healing attention.

Alone at last.

"Alone at last." Aurora was a wily thing of this world. She knew a little of many things, like cutting and slicing and singing and weeping, but also healing and the treating of wounds as well.

"You look in agony, friend," she whispered, pouring some dream syrup into a discarded cup by his bedside. It was a large cup. Closer to a mug. She filled it nearly to the brim. "Such a costly loss you were," she added, gritting her teeth.

His injury had taken the fight from the Riders. She had ordered them to retreat, but she would have preferred another hundred kills to her army's name before they did. As it was, the retreat before things turned rightly sour was her best tactic of the entire day. "You just had to flee like you did, didn't you?"

Such was his delirium, Nika did not answer. He merely stared in a haze at unseen things above his head. "Here, my friend, this tea will cure what ails you," she promised, tilting his head and lifting the cup to his lips. "Yes, yes, lap it up. Look at those lovely stars above your head. They are sparkling for you," she insisted, and he smiled and spluttered but mercifully continued drinking.

"Oh, I see them now. Mother, they are stunning," he breathed in a nearly inaudible whisper, and she grinned with all but her eyes. Those godly eyes stared into him, through him. Seeking something beautiful and natural and definite and eternal.

"They're all for you, Nika. Can you reach them?" she asked, and blessings upon him, he kept drinking as though it were ambrosia. And then he reached for those stars. "No, no, not with that hand. That hand can't do a thing… there we go."

Eventually, he drained the last of the cup, and she knew its potency. He would have a wonderful time, for a time, and then he wouldn't.

Anymore.

She might have stayed with him to watch the light slip from his eyes, but they were clouded and without true beauty. More than that, the coward had displayed his lack of nerve for all to see. Dying alone was a suitable end for him. She looked at the bottle and considered taking a little taste for herself. She pocketed it and slipped away from the doomed cur and out into the camp. She felt just wonderful about it.

Enjoying the smell of burning meat a little longer, she retired to her tent where, brewing a quick tea beverage, she thought less of losses and more of the excitement of the two days to come. Her god claimed she drank her tea like the king of hell: with a little honey and a dash of milk. She had no idea what that meant, but she, and whoever the king was, certainly knew the right way of brewing. Stretching her aching body, fighting off the call of food and sleep, she sat with crossed legs outside her tent's door, gazed at the motion all around her and began to relax.

She looked at buckets of water and dampened tarps steaming upon the flames; at limping and dying warriors screaming and suffering as they were tended to outside the healer's tent. She looked at the sombre actions of the Riders who had suffered the greatest losses, even in considered victory, and thought them glorious, wretched and superfluous to her vision of war.

She watched a thousand and one soldiers retire for the morning to sleep, eat, treat scrapes, tend to urges and itches, or else furrow with willing bed mates, and through it all, she smiled and loved her home, loved her life and all its death.

It didn't take long for Ferat to find her. In his hands, he carried a plate of bread, cheeses and freshly scorched boar meat. He offered the plate to her, and she took what she needed. Dropping down beside her, he sat as she did, resting his knee ever so against hers.

Only a god should have been allowed such familiarity.

"You are sitting very close, dear friend," she said softly.

"Oh, I'm sorry, Aurora. Will I move?"

"No, you may sit as you are."

He smiled, and she could only feel his knee against hers. It was ever so warm, ever so welcome.

"An interesting night," he offered after a time.

She thought so, too. "I call it a fairer fight than I expected."

"You appreciate such things, don't you?" He was clad in fine general's armour. He had no blood upon him. He was smarter than that. He hadn't been far from her the entire night. For the duel at dawn, though, he'd begun his march back to the camp, such was his irritation at her actions. Not that he'd bothered to argue with her long on the matter. She was denied a little blood; it was her right to take it for herself. The fight had been a good one, too. Only divine grace and the blessings of sunshine had made the difference. In another world, of another god's mind, she might have fallen to the boy's blade. Ferat had pledged he would honour her orders to retreat, and she found this interesting and appealing.

Probably a good thing she'd spotted the sun trap.

Probably a good thing she'd won as well.

They ate for a time as the fires were extinguished.

"What a peculiar thing," she said as the blazing furnaces succumbed to her soldiers' endeavours.

"Aye, three tents of supplies." He held the still-steaming plate of scorched boar, and she smiled.

"How much did we lose?"

"Three-quarters of our rations."

"And were the new prisoners freed?"

"No, luckily, we had them all locked up snug and safe in other tents."

She wasn't annoyed, merely amused. "See to it that the prisoners are chained and left out in the centre of the camp."

"It will be done."

"And feed the troops with whatever remains of the stocks.

They've earned it. It'll take the sting out of this morning's setback." She thought on this a moment. "In the meantime, gather some hunters to seek out some fresh game while the rest of us go to war."

He grinned. "It was the first thing I did. We might have a few lean days in between, but it won't affect us greatly."

She was pleased. She stroked his leg ever so and offered him a swig of the dream syrup that sat beside her, just waiting for such an occasion.

Smelling the bottle, he grinned. "So… you probably already know that Nika has gone to Valhal." He drank a little and recoiled, fighting the taste. "The healer was a bit surprised by his passing."

She raised an eyebrow but said nothing.

"She will say nothing; she too knows the value of a coward," he continued.

"Many will step into Valhal, but Nika won't be one of them."

"We lost many. I would say about we lost about—"

"Whist, my dear friend. I don't wish to know the terrible number. At least not yet."

"As you wish, Aurora."

They sat for a time, sipping a little dream syrup between them, until the world warmed and the sky cleared to a blazing blue.

"Do we know how many died from the fire?" she asked suddenly.

He sighed in contentment. "Only three guards. We believe it occurred around the time the grand charge began."

"And those who committed this charming act of sabotage?"

"The guards at watch were slain in silence. We did not catch the bandits who did it. Nor do we know how they slipped in and out of the town without eyes falling upon them."

She thought this was wonderful. She imagined these savage bandits at play, waiting for the moment they rested. She might lie in bed and feel the taste of steel as she slept—a pleasing thing to wake up to such death. Yet still, she might feel cheated to die in such a compassionate way.

"My dear Ferat, we might be hunted this very moment."

"Do you think?"

"I do hope so."

Sighing again, he looked into her eyes, and she could see he was as tired as she was. She took his hand and led him to her chambers. Not bothering to strip or bathe, she climbed into bed and nestled herself into his arms. He was again closer than he needed to be.

"Just an hour's sleep is all," she pledged. He ran his fingers through her hair and dared a gentle kiss upon her forehead before closing his eyes to her.

"And the grand machines are ready?" she asked as the syrup began taking them both.

"They move whenever you declare," he whispered.

"Oh, that's just positively wonderful," she whispered, kissing him once upon his lips before resting her head back on his arm, where she fell into a marvellous sleep of blood and death and rolling thunderous murder.

20

MEANWHILE, BACK AT THE ROCK

"Look, I know the ripping apart of Lucian wasn't the greatest boost for morale, but, in all fairness," Simeon said, then lowered his voice and looked around the room, "he was a fuken asshole."

"That is a fuken shocking thing to say, even for you," Kaya offered.

It was a fair point on her part, but Simeon couldn't help himself. "Hey, look, if I die, you all are free to mock my death," he offered, stretching out his arms in mock frustration. He drew them back in just as swiftly, such was their shaking. Hard to come off as unbothered with limbs shivering like that.

"Everyone is saying bad words," Whisper mumbled. Whisper wasn't part of the council. This was probably a good thing. However, their manners and bad language might have been somewhat better if she had. She sat in a chair behind Devitt. With a small blunt knife, she was eagerly carving a stick into a slightly more lethal stick. It was something to alleviate the boredom of listening to adults argue over the fate of the entire town. She wasn't to know that's what adults

280

usually did when the fate of great things was being decided and no one was doing a thing about it.

"Oh fuk, sorry… shit… ah—sorry, ugh… sorry, little one," Simeon said, bowing to Devitt, her apparent protector and guardian, and then Simeon bowed to the child herself.

Despite the tragedy, Simeon thought seeing Devitt with a child was a little funny. Of all the people he'd never believed to be father material, it was that idiot. Good man that he was. But an idiot, regardless.

Simeon remembered seeing the child carried by her father in the first attacks. Off to the trees the family had run. Simeon shut down that horrid vision right there. Instead, he enjoyed Kaya's smile every time she watched the little one grasp hold of Devitt. Simeon thought this, too, was a funny thing. Kaya looked almost human. He had always believed her colder than that.

Devitt had left Whisper at the door, pledging to return. The little one had screamed the house down. Simeon would have insisted she attend the meeting if Kaya hadn't stepped in and demanded that Devitt allow her to sit and wait in silence while the adults discussed what little chance any of them had of living through this.

No one else had minded. Apart from Silas, who had muttered a few curses under his breath, and, pardoning the bad word, but, fuk him.

"That's alright, Simon," the girl replied.

It's Simeon!

There were no drinks at the table. The chambers felt heavier than ever. Exhaustion and weariness had taken all members in their own way. Perhaps it was because they knew every single one of the bandits still alive knew they were in council. All of them would be eagerly waiting for a course of action. Were Simeon sharper, he might have brought along a little pouch of tobacco weed to ease the mood. And six hours later, when they emerged with no further plan but feeling rested and refreshed, having all slept soundly under its seductive charm, there may have been another attack to distract the waiting crowd, if they hadn't all just become bored and fuked off home.

Pardon the language.

"Regardless," continued Simeon, throwing away dreams of more relaxed times to make a point. "We did well along the wall; we kicked the ever-living shit… sorry… spit—the *spit* out of them. Why should we consider fleeing?" It was a strong argument. It needed to be said. A few days before, he'd have rightly agreed that revealing the town's tunnel and scuttling out in the middle of the night was the right manoeuvre, but things had changed since then. Pride had taken a rightly nasty bite out of his rear, and he wasn't ready to give up the town just to save his skin. Bandits of the Four Factions held no bastion close to their heart. But they knew the Rock; they called it the proper bandit capital (though Adawan might have argued something different.) The entire world had settlements and belonging, and they all answered to a shimmering Spark. Rock was a thing of bastard beauty and brazenness in the face of such civilisation. Spark City had never fallen and never would fall. How much of that was down to foolish pride and stubborn heroism? Truly, Simeon had been named as a council member in her greatest, darkest hour. How shameful would it be to let that slip away without a real fight? How pathetic would it be to sail on down the river, leaving eternal stone behind, all for the paltry cost of their mortal lives? A few days ago, he'd have thought differently.

Fuk nobility.

Fuk me, too.

Pardon the language.

"That's rightly easy for you to say… Simon," Silas spat. Simeon thought he had a rather fetching name. Silas, though —that was the name you gave a right sticky piece of brown phlegm you hacked up the morning after a riotous night before. If that prick continued with saying his name like that, well, he'd tell him as much. "You weren't even in the thick of it. You and the whore were away at the far side, picking up the fledgling warriors unfit for a first charge.

"Spit on you; I did my part. We all did," Simeon countered, winking at little Whisper.

I didn't curse, little one.

Even when that bastard bit of phlegm got in my face.

"Easy, Silas," warned Devitt. "Kaya sent him to watch the far wall as Gray went to the gate, and I went to the rear. We did our part; we did all we could." It was a fine, calming speech and though he might have had more to say, Silas nodded grudgingly.

"Everyone held. Nothing else matters," Kaya agreed. "Can we get on with the matter at hand?"

"Another spitting vote," Silas countered, rapping his fingers on the table. "There should be no vote; it's the right thing to do. Our comrades deserve to know if there's an escape route."

"Are we sure it's really a tunnel?" Gray asked, shaking his head. He looked as exhausted as the rest but somehow wore it better than anyone else. He was wearing a shirt, which was nice. Perhaps he feared another cutting?

Or else he was just cold.

"Oh, it's a tunnel, alright," countered Daisy and hesitated for a breath. "Though I think, were people to know of its existence, there's no guarantee they would flee down it like cowards." She smiled sadly, and he wanted to hold her, kiss her and remind her that for all her weakness, she did not flee or leave him, the town, or duty behind. It was a strength to be close to desperation and pull oneself from purest relief or despair. He'd said as much, but she didn't seem ready to forgive herself. On the wall, she'd been terrified and still fought. Side by side, they'd taken on a dozen fiends at least and cut them to pieces. But she saw only her faults, not her victories. She always had.

Kaya had a colder notion. Necessary though, and born of a leader's mentality, to her credit. "I firmly believe most will stay, but a break in morale could sink us. Curses on me for thinking this, and doubly so for saying it aloud, but might Raven Rock have a better chance of standing if we collectively believe there is no recourse."

"There is that," muttered Silas.

"Fuk sake. It is wrong to hold out on those who trust you," Gray countered. He was right. Yet still, there was a terrible danger to knowledge, was there not? A caged rat will fight that bit harder, as they said. But if there was a crack in the wall, that rat might tear itself trying to escape and be no better off. "Oh, spit on me—sorry, little one."

"That's alright," Whisper replied and lowered her voice. "Though I'm not allowed to talk to city rats."

Gray placed his finger to his lips, and the child did the same, smiling as though they were in on some secret jest—a charming thing, really.

"I do not think we should vote," Simeon said. "I think they have earned the right to the truth. Let us tell them."

Kaya may have had more words but fell still instead.

"That fuken prick has finally made sense," Silas said, hammering down his fist heavily upon the table. After a moment, he softened. He offered a gentle smile that could break hearts where needed. "Um… sorry… Whisper… eh… Idiot… I meant to call him an idiot."

"You didn't need to shout, Silas, but it is alright. I think he's an idiot, too," Whisper said and returned to carving her sharpened stick.

"Thanks a fuken lot, you little shit," countered Simeon, standing to leave, standing to end the discussion. There were no plans to hold as Kaya desired. There were no plans to go on a grand counter-charge, as Gray suggested. There were no plans beyond waiting for the world to turn and the attackers to come a-calling again. It was probably the only thing they could agree on.

Surprisingly, his rise was enough to end the meeting. It hadn't even lasted an hour. Beyond the door lay the entire town, about to discover there was light in the shape of a concealed tunnel, and Simeon was willing to bet a small fortune that they would stand the wall for as long as it took to hold.

That few bandits would break.

That few bandits would flee.

He was right.

21

FEASTS AND FINE TIMES

"That is astonishing," said Gray, gazing at the bandits in all their simple glory. The mood in Raven Rock's centre was ever so elevated. If one listened closely, one would hear few tears, less wailing.

You legends.

Kaya also thought it strange, yet she was unsurprised. Oh, aye, they were still hurting. Everyone would feel this hurt for the rest of their lives, but some tragedy could be taken and used for the better. Bandits endured. There was an indomitable spirit to bandits that was rarely matched.

Kaya was proud of those she called her people.

Proud Gray could see their strength too.

Human, just more stubborn about it.

The council had gathered the masses and announced with trepidation the tunnel's existence. The pang of guilt Kaya felt was swiftly lost to the positive reaction. They took it well. Better than well. Most were grateful for the hope. Others even laughed it off, claiming to already know of its existence. Some even mocked the fact that the council's only mistake through this siege was revealing this grand secret at all. How else could the council have escaped while the lesser idiots created quite the distraction by being slaughtered when the gates finally fell?

Certainly, there were a thousand and one questions. A few aggrieved souls also lamented for the lives that had been lost, but really, they were few and less than vocal in their criticisms, despite their right. Their real anger was directed towards the bastards that had come attacking; it was a rare thing for people to direct their anger at the correct sources.

Who would have imagined that those in control would share the knowledge to the benefit of everyone?

Who knew the people could take the truth and not panic?

It was just as Daisy suggested. There was no dreadful rush on the tunnel, no panicked claims that children and the old be allowed to go first. They had no desire to rush out into the Wastes, where who knew what butchers lay in wait. Instead, plans for the retreat were deliberated and put in place. They would go at the right time, when all was lost. A few guards were stationed at the entrance. Easier to keep an eye on it and all that. But really, they took this news as warriors would. It was nice that it was there, but let's continue defending and killing.

"We are an impressive people," said Kaya, leading the astounded Alpha through the gathering at the centre of Rock's stuttering heart. It felt like a thousand miles from a town torn to shreds by heartbreak, terror and death.

"I'm seeing this more and more, my dear," Gray said, falling in beside her. As they walked, the sun above their heads lit the path with its afternoon rays. The crowd parted to let them pass.

It's good to be the king.

"Though I'm sorry you are part of this siege, I am glad you fight for us, giving us an edge," she said.

"I am truly glad to be here. Of all places to fall, it could be worse than this remarkable settlement," he said. His eyes were on the sizeable pyre burning in the centre of the town.

Instead of plotting their escape, the townspeople were doing what only a bandit town could do during a respite from war.

"I think I understand what you mean," she said, leading him towards the pyre. Though there was sorrow, there was still triumph, enjoyment and a little overindulgence. And they would live wonderfully before the end, were the end to come.

Feasts and fine times.

As they drew closer, they saw that the pyre had been lit by a trader who was having a feast and inviting everyone to join him. Kaya couldn't help but wonder how much that trader regretted having stayed in town for the funeral. But instead of cursing out the world, he offered a little hope. Legends were known for lesser things.

Upon the large pyre, strung out and sizzling wonderfully, was the largest carcass of boar Kaya had ever seen, and its salty, delicious aroma carried in the air. People helping themselves, indulging in the finest foods with this remarkable man was a welcomed thing. They needed only a few barrels of sine or ale and a fine sing-along to get this gathering going.

"This is my favourite," Kaya exclaimed, gazing at the spread. As before, the bandits gave the council members a clear path, and Gray appeared rightly confused. Perhaps he did not know how to construct such a meal, let alone eat it.

"So, instead of rationing, we feast?" he asked.

"If we die in the next attack, won't it be nice to have a full belly when its contents are spilled?" she jested.

Gray rubbed his own belly. He still looked confused as he moved over to the laden table. "Aye perhaps… So… um… how do I eat this?"

It was a sight, in fairness. Along the lengthy table sat platters of freshly sliced meat, still smoking. The platters were surrounded by similar plates of various colours and substances, each with a spoon or ladle.

"Follow your instincts," she said, laughing.

"They say I should seek a bowl of soup elsewhere instead."

"Oh, just eat."

The meat was alluring, and even an amateur would know to go for the meat first. This is exactly what Gray did, but she slapped his hand away, shaking her head. Laughing at his exasperation, she did what any skilled maker of these delicacies did. She led by example. To Kaya, it was an art, and she grinned as she went to task.

"Alright, Gray, we are going to start right over here," she said, directing him to a longboard piled with impossibly soft flat bread. "You must ensure that it's nice and pliable," she said, testing a soft, stretchy sheet of thin bread and watching him do the same with another, pulling it in his clumsy Alphaline fingers. "No, no… not like that," she scolded, as, testing the bread's pliability, he tore the piece in half.

"Just let me grab some meat," he pleaded.

"Oh, whisht, have a little adventure in you."

Finding a suitable sheet, she tossed it on his plate and put her piece on her own plate. All her life, she'd tried to bake this particular bread in such an inefficient yet thoroughly delightful way and never come close. However, she liked to pick up a few overpriced sheets during the festivals. They kept her going for a few nights until they went stale, but it was a small matter. More traditional bread worked almost as well.

Almost, but not quite.

Cooking these exotic meals throughout the years had

become a bit of an obsession for her. Unwilling to wait for every festival to gain a pouch of ambrosia, she'd spent many nights and a tiny fortune experimenting with the ingredients she had at hands. She'd never quite mastered the delicious meals the traders gave, but had come rather close with some smashing suppers altogether.

The bread, though, remained a mystery.

A pox on those traders and their secrets.

"Right. Next, you need to slather that tomato and lime shit all along the centre, like this… See? Just like this."

"What is that red shit?"

"It doesn't matter. It's delicious." He did as she did, and it was all coming together. "Grab a little… and I mean only a little… of those and those. Mush them in the sauce."

He grabbed a few pieces of chopped lettuce and dropped them along the red shit.

"Fuk sake. What did I say? That's far too much lettuce—half of that. And don't forget the tomatoes, you fool," she admonished.

"That's a lot of tomato. I don't like tomatoes."

"You won't taste them."

He begrudgingly added a few quarters of chopped tomatoes and spread them out evenly.

"Now, slide this white sauce along the edge. Not a lot, though; you'll need space for more at the end."

She loved the white sauce. She couldn't remember the name of the vegetable it was made from—some sort of pea—but she knew she needed to mash sesame seeds, garlic and a little lemon into it to make it work. Everyone did it their own way. This trader had a rightly salty brew, and her mouth watered as she went for the cheese.

Gray didn't seem impressed. "This is a lot of work."

"Shut up. Add some more cheese."

He added more cheese, and she picked up a few spicy sliced peppers that had no right to be in anyone's mouth. She threw six down upon hers. "No, no, just two or three for you," she warned.

"Are they hot?"

"Lick your fingers."

"Fuk me."

"Shit, I forgot to add the fried beans," she muttered and ladled a large brown scoop over the mush on her plate and then another one upon his. It was a foolish mistake on her part. She'd spent so long perfecting his that she'd forgotten to layer everything perfectly on her own. With the beans on top, the meal looked anything but enticing. It was a small matter; it would be amazing wherever the beans went. Everyone knew that. "When we go back for a second pouch, remind me that we put that bean shit in before the cheese."

"I'll be sure to remind you... Are we done?"

She grabbed a few slivers of sizzling meat and threw them into the mess before adding a fresh dollop of that white sauce.

Perfect.

Apart from the beans fiasco.

He did the same and looked at it as she led him away from the tables of wondrous delicacies. They sat upon some barrels that had been arranged around the pyre. "This is the best part," she said, wrapping the thin bread back over the food impossibly smoothly, as though wrapping a birthday gift for a lover.

"How did you do that?" he cried incredulously before looking down at his ruin of a meal.

"I'll do it slowly for you," she said, folding, holding, tucking and wrapping the concoction into the strangest, yet oddly appealing pouch.

He held it aloft and smelled it carefully.

"Hold it from the bottom, and hold it rightly tight. You'll get about three bites in before it all falls apart, but I promise not to look at you eating around then, as long as you don't look at me."

"That's fair," he said, leaning in and taking a bite.

"Well?"

He chewed for a time and swallowed and looked at the meal as though it had just professed its love for him. "I want three more."

They sat for a time, side by side, as young lovers might before either dared to engage in a kiss or more for the first time. When they finished eating, Kaya was sated and weak with contentment. She knew she should have taken the time to sleep, but it seemed more important to experience this afternoon for its humanity. They walked up to the top of the wall, where they sat looking down at the town, but also keeping an eye on the forest. It was strange to see her comrades of war so at ease.

Strangely, though, two separate factions, one answering to Silas, the other Simeon, ate heartily on either side of the town's centre. Before this invasion, she would have never thought either warmongering fiends would take their honour so seriously. It was a strange thing to read each man so badly.

Looking back to the forest, Kaya felt truly at peace for just a moment. Gray, for his part, carried no frown upon his forehead, and she had at last grown rather used to that glare. It was attractive and comforting.

"Where were those delicious pouches this last year?" Gray said after a time, and she laughed.

"That bad a year?"

"Aye, that bad a year." For just a moment, the frown returned, and she rested her head on his shoulder for a moment.

"Tell me of it, Alpha."

"I am an Alpha in blood but not in duty," he said quietly.

"I knew it," she whispered, and he laughed.

"Perhaps, after I die, I will tell my tale."

"That would be an interesting conversation."

"Among my belongings, there's a leather-bound journal; you have my blessings," he whispered, and she did not push the matter. That feeling of contentment began to sift away like the aroma of a feast after the guests had departed.

"For now, will you tell me why you came here?" she asked.

"I came here to die."

Somehow, she knew this to be the truth, and a cold anger came upon her. "So you knew we were to be attacked?"

He laughed again and leaned his head upon hers. "Not at all, dear Kaya. I am a bastard, but I would've had the good grace to warn you lot of an incoming attack… Not that you would have fled, wonderful lunatics that you lot are."

"You lot? You mean *us* lot."

"I came here to die by a bandit's blade. I didn't think it would be difficult. What with… us lot being such bastard, cutthroat fiends and all."

"That's what we are."

"The problem was, you fiends are incredible," he whispered and sat up. She looked to him and saw tears streaming from his eyes—a curious thing, really. "You, Kaya, most of all, enlightened me," he went on. "For this, I am eternally grateful—that I could step from the path and see your people as the intriguing beings you are." He was smiling now—a beautiful thing, and she could only smile in reply.

"I knew I'd earn a smile from you before the end," she jested.

"For all you have done, I offer my last ever smile as a gift. Do with it as you wish," he whispered, then took her hand, kissed it and placed it to his heart.

"If this is your way of enticing me into bed, rest assured, you have overplayed your hand. I have been rightly willing from about three days ago," she jested, but honestly, she was moved.

"Oh, to be a cur with a heart and desire. For you, above all else, are the most beautiful creature I have gazed at and desired these last years. In another life, I would have tried to charm your heart away from who you truly desire."

"Stop it," she gushed, despite herself.

His smile softened, lessened, and then disappeared. "Tell me this, Kaya. Here we are, at the end of the world. Why are you with a broken Alphaline, barely able to walk, when you could be in the arms of the man you truly love? If I can see it, how can you not?"

"I don't know what you mean," she said, looking away from him towards the small crowd in the centre of the town. Her eyes fell upon Devitt, wrapping a pouch for Whisper, who immediately made a right mess of his handiwork, and she smiled and wondered about wandering on down.

"What the fuk is that coming towards us?" Gray suddenly said, sitting up, shattering the peaceful moment once and for all.

22

____

GEARS OF WAR

"That can't be good at all," cried Ettien, retying his trousers as he leapt from the bed. Aimee was in a similar state of undress, or to be precise, not nearly undressed enough. Just a few buttons to re-clasp, some wisps of hair to tie back up. They slowed for a breath and gazed at each other. It was not love; it was merely convenient. He was gorgeous looking, but that wasn't all she cared about. Just half of her. Were there another like him in the town of similar allure, she might have brought them both to bed. That would have been nice. She had long desired to lose her virginity. With the entire world falling apart, it seemed like the right moment. And that moment had now been missed.

She had no regrets about the meal they'd devoured and the dessert after that. Nor did she regret the lengthy kissing they'd shared. It was lovely, comforting, and had been helping them both to get in the proper mood—to set the juices flowing and the heart a-pounding. But all for nought, as it turned out. She wasn't heartbroken to miss out on the act, however, for she knew she would survive this. She was

Aimee; she was invincible. She always had been. Always would be.

Ettien though?

"Those aren't mounts," she said, listening as she tightened her laces. "Not foot soldiers either." She watched as he struggled with his boots, then his armour after that. She wanted to savour this moment. Wanted to hold it for a breath and walk out, face whatever thundering force there was clamouring at the gates and never think of it again.

Why? Because she knew memories like this would take away her sanity. She knew a bandit's life was an arduous march at the best of times. She'd lost friends in recent days. Moreover, she'd lost her family years before. Orphans were left with less, and she'd always been happy with what she had. Overthinking about misery was likely to take whatever sanity remained in her fractured mind. Things were lost, and people died. It was best just to keep trudging on.

Invading army or no.

"I'm really scared," Ettien murmured, more to himself. He looked through the grubby window of the one-roomed hovel she called home.

"Whatever it is, we will hold against it," she lied, and it was a fine lie.

"I can't see a thing," he said, latching the last piece of his ancient bronze armour. Were this a tale of romance and honour, he would stand the gate with her, protecting her rear. They would hold off the hordes and win the day. Together. In love. "I need to go."

She was already slipping from his mind, too. A girl could tell these things. Aimee knew his father was out there on the wall, standing ready on the front line as he had from the beginning—no doubt in better-fitting armour and all. Mid-lustful touch,

Ettien had confided his terror and pride in his father, said that he considered Ettien a true man now, fierce and heroic enough to stand the wall with him. Aimee agreed with his father.

In the beginning, after the slaughter at the gates, Kaya had insisted Aimee remain concealed, hidden away like a porcelain doll. Aimee had been grateful for the respite. She had done her part. She was too young. Too unskilled. Too likely to get in the way. Pride be damned.

But these curs were likely to surge over the walls, and Aimee was damned if she was going to hide away listening to the roar and horror as her friends, comrades and strangers went to war protecting her life.

I am invincible, after all.

Until I'm not.

Aimee feared death as much as any youth, but she was calm about such things. If she died, well… that would be that. There would be no life in the darkness afterwards nor rebirth in the moments after that. The absent gods were a myth. She passionately believed that the dead were dead, and that was alright. It sounded quiet and restful.

"You look fine in your armour," she said to her almost-lover.

"You look beautiful."

"I know. I always do."

They held for a breath and then ran out the door, down the stairs, out into the light of the day with so many others. Outside, the roar of coming death was tenfold what it had been behind grubby windows with a lover at her side. Ettien ran a step behind her, and she thought this strange. He had a bigger build and a longer stride. An athlete, really. Perhaps it was the ill-fitting armour. He looked pale as he ran. His eyes were turned to the wall, and he seemed to be transfixed by the screams of alarm and panic from those already gazing at their doom.

What do they see that I cannot?

When she saw Kaya running atop the wall alongside them, Aimee felt her adoration for her grow that little more. Kaya was Aimee's hero—she always had been and always would be. Kaya's leadership during this siege had not added to that adoration; it had merely reaffirmed what she had always known. She had not been born into this life, but she was more of a bandit than any of the others.

Aimee could have said these things, but she never would. She'd never give the sly witch that much ammunition to use in life. It simply wasn't her way, or theirs. What was their way was standing beside each other at the end. She sprinted towards the ladder and grabbed hold, taking the rungs two at a time.

She left Ettien behind, and that was fine. They did not even say goodbye. It wasn't Aimee the boy desired to stand the wall with, was it? It wasn't Aimee he sought out among the defenders.

I'll see you after the end of the world, my dear.

"What are you doing here?" Kaya shouted, stopping to take hold of the younger girl.

"I will not hide away another moment," Aimee said resolutely, and Kaya cursed loudly, seeing her defiance. She should have recognised it in the way she had been brought up, in the way she was instructed by her master.

They stood still a moment as their comrades sprinted along the wall, and only Gray hesitated as he made to pass them. His place was by Kaya's side, and Aimee thought him a potent ally to the cause.

"Fine, you little witch," Kaya spat. She looked shaken.

"Stay behind me every step of the fuken way. Do you hear me?"

"You said the bad words," Aimee mocked, for that's what terrified warriors did when gratitude was not forthcoming. When the prospect of war and murder was all-engulfing.

Beyond, where the crowd gathered at the front of the gate, there were further screams of panic combined with a new note of bewilderment, for that terrible rumbling sound was growing.

"What is that?" Aimee cried. Pushing her way through the staring crowd to the edge of the wall, Aimee gazed into the forest from where the fierce rumbling came. At first, she could only see a peaked tower of wood and leather. And then, as it emerged into the open, she finally saw it for the mysterious threat it was. It was as large as her shabby bedroom, and its height loomed over them all; it was at least twenty feet high: a great big tower on great big menacing wheels.

"What is that?" Aimee repeated.

"I don't know, Aimee. I don't know."

It bobbled slowly along upon wheels of hardened wood, as large as a tall man, rumbling onwards, denting the ground with every inch it moved, every foot it was pushed. The front of the tower was no more than a shell of a structure. It was a thick leather skin of sorts, hammered and reinforced with long support beams that protected the dozens of soldiers at its rear, heaving, huffing, marching and shoving. It was protected on either flank by shield bearers. They drove forward as one, and soon, its monstrous shadow touched the wall and kept coming.

Though the lower part of the tower was little more than a skeleton, the upper section was a mighty defensive beast. It was a reinforced room of thick wood on all sides, with only a thin slit in a wall at the front, where a dozen archers stood side by side with weapons raised and ready.

Upon that tower was the place to be.

Standing at the wall above the gate was not, and it was here the archers attacked first.

Aimee remembered the screams from that first horrid night. They returned now, as piercing as before, as half a dozen defenders, far too slow to gather their wits, fell away from the front, screaming, grasping at arrows protruding from their limbs. Immediately, a fresh salvo of deadly projectiles came raining down upon them.

"To cover," Kaya screamed, but it was all too late. Those fiends pushing the beast gathered pace, and the archers replied in kind. No longer in formation, they fired quickly upon those few still along the top who could only drop down behind the gate or lie there dying. It had taken only moments, but thanks to the vile machine, the bandits, who had not even had time to get in the fight, were already losing ground.

"How can we stop that thing?" Aimee cried as bandits charged and dropped all around her. She stood frozen as the world around her drew to a stillness, and her limbs were heavy, like she was in an awful dream that she could not escape.

I am invincible.

"Get out of range," roared Gray, sprinting along the top, away from Kaya and Aimee, towards certain death. He drew a dozen or so arrows from one of his quivers as he flew. He was swift; he ducked incoming arrows, and *he* looked invincible.

Kaya grabbed Aimee, pulling her from her stupor, and dragged her down towards the corner, as far from the rolling beast as they could. From here, Aimee could more clearly see this monster's curious design, and the legions of those who accompanied it. A platoon of invaders heaved and pushed the beast forward, and a thousand warriors in full invasion attire marched behind them. Some moved around to the back and were climbing steep wooden stairs up to the wooden room at the top. A curious thing, she thought coldly, that none carried bows or crossbows.

Are they climbing up to get a better look at the mayhem?

She knew there was something peculiar that she was missing. She tried to understand their actions but her mind was blank.

She heard a yell and turned in amazement to see Gray attacking the tower alone. He ran among his comrades on the wall, drawing and firing at lightning speed as he went. His movements were a blur, and Aimee was amazed. His screams were threatening and primal; he called for death and outright demanded it. The archers attempted to strike down this solitary guardian and died for their attempts.

He is incredible.

Though the slit in the wood was barely enough for a fiend to poke his head through, Gray fired twelve arrows directly inside without taking a breath, and with the curs clustered so closely there, he struck down at least half of them. Instead of celebrating, he spun back along the wall, firing sublimely as he did. He alone held the archer assault as they cowered below the wall's cover.

"He stopped them," Aimee shouted jubilantly.

"No, no, he didn't. He only stopped the archers," Kaya cried. Her eyes grew wide as Gray suddenly fell to a knee. From his leg, there protruded a solitary arrow. He half-rose again and staggered backwards, and Kaya rushed to tend to him. He hobbled along the wall, and once clear of the tower and its archers, who were as yet unaware their vanquisher was injured, he turned and snapped the arrow off.

"Didn't even notice I was hit until I fell," he muttered, angry at himself for taking an arrow in that way.

"Calm yourself, fool," Kaya hissed, dropping beside him and cutting free a strip of her shirt. Swiftly, she began to wrap it around the arrow piece sticking out from his leg. "Stop pulling at it," she warned. "It needs to stay in, in case it has hit a bad vein." She was calm, and he screamed aloud in frustration, cursing his luck. Kaya tended to him with near tenderness. She was calm in the mayhem of war, while Aimee could only look to the tower as it continued to roll down upon them.

Be great.

Taking Gray's bow, Aimee alone fired at the monstrous tower now. Not at the archers but at the fiends pushing the great beast. Easy strikes, really, and she killed thrice before the rest of her comrades, no doubt buoyed on by the sudden lack of attacking archers, climbed back up the wall and began to rain arrows upon those heaving the tower forward. These were the easiest kills any of them would get, but their kills were far too few to affect the beast's momentum. Beneath the rumble, Aimee could hear the beat of a drum and the heaving chants from the attackers as they faced a hail of arrows but kept on coming. Were this chant not the most terrifying thing she'd ever heard, she might have appreciated their drive and desire. And the rhythm, too.

They kept chanting, pushing and dying—until, with a mighty groan, the beast stopped just a few feet short of the wall.

"They did it," cried Aimee, looking to Kaya hopefully. Around them, the gathered defenders began to cheer and roar. They claimed another stout defence, another defining moment for the Rock, but Kaya looked worried.

"Get your sword ready, little one," she hissed.

"We need to get to the front of that tower," gasped Gray, climbing to his unsteady feet despite Kaya's protestations.

"On me," Kaya cried, edging back down the wall. Those who realised the threat was alive followed up, gathered around her, blades drawn, hands quivering.

With a clunking boom, the front of the tower wall collapsed forward, dropped down and held upon the wall's surface. A thing of genius, in truth. But weren't all bridges a touch of genius?

It held and steadied, and from the front, the warriors within the machine gushed out screaming and swinging, and without raising a sword in reply, the defences of Raven Rock were fully breached.

But the bandits would not be undone so easily by this terrible machine, for upon each side of the wall and from below, the bandits went a-defending.

"Get up," voices cried.

"Get up here," more voices cried.

"Get up here, or we are lost…" Kaya's war cry rose above them all, spurring them to action. The defenders lined up on both sides in rows three warriors deep, and, running at the pace of an injured Alphaline, they rushed the defenders.

I will survive this.

The attackers were unprepared for this style of warfare, and most had never trained upon this machine—or a wall for that matter. They were no match for the defenders flanking them on both sides. Some met their end at the first step. Others just kept running down the bridge and, perhaps, blinded by war and blood, stumbled, dropped into the space between the bridge and the wall and met their end at the hands of the aggrieved bandits who waited for them below.

I am invincible.

Rushing forward, Aimee swung and struck and cut

through skin and muscle. With so little space to move, there was only a limited ability to attack, but a bandit was used to such things as unsteady footholds and unfair disadvantage. On both sides, the defenders dove into them and held their charge.

In her ears, she could hear Kaya's cries. A true leader, killing, leading and rallying the defenders mid-blow. On the other side, Gray, balancing upon a shattered leg, could only roar in frustration that his strikes were without the speed and strength he was capable of. She thought him heroic, brave and determined, regardless.

Invincible.

They held for a time, but for every attacker they held off, there were a thousand more willing soldiers to replace them, all patiently waiting for their turn.

The world became nothing but the plunge of blade on flesh.

Though Aurora had appeared to be quite the warrior, these soldiers of hers were far from elite. The outnumbered defenders however were disciplined. Groups of three or so at each side of the bridge faced the attackers as their patient reinforcements stood behind waiting just eager to step in and relieve them. Every few engagements, each group retreated as one, allowing fresher defenders to step forward and replace them and grant them breath. Kaya however, barely rested for she was determined to lead, and Gray, despite the pain and ruin, was dominating with the blade.

And Aimee?

Well, she tucked in and was willing to kill the easier targets the other two legends left in their wake.

We are invincible.

They stood longer on the line than any others. They worked like a well-oiled machine, as well as any group of seasoned Runners might have done. They slew all who stood before them, and Aimee felt a surge of pride as she realised that Kaya kept her at her side, despite the motherly fear, despite the blood, despite the brutality.

They all went to war against impossible odds and, for a time, held the line.

And they weren't alone.

On the far side, Silas near singlehandedly held the attackers. Swinging his massive axe, he battered the brutes back something fierce. He, too, fell into a routine of murder and destruction, legend and heroism.

But mostly brutality.

Every few blows, and after every fresh kill, he would drop to a knee and catch a breath, while his comrades behind him would flood around him, driving forward with long pikes impaling the attackers, or simply knocking back those who attempted to break through the line. A few archers aligned with his leadership would release into the mass of invading soldiers, killing and maiming. And then, Silas would return to his feet, swinging and roaring, killing and winning. Though it was a carelessly conceived plan of defence, it was effective.

If energy had been boundless, ammunition plentiful, luck limitless and the defenders' strikes blessed by the absent gods, the defenders might well have won the day. However, such were the numbers surging down from the great machine and filling the centre of the wall that the defenders were slowly pushed back.

Until Simeon changed the entire battle.

Nobody but Aimee, who happened to glance down the street mid-skirmish, might have noticed the fiend of fire at task, but he charged swiftly through the streets of Raven Rock, through the square at its heart and on towards the wall.

He was screaming his intentions, but who would have been listening?

Nobody but Aimee, who sucked in a breath and tried to make sense of his actions.

From his hand hung a large oil lamp on a long swinging chain, likely filled to the brim with the finest oil or a potent concoction of unrefined sine. It was no secret he was attempting to brew such a thing in his building's basement. He'd likely overfilled the lamp, for burning liquid dripped out as he ran. He halted near the wall and, with a mighty yell, began to swing it around his head, loop after deadly loop, creating a perfect circle of flames.

Kill them all.

"What is he doing?" she gasped as he suddenly released the chain, sending the flaming lantern like a comet into the sky. The chain, drenched in burning liquid, became a tail of purest fire as it reached its pinnacle, somewhere above the defenders and a little above the attackers.

And then it dropped and, with a silent smash lost beneath the symphony of war, it exploded.

The idiot missed.

All along the roof of the tower, the volatile liquid spread, settled and came alive in fire, but somehow didn't manage to burn a single fiend, and Aimee howled in frustration. And then she saw Daisy running up from behind him, armed with a similar flaming lantern. She climbed a ladder and all, screaming as she did, and hurled the thing over the wall. Her throw was a little less aggressive, and the lantern plummeted down upon the leather coverings at the front of the tower, where the flame ignited as the first one had.

The attackers kept surging, but the fire along the top of the tower grew, and suddenly there was confusion, a slowing of the numbers, as smoke billowed from below and caught in the inner roof at the top.

And then Aimee stumbled upon Ettien's body.

Oh god, no.

He was at the bottom of the wall, with two arrows through his chest where a better suit should have protected him. He lay spread out, unmoving. Beside him lay his father. Though he was a superior warrior, it had taken only one arrow through the throat to kill him. A terrible, wrenching sorrow came upon Aimee, and her hatred grew. She wanted to kill them all. To break free from the line, charge up that bridge and keep killing until that slag Aurora was on her knees. And then she would truly get to killing.

And then the attackers turned their attention to Kaya, and the world slowed to nothing.

Please, God, no.

The biggest brute Aimee had seen in her life charged down the bridge. Under the cover of a deathly plume of smoke, he shoulder-barged through the defenders and fell upon a resting Kaya, knocking her away from the defensive line.

Behind him followed a dozen warriors, no doubt eager to take advantage of the break. They engaged the defenders with shields and blades. The piercing clatter of steel rose all around her, but Aimee could only hear the struggles of her master as the massive fiend attempted to murder her.

He lunged his blade at her, and only luck and reflexes saved her. She slipped wide of the blow and blocked the strike, but she was knocked down, and he stood over her with sword raised.

Not like this.

Kaya did not scream; she merely stared at her killer as he roared—and Aimee moved swiftly to her side. Throwing her entire body upon the fiend, she blocked his strike and dragged him over the edge.

Falling.

Spinning.

Crashing.

Hurting.

The world spun and nearly went dark, but she held her consciousness long enough to see that her attack had sent him over at the wrong angle. His head hung in an unnatural position; his eyes were glazed and gone.

Only then, as she looked around at the many bodies among which she herself had landed, did she realise she had fallen on the wrong side of the wall. She was as far from safety as she could get. Around her, the screams of the dying were a pleasing thing, but she dared not move, even though she heard Kaya's wails from a few feet above. Daring a careful look lest the boots around her stamp her to mush, she saw Gray holding Kaya, preventing her from leaping down; indeed, it was the finest move on his part. Glancing the other way, she stared at the lone figure whose attention was drawn to the burning tower as it fought the flames.

Do it.

Aimee had a plan.

It was a stupid plan.

It could never work.

But she went for it.

With nearly all eyes upon the wall and the flaming tower, it was rightly easy for a sneaky little bitch of a thing to stalk up on that slag, and this is precisely what Aimee did. Despite the strain on her body and the agony in her heart. Despite the terror in every cell of her being and her fierce desire to live another moment.

She crawled the first few feet through a sea of boots, keeping her eyes trained on her target above.

Twelve feet away and at an angle, she rose and stumbled forward.

Ten feet away, she drew her blade.

When she was just six feet away, Aurora started to turn.

Two feet. Oh, those eyes were glorious.

Aurora suddenly became a wave of motion, a tempest of violence as she leapt away, swinging her blade and screaming as she did. She was a blur of movement and little more. She was incredible, and she was terrifying. Their blades clashed, and Aimee knew she had no chance. It didn't matter. She could take no more of this horror.

She tried her best; she really did.

The battle was over before it began. The slag spun and turned with Aimee's every drive, and from her glee, Aimee knew she was being toyed with. She considered fleeing, tossing her blade at her vanquisher and sprinting back towards the wall in the hope she was agile enough to reach a waiting hand. Really, though, she was dead. Dead the moment Aurora met her strike.

All too swiftly, Aurora disarmed her and followed through with a blow to the chin that took her knees. Then, standing over Aimee, Aurora held her blade to the girl's throat.

"I know you, don't I, little one?" she asked, kneeling to run her fingers through Aimee's hair. Truly, Aimee felt a terrible coldness come upon her.

23

THE END OF IT ALL

nd so began the end of it all, or so it felt to Kaya. She screamed as she collapsed to her knees, while all around her, the war continued. And why wouldn't it? They were winning, or it had felt like as much. Until a brute had charged her and a young, foolish goddess had saved her.

"No," she screamed again, seeing Aurora strike the child once, twice, and then a third time after that, and then she fell still. In that moment, she despised Devitt for bringing her into the town, for bringing her into their world. It was all she could do. Anger was a gift, and hate was much the same.

This is too much.

She wanted to leap from the wall, fight her way through the hundreds and get to her girl. The girl had been alone her entire life. No one else would fight for her. If Kaya wouldn't, then who would?

You can't.

Gray thought so, too. He took hold of her and wrapped his arms tight. "You are too important," he whispered, and oh, in that moment, she hated him too. Even if he was right. She loved Aimee above all else, but that selfish love could jeopardise their defences. Aimee was more important to her than anyone else, but that meant little to the greater cause, and curses upon Gray and herself for seeing it.

Just kill her quick.

"Leave me be," Kaya warned, and he released her. She did not hesitate. She charged towards the attackers moving up along the wall tearing into her brethren. She did this to distract herself from the moment of purest horror yet to come. She knew Aurora would kill the child. At that moment, she pledged to kill Aurora when they met face to face. It was a terrible pledge. Were the absent gods caring enough to give her a glimpse into the future and allow her to see the turning of events, she might have held that pledge and attempted to save the town instead. But vengeance was too potent a sauce and the absent gods were not that kind.

"Kill them all," she cried, and it was enough to rouse a little fight in her comrades. With the last of their energies, these brave defenders gave up their lives attempting to stem the tide. They rushed with her. They swung and struck and bled and died. Swords clashed, and the attackers became frenzied like hornets aggrieved by a careless fool. Their desperation to finish the task became apparent as smoke and fire enveloped their tower. They panicked, they gave ground, they suffered to the driving bandits and were beaten back towards the bridge until, with a terrible creaking crash, the tower began to buckle beneath the flame. This brought fresh drive to the defenders, who pushed hard, swinging freely, believing themselves victorious, and indeed, they were.

Though Kaya was heartbroken at the cost.

The attacking reinforcements slowed their climb through the burning tower as it began to lean to one side and shake throughout.

"Send them back into the fire," she cried, leading the line, stabbing and swinging. On the other side, seeing the tower struggle must have given wind to Silas's axe, for he returned upon them tenfold the devastation she could inflict.

The world became nothing but the sway of swords and the killing of brutes, and Kaya was impressive. Continuing to step forward, she howled her hate and won each clash she engaged in, but the tower's collapse truly ended the impressive invasion.

With a thunderous crash, louder than any charging army, the tower fell in upon itself, like an egg smashed by a fist. Those within were engulfed in a deadly ball of fire. Dozens were burned alive in the first few moments. As the tower crumbled and burned, the attackers upon the wall had no choice but to leap down into the town and meet their doom, or drop back down behind into the flames and meet their death in the fire.

Most attempted to stand their ground, and all were slain.

The slaughter was rampant; it was savage; it was easy.

The attackers must have gazed upon their brethren falling and thought this invasion was rightly cursed, such were the devastating numbers lost.

Swiftly enough, the roar of battle subsided to the delicate flapping of flame and the muted groans of the dying.

Kaya, wiping the warm spray from her brow, turned to the nightmare in the furnace below. Many rolled, wailing in agony, as their comrades attempted to beat down the flames charring their skin, and it was a fine sight indeed. Without a nearby source of water, the smell of burned flesh filled the air, and, enjoying their anguish, Kaya imagined it a most dreadful way to die.

No amount of aloe leaf will fix that shit, no matter how hard you rub.

Bitterly, Kaya looked to Aurora in the grim hope the deed

was done. Through the smoke, she caught sight of the witch gesturing wildly. Then, suddenly, the great horns of retreat were blown, and it was a tonic to her ears. Witnessing a thousand battered and burning warriors hobbling back towards the treeline near brought a smile to Kaya's face. Then, once again, she looked to Aurora.

She could not see if Aimee took breath or had suffered a dagger's strike. She tried not to hope lest she lose the run of herself.

"Oh, Kaya, I see you, girl," Aurora cried in delight, standing over Aimee's body. Kaya wanted to hide away, to avoid her gaze altogether, lest she turn to torturing Aimee while she watched on helplessly. She sheathed her blade, swallowed her anguish and begged the absent gods for mediation, mercy, and a miracle. She merely had to find the impossible words to attain all three.

"I see you there, charred and glorious and rightly covered in blood," Aurora called gleefully.

The defenders around Kaya knew her torment; they looked to her warily, lest she give it all up so Aimee might walk free. They didn't realise how cold-hearted she could be. Even at the cost of her soul. Her sanity.

"Here I am," she said, and her voice was raw and aching. Gray hobbled up beside her and immediately went to pick again at the shard of wood embedded in his leg. Kaya couldn't imagine the agony he found himself in, yet here he stood, waiting to die with a sword in his hand. "What is it you want?" demanded Kaya. She tried to sound firm, but her world was a torment, and that bitch was about to engineer its end.

"Well, I want to kill every single one of you heroic bastards, but I'll be satisfied with this one."

"She's just a child," cried Kaya, and Aurora laughed.

"Such a child could have value in ways you could never understand."

"To the fires with you, witch," Kaya wailed, knowing this would end in tears and blood.

Aurora hesitated. "What will you give me for the little one?"

Don't kill her, don't kill her.

I'll give you anything you want.

"What is it you desire?" Kaya countered carefully.

For a breath, she wondered if Aurora desired Kaya's head; she might indeed offer it willingly. She would merely ask her killer to murder her clean and quick. Visions of Lucian's death came to mind. She remembered the red spray covering Aurora. No, she didn't want the bitch bathing in her blood, as she most certainly would do.

"I want you in battle, Kaya; I want to tear your head off. Flay that beautiful skin of yours. I want you, Kaya. I fuken want *you*," the diminutive woman replied, and Kaya nearly leapt down then and there.

I'll tear your husk of a heart out, slag.

"Do not do this," Gray warned from beside her. He could barely stand, but he looked to be less in pain than before, as though he controlled it, as though pain was nothing more than an obstacle to overcome. "Do not give in to her."

"I must," Kaya whispered.

"Look around at those who trust in you; do not lose yourself to this madness," he urged, taking hold of her shoulder. He might have been leaning on her. Might have been holding her back, too. She never knew where she stood with him. Not even now, at the end.

She did look around. She saw her comrades waiting, watching breathlessly; they were triumphant and heroic and wary. She was their leader. Of that, there was no question now.

How could they ask me not to die for Aimee?

"Will you fight for her, Kaya?" Aurora cried, dragging the girl into her arms, holding a small crossbow bolt to the girl's throat. She looked like she knew where to plunge it to get the right reaction—real deep.

"She will not," roared Simeon, taking the choice from Kaya, and oh, Kaya wanted to tear his throat out. But also, he was right. Not that she would ever forgive him.

Aurora didn't seem surprised or upset by Simeon's words. She merely looked at the girl and the bolt's tip. "I offer you a chance to earn a little grace," she said after a while and stared at the wall—at Gray, to be precise.

"Would you fight for this girl's life?" Aurora called out to him.

He never gave Kaya a chance. She reached for him, but he dropped from the wall silently. He rolled ever so as he landed, and this delighted Aurora, who cast Aimee aside as though she meant little. Compared to the Alphaline, she probably did.

"Will your brutes honour your retreat?" he called out, and she thought about it for a breath.

"I give my word, Alphaline," she spat, and Kaya saw her wipe a little drool from her mouth.

"Then to the death," he boomed, and he sounded strong and fierce, and she knew in that moment just how deeply she cared for him. If not as a lover, then as a dear friend. A friend who leapt into death's grip to save a girl. To save an entire town.

"A fight to the death it is," Aurora cried, and for a breath, Kaya worried a line of archers would appear from the forest, keen to deliver retribution. It felt like a trap; it had to be a trap.

But no such fiends appeared.

Aurora drew her sword, walked out into the mud between the forest and the wall and stood in a pose with her sword out in front of her, offering an honourable challenge.

Kill her, you legend.

Gray ripped away the bandage from his leg without so much as a grunt. Flexing his leg to test its movement and leaking crimson as he did, he drew his sword and began jogging, and Kaya's heart raced. She had seen him half lame in battle; he had still been a far better fighter than Lucian. Or Aurora. More than that, he kept his back to the sun. But that trick wouldn't work twice.

"Kill her," Kaya roared, and the crowd chanted his name as he ran. And why wouldn't they? He was impressive, elite and ready to save one of their kin and possibly them all. The world slowed as he formed up upon her. Still, she didn't move; she merely bent low, with blade out, with her eyes upon his gait, studying him, timing him.

Setting him up.

It happened in a flash. Instead of the clatter of blades and brute strength, there was the delicate double clunk of her wrists as they shot out and aimed at his chest. It was curious that as she cast aside her sword, her cloak caught in the wind, whipping out behind her, exposing what appeared to be miniature crossbows attached to each wrist.

"Oh no," Kaya screamed, but the weapons had already been released. Aurora was already spinning away, reloading for the next strike.

Gray dodged the first, spinning awkwardly, then whipped his blade around in a desperate attempt to knock away the second strike. Problem was Aurora was rather assured with these foul weapons. She delivered the strikes at the exact moment. It was near impossible to block and avoid both bolts coming from the angles she'd chosen. Perhaps he might have slipped the second if he were uninjured and warier of her threat and not so far beyond the point of fatigue. Might have ended the invasion there and then.

As it was, he took the shot in his right arm, and his blade fell pathetically onto the grass.

"Mercy," cried Kaya immediately, but Aurora wasn't listening. She was taken up with altogether ending Kaya's world.

Gray reached for his sword with his uninjured arm, and Aurora shot him through the elbow from behind. The next shot she saved for his other leg behind the knee.

She seemed very happy with that.

Gray showed little fear; he merely cursed her as he collapsed to his weakened knees. Whatever words Aurora shared with her vanquished opponent, she said them quietly so that only the Alpha would hear. Behind her, a few Riders emerged through the trees, and Kaya's heart sank. This was the end. There was no hope left.

Devitt took this moment to take hold of her, wrapping his arms around her lest she leap over the wall. "He's already dead," Devitt said softly, and her hate for him grew. His only sin was in bedding a whore. And bringing ruin upon them all.

"Do not look," Devitt said, and he spun her away from the sight as Aurora towered over Gray, who, unable to rise, could only drop his head and prepare for whatever evils she had upon her mind.

"I will not shy away from this," Kaya roared, and hated and wailed but would not weep, would not be broken. She pledged to lead her comrades until they killed every one of the attackers.

This, too, was a terrible pledge.

She pulled herself free of Devitt's hold and dropped to a knee once more, willing the absent gods to somehow save Gray. But also…

Take him, not Aimee.

The Riders separated, and Aurora motioned to them to tend to Aimee with care. Gently, they lifted her onto a mount, then sprawled her out while wrapping her arms and legs in rope.

Do not take her.

They saved the rest of the rope for Gray. Wrapping a length of it around his neck, leaving him scarcely room to breathe, they dragged him towards the treeline, and for a breath, Kaya formulated a grand charge as he had once suggested.

"Oh, not like this," Devitt moaned as they wrapped the other end of the rope around a far-above branch and began to pull him skywards. "We can't allow this to happen," he cried.

"I'll kill them all," Silas roared as a dozen hands kept him in place. Kept him on the wall. Kept him from starting towards the Riders and likely sacrificing himself in the effort.

Let us leap together, cur.

But no one leapt. They could only chant Gray's name. It was a kindness they could offer only kin. Perhaps he might know he wasn't alone, even at the end.

Gray did not scream as they pulled him aloft. He simply shuddered for a time, allowing his injured arms to hang limply down at each side, and Kaya thought the bravest act on his part was giving Aurora no joy.

For a time, he merely hung until Aurora couldn't help herself. She swung his struggling body as though it were a game for children. She also seemed rather displeased with his lack of reaction, and Kaya could no longer control herself.

She fought those tears something awful and her body began to shake.

And then Gray began to tremble uncontrollably, and Aurora cackled in delight until suddenly, with a gasp, he fell deathly still, but for the gentle swing she had given him. She plunged her blade through his belly and cut downwards, and Kaya became dizzy. Some blood and innards fell free, but still, this was less a horror than Lucian's end.

They did not cut him down. They left him where he died before simply turning their mounts and disappearing into the forest with their ill-gotten gains, leaving Kaya broken and ruined, lost and alone.

Though they left devastation behind them, Raven Rock stood proudly.

24

THE PHANTOMS

For too long, they had considered what to do. It was all they could do while hiding in their sanctuary, staving off boredom and trying not to think about their hunger. They had considered finding some mounts and making a run for the city. That thought lasted no more than a moment.

To the fires with Spark City.

Hiding in the camp, Rua desired safety, life and hope. However, the bandit in her was disgusted with the invaders' gall. She wanted to punish them and exact what revenge they could, minuscule as it might be.

From deep among the trees where no fiend dared to tread, they had watched the horror unfold at the funeral. Instinct had driven them, not back to the gates to die with their comrades, but to the trees to wait until the camp had near emptied itself.

They'd killed three guards without taking a scratch. It was no great feat; it was simply desperation as they raced through the camp, seeking a way to turn this minor incursion into something of substance.

"Will this have any effect?" she had asked in those first few frantic moments.

"I do not know, Rua, but that is all I can imagine doing."

"Should we at least take some meat before setting it ablaze? I haven't eaten in so fuken long."

"Fine, but don't be seen," Rook hissed as she slipped into the supply tent and stripped healthy portions from some choice cuts—enough to feed them for a couple of days. At the time, she had grand ideas about surviving this ordeal.

"Oh, come on, hurry. Someone is walking over," Rook hissed from outside. She suddenly smelled the stench of burning oil, and around her, the darkness gave way to a bright, dancing flicker.

"Have you set this on fire before I'm out of here?" she whispered hoarsely, slipping back under the tarp. She watched another guard walk through the camp with his back to the flickering flames Rook had set upon the tent.

"I needed you to hurry," he had said, grinning. They had done all they could think to do, burning their supplies as dawn hit before sneaking back into the grass and green, where no one could see two little bandits up to some mischief. They were far away before the cries of alarm filled the air.

Even if little had been achieved, they took it as success. More than that, they grew bolder, and such a thing was a danger to any Runner. But those exact Runners who lived to tell the tale of such boldness usually had more wealth to draw on than most others.

———

The second time the duo invaded the camp was that very afternoon. It was opportunity and a little vengeance on their mind which emboldened their careless actions. Seeing the army march in the daytime with that awful war machine leading the line had stirred them. It was more precarious to attempt guerrilla warfare with the sun at their backs, even if most Riders had taken to their tents to avoid the burning sun. They had glided through the treeline, studied the remaining three war machines in silence and set upon their reprehensible target. In truth, it had been Rua's suggestion, and shame upon her for imagining such a thing.

They started it.

Somehow, it was easier to kill a cur than a thoughtless beast. Humankind was far from innocent, while beasts simply answered their masters.

It needed doing.

They had known they could do little for the war effort, but after seeing the horrors the mounts had inflicted upon their comrades, it was the horses they'd focused on. Easier to kill a few hundred beasts than a hundred sword-waving lunatics. Moving swiftly along the pen holding the many mounts within, they saw that there were fewer guards than there had been the night before. To burn the beasts where they stood was cruelty most vile, and for a time, as they stole into a remaining supply tent with another two guards slain, they hesitated.

"I'm not sure I can do this," Rook had said.

"It seems a savage thing," Rua had agreed, looking into the wise old eyes of a stallion.

"We can't just let them charge down upon our people again, though, can we?"

Another guard had the temerity to pass their way, and Rua had killed her and left her in the paddock. When Rua had returned, Rook had been rubbing down one of the beasts with affection.

"Perhaps there is another solution," Rua finally suggested,

easing towards the edge of the paddock. With a knife, she had cut the knotted wires holding the walls together.

Rook must have understood her actions for, rounding up on the beasts, he had begun whipping the closest ones into a frenzy, and they had taken off through the encampment en masse in a dozen different directions, trampling their masters as they went, scattering where they could.

"We should go," she cried, slipping out of the pen as many of the Riders, alerted by the noise—some in the moments before their death as a hoof went through their skulls— emerged from their tents.

Only in those last few moments, as they fled, did they notice some prisoners trapped at the centre of the camp. The realisation took a shine from their victory.

———

This third time, they were determined to throw caution to the wind, hoping to create a little havoc that might tilt the favour in Raven Rock's way. It was all they could do. Even if, in the grander scheme of things, it was little more than a drop of rain against a forest fire.

"Watch it," Rua muttered when Rook stopped moving suddenly, causing her to twist her ankle ever so. Rook had an uncanny ability to know every step, while she was more tentative. He led, and she followed.

"Whisht, woman," he mumbled, ducking low, watching the world, setting their path through treacherous terrain. Massaging her ankle until the sting passed, she matched his step once more. He moved like a master tracker, gliding along the edges of the treeline, seeking a path through.

"Easy," she suddenly whispered, and he stopped dead in

mid-step. His job was to lead the way; hers was to keep an eye on potential threats. She tapped his shoulder on the right, and he looked around as a guard approached them.

Where did he come from?

She did not panic. They remained still, hidden in shadows, little more than shapes in the murk.

Nothing to see here. Move along.

"We're just going to let him march right by?" Rook whispered.

"It's dark; we may as well take him," she said. She liked this part. If they failed at their overall endeavour, killing a few of the curs along the way would simply add some spice to their misdeeds. "Fuk him."

"A good point."

The guard strolled along, unaware of the precarious nature of his steps. He stopped to stretch a mere three feet from their hiding place. Rook had the good grace to let the man finish his stretch before stepping out of the dark, wrapping his arms around the cur and dragging him back into the cover of the treeline, where Rua waited with a dagger. It was a simple kill, and he died without a sound. For a moment, Rua wondered how smooth they two might have been had they ever paired up as Runners. Saying that, she missed her forge, missed the simplicity of steel and ore and burning and sweat.

And none of this sneaking-around shite.

They left the body to quiver its last and she looked out upon the camp again, watching for threat. All she found were some exhausted guards, an innocent-looking tree trunk and a few abandoned campfires.

It's almost too easy.

"That way—go now," she whispered, and he slipped

through the treeline out into the open with her on his heels. Ducking low, hiding from the shine of the shattered moon and listening for movement, they were brave, foolish and wonderfully reckless. There were more fiends awake and aware than there had been the previous times, but their route was clear; the gods were with them. And besides, who would expect an invasion from such paltry numbers?

Slipping beneath a massive cart, they lay beside each other and waited for their moment.

"Rook, you need a wash."

"I fit in better smelling like this," he countered.

While Rook was happy to smell like the road, Rua regularly allowed herself a brief respite from the planning and worrying to bathe the stench of panic from her body in a nearby river, not far from their tree camp. It was the one time in the day she felt more like herself. If she were to die, she would die looking—and smelling—her best.

"Pride, my friend. Have a little pride," she mocked, and he laughed, and the sound caught in his throat. They had never been the greatest of comrades, and they were rarely allies in council, either. But these last few days, they had become firm friends.

"I'm not trying to find a wife among these brutes," he said, eyeing her. "Are you attempting to find a lover?"

"Perhaps I'm just attempting to charm you?"

Lesser fiends might have taken to lying with each other as a way to while away the hours. It wasn't that Rook was too old for her, or unappealing. It simply never came up. Little chemistry, little need. They slept side by side in their little encampment, and not once did she fantasise about awkward moments turning to more. He certainly never pushed it, either.

Perhaps he didn't favour her kind, her race or her attachments. Regardless, it didn't matter, and it didn't bother her.

"Maybe if you didn't wash every day, I'd bother to look at you," he whispered as two Southern curs wandered by. From the stench of scorch off them, Rua imagined they had suffered quite the tanning from the flames.

"So what do you think?" he asked.

"About?"

"About our targets?"

"Let's do all three."

He grinned and approved of her daring. They had argued and agonised over which exact target to attempt and settled upon the prisoners. Indeed, it was the only thing they needed to do. Had they not charged out in the days before in search of Smit and Fitz? They had seemed so driven and wild, like fire upon dry grass. Now, these dozen prisoners sat huddled and listless, heavy with chains and knowing their doom was upon them.

In truth, it was the riskier of their three objectives, but were they to succeed in their primary mission of assassinating that diminutive whore as she slept, the prisoners would likely be punished something awful in retaliation.

And if they saved the prisoners and somehow found time to kill the bitch while they were at it, they could always attempt to sabotage those last three massive war machines as a parting gift before skipping off home.

"This could be it," Rook said after a moment. There was a cold, definite tone to his words. It was easy to decide upon these missions in the safety of their camp. Out here, though, knowing death was so close was a sobering thing.

Forget the prisoners.

Turn around.

Save yourself.

She knew better. She could think of no life worse than one in chains. Rook thought so, too, from his own time in jail. There were worse ways to die. If nothing else, dying while trying to do a good deed was a heroic end.

The wind blew, the moon dipped in behind a cloud and they slipped forward without further word. They scampered through the heart of the camp, along pathways between the sealed tents, where snores and the sounds of furrowing were prevalent, past the burned-down pyres once bubbling with pots of stew and boar.

Sliding low, they dropped behind the two guards sitting glumly in front of the fire and killed them as swiftly as they could. Rua slit her victim across the throat while holding his mouth; he bled out nice and quick.

Rook's victim saw the attack coming, though, and managed a half scream before Rook fell upon him. They struggled until, getting atop the smaller guard, Rook pinned him, and Rua finished him off with her blade.

They held in silence as the cur died in their arms, watching the camp for further threats. They believed the gods were with them, for there was no sight or sound.

At least for a time.

"That was your fault," Rook mocked as they slipped toward the semi-conscious prisoners, who barely roused themselves.

"Of course it was."

"He saw you approach and got rightly aroused by your scent."

"That was my plan to distract," she whispered, sliding up beside him.

Rook's fingers were a blur of motion as he went to work unlocking the prisoners' chains with a little set of thief's pins.

All the while, Rua gently woke each prisoner lest they scream out before they had a chance to escape.

It was all going so well.

"We can do this," he murmured, and the camp exploded in screams and horror around them.

25

———

DECISIONS, DECISIONS

Her name was Aurora, and she was having a positively marvellous day. She watched the Riders charging through the undergrowth. The tower had created quite the path, and from here, she could see the edges of her wonderful camp.

You are almost mine, Raven Rock.

She wondered how furious her god would be upon discovering that his siege engine had been destroyed for such a low price.

"It did what it was supposed to do, my love," she whispered to the wind in the hope that her god, who saw everything, might listen close and hear her words in the breeze.

She thought about the swinging Alphaline, and her mouth watered so much she spat once and then a second time after that. His eyes had told a tale that was not for her, and as they faded, they had been beautiful. As had that strange, loving smile as he looked past her to something beyond—a curious thing, really.

She might have torn him limb from limb at the end, just

like the boy before, but that would have been adding injury to insult. She liked to think that, in the end, he respected her fiercely for deceiving him as she had. She might have whispered in his ear just how many Alphalines she'd slain these last few seasons.

Probably more than any living fiend.

After Magnus, of course.

That fantastic bastard.

She froze, thinking of that cur. Her god did not approve of Magnus and his brutal ways. She hoped Uden hadn't taken that exact moment to listen to her thoughts.

Blood and gore, and bodies and death.

All the death.

"There are much better things to think about," she whispered, enjoying the sun on her face as she walked. The South was frozen and beautiful, but this warmth was a familiar, lost thing. And just as swiftly as before, she froze, thinking of such things. Her god wouldn't approve of that either.

She stopped to pick a few flowers on the way home, eating their petals as she reached the camp, where she could only laugh at what awaited her. Or, more aptly, laugh at that which nearly trampled her as it charged by.

How superb.

She recognised these beautiful beasts the moment she saw them and giggled with delight that some fiend had taken to freeing them, causing all manner of havoc to her serene camp. Of course, the giggle was also for the joy she would get from punishing the new general for this chaos.

Looking along the pen, she saw the spot where the mounts had been released. Even now, a hundred Riders were sprinting through the Wastes seeking to recapture them. That so many had no harnesses when they were released was shocking, and she enjoyed the Riders' distress that little more.

Many of her returning warriors, both wounded and fighting, watched on with equal mirth at their misfortune. A devious leader like herself would usually allow them to.

However.

"Those who can," she called out to her comrades, "will gather some rope and assist the Riders in tending to their beasties." With low mutterings of discontent, her boys went to task, seeking out the mounts as she commanded.

She walked among the injured as any goddess would after a battle that had swung against them. Listening to their tales of woe about the fires, the hiss of arrows or the clash and cut of steel, she feigned interest and false compassion. It was a lesser thing to do, but it's what Uden would have desired, all to hold firm her leadership. Give them a foot of rope and a glimmer of hope with a few simple words of kindness.

All while displaying the strength and brutality needed later on.

She looked past the half-empty pen to the centre of the camp, where the rest of the prisoners slowly starved to death. Aimee lay amongst them, her keepers tending to the chains she would require. Such a fate for the girl disgusted Aurora, for she was special, blessed; at least she would eat well for a time.

"Oh no, no—have her bound properly and left in my quarters," she ordered, and with barely a shrug, her keepers immediately set to work.

An hour before nightfall, Ferat came to her. He did not wear his charming smile, for in his hands was an almost-sealed missive from the deepest South. She recognised the colours and the seal as Ferat offered the words of her god.

"You look unhappy, dear friend," she muttered.

"I would not have expected word from the Woodin Man this deep into the North."

It was a fine point; she smiled with all but her beautiful eyes. Perhaps he feared Aurora had admitted to her lover that she had lain with a man many nights in the season. Perhaps he feared Uden himself could see the actions of his acolytes as they lay beside each other all innocent-like.

As if it won't lead to something more beautiful and thoroughly confusing.

Perhaps Ferat had simply read the words within.

Aurora took the letter, read its contents and collapsed where she stood, against a freshly cut tree stump—a fine place to drop, in truth, with just the right amount of back support for a girl still growing into herself. This letter, though, took her strength and will and made her feel far less than she was.

I will be blamed for this.

Ferat dropped to a knee with her as though they were in mere conversation, and she was grateful for his quick reaction. It wouldn't serve her cause to be seen collapsing onto her rear, no matter how shapely it was.

"My dear friend," he mumbled beneath his breath, and she could only read the words repeatedly.

Aurora, most vile.

I write this at a late hour.

It has been long enough since you last sent word of your doings.

I wonder what terrible evils you have been doing in our god's name?

He loves you, little witch one, but he loves me too.

For once, let your disgust of me be put aside.

There is word of dissent growing in our home.

There are whispers of a king still walking the South.

A bad time, and we must regather before we follow his grand march.

He calls for you, Aurora. He demands you forsake whatever vile Alphaline house you stalk.

And most importantly, he has decided on other plans for Raven Rock.

He does not wish to weaken your army lest it be needed in the months ahead.

Every life matters should there be a civil war.

Leave now, oh most vile witch.

Do not stray from the river, and make your way back home by way of "Little Rose."

In Uden, we trust.

In Uden, we rise eternally.

Yours, with regret.

Gemmil.

"Oh dear." It was all she had in her. She looked to the horizon, where the birthing of the night painted itself a beautiful sky, and she held her mind lest it fall apart.

Where was this message a week ago?

Why did I not receive this message a week from now?

She could not leave these matters as they were. She could not deny her god's wishes either. Her mind turned on itself, filling with vacant rage and a tragic sorrow. She stared at that sky and the natural beauty of the setting sun, and she wanted to wail, to laugh, to kill them all, and race back home to be slain or be saved by Uden.

She also wanted to dip her head and honour these fine bandits for the beautiful brutality they had cast upon her kin. They had dashed themselves against those damned walls, and the bandits had kept them out.

"Is he displeased with our actions?" Ferat asked, as though he hadn't read the message, as though she wasn't stuck in a precarious place altogether. Aurora, playing along, offered the parchment so he might read it.

"So everything we have done here will be for nothing but for a god's will?" he said when he had finished.

"He sees all," she replied immediately. "He will have us gather ourselves this night and flee."

"He does not see everything, Aurora." Ferat took her hand gently. No one would notice this affection. Not even a god with an all-seeing eye in a frozen castle a thousand miles away. "Look at those walls; they are near crumbling. We have come so far."

She did not like these thoughts or words because she agreed with him. She was no fool.

"Perhaps I can see," Uden whispered in her mind, and she bit the inside of her cheek and fought for sanity.

Plenty of their plans relied on this bastion falling. Others relied on their secret march. Aurora was trapped in the middle. Word would spread like a sickness in the wind of a force that had dashed itself against the walls and failed. How pleased would Uden be then?

"This siege might drag on for another week at most," Ferat offered.

"Or the Rock might fall tomorrow," she offered.

"Exactly. What difference is a few days? We can make the time up upon the march."

"The point is defying him."

"You take lovers, Aurora; how does that not defy him?"

Shut up.

"That's a different issue altogether; I tell him of my actions, and he expects as much. I am punished for such things. And besides, I kill those I lie with."

"I'm aware of this."

"I must think on this," she said, and he sat beside her.

Her mind was awash with dreadful things as the hours passed. Her only distraction was the punishing of the new Riders' general. It was a most welcome event. She tried to remember his name. "Caden" it might have been, but it was a small matter.

It was Ferat who tended to the punishment. And why not? He was her savage right hand. He acted for her on these matters. Oh, the Riders had been rightly riled up about her decision. A brave fool named Evren had even beseeched her to reconsider, and she had allowed him time to present his well-constructed argument. She had listened from her throne in the grass and dismissed him at the end. She would keep him in mind though.

As for Caden, he took the whipping well. A good thing too. No general should weep as the whip-crack scorched their skin. Perhaps he was an honourable man, and that, too, was fine. Honourable or not, however, he had allowed his mounts to escape. Nearly half had already been recovered, but it was a small matter. Weakness and carelessness were unacceptable. It wasn't enough of a punishment that the Rider's guards were slain in the attack.

Ferat was rhythmic and brutal as he slashed the young general's back.

She counted the blows as he did, and it was a sight for the entire camp. They counted with her, and after the slaying of the Alphaline, it was quite the highlight of the day.

Eventually, he began to scream, and she was happy that he had lasted as long as he did. She licked her lips and counted aloud.

"Sixteen, seventeen, eighteen…"

Delicious.

Ferat adjusted his stance and lashed again.

"Nineteen, twenty…"

"Enough!" she shouted, and Ferat heard her, but his wrist did not.

"Twenty-one…"

He held for a breath. The man moaned quietly, and she thought his back a suitable ruin.

"One more," she insisted, and bless Ferat, he struck that fiend viciously, and she clapped in delight as her gathered kin intoned the even number. "He has endured enough," she announced, and immediately, the Riders standing around their pen began to plead for mercy. They were angry and ill-disciplined, and she greatly hated them. She might speak of this ill-discipline to Uden when she returned. Perhaps then, Gemmil wouldn't have the temerity to insist they ride with her boys and girls.

Ferat nodded and, drawing a blade to the man, struck him three times in the ribs on either side before slicing his throat. A needless taste of violence that he knew she'd appreciate, and as Caden slumped limply in the hanging ropes, spilling crimson, Ferat stared down the aggrieved Riders, looking rather impressive. He beckoned to Evren to approach. And Aurora smiled, for this was the settling part.

"So ends the unimpressive rule of Caden…" He handed Evren the blade and muttered a warning to the man to keep his Riders in line. It was her command, and spoken low enough that only Evren would hear. "All hail the new Rider General, Evren," he declared, raising the man's hand, and Evren bowed to his Riders and then to Aurora. He knew how to play this game well enough. She wondered how long he might last.

At least until the fall of Raven Rock.

The rest of the night was a right settled pleasure. She sat upon the grass with her back to the log and her cloak draped lazily over her. To any casual onlooker, she may as well have been a log surrounded by burly warriors on all sides. She thought this seat a fine place to rest. It was a distance from any tree, a distance from any tent, a greater distance from any concealing obstacle. As the night drew in, she ate heartily of the last of their supplies, as did the rest of her kin, all the while keeping a watchful eye on the trees, the prisoners, the machines of war and the night itself.

After midnight, the camp settled in for some well-earned rest after a long day of losing ground to the bastard bandits. It was at this witching hour that she caught sight of movement —nothing much and gone in the blink of an eye.

"You there," she hissed at a Rider guard sitting by a fire a little further away. He was sipping tea, lost in his thoughts and imaginings. "Wander around the edge of the treeline of the camp," she said, and the Rider nodded and got swiftly to his feet.

He wandered down through the camp, and she watched with excited glee.

Oh please, oh please.

He followed her orders, keeping an eye on the treeline,

stepping softly. He did not draw his sword as he passed the trees. She caught no movement, and her heart dropped.

Just the wind.

And then, a few steps on, he suddenly disappeared. She clapped her hands four times in delirium as the trees rustled for just a moment. She suddenly envisioned the torment and fear the man must have felt as he was dragged in. And the pain.

"You did that on purpose, didn't you?" Ferat whispered from beside her, and she grinned mischievously.

"Do you think it's them?" she asked.

"I do."

"Do you think they slit his throat, bled him dead?"

"I do," Ferat muttered and turned to rise, but she caught his hand, drew his fingers to her lips and, ever so gently, sucked on them a moment.

She released his fingers by kissing each one, and he quivered. He knew her threat, so he played with her fire. Perhaps that was true love or simply true desire. Whatever it was, it was more beautiful than any godly touch, though she did not understand why.

"Don't go just yet. Wait a little time so we might watch these rats all scurrying."

"As you wish, my dear friend," he whispered. He did not draw away, and he did not even pull his hand back. He didn't know that, if they furrowed, she would probably never betray him, kill him, as she did the others. Probably. She wasn't likely to tell him that, either way. That was the fun of it.

They sat side by side as the two brave rats crept through the camp, hiding where they needed to.

"Oh, please let them stumble upon us," she whispered, and he laughed ever so, and it was a delightful laugh.

Tragically, they did not stumble upon the watchers in the

dark. Nor did they attempt to assassinate her, which would have been a truly godly thing. And despite the alluring nature of the war machines, sitting there all but unattended, watched by only two humble Riders, they turned their attentions upon the prisoners, and Aurora giggled with glee as they killed both guards, albeit with a struggle.

"They are rather skilled, aren't they?" Ferat noted, and she agreed. She thought them heroic, too. It was almost a shame to have to end them.

"I admire them greatly… Take them."

"As you wish," Ferat said, climbing to his feet and adjusting his belt before striding into the camp and announcing to those waiting behind the flaps of tents that invasion was afoot.

"Put up a fight," she willed the interlopers as a few dozen warriors streamed from their tents with weapons raised. There were screams and violence, and then, with some bloodshed and much defiance, the interlopers were felled by the rushing warriors. Aurora looked back to the letter from Gemmil and thought again about the decisions to be made. She watched as both warriors were taken away in chains, and she wondered a little more.

"What will I do with you?" she asked the wind and heard no reply.

26

DEAR DIARY

Solstice 25th

Greetings from the road, dear journal. It is me, Gray, line of Natale. Though it seems only a fragment of time has passed since I last scribed on these most hallowed pages, it has in fact been almost a month. But why have I been quiet? I hear you ask. Well, it has been wet. Real fuken wet. If all the wetness in the world were to make a home for itself, it would be in my boots. And undergarments. I swear it will never stop raining again. If it does, I'll send a prayer to the absent gods. Ask them why it has stopped raining.

Honestly, these last few weeks have been an awful trudging nightmare. That said, Arlen and I have loved every spitting moment of it. As I write this, no surprise it is raining again. I'm hiding here in cover as she goes to work, trying (and failing) to set alight a fire for the night. Honestly, I don't know why she bothers. She's terrible at it. I'm watching her mid-stroke; back and forth, she rubs those pieces of wood, blowing, praying and failing. She's getting rather soaked in the haze of rain and all. Meanwhile, I'm tucked in here, beneath the canopy. Merely damp.

Spit on me.

She must have heard my mocking. She just asked me to go and pick a few logs for the fire.

Well, I'm soaked through again, and that fire looks less and less likely. I've long believed that the genius who invents fire in a box will be rich enough to own the world.

I'm just happy I have a heavy cloak thick enough to keep out the wind and rain. Especially the rain. I've said it already in this journal, but I'll repeat it. The North is a rightly shitty place to try and march. Yet here we are. Having the time of our lives. All wet and shit. Fighting the chill and marching the Wastes.

Well, what do you know?

She just caught a spark with that incessant rubbing. There's a full little flame growing and all. I had hoped to avoid cooking the meal tonight. What's wrong with some cold salted boar and a little buttered bread to stave off hunger, anyway?

She's built that fire up rightly fine. That hazy rain hasn't a chance. She's already looked at me three times, muttering under her breath.

Fine, my love. I'll put on the meal.

Well, I would hardly call the stew I brewed a masterpiece, but Arlen appears happy with her bowl—and her second bowl as well.

She's been eating a lot these last few days.

A lot.

More than one person should.

Yes, dear journal. I know what you are thinking, and you are right.

Arlen is near two weeks late of bleeding. At last!

Now, let's not get too far ahead of ourselves. We aren't fully convinced she is with child, just yet. But if she is, well, things will change something fierce. For one, I will diligently return to scribing frequently. If not for me, then for my unborn son. Or daughter.

If it's a son, I will become his master, and that is a terrifying thing. If I sire a daughter, well, she will go to the city and make her life there. I do not know which life I would prefer or regret.

Of course, Arlen might simply be ready to bleed this very night.

Her mood, however, suggests there is something in the air.

If you are reading this, Arlen, my goddess mate. My beautiful beo. My soul mate eternal.

And other such syrupy shit.

I am truly excited.

And terrified.

———

Solstice 26th

It is still raining. My hands are nearly wrinkled, such is the downpour. She's at it again and has no chance of bringing a fire to light, but that's alright. Perhaps it's a sign to limp on home. A girl in her condition should be warm and relaxed. Not marching through the Wastes every day. I know, I know, it was her choice to come and march the road. "Why should the boys enjoy such adventures while I was stuck in the city?" I'll tell you why: most of our adventures involve little more than stubbing our toes, keeping the wind off our back, eating next to nothing, and all manner of a thousand other annoying things. Oh, and the rain. So much rain. Well, she wanted this, so here we are.

Alright, alright. I'll stop complaining. It's just something to do beyond writing about the same old shit every day.

The truth is, home is calling, and we've been away too long. It has been wonderful, tedious, beautiful and exhausting. It has been a glorious year upon the march, but I am a male, and a very potent male at that, it would appear. (She had counted the days, but sometimes, the gods bless us with miracles.) It is time to go.

But not before one more stop.

There is a town on the horizon that is calling to us. We need some flint to help us with fires going forward. Perhaps after that, we might have a pint or two of ale. Well, I will have a pint or two, and Arlen can eat a finely creamed boar. Perfect, really.

———

Solstice 33rd

I am a murderer.

———

Solstice 35th

I do not wish to scribe these words. Arlen insists upon it. Perhaps it is my punishment. And it is my fault, no matter how often she tells me differently. My soul is heavy, broken and lost. I have never taken a life, yet here I am, running free, wanted for this terrible deed. It is still raining, and I am truly miserable. I look over at my goddess and love her with all my heart. I do so because it is all I can offer.

We are hunted. It is a terrible thing to run for our lives as we do. Do we deserve it? Perhaps not.

Do I?

Perhaps.

Where do I begin that I can explain myself?

That town knew our kind the moment we stepped upon its treacherous land. They may as well have been Southern; such was the warmth and kindness within. Aye, they left us alone for a time. We even managed a full meal and a few pints for me. Fine ale, too, and I partook a little heavily. It had been many a month, and in truth, I should have kept my wits about me.

Oh, the regrets.

We should have concealed our blades and their regal seals. Those lowerlines just couldn't help themselves, though, could they? A pair of Alphalines in their little shithole of a town was just too much of a temptation.

It began as a few muted jests from a group sitting at the far end of the bar. Probably where the regulars sat and all. A sober Gray would have grabbed his belongings and marched back into the rain. But there had been so much rain, and the fire was right beside us. Besides, Arlen had desired a few honey cakes, and who am I to deny the girl a treat?

The night went on, and the drunkards fell silent. All but one, of course. A right prick who muttered his hate for the city, for our kind, for our whore standing in office.

I should have known better.

The mayor's eldest.

Of course it was.

He claimed to be a blade master, and his comrades cheered him on.

He came at me, a-threatening.

It didn't matter that he drew his blade first, either.

It was instinct, and it was over in a flash.

Arlen was screaming, and I was in a drunken haze of anger. The boy was dead, and I was a murderer.

We set no fire tonight. We do not even rest, either. I can barely hold my quill. Arlen looks like she could eat a hot meal. This salted boar will only keep her going for so long. I could write more, but I must rest. Close my eyes for a few hours if I can. Wrap my cloak around us both and regret my steps.

———

Solstice 36th

The hunting party found us this afternoon, and only a miracle saved us. Upon mounts, we could have stayed ahead of them, but on foot, we had to rely on hiding among the green, moving through rivers to keep them from our trail. It could only protect us for so long. They fired upon us with bows, and we were lucky enough to escape. I did not fight the dozen hunting curs, though I wanted to. I could have killed them all, be damned.

We lost them by leaping from a great height to a river below. They never even saw us, but the damage had already been done. Arlen was so brave; she barely screamed as the arrow struck her shoulder.

A mild strike. Once clear of the curs, we tended to her wounds. It didn't go deep, and she took the pain.

I'm so proud of her.

It isn't raining this night. The path is dry, and we are merely resting instead of sleeping away our advantage. We have a fine route, and the shattered moon is glimmering tonight. We will make the miles over marshy terrain; it is better suited to a couple of shattered Alphalines than a dozen mounts likely to fall and break their legs.

———

Solstice 39th

I am no father. I don't wish to write much tonight. I am empty and lost. We drove hard, and Arlen's body could not take the rush. I am less of a man today than I've ever been. I can't write any more.

———

Solstice 40th

The area around Arlen's shoulder has turned an unsightly red, and she has become rather weak. I lit a fire this night, and I do not care who comes to gaze upon it. That emptiness is gone, replaced by only a depthless rage for all that has happened. We have travelled far, and these stubborn fiends will not cease their charge. I have agonised over running that first night, but truly, what judge wouldn't hang an outsider for the senseless murder of their most loved, most virtuous babe?

I feel that fury rise as I sit here feeling more lost and alone than I ever did in those terrible days before I reached the city, before I faced the awfulness of the Cull. Many miles have I walked since then. I pray to the absent gods to give Arlen strength to walk quicker.

It is late; I must eat. I must put out this fire and sleep.

———

Solstice 41st

Arlen wasn't able to walk very far today. I do not know what to do. I wish my father were here. He always knew what to do. If he were here, we would fight. If Mother were here, she would have a cure for whatever affected Arlen. But they are dead, and I am alone with a sickly mate, and it is not fair. No matter how many times I tried, I could not set a fire tonight. The wood was too wet, and I am unskilled in such things. The heat resonating from Arlen might suggest she needs no fire anyway. I do not know if this is a precarious thing.

———

Solstice 41st

I do not know what to do this evening. Arlen has been unable to rise from her bedding, and she wheezes and speaks in tongues of unknown things. The hunters have also caught our scent, and I am lost.

What do I do?????

I would give the world to know what herb or tonic I could use to sever the delirium she is in. I want my love back with me. I need her most dreadfully this terrible night. I light a fire, not for the cold, but for mercy. I call a beacon down upon us, down upon her.

She just reached out and grabbed my hand. "Let me go," she whispered, and I am beside myself. I stoke the flames as she fights bravely, and I fear the worst.

Please do not take her from me.

Please let them see mercy.

———

Solstice 50th

I have nothing left.

————

Solstice 60th

I do not know why I even bother to write this. These last few weeks have been the worst of any wretched cur's life, and I am a breath from death. I have only to climb up a tree and finish myself off. For so long, I have stayed in this dreadful place. Why should I move from here? I have no reason to live.

————

Solstice 63rd

I barely have the desire to scribe this, yet here I am. Heartbroken. Broken. I once believed in humanity and goodness. I believed in mercy, too. I knew those curs would show me no mercy, so, curses upon me, I fled as they approached. I knew in my heart it was a colder decision but a needful one. Deep down where my heart used to be, I knew I could track her down when she recovered. No prison would deny me should I need to break her out, no hunting party too large to overcome. They believed I had fled, and it was the finer move on my part.

I waited as they approached, quivering and praying to those damned absent gods.

They did not tend to her. Instead, they ripped my love from her bedding, and I was too far from them. I ran, but it was all for nothing. They must have loved that boy to near madness, for, as a frenzied group, they murdered her.

She was brave; she did not cry out or betray me as I

charged. They wrapped that rope around her neck and hoisted her high, and she fought them until they took her breath. She fell still and fell to peace in no time. That is the one relief I hold.

It didn't save them, though.

My name is Gray, line of Natale, and I am a murderer most foul. I fell upon them and showed no mercy. I cut and stabbed and tore them asunder, and it was easy, and it was justified.

It was the mayor I killed last, and I punished him with more brutality in return for the torment he caused me.

I do not regret my actions—only that I could not have done it twice.

For days now, I have feasted on their rations. Today is the first day I have climbed from my bedding and gone to her fresh grave.

I want to die, but she would want me to live.

So I will live a while.

Until I find a way to die.

———

Equinox 70th

I have lived no life these last seasons. I have walked many a mile and still found no way to leave. I miss her every day and dream of her every night. I feel a terrible emptiness come upon me. They say time heals all wounds, but I do not wish to heal. I lit no fire tonight, nor did I bother to eat. I remember when things like that mattered. Nothing really fuken matters. I wonder if this journal will end up in a river, ruined and unread. What a fine, unimportant end that would be for me.

———

Solstice 25th

It has been long enough since her passing that I feel I can scribe words coherently. May curses be upon me, but the pain is lessened. But I know well it will never leave. I find myself out in the world, enjoying things more than I have done of late, and yet I feel it is a crime. I still wish to die, but I no longer demand it silently in every tavern I enter or upon every lonely road I tread, eager for some cur to rob or challenge me. Perhaps they recognise a broken soul and know the dangers. Perhaps they feel sorry for the wretch, which is why so many sit with their heads bowed when I approach. Perhaps they do not deserve such a murder on their conscience. I wonder—if I told them I had no will to live, would they take pity on me? Would I allow them, though? It is a small matter.

Regardless, no fiend has stabbed, robbed or ended me. And I find myself with many a mile walked, closer to the city than I'd ever expected.

But I see an opportunity, for I have learned of a town not far from here. Only a few nights' walk and all. They whisper that it is a town of cutthroats and thieves and raiders and rapists. I wonder if I can finally find rest here. Such a thing would be a relief.

Wherever you are, Arlen, I am sorry.

I have walked for as long as I can. It is time to step into the darkness. I hope I will see you as I go. I hope you will be waiting with open arms and love. I will not fight this death if I feel you near. I will simply smile at your waiting hand and allow it to happen.

———

Solstice 31st

These fiends are wild. I do not hate this town as I expected I would. I might stay a little longer than I'd planned.

———

Solstice 37th

I will die today. This, I know, and I look upon it with relish. I do not believe my death will be at the hand of the city either, though the stealing of Spark's lights might suggest a motive.

Regardless of the reason, I have learned the art of heroism, though it is at times most wretched. Some foul witch has set her sights upon the Rock and its soul.

A soul.

What a precarious thing.

I cannot believe a town has such a thing, but I feel it in every warrior standing the line. I feel it in the wall as well. Perhaps knowing I am so close to death grants me an understanding of such things. This witch is mistaken if she believes she can tear apart such a priceless thing as this town's soul. I have made friends and earned respect from fiends considered the foulest. I am home here, at the end.

I know Arlen waits for me in the darkness. I can almost smell her perfume. Feel her presence at my back.

Today, Arlen, I will step in to meet you.

But it is not to Arlen that I write these last few words.

It is to you, Kaya.

I believe in my shattered heart that you will live through this. Your bravery and affection have been a revelation to one so lost. You gave me moments of peace, and I thank you from beyond the dark. Keep fighting. Keep living.

I will wait for you in the darkness beyond.
Decades from now.
Do not disappoint me.

Your dearest comrade of war,
Gray, of Raven Rock.

27

—————

CLEANING UP

Kaya ran her fingers along the journal as though it were a dear friend. It wasn't. It was his goodbye, and she felt a terrible sorrow. It wasn't just for the Alphaline; there were comrades she'd known more closely these last few years. It was for the horror of it all. It wasn't fair—any of it.

She stretched her arms out lazily and took in the morning. *Mourning.*

She had slept through the night. She hadn't expected her racing heart to allow her, but sleep she did. No attack came, though Kaya knew it was a simply a reprieve from the storm. That witch Aurora was up to all manner of tormenting Aimee, no doubt, and Kaya felt the tears coming.

Kaya had wept loudly into her pillows, away from the world and those needing her strength. A truly pathetic thing, and now, in the light of day, she could cover that agony a little more easily. She placed the journal back among his belongings, stripped off her ruined garments and sponged off what layers of grime, sweat and blood she could. A girl wanted to look her best when she did tasteless things. It seemed like the only thing she could do.

She picked out one of her better leather garments and stepped into it, then tended to her hair, styling and tying it back where needed. Catching a glimpse of herself in the mirror, she was shaken by the woman looking back. She looked far older, as though she had aged a decade in a few days. Haggard and ruined.

Battered.

She thought of the emptiness that had taken Gray, and she wondered if that was her future. Moreover, she wondered if it was such a bad thing to simply not care.

Broken.

Her stomach growled despite her lack of desire to eat. Sitting in the middle of her table was her breakfast, wrapped in a cloth. She needed no plate; she simply unwrapped the half-eaten pouch and bit into it. She thought of the glimmer in his eyes and her bemusement. The food wasn't up to her high standard of preparation, but he had done well enough. "It will take the sting off surviving if I return to eat it," he had jested, and she too had jested, right before it had all gone wrong.

"You died well," she whispered to the silence, and knew it was time to tend to grisly tasks.

Walking through the abandoned streets, she couldn't help but shudder at the desolation. All along the wall lay the sleeping warriors, those too stubborn to return to their proper beds lest an attack come. As for the strangers whose only sin was staying a day too long in the town, they slept where they could, and it was a shame. She might have ordered them to take beds where they could, but the effort seemed too much. Perhaps, if they survived another day, they would be welcome to find a home for themselves here. They had certainly earned it. There was certainly space. She loved and respected them all in that moment, her band of brothers and sisters. They might die, but nothing would diminish their spirit.

She straightened up as she marched and reached the gate where two factions of defenders stood on opposite sides of the wall. She thought it was funny that Simeon and Silas had caused such a separation. It was good for morale, she believed. Each group was trying to outfight the other. It was something to hold onto, what with such misery around. On the right side, Silas had finally succumbed to fatigue, no doubt mid-march, and lay asleep in a heap upon the cold stone overlooking the battlefield. A woman lay strewn across him. Her shirt was unbuttoned, Silas's unconscious hand resting within it. Kaya could only smile at their indifference to decorum.

On the left side, beneath blankets and resting on pillows, Simeon lay tucked into a corner with Daisy wrapped around him. Like Silas, he too had probably stayed awake as long as he needed to before some tobacco weed and exhaustion took him as well. They looked impossibly comfortable and ever so saccharine and honey-sweet. Were Silas to wake first and see the lovers at rest, Kaya could imagine quite the fury coming upon him, regardless of where his hand had rested the entire night. He might well put that fury to good use when the attackers came a-charging.

"Good morning, General. Not a sign all night," a guard muttered as she climbed the gate and walked to the edge above, where the pyre had burned away to little more than ash and charred wood. A few days of heavy wind would make it appear as though the dreadful machine had never rolled its way upon them. "What are you doing?" he asked warily as she slid the inner ladder over the wall and eased it down to the other side.

"I'm going for a little walk," she replied, stepping over, climbing and dropping before her nerve left her.

Stepping among the dead was an awful thing. They all

looked the same in death. The bodies of both armies lay twisted and entangled with one other, all ruined and lost eternally. She tried not to gaze at their awful grimaces as decay began its nasty task. She suffered the stench and endured it. A few ravens rose from their feast as she wandered, and it turned her stomach. Death was good for the land and nature, she reminded herself. It was the grim way of things. Through the awfulness she marched, determined and desolate, until her feet touched the grass of the Wastes. Near the treeline, she imagined a thousand eyes upon her, and half that number about to step in and strike her down. It was a lovely day to face a charge, and if they took her life, she would take a number of those brutes with her; if they took her captive, well, she would be with Aimee at least.

But no attack came. The world was still, and that was almost worse. In war and horror, one's thoughts turned only to survival and killing, but in silence, the soul went to task, tearing the heart apart.

Do not weep.

Be brave.

Do it for him.

He deserves it.

Gray still hung where they left him. A terrible thing. His mouth was agape, his eyes were glistening and distant, yet he looked almost peaceful. "You died well, my friend," she reminded him. This time in person. It seemed important. She wondered if he was in Arlen's ghostly arms right now. Perhaps watching with ease the last days of the battle, taking bets on who would survive, favouring the scrappy upstart over the subtle master just biding their time. "Who's your money on, friend?" She liked to think he'd have placed a side wager on her surviving. That would be nice. "She cheated you," Kaya whispered, tending to the stubborn knots on the rope. He swung in the breeze, tipping gently against her shoulder, and she shuddered at the coldness, the finality of it.

Awfulness.

She heard no reply, and that was fine. She hoped he had been taken up by Arlen. She sounded like a strong female Alphaline, and well suited to his fire. Her fingers began to tremble as she tugged, and her stomach turned on itself.

"Let me help," a familiar voice from beside her said. It was Devitt; he looked as she had in the mirror—old before his time. Beyond him, standing upon the wall, she could see a gathering of warriors at watch, reverently observing their general as she tended to final things. Alone. Then she saw Whisper among them. The child would carry the scars of these last few days further than most. She looked to Devitt, and a modicum of Kaya's anger flitted away.

"Take his legs," Kaya whispered, when the rope became tight under his weight. Devitt did as she asked, and they eased the Alpha to the ground. More warriors dropped from the ladder and walked out to the battlefield. Without announcing it, they began tending to the rest of the dead. With a creak, the gates opened ever so—just enough to allow a person through, or worse, a person back in, laden with their dead.

Tears began to flow as the warriors picked at their lost, but Kaya would not cry. They hoisted Gray aloft, and he was dreadfully heavy. With a grunt every few breaths between them, they carried him back through the gates. There, the dead could rest side by side and be mourned without the threat of an attack.

For hours, the surviving bandits dug shallow graves at the rear of the town where the wealthy might have planted crops in between their grander structures. It was an awful but necessary task, and Kaya and Devitt barely spoke throughout the ordeal. Whisper, though, did speak, saying sad words of goodbye as her parents were placed side by side.

"They will have plenty of friends now," she mumbled as the first shovel of soil was placed upon their heads.

Even Silas attended this mass funeral with reverence. He shared no disdainful gazes with Simeon, either. Instead, he looked at the many bodies, counting them aloud so that he might remember the number of murders he would need to inflict to balance the debt.

And then take a few more for good measure.

Hours passed, and there came a faint but growing rumble of hope that no further attacks would befall them. Kaya knew better. She wasn't inclined to wait and see either. Though they had scouts hidden in the forest, keeping an eye on the distant camp, she wouldn't wait. Come nightfall, with the dark as her ally, she alone would plunder that camp. If she died, she fuken died. It was a small matter. She'd have great company in the twilight beyond.

They saved Andreas for last.

It was fitting, really, that he alone was the only warrior to be buried out beyond the wall. He was delivered to his final resting place, where he would become a fine pouch of potatoes the following season. They eased him gently into the ground and began to cover him up from the world forever.

"We could've used you," Devitt muttered in between shovels.

"We would have won by now and all," Kaya added.

"I think he would've done as well as you," Devitt offered, and she nodded and thought him a fine liar.

Patting the ground, ready to break down once more in the privacy of her hovel, Kaya turned to leave and only then heard shouts of alarm.

Walking from the treeline, no more than a few dozen feet from her, was Aurora Borealis, who liked to kill people.

She wasn't alone.

28

SAVAGE

 er name was Aurora.

She liked to count, and today, she counted many things. In truth, the desire to count always came upon her at the most stressful of times. Deciding the fate of an entire town was nothing next to the decision to deceive her god lover. It had never been done.

She was terrified.

That last thought involved three words.

That one a delightful six.

That one was five, and that was no good at all.

She stopped counting and looked to the light emerging from the tent's open flap. "No one came to kill me during the night; I'm almost sad about that," she muttered, and her guest said nothing. That was fine, too. The girl didn't need to say anything. She was merely a child, and though children thought themselves most enlightened and opinionated, they rarely had anything interesting to say.

Kill a few people, furrow a few more, and then you'll have something to say.

Aurora left the girl to slumber where she sat. She looked

like a caged rat on a wooden chair, wrapped in rope and attached by sturdy bindings that held her still.

Deathly still.

With her head drooping forward, Aimee might have been feigning sleep, or possibly feigning death and all. It was a small matter, in truth. Delicately, Aurora slipped behind the girl to gaze at her bindings. The knots were expertly tied, but the girl had tried to slip out of them. Moving around in front of the girl to face her, Aurora stroked her cheek and then the other.

Little Miss tired herself out struggling.

And she had struggled. A right little fighter she had been, with a crude tongue, and this had pleased Aurora something fierce. Her gift to her god would be only one of many. But this child had the potential to outlive the rest.

At least for a time.

"Sleep well, little one. Everything changes today," she whispered, and despite her ruse, Aimee looked up at this, so Aurora took the girl's head in her hands, kissed her sweaty forehead and thought her most beautiful. Dried tracks of tears marred the grubby finish to her face. She'd had quite the night as Aurora slept. "Oh, my dear, don't cry. It will be wonderful—I pledge you this." It was a terrible pledge. Any tears were a waste in Aurora's mind. Her god didn't like tears unless they were delivered involuntarily, along with gasping breaths, as your life was strangled out of you.

Aurora wanted that so much.

"Fuk you, you fuken slag, I'll fuken kill you! I'll fuken tear your fuken eyes out!" Aimee screamed.

"And then what?"

"I'll kill your entire army. I'll slit every throat. I give you my word."

"That's a terrible pledge, little girl. You can't even get out of those ropes," Aurora said softly, placing her hands on the girl's shaking knees. "But keep that fire; you'll need it in the coming months."

Aurora turned and walked away without another word. She strolled through the camp, stretching and leaving the muttering child to her curses. As before, the entire army waited with bated breath for word of her decision. Despite her best efforts, the warriors had learned there was a grand decision to be made. Some favoured a retreat back home, back to the cold. Others demanded that the town be felled by fire.

She had agonised over the decision to leave or to fight. So far, she was adamant she would fight, that they would follow through with the final attacks. Uden would beat her regardless. At least with the task done, there would be a few more kills to her name.

He will understand.

Even if I return with a shell of a force.

Won't he?

Around her, the camp was less frantic than any morning before. They suffered in defeat as any army would and were slower in their actions, feeling the fatigue that little more. Feeling those scrapes and bruises a little more too.

It was three dozen steps to the centre of the camp, and it was there that she intended to spend a little time getting to know the prisoners. Before the decision. Before the killing. Before she deceived her god. Before all things ended.

It was a fine place to start any day, and Ferat must have thought so, too, for he was already among them, feeding a ladle of fresh water to each gasping fiend. She thought it a terrible kindness but also a nasty act of cruelty. Without his interference, they might have slipped from this life a few days before. Dehydration was no way to die, but dead was dead.

And sometimes, death was an escape. The prisoners took their water with weakened relish before collapsing back upon the ground, into the mud and waste and awfulness.

She allowed him to finish his cruel charity before greeting her dear friend. "A fine day for war and death," she mused, and he smiled.

I have made my choice.

And I am wrong.

"Whatever you decide," he offered, casting aside the ladle. Only one prisoner rejected the offer. He stared at Ferat in silent hate and she tried to remember his name. Aimee had called for him. For them both.

Both.

Aurora did not see his feminine companion among them and thought on this a moment.

"Where is the other girl?" she asked.

"I do not know. I assumed you had taken an interest in her," Ferat said, looking around. It was a fair assumption. No one ever knew who Aurora would take an interest in at any time. "Do not worry, I will seek her out," he said.

"Before you do, tend to the child."

He looked at her with a frown.

"I didn't do anything to her. She needs to be properly bound once more. And use chains this time. Plenty of chains."

"It will be done," he said, bowing and marching off.

As Ferat went off in search of decent chains, Aurora glanced around the camp, looking for the missing prisoner. Usually, she'd take little interest in any escapee beyond their natural ability, but the girl stood out. Aurora really liked her dress. She would really have liked that dress for herself. They were of similar builds, she and the girl; perhaps Aurora's hips were somewhat narrower, but it was a small matter. She was decent with a needle and thread if needed. She thought more on the girl and remembered that she was the smith as well. She tried to remember her name but could not. She did remember her rather charming accent, though. Wonderfully charming.

Particularly when she was screaming abuse at her.

Particularly when fighting for her life as Aurora's kin formed up around her.

Oh, yes, this wild bitch had swung and cut and drawn blood. Fierce for a woman her size. Aurora could respect that.

"Do any of you know where the girl has gone?" she asked the prisoners, who stared absently into space. She wasn't offering water or food; they didn't care.

"You foul, evil witch," one of them growled. It was the other little sneaky snake in the grass from the night before. He, too, had put up quite the fight. He had killed two more Riders and battered three of her boys to near unconsciousness before they finally placed the chains around him. This name she suddenly remembered.

"Do not call me that," she warned.

"Fuk you, you fuken whore."

Better.

"You are Rook, aren't you?" she muttered. *He is on the council with Kaya, Devitt, with... ugh... What was it?... Rua. That's it.*

Great accent altogether.

"To the fires with you and your raping kind," he roared, loud enough that anyone in the camp could hear his lies. Aurora thought him very much mistaken. They didn't do such awful things to prisoners. They didn't even do it in the South. That was a cardinal sin against Uden's will. Burn the women, aye. But rape them? Being caught at such an act was a death sentence.

"We don't do that," she explained carefully.

He spat in the dirt, and she spun away, preparing to seek out the girl. It wasn't the largest of camps, and its numbers were thinner with so many soldiers fallen and so many of their mounts gone.

"Four fiends, in the last hour, took her into the forest," he hissed, and she turned back to see him pointing to the dark green beyond. It looked like a fine place to get a little privacy and all.

No, no, that can't be right.

She wouldn't believe it. She refused it. She even hissed at the lying cur before taking off towards the forest. She walked resolutely, holding herself back from running, but his cold words stuck with her.

Why would he lie?

Aurora prided herself on decorum, honour and fairness. Even in war. Even in chains.

Why would he lie?

"Four fiends."

She increased her pace.

Why would he lie?

She began to run.

"No," hissed Aurora, refusing to believe her soldiers capable of such a revolting thing. She had her blades already drawn as she charged through the green, listening to the silence of the woods and the camp's rumble. She kept running, listening, disbelieving.

They will not do this.

We are better than this.

We must be.

She charged through the forest for a time, long enough that she began to doubt, until, stopping to take a breath, she heard them. A low rumble of bitter noises. Male and female noises, to be exact, and she was disgusted.

Aurora did not scream. Silently, she stalked towards the sound; her decision had already been made. They were four and she was simply a killer of gods.

She came upon them in a little dell. They must have taken very little time to find such a mediocre place in which to attempt a rape.

Attempt.

I'm not too late.

She wasn't too late, but damage and cruelty had already been inflicted upon the woman. Rua remained in her chains, arms aloft, suspended from a branch on a seeping oak tree. Her shirt had been opened, and her unprotected breasts lay out in the open for their fondling. Mercifully, the rest of her dress remained strapped tight. It was a really nice dress and deserved to be worn appropriately.

They stood around her, striking her with open palms, laughing, mocking and threatening. Three of them had already removed their trousers and stood displaying their far-from-impressive manhoods. The fourth stood holding the chain, and began releasing it, lowering her to her knees.

He wore the same vile grin. His fate too was sealed.

Rua didn't take this assault with ease, though. She swung her legs ferociously, kicking out at her attackers, spitting her hate, challenging them all. Aurora was ashamed and not at all surprised at the Riders' behaviour, at the foul deed they were attempting. Ill-disciplined, foul fiends, all of them—better left dead by the side of the road.

"Stop this," she roared, bursting out of the trees. The bastards spun to face her in their nudity, all proud and pathetic—caught in the act.

"Aurora, we were just punishing this bitch…" began the

nearest Rider, then saw her threat for what it was. In her hands, she held her sword and dagger. He attempted to grab his trousers, reach for his sword and plead with her for mercy, and managed to do none of them. She struck a glancing blow upon him as she raced past, slicing him neatly in his most delicate of appendages. He screamed as he caught hold of his half-severed piece, but she was already on to the second, who reached for his blade and managed only a blow upon the ground as she spun past him, plunging her blade deep into his kidneys, then releasing him and knocking him to the ground.

The remaining two begged pathetically as though she might be swayed. Really, though, they knew their fate, and she took her time with their killing. She was on the first in a flash, gripping his manhood in her fist and deftly removing the source of his evil desires for the rest of his life. However long that might be.

It wouldn't be long.

With the screams of the dying filling the glade, she fell upon the last—the fiend who had lowered the chain and was now attempting to run away. She fired her wristbows at him as he ran and caught him in the rear and ankle. She knew the ankle to be a wonderfully painful place to receive a blow.

He screamed for mercy and pledged that he was innocent, declaring he "did nothing more than hold her in place."

"I don't care, you piece of shit," she screamed, falling upon him. His manhood was still protected beneath his clothing. It made no difference. "But I will give you more mercy than the rest," she pledged, and spat upon his face as she dug that dagger in low, real low, driving it through his groin. He squealed as she twisted the blade, tore and rummaged a little more. She knew there was a way to bleed him out a little more if she kept searching.

She searched for the killing slice.

For a time.

She found it.

And he bled out swiftly after that, and died shitting out his bowels, and it was a fitting end.

Aurora got to her feet and went to Rua. "Are you alright?" she asked the girl, still fighting in her chains as Aurora released her.

"Fuk you and your kind," Rua hissed, sitting down against the trunk of the tree that had entrapped her.

"I did all this for you, dear Rua," Aurora whispered, then gently pulled her blouse closed over her chest before buttoning her leather dress back up. It really was a fine dress. She might have said as much but thought better of it. Perhaps later.

"To the fires with you."

"Oh, aye. Eventually, that will befall us all."

She turned to the curs who were still breathing, then went to task severing the last of their manhoods. To their credit, they lasted a time, bleeding profusely, as she placed each severed piece in its owner's mouth. It seemed a fitting end, and she watched them splutter and bleed out swiftly enough. Such was the fear, the horror, the justice.

"They died like cowards," Rua said after all the bodies had fallen still.

Four manhoods, all severed and ruined.

That will do.

She was glad they were an equal number as well.

"Deservedly so," Aurora said, and from her pocket she took a mostly clean handkerchief and daubed at the blood on Rua's lip. It was something to do while she waited for the haze to clear itself from her mind. Rua might have said more, but she stayed silent and let Aurora tend to her. Out of fear?

Out of respect? Aurora might have asked, but the girl looked shaken.

It didn't take Ferat long to discover the horrific scene, even after the screams of the dying were lost in the wind.

He offered water for Rua's injuries, and Aurora called for food as well. It was all she could do.

"Was he among the prisoners when they came for you?" Aurora asked Rua, jerking her chin at Ferat. She dreaded learning her dear friend could do such a thing, or allow such a thing to occur. Each was as bad as the other, in her mind. She'd inflict the same punishment on him if he had been a part of this, regardless of friendship.

Rua shrugged indifferently. "I don't recall," she muttered, and Aurora smiled. That was enough for her. It was unlikely Ferat was capable of something like that. He didn't have the look to him. Those four curs, though, had most certainly had the look.

Riders.

Rua ate little as Aurora doted upon her. Aurora, for her part, tried all manner of conversation in a vain attempt to win her favour. It wasn't in Aurora to ignore her failings as a leader. This was on her.

As were the four savage killings. Such brutality would likely earn the ire of the remaining Riders when they discovered the bodies of their comrades in such a state. Normally, Aurora wouldn't have cared, but they had been ferocious on this campaign, and she wasn't confident they would take this act of hers in silence. Regardless of the fact that their punishment had been justified. They were dead, and they deserved it. But still, best not to rub it in the faces of those who came enquiring.

Ferat called three of his most trusted warriors to tend to

the dead. They buried them deep enough that no one would notice, but not deep enough that beasts wouldn't sniff their remains out and go a-feasting.

It is what they deserved, the absolute scum fuks.

The absent gods agreed.

All the time, Aurora's mind was awash with thoughts, until, like a gushing surge of water, she came upon her answer and felt the weight of the arth fall from her shapely chest. Even if Uden was displeased with her, surely the vile actions of these four mounted warriors would direct his anger away from her.

"I like your dress," Aurora said eventually.

"When you kill me, you are welcome to it," Rua snapped back.

"Thank you very much," Aurora whispered, patting the girl's grubby hand.

Rua looked like she had more to say but gave up before the words formed. It didn't matter though.

Aurora dropped to a knee. "I very much wished to kill you all. Burn your sanctuary to the ground. However…" She looked around at the mounds where the vile scum lay, minus their manhoods and soon to be forgotten. "They are a pox upon my Southern house," she said, and spat on the ground. She didn't know exactly what that meant, only that Uden sometimes spoke those words when dealing with a cur who had displeased him greatly. It was a fine-sounding thing altogether. "They have robbed me of my pride and our honour."

"What are you saying, vile witch?"

Please don't call me that.

"We are unworthy of victory; I will surrender our charge. I will meet with this Kaya and offer a knee."

"She will not fall for that deceit," warned Rua, baring her teeth.

"She will listen to me," Aurora offered, and felt just fine about herself.

29

ACCORD

No matter how much he'd scrubbed, Simeon couldn't get rid of the burning smell. He'd changed clothes twice and bathed once; he'd even used his most potent aromatic oils to cover the stench, but it wouldn't leave his skin. Daisy had insisted she didn't notice it, but Simeon could smell it constantly, and every time he breathed in deeply, he smelled that stink of death. He tried not to, but he couldn't help imagining how many fiends had burned to death at his hands. Any way to die was no way to die, but that way seemed way worse than most.

Walking briskly through the town, he clenched his fists. Even the air was rough on his fingers. They were still blistered where the oil had spilled over. They would scar, no doubt, and he would constantly be reminded of his most savage attack. He should have been proud, and perhaps he was, but also, he remembered the screams, the panic as they had writhed and burned, and he watched it from above, delirious and broken and shaken.

The defenders of the town, however, thought highly of his actions. Well, most of them did. Those who followed Silas thought very little of him, which was fine. No matter what deeds he accomplished, they would answer only to the most dominant voice of them all. They followed Silas as though he were a god. Perhaps he was. A god of war, at least. And their god decreed that Simeon was a proper wretch, which was fine too.

Besides, Simeon had his own little army that followed him and held onto his words and thoughts. It was unsettling and comforting all at once. He could not march through the town as he did this afternoon without a few following along, eager to compliment him and swear that they had his back. They were working on a nickname and everything for him. "Firestick" was one such mocking term. "Sparky" was another. He was no fan of that one.

Overall, his stock had risen relatively high in Raven Rock these last few days, but now, after the burning of the tower, he was quite the legend.

If truth be told, it hadn't been his idea to fill and burn the lanterns. He was just the quicker Runner, the more accurate thrower. The master plan was Daisy's. Though he wanted to tell them this, she swiftly forbade him to direct any attention or praise onto her. She considered his legend a greater thing than her glory. A peculiar thing, Simeon marvelled. He argued, but strength was returning to her, and she would not be moved. She held him aloft to take the credit while she remained hidden in the shadows—although neither could in fact do this at all, for precarious things were afoot. His heart hoped for a treaty, a resolution—some end to the fighting. Really, though, he had a terrible, sinking feeling. Looking at Daisy as she led the way, so did she.

"Go get her, Sparky," one of his comrades shouted as they passed the grand office of the council.

A crowd of wretched, battered fighters surrounded the

council chambers. They did not cheer; they waited in stony silence for an outcome. It was said that Aurora had come offering terms of surrender.

To those who would listen, he would claim that he wanted to fight for this town until they won. That he wanted to stand atop the wall and give everything, including his life.

But he also wanted to live.

That tunnel was looking more than a little alluring.

The forest more than a little tantalising.

Who would even notice?

All eyes were on the last two council members as they reached the council stairs and began to climb. Stopping the doors to ready themselves, they kissed once, a delicate, passionate moment for them alone, before stepping into the arena of the council to face the horror to come.

"About time, too," Devitt hissed, ushering them in the door. He was pale, sweating—never a good sign. The child Whisper was not in the room this time, and a good thing, too. It was no place for a child, what with that lunatic Aurora sniffing around. What with there being a chance they'd slay the interlopers if it all came to blows. What with the chance there would be some rightly fuken bad language spoken.

The meeting room appeared perfectly dignified inside. There were even a few glasses of water on the table. That was the level of hospitality offered. It was Rua he spotted first, and he couldn't help but beam a smile. She had been returned to them in chains. Simeon had thought her long gone—hiding from the invasion, dead, or hacking at those fukers, Smit and Fitz. Returned alive was a decent enough outcome. She sat at the table, frozen, with her head bowed, but that was alright. Alive was alive.

Silas sat with his back to the door. His battle axe sat prominently on the council table, making clear his message of threat. Beside him, Kaya stared with unbridled hate at the unsettlingly calm Aurora Borealis, who liked to kill. She sat at the head of the table where Andreas might have sat. Behind her stood an unimpressive man. As young as any of them, he was impeccably dressed in fresh armour. He was muttering some incomprehensible words to his master, and Simeon could feel the tension in the room.

"So, is this it?" Aurora asked. She eyed Simeon indifferently, then eyed Daisy and lingered. "Is this the grand council that has scuppered my plans, brought fire to my kin, declared yourselves fierce, stubborn defenders?"

"Only Rook is missing," Rua muttered, and Simeon saw the swelling around her eyes, the cuts on her lips and all. He recognised the signs of a subtle beating, and a fury came upon him. He reached for his sword's grip but did not release it. Aurora wasn't wearing a silk scarf. Apparently, that was all it took.

"And Gray, but you already saw to that," Kaya hissed. She looked ready to kill. Peace be damned.

"Who is Gray?" Rua muttered and fell silent. Simeon had never seen her as subdued as this.

Silas slammed his hand down upon the table. "How dare you step upon our territory?" he snarled, which amused Aurora. She gave him a long look, not as though she were undressing him with her eyes, but rather as though she were removing his very skin. Simeon reflected that he would live a happy life if he both survived this siege and never had a woman look at him the way she looked at Silas.

"I bought my way in," she said dreamily, eyeing Rua, her gift.

Kaya wasn't intimidated in any way. "I want Aimee back as well."

Simeon thought her a little subdued, considering what had been taken from her.

"The child is inconsequential; be happy with what I have brought as an attempt to commence talks of peace," Aurora said softly.

Peace?

Devitt finally took a seat—a little too close to Aurora. There were rumours that the idiot had allowed Aurora entry into the town in the days before. Further rumours suggested he had bedded the evil witch. Still, though, sitting here and holding onto his hate as best he could, Simeon considered her quite the looker.

You are an idiot, Devitt.

But also, well done.

"Is Aimee alive?" Devitt demanded, and she purred ever so.

"Never mind the child, dear Devitt." She tilted her head slightly, looked to Kaya and then looked to Devitt. "Through all this horror, did you confess your love for Kaya in the end? I see now that she is quite the catch," she said, smiling. It certainly appeared Devitt and Kaya remained unmoved by her implications, and Simeon thought these the strangest peace talks that had ever occurred.

"Fuk you," Devitt muttered.

"You already did, remember? It was… perfectly fine."

Kaya looked at Devitt for just a brief moment. She might have growled under her breath.

Aurora's companion behind her seemed just as displeased with this confession. He muttered some words and placed his hand on her shoulder, and she muttered an incomprehensible few words in reply. He didn't seem satisfied. Aurora spread her arms out wide. "Let us not bicker, my friends. I bring fine tidings and friendship. An honourable thing after days of war." She gestured to Rua, slumped in her chair, her chains clinking with every breath she took. That was no place for a council member to find herself. Not here. Simeon might have said something, but the room was volatile. "I come with gifts; surely that is a sign of peace?"

"And what of Rook?" Rua asked.

Aurora countered without missing a beat. "I did not know he was in such a privileged position; I will return him as swiftly as I return."

Simeon couldn't help himself. "*If* you return."

Shut up, idiot.

Threats help no one.

Aurora's comrade didn't like that, not one little bit, and Aurora eyed Simeon in a particularly familiar way, and he felt a sinking sensation in his gut.

Oh, well.

I'll still be happy if I survive this siege.

"I will leave this room alive," she said quietly. "I will clear these walls with no wound suffered." Simeon didn't like that tone either. It felt like the world was on a precipice, and the next careless step would send them all plunging into an abyss. "How I leave is down to you." She held up one hand. "One choice delivers peace." She held up the other. "The other choice delivers the end of you all." It certainly seemed as though she had made similar speeches in her time. It was an intimidating thing to have intimidated her so little.

It's all about to go to spit.

Kaya stood up. "We accept your peace and would have you leave, but not without bringing us the child." It was a fair exchange, thought Simeon.

"To the fires with you, Kaya," Aurora suddenly snapped,

and her comrade looked ready to draw a sword—and likely receive an axe through the chest for his actions. There wouldn't be much peace brokered after that. But Aurora wasn't done. "Go make another of your own, you whore," the vile witch added, standing to face Kaya. They glared at each other, two explosive warriors ready to spit bile and swing swords. Kill everyone.

And it was contagious.

They'd spent days in fear and worry, and then this vile woman had strolled on in as though it were no matter. Simeon felt the urge to draw his sword. Show some teeth.

Both women stared at each other. There was blood, violence and death in the air. It was hard to tell for certain, as they all felt the same.

"You think we will simply believe you offer peace?" Kaya roared. "Tell me of the honour in Gray's death."

"We fought; I won."

"You pledged a fair fight," Kaya hissed. Simeon thought it a fair point.

"I promised no such thing," Aurora snapped in reply. Truthfully, Simeon couldn't remember the words they'd shared before it all went to hell. It had certainly appeared a fair fight was to occur. It mattered little now. Dead was dead.

From behind Simeon stepped Daisy. She faced both women and waited for silence. She did not quake; she did not shrink away. She sounded like herself again—strong, wise, fierce and brilliant. "Can we all just calm ourselves?" she entreated, and Aurora stopped to look at her. Ever so gently, she reached out and took a few locks of Daisy's hair in her hand before releasing them.

"I would scalp your head and wear your locks for a crown. You are beautiful."

"You lunatic," cried Daisy, and Silas was up on his feet,

axe in hand and face red with rage. Simeon wasn't too far behind. He pulled his sword as Aurora drew hers and backed away from the table.

"Whoa," cried Devitt, attempting and failing to calm the room.

A few strange things occurred in that moment. Kaya pushed past him, sword outstretched. Rua leapt from the table and dove for Aurora, missed, and collapsed on the floor. Daisy shrieked as though struck, before retreating away from the violence to come. Aurora, avoiding Kaya, stood back, shoving her comrade in front of her as Silas swiftly swung his battle axe and cleaved Aurora's unimpressive comrade through the head.

A primal cry emerged from Aurora as the man shuddered and collapsed at her feet, spilling crimson all over her boots, and Simeon charged in from the side. He had the advantage at this angle, and he swung wildly, knowing he or Kaya or even Silas would kill her. Afterwards, they could deal with the fallout from her aggrieved soldiers.

She never came into the town.

Swear to the absent gods I do.

"Kill her," Simeon screamed.

30

WRATH

Her name was Aurora, and she was wrath incarnate. She stood in stillness for a breath as they formed up around her, and she was not scared. Far from it: she was blessed and righteous and filled with a terrible rage. She could see Ferat trembling as he died. Deep down where a soul might have rotted, she felt a shudder, a stir.

Ferat had opposed the accord and demanded without words that they take this town for its defiance, torch the buildings, flail the inhabitants and other such lovely things. He had been right, and it had been sacrilege on his part. And she had forgiven him this sin.

You are beautiful in death, dear friend.

You were beautiful in life, too.

His legs twitched, and his blood spurted. She'd seen such a stunning sight at least a hundred times over, and usually by her own hand. But as Ferat died, a grief so maddening came upon her that she was numbed. She felt herself shiver. Felt a whisper of a name from a lifetime ago that she could no longer speak. Would no longer speak, lest her god deliver his wrath upon her.

Fyre.

She wanted to kill, to avenge, to weep, to tear apart some skin and limbs and bathe in blood and howl and be dead.

Merciful peace.

Ferat struggled his last and fell still in a pool of his own blood, no more than a foot from her. She thought there was the purest beauty in the spectacle of his skull split apart like a melon for the entire world to see.

Like reassuring tears in violence.

His killer, the foul, drunken brute, heaved at the battle axe to pull it free, and Ferat's body was dragged and battered, sending all manner of matter around the room, upon the table, upon Aurora's face, and she licked her lips and tasted salty warmth and wanted to die all over again.

She also wanted to dance. To raise her bows and kill them all, to spin and pirouette with dagger and sword and slay each of them until the floor was a slick red river she might float upon.

They screamed, they cursed, they came upon her, and she did not raise her blade, nor a wristbow either, for they did not deserve such brutal mercy.

"Kill her," someone screamed, and she was roused from her stupor of hate. She already knew what to do. Knew the moment she'd stepped into this room. A girl like Aurora was never one to let herself be trapped in any way. Spinning on her heels, she took a chair and swung it behind her with enough force to send it through a nearby window, which did what most perfectly fine windows did when struck in such a way. It shattered outward in a thousand pieces.

It's time to go.

Wrapping her cloak around her, she retreated, not out of fear but out of cruelty. She had plans, all the plans, and she did not want these fiends to die at her blade. Not yet. Not until everything was burned, and they alone were left to gaze at the fruits of her vengeance. Uden willing, she would then turn upon them and punish them terribly. Bathe in their blood and never raise her head above the surface again.

Born in blood.

Bathe in blood.

Die in blood.

She leapt and made herself small as she spun. Through the window she went, flying from the claustrophobic, smoky room out into the brightness of the day. Why walk all drenched in blood when one could fly?

She smiled as she leapt to her doom.

Falling.

Spinning.

A little bit of twisting.

She saw the next building's roof rise to meet her, and she smiled again, knowing the pain to come. She hit hard as she landed, rolling a little as she did. Wonderfully, she did not rip open her fingers as she hit, either. They merely grazed the surface of the flat roof and lifted off again, unharmed. Rising, she spun back to gaze at the room above and caught sight of Kaya climbing through the frame less gracefully than she had.

She is no goddess.

Panicked shouts erupted in the streets below at the sight of a goddess in flight, and wonderfully, Aurora felt the thrill of being hunted. She hadn't endured such a thing in a lifetime. Her heart raced in excitement. She saw the gates far down at the other end of the town—quite the distance and all. The wall was only a few buildings away.

To the fires with this town.

It was seventeen steps to the edge of the roof, and she dropped to the adjacent one a few feet below and kept running, counting her steps as she went. Behind her, Kaya landed and began to chase and oh, the temptation to turn and gut her in mid-flight was near maddening. Instead, she counted another few dozen steps and dropped to the roof after that, all the while enjoying the rising cries of alarm around her.

That's it, fools.

I'm right over here.

Though anguish plagued her mind, she was positively giddy hearing the voices and seeing the movement in the streets below as she leapt over to her next perch. And once Kaya began to catch up, that was ambrosia for her husk of a soul. Bigger, thicker, longer legs served the bitch, no doubt. It was a small matter.

She reached the last roof beside the wall and almost went for it, almost allowed carelessness and excitement to guide her step. A girl could land short and break her ankle that way, and that was no end for Aurora.

Carefully, she dropped to the ground. Alas, she landed hard upon a running defender, alert enough to follow the shrill cries of panic but not sharp enough to bother looking up. She felt bones shatter as she fell upon him. He made a perfectly acceptable cushion and all. Aurora's sword was drawn before he knew his injuries, before he knew his attacker, before he could raise his shield, before he could scream in alarm.

He died with the third strike. Her sword went deep into his lungs, all the way through and into the ground beneath him. She kept driving that blade in, though. It was all she could do. Her comrade of so long was lost to darkness, and she was a thousand miles from home, from her god and from everything she held precious.

Hide it away, Aurora.

Use it and be fierce.

She thought about this as she pulled her sword free and felt a little better about herself. Eyeing the ladder and ignoring it, she gazed at the impressive wall. She'd seen a few bandits scale it in that wonderful first attack, and fancied her own chances despite her size. Sheathing her sword, she drew back and then sprinted on the looming wall and leapt high. She kicked once. Her foot slipped ever so, scraped a little more, found purchase after that, and up she leapt, gripping the top and heaving herself over as though it were nothing at all.

At either end of the wall, she caught sight of guards seeking her out. They looked so many, and she was but one little savage killer. The depthless green stretched out before her. All she needed to do was drop down into the forest and be little more than a gust of wind against the many waving leaves. No one would see little Aurora disappear into the nothing. Until she returned. With death behind her.

"You whore," hissed Kaya from the building opposite. She eyed the distance, and Aurora grinned, feeling a terrible itch where her wristbows remained unused.

Come play.

"I know exactly what I am," Aurora countered, and Kaya took another long, hard look at the distance between the wall and the roof.

Let her fall and break herself.

"You brought this storm upon your town," Aurora hissed, eyeing the wall. There were a lot of guards with simple swords and shields that could do with a fine bit of killing, she thought. Something to do, something to make this horrific visit somewhat worthwhile, something to remind them of her.

Kaya rushed forward with those tree trunk legs and took flight surprisingly gracefully. For a breath, Aurora watched her as she soared over, up, and then dropped hard as she neared the other side. She did not fall. It was a small matter, and Aurora sprinted towards her. As Kaya scrambled over, Aurora simply leapt over her, drawing her sword, her eyes upon lesser, unimportant prey.

To their credit, the guards along the wall were brave, hardened and skilled. But they still fell, one by one, as she drove past them. Her blade was a blur where needed, but her wristbows were most accurate. Firing bolt after bolt at the charging bandits, she left them behind, mostly dead or dying, and screamed shrilly, taunting Kaya as she did. It was all she could do. Ferat was gone, and the world needed to burn.

"Six to my name," she screamed triumphantly, raising her arms. She desired to be seen upon this wall. Let them fear the coming of the witch. Let them see her grace and know the end. She was a portent of things to come. A warning that this was the end.

By the time Kaya caught up with her, she had taken out two more guards along her charge—a fine number and a fine distance, too. They met at the front of the town, and Aurora spun to meet her charge.

This is too easy.

"I'll kill every last one of you fiends," Kaya hissed, and Aurora did not reload her bolts; there was no need. Aurora had the killing of her. She was no Alpha requiring the darker arts of assassination. She would be dispatched with merely a few parries of the blade and a deadly thrust.

"You will regret your actions today," Aurora whispered, and Kaya charged. Aurora offered little resistance to her attacks. She simply took every blow as though it was coated in honey. Yes, this would be the easiest kill of the day. Most enjoyable, too, for she punished the bandit beauty as though she were a master humiliating an acolyte. It was perfect and godly, and as their swords clinked loudly with every engagement, Aurora howled in delirium—all for the show, all for gathering attention.

And those fools along the wall, upon the buildings, in the streets and below the wall watched on with a crushing hope. They cried out for Kaya, believing her good enough and commending her to the absent gods that had no business rearing their heads for this round. But after a time, it became all too apparent that if Kaya was their last champion, all hope was gone.

Unlike her fallen kin, who found themselves clumsy upon the wall, Aurora was lithe on her feet, spinning and dodging Kaya's loose strikes. All the while, she countered and beat her back with twice the fervour. Every skirmish became a desperate dance to knock Kaya from the wall, and there was only one leader in this movement.

"I have you," Kaya cried, playing the part of a deceiving cur to no one but the most dim-witted fighter. It was all she had, and Aurora thought this almost endearing.

"You have nothing, wench."

Kaya's brazen lies fell silent, replaced only by the sounds of her own gasping and Aurora's shrill cries, and it became embarrassing. Aurora presented herself as a divine goddess of war, and some of the onlookers dropped their heads unable to watch a moment more.

At the end, Aurora drew her in, hissing in her face. Panting desperately, Kaya leapt forward and met a blade through her arm.

"I'm not done," Aurora hissed as the girl fell to her knees.

"You will die this very day," hissed Kaya, reaching for her fallen blade with her weakened hand. Aurora let her rise, and she looked at the sky and the fading sun.

"You had best get to it swiftly, so," she mocked before

stepping past a wild lunge and countering by slicing across Kaya's shapely leg, making her stumble to her knees again. "Get up now, or I shall skin the child."

Swallowing deeply and showing a stubborn side Aurora approved of, Kaya leapt for her and took another strike to the arm. This one on the other side. Again, the sword fell, but Aurora followed through and sliced across the other leg. She cut lightly, for she had no interest in taking Kaya from the battle. Merely taking her will. Kaya, screaming and shamed, stumbled over the wall, where Aurora swiftly caught her, dragged her to her knees and placed her sword to her neck.

"No, no, dear Kaya, you will die this night, come the moon's first glimmer," she pledged.

"You have no honour, witch."

On either side, the defenders had ceased shouting. They took to climbing the wall, seeking a little revenge and a little killing as well. Aurora loved their foolish bravado. She even imagined taking them all on—from each side—at the same time.

What a beautiful way to die.

Perhaps by way of a battle axe in the head.

She thought that would be the most satisfying way to slip from this world. But instead, she leaned in close and whispered in Kaya's ear. "Look to each of your friends, and know I offered peace. I offered the world. All of their deaths are on you." She shoved the girl from the wall, back into the inside of the town where she belonged.

As the defenders surged up, she absently counted their paltry numbers and knew this town could hardly withstand a full attack.

Dropping down before the nearest cur neared her, she landed smoothly, without any injury, and kept running.

They did not let loose in time, and she darted through the

treeline towards the camp, her wrath driving her forward. She did not count her steps; she simply thought on her god and prayed to him for the first time in a while.

"Send me a sign that you see," she demanded, certain he might interject.

"Send me a sign that you see it all," she roared, seeing the camp far ahead.

She received no sign, and again, she was shaken by the realisation that she could openly decide to deceive her god without recourse.

She thought again of that name, once lost to her, and it shook her.

Fyre of night.

"I hear nothing," she whispered, pushing that name far down into the dark and wondering if Uden was actually there at all. Such a thing was all-encompassing and claustrophobic. She might have dropped to a knee, thought a little more, and feared a little more. Instead, she heard his voice in her mind, distant and all-controlling. A shudder overcame her and, with it, a dreadful, eternal calm.

Is that you, my love?

Are you simply watching to see how far I might stray from you?

How disobedient I might become?

"On the night I was born…" she whispered, then swallowed deeply and kept walking.

She was nearly breathless when she reached the camp. Immediately, she ran to the centre, where she came upon the prisoners and their keepers. She felt a hate come upon her, a ferocious thirst that desired more than the shedding of blood. She wanted death, she wanted cruelty, she wanted havoc, she wanted it all.

She gazed at the prisoners' listless faces and thought this

was no good at all. "Feed them shards of meat so that they might come to life, so they might be aware as they fall into the town," she hissed to their keepers.

Around her, the soldiers gathered up, no doubt wary of her sudden frantic appearance. No doubt interested to know her final decision.

"Bring the machines forward," she roared, indicating the last siege weapons she had been cursed with bringing into battle.

"Ready the mounts," she roared, and the Riders nodded. They did not respect her leadership, but they were willing to fight.

"Prepare yourselves, my beautiful warriors, for we will take Raven Rock this very night," she roared. The entire camp was united in its cheers, and Aurora Borealis left Ferat's memory to wither away like the many before it, and she felt fabulous about it.

31

ALL HOPE IS LOST, WHO SAIL
THESE SEAS

The low rumbling of menace signalled the end of all things. Rook knew this, just as he knew there was no escaping this horror. He licked his lips and savoured the taste of salted boar meat ever so. A fine meal. Last or no.

Would have been nicer during the festival.

He closed his eyes and thought of better things and grander times—good laughs and joy among friends. Better that than dwelling on the terrible fate that was rolling towards them all. It was something to do while waiting for the darkness.

I'm on my way, Rua.

Through the bodies marching ahead, he could just make the witch out. Marching with head held high, rightly proud of herself. She led this group, and it was a pitiful march altogether. His comrades were barely coherent, after days spent starving and terrified. In truth, the latest meal, steaming and delicious food served on metal platters, had stirred a little liveliness in them, but still, they stared ahead with a vacant gaze, their limbs barely moving, their feet shuffling. Conversation was little more than muttered speculations or prayers to the gods. They were the beaten and lost. No fine meal could restore their will. He wondered if their lack of awareness was a blessing in the end. Was it better not to see the rope as it was placed around the neck?

With heads bowed, they followed the great rumbling machines heaved by warriors through the foliage towards the town. Their roar was a terror, and any fool with notions of war knew their history and menace.

This is the end.

A solitary clinking chain kept each beaten prisoner in place. They shuffled along in one solitary line, and Rook, last to be captured, brought up the rear. He fidgeted with the chains as he trudged along, subtly trying to find a break, a weakness, anything really, but without a tool to help him, he may as well have tried to gnaw his hands off and slip out that way.

Another day of starvation, and I might have.

In truth, Rook was broken.

He had broken the moment they took Rua from him. He'd fought for her, screamed, roared and met little more than a few strikes for his efforts, delivered with an open palm and intended to subdue him, put him in his place, remind him of his lack of threat. It was only long after they'd disappeared into the forest that he'd indeed given in. When the vile witch followed after and did not return, Rook knew the terrible, terrible truth.

Rook's stomach churned in his belly, and he fought the urge to throw up. It would be an awful waste of a last meal. And walking with the taste of vomit on his lips was no way to enter the darkness. He fought that churning like a hero. It was that or gaze at the three monstrous catapults that ensured the end of Raven Rock. He wasted a little spit on the nearest one as he walked. He knew his fate would be loading these beasts with heavy boulders to crush his comrades hiding behind the wall.

Such a thing was bad for the soul, whatever remained of it.

Aurora had not brought with her a significant number of warriors. The monstrous machines were heaved by ten apiece, and a few able Riders were on their own mounts, hauling from the front. The rest of the army was likely preparing for the final battle. Rook felt it in his gut. Every decent siege ended in a massacre, and there was something in the air.

The absent gods agreed.

Perhaps, were Rook a part of a fitter and feistier few dozen, they might have fought their way out of this, their lack of weapons be damned, but honestly, they'd lost their spirit. And Rook? Well, at this late hour, he just didn't want another beating. His soul had taken enough the last few days.

Aurora barked out orders in their foul language, and many heads nodded in reply, and truly, of all the regrets in his life, the strongest was that he had not killed her the first chance he'd had.

It's what you would have done, Andreas, isn't it?

Unsurprisingly, his dead friend offered no reply, and Rook was left to dwell on roads not taken. Oh, to have gone against his better notions and thrown caution to the wind, he mused.

She'd be dead, and she'd be alive.

In a little clearing not too far from the town, Aurora barked another order. The machines slowed and then rolled to a standstill, and Rook looked around warily for the ammunition. He reckoned those felled trees would make it easier for them to aim for the town.

His keepers went to task on the machines, manoeuvring them into place side by side at slightly different angles.

Despite his appearance, Rook was inclined to educate himself on ancient things, and he knew that these monstrous weapons were already ancient when they had first been used. Yet somehow, they were a potent source of menacing violence in these times. If one had the know-how to build one, that is. Until this day, he'd never actually seen a catapult in his life. Now that he'd met them up close, he hated them.

An old drunkard in a tavern had once claimed that everything came around in cycles. Perhaps the smelly old prick had a point.

Catapults had come, catapults had gone; catapults had come right back again.

Just like lights in glass.

Just like war.

Distantly, Rook saw the glow of the town fall to darkness, and he thought it was a welcome thing. Upon the machines, the engineers tended to the levering, the aiming, the perfect weight of ammunition needed for such a distance, and the awful truth dawned on him even if it did not dawn on his comrades.

Better they don't know it yet.

"We are going home, friends," he whispered to them, to the wind, to the gods as well, that they might guide him home most painlessly.

They unlocked the first man from the chain and urged him up onto the catapult with a sharpened stick. He argued a little, but there was no fire in his eyes; only resignation and melancholy. Only when he sat on the little platform, which clunked down ever so as ropes were pulled tight, did the realisation come upon him. He wailed and begged, and Aurora laughed. And then she barked a fresh order, and with a terrible roar, he took flight high over the canopy of trees into the sky, screaming.

Rook watched that one comrade on his final journey. He counted the moments in his mind as the dark, screaming shape disappeared over the wall and fell to a dreadful silence somewhere within.

Swiftly, the second and third prisoners were released and delivered back home by the cackling witch. They took flight at different angles and trajectories. There was a cold intelligence to it.

No one will be able to see them coming.

Suddenly finding a little bit of fight within himself, Rook leapt upon the nearest keeper, punching, kicking, snarling and spitting. He took hold of the cur and smashed his head against that damned catapult's side and coloured it crimson ever so. Countless fists came for him, punishing and battering, and he met as many as he could. Through the many strikes, he took hold of one more fiend, dragged her in close and, wrapping his arms around her neck, twisted with all his anguished strength until there was a sudden give, and one screaming voice fell still in his ears. Knowing he had stolen at least one of their lives was a comfort as her comrades closed in and thrashed him senseless. Only Aurora saved him, stepping among them with a howling threat, and they left him in a messy heap to listen as every comrade ahead of him was hoisted upon a platform and fired into the night.

All of them went without a fight.

Eventually, they came for him, and he was helpless to stop. Gloved curs picked him up from where he lay in ruin and carried him up onto the catapult of wood, now splashed with crimson. Spitting blood and, no doubt, suffering broken ribs, he gasped, cursed and eventually settled as they placed him upon the awful machine's platform.

"May you all burn," he cried hysterically, trying to find the will to move, to fight one last time, but alas, he was too beaten in body and soul. He listened as they mocked him, cursed him and condemned him, and then all he could hear was the crank of the mechanisms. He felt a slight lurch as the platform lowered a few feet.

And then a terrible silence.

I'm so afraid.

Then, her words.

And the world exploded as a cart struck him, or what felt like it, and his limbs betrayed him as they were flung wide, and nothing was below him. The world was freezing, and he could hear nothing but the rush of wind and his own screams caught in his throat.

Flying.

He caught himself as the ground rose up at him. He looked to the night and the stars, the rise and rush of the unlit wall as he cleared it, and he kept going. He looked below him, heard the screams, saw people gesture to his flailing limbs, and screamed a warning to those below who might not see a deathly projectile about to land on them: "Watch out!"

In the end, he looked to the world and caught sight of a familiar friend, a comrade, a bed-mate in everything but the act.

It was only a flash, and their eyes did not meet, but in that moment, he felt a puzzled relief that she was upon the wall, screaming, warning her comrades of the horrors. As he neared his end, with a large building and certain death looming, for a frozen moment, he took heart in Rua's survival, and he landed hard, and that was the end.

———

Rua listened to the hum for a few moments before taking the spanner to the lever and getting to work rightly ruining the beast. They knew the town would fall this night. As the world around her ended, the last thing she wanted to do was gift Aurora an advantage of the cover of darkness. Besides, there would be survivors who fled this place. She thought they might have a better chance of escaping in the dark.

Let the attackers light their own way.

She could slash a few wires along the many lines of lights strung throughout the town, but it wouldn't take a genius to understand the finer designs of wiring and repair them again, so instead, Rua went to task tearing the generator apart. She used a delicate touch—aiming merely to sabotage, not destroy, mind, so that only a genius with the aptitude for such things could restore it when the time came.

As the whirring grew still, she removed a few key pieces and tossed them in among a thousand similar mechanisms strewn throughout the room. It was all she could do. Andreas would have wanted it done this way, and she would honour him at the end.

"These cursed lights," she muttered, then thought again of Andreas and fought a sob. Since Aurora had fled, Rua had stolen a few moments to honour her beautiful Andreas and visit him where he rested. It was easier to say goodbye without facing the cold body itself. She'd wept all she needed, wiped up those tears and then climbed back into town and prepared for war.

She had taken for herself her heaviest armour. A fine piece, though not her finest work. She wore it well and welcomed the blood-covered sheen it would wear before she fell. Her sword was an easier choice. It was hidden beneath the counter in a long box with a lock even Rook might have struggled with; she opened it and drew out her longsword. She'd made it for Andreas, but payment hadn't come by the time of his death. It was no matter. If she couldn't wear the armour that should have been his, she would die with his steel in her grip.

"Things would have been different with you here," she whispered and missed him once more. Listening to the clink in every step, she closed the door of the building and walked out into the cool night.

Walking through the streets, she could feel that the town had an edge to it now. Perhaps the defenders were wary of the lights dimming; perhaps they saw it as a sign. Kaya had already announced the killing of the lights. They should have used their heads.

Looking along the walls, however, she saw that each brave fiend looked as though they knew their place. Perhaps, were they to realise she was new to this siege, she might have been given a station of her own. As it was, she had decided to stand at one section of the wall and kill any brute who stepped near. It was a simple enough plan.

Distantly, she heard a shriek, and it unnerved her. It had come from somewhere in the forest. She strained her eyes in the dark but saw nothing beyond the treeline. That scream grew louder, though, and it was disturbing. It continued to rise, and a terrible realisation came upon her.

Aurora Borealis.

"Who is that?" she cried, but no one replied. They probably couldn't hear her above the wail they were making. It became a piercing screech that echoed in the quiet streets. She looked to the sky, though she did not know why, and near the wall, she thought she saw something. Then the scream sounded almost directly above her, and just as quickly it was behind her. Abruptly, it fell silent, and she wondered what evil this was.

She wasn't alone in her wondering. Desperate, confused voices echoed around the four corners of the town.

What has Aurora planned next?

And suddenly, there came another shrill cry. This one, though, came from the far side of the town, and it rose and it was terrible. Then, in the shattered light of an ancient moon, she caught sight of a flying beast waving in the night, and only then did she realise the terrible things afoot.

Those machines Rook spoke of.

"From above," she howled, seeing the figure clear the walls at a terrifying speed that no human could survive. Not even an Alphaline. The figure hit the side of a building like a rotten apple flung angrily upon a seeping oak. There was an explosion of blood and limbs and innards, and then a dreadful silence as the body spun a dozen times in a breath and collapsed in a pool of ruin upon the centre of the town, and she fell to her knees, knowing the cruelty in Aurora and her war machines.

We should have set alight the beasts first.

She thought of Rook, and wept loudly as another body flew through the night, smashing loudly against the wall and sticking where he struck. He landed legs first, and truly, it was an awful end, for he did not die, at least, at first. He spluttered, spat blood, looked to rise, and reached for no one. Rua could only howl for him. She knew him to be a prisoner. And her failure stung that little bit more.

"I'm sorry," she whimpered, hurrying to his side delicately taking his broken fingers in hers. He merely exhaled, looked around and died looking to nothing.

She could only look on in anguish, howling her misery, as more and more prisoners fell through the darkness. She counted them as they landed, she listened to the screams of her comrades who ran to where they fell, and she could only hope that Rook would come to a better end than this.

When she had counted the last remaining prisoner, and Rook was not among them, she hesitated and hoped.

Please, please, please.

And then she heard him—she recognised that stubborn roar. She demanded the absent gods carry him to a greater place, but alas, in the darkness, she only heard his cry nearby, and she called for him, until suddenly there was stillness.

And the town became silent for a time.

Until the rumble of war rose in the distance one last time, and she took that anguish, fear, horror and hate and went to stand along the front of the wall with the rest of her comrades as the invading army surged down towards Raven Rock.

"This is the end," she whispered as those around her called for defiance, for honour, for all manner of impressive things. Rua accepted her fate, gruesome as it would be. As long as she took as many invaders' lives as she could along the way, her final journey would be welcomed. "For you, Rook, and for you, dear Andreas," she whispered, ready to meet her comrades in the dark beyond.

And in the darkness, her lost ones waited with glass in hand, ready to welcome her in.

Devitt placed his burning torch back upon its cradle at his feet. He might have desired to stand in darkness with his weapon raised, might have preferred to skip away unseen. The body below the wall had long since stopped moving, and there was little he could do to help the man. Devitt thought it no kind of end for anyone. He imagined the terrible fear each prisoner must have felt while dropping to the ground, and knew this was a cruelty most vile.

"You brutal bitch," he muttered, hating himself ever so,

swallowing his guilt, lest it take his soul. Perhaps, were he a braver and more selfish man, he might have looked to the sword in his hands as a way of repaying his horrors to all who had committed these foul deeds. As it was, Devitt had greater things to worry about than the mere desire to kill Aurora where she stood.

Besides, from where Devitt stood, there would be far too many fiends in between them, anyway. Attempting to kill her was a sure way to end up dead. He'd seen that for himself.

Devitt had never felt more alone in the world than he did now, watching the turning of the tide and the approach of the end. He smelled it in the wind, and he saw it in the terror around him. His doomed comrades were fierce and heroic but too stubborn to know any better. As he fought the desire to step from the wall, each of them dug in and awaited the wave as it surged from the forest all at once.

Oh god.

"To arms," he heard people cry as Aurora and her entire army announced themselves. They rushed from the dark towards the dark. Some held torches to light their way, but it didn't matter. They knew the way. They'd all been here before.

The army came not as a disciplined beast, relying on tactics and a plan, but like a rabid bear, without care or thought. Perhaps they had caught the fury of Aurora's wildness—a terrifying thing, really.

The mounts charged ahead first. Their riders carried javelins, and they raced up along the wall from every side, flinging these wooden missiles upon the defenders, causing all manner of havoc. Those curs without javelins chose to bring their mounts close along the wall, where they leapt from their horses' backs and took hold along the top where no defender stood. In a few frantic breaths, the wall became the finish line between desperate defenders holding the line and scrambling invaders, desperate to break it.

And break it they did.

As the Riders went invading, countless foot soldiers surged from the treeline. Some carried hooks like before, and Devitt's heart dropped as he saw a hundred or more long wooden siege ladders, raised and nearing the wall, each carried by three fiends. The ladder-bearers charged along the wall, placing and climbing, screaming and cursing, killing and dying.

Winning.

Another wave of attackers surged down upon the front gate, and the entire wall resembled a frenzied hive of warfare.

Clunk.

Devitt looked down in horror to see that a ladder was braced up at his feet, and immediately, a brazen fiend appeared, screaming and swinging, and Devitt could only hack at the man until he knocked him free. By then, though, it was already over. Or felt as such. All along the walls, the invading army flooded over, and his comrades held and died where they stood. Aye, they were brave, and he considered them kin and worthy of a bard sonnet or historic tale delivered by a wise old master, but in truth, after this night, no one would ever speak their names again. It was a sobering thing to realise the inevitability of nothingness. An awful thing to think of it while delivering a killing blow to a vile bastard, screaming as he died.

Not like this.

He stood for as long as he could, killing and holding, but the attackers were endless, and after a time, Devitt simply gave up the fight, not out of cowardice but out of necessity.

I must do this.

When he spied a break in the charge, Devitt simply

slipped from the wall, using the violence and chaos as a shield as he escaped this nightmare. He dropped and kept running. No one followed, and it was a blessing. The longer his escape went unnoticed, the further he could flee without the threat of being followed.

The invaders poured through the streets, screaming and hunting, charging through buildings and setting fires where they could. The screams at the healers' bay were worse, and Devitt closed his eyes and ears to such awfulness. Oh, aye, the defenders didn't allow the attackers free rein; some brave souls followed after, hunting them down. And indeed, were anyone to notice his escaping, they would think him hunting too. He didn't care, regardless. He had greater things on his mind.

Goodbye, Raven Rock.

Near the centre of the town, he came upon a terrible thing. Outside his house stood little Jak, screaming as loud as any war cry. The sound drew his attention above all the other thundering noises. And why wouldn't he scream? It was all he could do, with his mother lying in a pool of blood while his father struggled against an invading cur. Devitt barely knew Jak's parents, apart from them being neither decent thieves nor battle-worn defenders. They ran the tavern, but dealing with troublesome, drunken bandits hadn't prepared them at all for an attack like this one. Though large and sturdy, Jak's father was no match in skill to the far smaller woman, who ducked his clumsy attempts at swordplay before she drove her blade thrice into his impressive belly.

Devitt had never thought himself capable or interested enough to be a father, but instinct took him, and he never hesitated. He attacked her from behind as she turned to tower over the boy, pulling at her long blonde hair while stabbing ferociously at her. It was the easiest kill of the day, all to the echoes of the boy's terrified screams.

"Hush, little one," he mumbled, tending to Jak's father and finding him gone. It was the same with his mother, too. A cruel thing to be orphaned in a brief few moments. A crueller thing to be present as it occurred.

"Mum… Dad…" the boy howled and stood against the wall, frozen, with eyes upon his dead father. Around his shoulders was a little pack. No doubt, they had chosen to flee at the end. A tragedy they hadn't left a little sooner.

"Come here, Jak," Devitt said, trying to lead the boy away from their bodies, but he wouldn't budge.

He grabbed the boy, hoisted him up and began running. Jak did not fight, but he screamed something terrible. Through the streets they ran, announcing themselves with every wail from the child, and truly, Devitt considered knocking the boy out cold—a vile thing, but necessary if he couldn't calm him down.

Running as fast as he could with his screaming burden, Devitt eventually turned the corner and began to sprint towards the entrance to the tunnel.

A few remaining guards stood at its entrance, and he thought them as heroic as those standing the wall. Around them were the bodies of foolish attackers who had charged them and met either a rain of arrows or the sharp ends of the guards' pikes.

Devitt and Jak weren't alone. A few other bandits, most with children, were busy climbing down the tunnel into the darkness beyond. No doubt, they would seek safety in Adawan, but Devitt had little interest in journeying to such a place. He would go to the Deep North, he had decided. He'd even told Kaya, who thought him a fool. It was no matter. Love was love, and his love was not to her liking. Not anymore. But he would miss her regardless. This, too, was no matter.

War would never come to the Deep North, he imagined. It was a precarious route to travel with a child, but no army would get through at any great pace. Staying ahead of any army seemed a mighty fine idea at that moment.

As did getting into that tunnel and getting gone from here.

The guards did their duty well, as a couple of attackers appeared from the darkness and charged them down. The guards spread out, aiming their bows, and released and killed before swiftly recovering the arrows for further use. They did it as though it was the most leisurely part of their day—and perhaps, to them, it was.

As Devitt approached them, they glared at the screaming boy.

"Devitt, sir, she still remains," one of the guards said, pointing to the tunnel's open entrance. A delicate weight was lifted from his chest, but not so much that it made carrying the boy any easier.

"Thank you, my friends," Devitt offered, shifting his grip on the squirming, crying boy.

"Sir, you can't go through there with the boy screaming like that."

It was a fair point, and Devitt produced a handkerchief from his pocket. The guard nodded grimly.

A moment later, the boy's shrill cries were bettered by a boom of thunder from the front of the gate, and Devitt's heart dropped again.

That cannot be good at all.

A second boom rang out in the night, and the guard quickly ushered the boy and the wary council member down into the dark tunnel.

"Fuk it," Devitt hissed, nearly slipping off the ladder as he dropped down to the floor of the tunnel.

"You said the bad word," a voice from the dark muttered.

"I did, Whisper," Devitt replied. "I'm sorry."

Whisper wasn't listening. She was already upon Jak, hugging him as only a soulmate could and tearing the handkerchief away from his mouth. Through tragedy and terror, Devitt didn't wonder if these two little ones weren't destined to always be together. He did not think how terrifying caring for two children might be, and he didn't want to think of it either.

"My mum and dad went to the dark," Jak said, then began to weep again. Whisper didn't let go of him. It seemed to work.

"So did mine," Whisper insisted. "They went sooner, and they'll know what to do now." Her voice turned soft. "They will look after your parents when they get there," she added, hugging Jak, who did not fight her hold.

"I want them to look after me."

"It's alright. Devitt will look after us now."

"Yes, I will," Devitt said gently.

Whisper released the little boy. "You must stay quiet, Jak. Or else they'll find us when we sneak away," she insisted, and Jak wiped his tears and nodded.

Whisper looked to Devitt, smiling in the dim light. "I waited as everyone went past; I knew you would come for me," she said, and Devitt squeezed her hand. She'd chosen him as her guardian; he didn't know why. He couldn't argue against it either. Acting as her father these last days had been the finest time of his life. He didn't know what to do but pledged to save her. It was a good pledge. He pledged to do everything to give her and Jak the entire world. That, too, was a good pledge.

"Good girl. Grab your pack, and we will march from this place."

By the time they reached the exit and slipped through its silent concealed hatch, the roar of Raven Rock had reached its crescendo. Devitt refused to look back. Instead, he took the childrens' hands and followed the tracks taken by the lucky ones who had gone before him.

Goodbye, Kaya.

Forgive me.

"On to the Deep North," he pledged.

It was a good pledge.

————

We are winning.

No.

That's not true.

We are not entirely losing as we once were.

That made sense to Simeon, so he went with it, despite the horrors at the front of the gate.

"We are holding them," he roared, which was probably more accurate. Simeon had never been more frightened in his life. He'd also never felt as alive, either. He was art in motion, and his masterpiece was battle. He might have said as much to Daisy as they lay together after this final battle. And it was the final battle. And they would lie together. And he would speak poetry in her ear, for she loved that shit. And he, well, he loved her.

This is not the end of the world.

I will save us both.

It was a terrible pledge.

But he didn't know that yet.

At first, when those brutes had driven down upon the

gate, he had despaired like everyone else. Hard not to as they surged up and over the wall, killing everyone and all.

But like a master pugilist caught with a cold punch in the opening bout, they caught their wind, started punching back and discovered a belly far softer than it had first appeared.

Looking around, he could see that the remaining defenders were paltry in number but plentiful in guts, hardness and brutality. They were worth ten to every attacker on a ladder. They had better-suited skills, greater determination and a home to defend stubbornly. Such things mattered far more in war than sheer numbers.

"Keep going, you legends," he screamed in a voice that seemed to belong less to his timid self and more to a fiend built for murder and pillaging. He had never understood the measure of himself until these last few days. Never recognised the benefit of honour and bravery either. It was an unsettling thing, but intriguing.

As was the constant flow of killing on the wall. It did not feel like war, this battle. It felt like a glorious massacre, and Simeon thought himself a right bloodthirsty fiend altogether. His pike felt unnaturally heavy and slippery in his hands. Every time he drove that bastard weapon into one of the fiends, every time he tore through skin and muscle, bone and organ, he felt like a machine a-rolling. Never stopping, no matter the labour or the terror. He killed and led upon the wall, and they followed.

Because no one was better suited to the job.

"Is this all there is?" Simeon demanded in mock triumph. Perhaps, were his comrades to cast a glance at his bloody weapon's tip, they might see how much it quivered in his hands.

Just the adrenaline.

Instead, they roared with him and went to killing as

efficiently as he did. And those bastards kept a-coming. He had lost count long ago of the murders to his name, though it was a mighty number. Some beside him shouted tallies, and he knew they were nothing to his crimes. And that was fine. That was how it was in war. And massacres, too. He wanted to kill them all. And they probably felt the same. It was nothing personal.

He had already lost three brothers of the wall upon this final charge, and each loss was a harrowing thing. They had been pulled from the top as they lunged forward by eager attacking hands. Those hands were treacherous things, and when they pulled as one, they were enough to unseat the most secure of defenders. It was no way to be taken, he thought bitterly, looking to the mass of dead in the shadows below.

Though Daisy stood with him, it wasn't on her he kept his eye. It was Silas. The cur held the other front of the wall. And he held it well.

As they had all during the siege, they balanced each other perfectly. Though Simeon despised him for all he was, he marvelled at his fierceness. Silas never appeared to tire once there was killing to be done, and indeed, with both groups of their followers fighting together, Simeon was inclined to believe no man was fierce enough to kill Silas.

The absent gods thought so, too.

Even if they, too, despised the man.

"What else do you have?" Simeon demanded of the fiends that attacked. He knew they understood. "You understand me. Don't you?" he roared, and really, the attackers offered little suggestion either way. They simply continued to climb and die.

"Come on. Just tell me. No one else is listening. What else do you have?"

It was a fair question.

They had more.

One more, in fact.

The last of the siege weapons rolled through the trees and began to pick up speed.

"Oh," cried Simeon, wishing he had a flaming lantern, although he was not confident it would make any difference. "I suppose they have that."

Its shaft was the length of a thick, seeping oak.

Made from one as well.

Like a clenched wooden fist, it rumbled forward upon massive heavy wheels, built for sturdiness but also speed, as dozens drove the ramming beast forward. The ground quaked, and a cold knowing came upon Simeon as he understood that this was the end.

Fuk me. Now what?

He edged along the wall as the beast neared; the attackers fell away lest they be dragged along by the beast or crushed beneath its charge.

"Be ready, my comrades," Simeon cried, lest the monster's appearance take their heart and send them running. He grabbed his pike tightly and stood up beside Silas. No better fiend to hold the line with, he decided at the end.

And besides, if any curs could lead a defiant defence, it was them. Honour be damned.

Enemy of my enemy and all that spitting nonsense.

And then the ramming beast struck.

The wall shook with the force of it, and the gates boomed loudly as they were knocked nearly free of their moorings but miraculously held. The siege weapon bounced backwards through the attackers, crushing many under its wheels.

Perhaps it was exhaustion, drunkenness or even bad luck, but Silas tumbled forward and nearly went with them.

Let him die.

It was instinct that moved Simeon as he leapt upon him and held him away from the fall and certain death below. "I have you, cur," Simeon cried, dragging the scrambling defender back to sturdier ground. "That's twice now I've saved you."

"You think us even, so?" Silas snarled, his voice full of hate.

As the ramming beast was pulled back through the battlefield, Simeon's comrades plunged their pikes down upon those attempting to move it. Silas's comrades fired arrow after arrow down upon the curs.

We fight well together.

Simeon stepped between both groups of defenders, keeping his hand upon Silas's shoulders so all could see. Even though they hated each other, they might still unite as brothers and win the day.

Stronger.

"Do you see how we all can do this, friends?" he cried as the ramming beast began its next charge, and he steadied himself, just in case. He wasn't afraid; he believed he would survive this with a victory to his name. He only needed them to believe the same. They gazed to him for leadership. And why not? Kaya was their leader, but she was diminished since Gray, since Aimee, and since failing to kill Aurora, too.

He could lead, and they would follow.

Fiercer.

"All of us are exactly the same," he continued, and the words began to flow easily. He gripped Silas tightly as the beast hammered the gate again with just as much force, yet once again the wall and gate held.

Braver.

He could see both groups of defenders, his and Silas's,

looking at each other. And he wondered did they realise, at the end, that there was no difference between them?

"That's it, my friends. We together can hold these bastards all night."

Some of his comrades cheered.

"Are you with me?"

A few were. They said as much with a few cries.

"Come on, you legends. Are you all with me?" he demanded, and more cheered.

Even a few of Silas's did too.

"We will win this," he declared, and they believed in it, too.

United.

It was Simeon's finest moment ever. He raised his arm and Silas's in the air. Defiant and proud. They would win. He was sure of it—until Silas grabbed him roughly and heaved him over the edge into the waiting arms of a thousand and one killers to die a grisly death.

———

The moment held still, and Daisy with it. Frozen, lost, destroyed. She fell to her knees as Simeon fell to his death. The absent gods had played their cruel hand, and it was the end of the world. She might have ended herself in that moment, plunging her dagger into her chest or slicing her wrists deep and long and running upon the man who killed her, before ripping his fuken throat from his fuken neck in her final fuken moments.

Everything held in a cruel stillness as though the war wasn't turning, as though the fiends weren't knocking at the door, asking to come on in. In that moment, they would have been welcome.

Why?

Because Silas had destroyed her life, and now he had destroyed her soul. He did not laugh; he did not cheer. No one did. He merely looked over the edge at his fallen victim, and it was too much.

Why?

Silas had never loved her. This, she'd always known. He'd merely loved destroying her, and a curse upon her weak will, she had allowed him to. Perhaps a child might have stirred her to life, might have allowed her to see past the bastard she lay with, lived with, bled with and died with.

As it was, the awkward flirtation all those many years ago with a right charming cad had stirred her from within. How could she not have fallen in love with such a disaster? Simeon, by contrast, had thrown caution to the end and owned his failures as though they were treasures to be stolen. He had offered her kindness, loyalty, comfort and devotion. He'd offered his soul and demanded simple desire in return. He had made her fall for him, and he had fallen for her against his own better judgements. He was the best of them all, really, mostly because he didn't know it.

And I killed him for it.

She wanted to collapse where she stood, give up and cower beneath Silas's cruel glare and vengeful hate. She wanted to weep loud enough that even Aurora would hear her anguish and cease the assault, lest the gods condemn her for cruelty beyond the realms of acceptability.

But also, deep down, where the real part of her hid away in a cage of her own making, she felt a breaking of the bars. An emergence of fire. A spark against the night.

"You animal," she snarled, and as that spark grew to a fire most justified, she felt her fingers tingle, felt her limbs strengthen, felt that fire burn a raging hate, and oh, she despised the brute in front of her—despised his very soul. She looked through him and fought that urge to recoil from his fists, his gaze and his vileness.

"May he burn in fire, you spitting whore," Silas roared, and she could only step to him. Eager to strike, to punish, to avenge.

Then, the battering ram thundered through the battlefield one last time, and she barely noticed. Even when it reared up and took those legendary gates from their moorings and drove them back into the town.

Around her rose screams of terror and grief, and she was suddenly jolted back to the present. There was a mighty rumble and roar as the attackers on the other side of the wall rolled the ram back into position, while those who assailed the wall fell upon the growing gap, and at last the town of Raven Rock fell.

"So will you burn, cur," Daisy cried and ran to Silas. For a breath, she remembered their courting so long ago. Back when she had a soul, not the pitiful husk that lay within her now, but a life force that had fuelled her will and desires. She did not care that she warned Silas at the end, nor what the defence of Raven Rock would suffer without him standing tall. She didn't care.

He'd killed her by killing Simeon.

He'd die for the act.

It wasn't the finest attack. It didn't need to be. She heaved her pike in her arms and rushed him—just as he saw her intentions.

"Fuk you, whore—"

She sent that pike right through his belly and left him to die in ruin.

Spinning towards the wall, she looked at the bodies below and yearned to be with her man at the end. She heard their screams behind her. They called for her, for him, some even for Simeon, but none of it mattered. This was the end.

Stepping over the edge of the wall, she dropped into the midst of the attackers below. She drew her blade as she did, swinging and slicing and killing and missing. Perhaps it was sheer luck that she survived those first few bloody moments. Perhaps it was the will of the absent gods that the gates fell in that moment, too, for their eyes were turned as one towards the inviting entrance, their swords drawn away from feminine assassins appearing from the sky, killing all who failed to notice her.

Perhaps she was fated to die.

Perhaps she deserved to die.

Perhaps, in the retelling of her tale, she *would* die.

A fitting end for young lovers who had given everything for each other.

But she didn't die.

And neither had he.

"What the fuk are you doing?" Simeon cried behind her. She whirled to see her love still standing, dug in, swinging and living and killing and living and screaming and living and fuken living.

Let this be real.

Around him were the bodies of those who hadn't noticed the fiend fall among them. Or, if they had, they'd considered him already dead before he landed. Or perhaps they hadn't looked closely at his armour to see his allegiance. In the dark, who knew who one's enemy was? No matter the reason, it was a miracle, and she took it as such. All around them, soldiers surged and charged, unaware they passed by two perfectly acceptable victims so close to the open gate.

The two lovers were nearly dragged along in the crush of attackers, but Daisy grabbed for Simeon and pulled him back to the spot near the wall where he'd made a perfectly acceptable defence with little more than a sword and shield.

"What are you doing?" he repeated, but she didn't answer. Though the fates had granted them a breath, it wouldn't take long for everything to go terribly wrong. Daisy dragged her man up along the wall, through the surging crowd, towards the corner, towards open ground. Ducking low, they growled as though in war, as though attacking, as though they were Southern, and he fought her only when they reached the edge of the battle.

"Whisht," she snapped. Around them, the soldiers thinned out. The mounted warriors were all screaming in victory, not giving the two intruders so much as a glance, and Daisy and Simeon braced themselves for the last leg of their flight.

Gripping each other's hands tightly, they sprinted, and they were thieves in a crowded tavern, there for a flash and gone the next.

We are just going to dash right out of here.

Nothing to see here.

The ground under their feet softened, the thunder lessened, and suddenly they were alone. Certainly, a few foreign voices shouted their way, but no fiend charged them down; no vile witch appeared and gutted them.

"We cannot abandon the town," he said eventually, but she continued to drag him through the trees where they had been just a few days before. There was no line of hunters waiting though, this time, was there? There was only blissful silence, like the quiet after a storm.

"The town is lost," she lamented, spinning him around so he might see the loss and realise the end was upon them. Silas had granted them escape in his last act, she reflected grimly. *May he burn for it.* "But this is not our end," she pledged, and it was a good pledge.

She pulled him to her, and they kissed for a glorious, sorrowful moment.

"So lead us to safety, my love," he whispered.

"As you wish, my darling."

———

"Fuk."

Silas had seen enough in his life to know it was a fatal blow. He wished she'd plunged the pike a little higher, right through his heart. Spill him dry and be done with him. Instead, she had merely wounded him enough that he took a breath, died a little, took another breath, and there was piss all anybody could do about it.

A fine strike it was and all, you wench.

The pike held him up, pinned him in place, and though his knees demanded it, he could not fall. He could only look forward as all around him stood frozen in shock, watching as their greatest warrior breathed his last, felled by one of their own.

I told you she would be the death of me.

In the same way, he could only look on as Daisy, his once beloved, had stepped to her death. He had reached for her as she dropped but been pinned by the pike. It was strange to see her alive and full of fire at the end, and then, in a blink, gone into the eager jaws of death.

Choosing death over facing him was the final act of cruelty on her part, and he hated her more now than he ever had before. He was glad she had died. He only wished Simeon could have seen her die as he had. That was the type of justice he deserved.

Killing me wasn't enough, was it, darling mine?

"Get him some help," a voice cried, and he tried weakly

to look around. A hard thing with the blade's sharp tip tearing him inside out. His comrades appeared at his side. He had never felt more beaten, more pathetic.

"Let him burn," a second voice howled, and he recognised the man as Simeon's comrade. They few remaining brutes stood to one side, watching his downfall, and he truly hated them all as well.

They turned from defending the wall just to watch him, and Silas died a little more.

I don't deserve this agony.

Both groups argued as he died in the midst of them.

Both groups avoided the thunder below.

Both groups ignored the attacking fiends as they surged through the broken gates.

"You are alright, Silas. We have you," a voice said soothingly, and he reached for his flask in his pocket. A difficult thing with a pike pinning the front of his coat so tight. He wanted a drink. He also wanted to live. More than that, he wanted to fight and kill.

Not like this.

Still, they argued, and all was lost, and Silas spat blood from his mouth.

"He's a murderer," a spokesman for Simeon's side declared.

"Simeon had it coming," countered one of Silas's better generals. Though his mind was fading, with the pain taking his sanity, Silas agreed with that notion.

"Silas had it coming more than anyone."

Did I really, though?

"Well, so did that murdering whore, Daisy."

"She was justified, you cur."

Things started to take a precarious turn, and still, below them, the fiends surged through into the town, assailing the paltry few who stood at the gates and were swallowed up beneath the first wave. Perhaps, had the defenders held with the same discipline, heroism and ungodly luck, they might have stood at the gate and held those bastards.

Alas, they were too busy hating their own kin and proving themselves better than their brother or sister.

"Daisy was a fuken tramp."

"Daisy was the best of us."

"They said the same about your mother, but we all knew better."

"My mother was a saint."

"Your mother was no saint."

"You'd best watch your mouth."

"I said the same to your mother… when she was down on her knees."

"I'll kill you and all."

"I'll fuken kill every last fuken one of you."

Silas had enough. As both groups gave up the defence and drew blades, he collapsed on the ground between them. The agony was too much, the call of death too irresistible. But most of all, perhaps, the terrible truth of where hatred led killed him as cruelly as a blade through flesh.

With all his strength, he heaved the barbed tip from his belly and left it to drop to the fiends below. The agony was maddening, and he could do little more than wad his scarf into the fist-sized hole and wriggle his feet painfully over the edge. Grimacing, he gazed at the attackers below.

Behind him, his comrades went to war, stabbing and screaming, maddened by their leaders' last stand. For just a breath, Silas considered Simeon's foolish words of faux heroism, and he hated the bastard, even if he admired his attempt to convince the defenders they might live.

I did all of this.

It was a sobering thought, and his body began to tremble, such was the trauma he had suffered. Such was the sudden guilt. With shaking hands and no pike pinning his coat, he reached in, removed his flask, unscrewed the top and drank deeply of the last beverage he'd ever have.

I have only hate to drive me.

Beside him, a woman fell, gasping and lost, a blade cleaved halfway through her skull. She stared past him, and he was unmoved, even if she had once furrowed with him like a champion. None of it mattered anymore. Not even the searing pain that took his mind.

Drinking his fill and tossing the flask away, he grabbed his battle axe and simply let himself drop to the army below him. He had no plan beyond swinging and killing. It was all he could do, even as his comrades above killed themselves and wasted their wretched lives at the worst possible moment.

Hitting the ground beside the gate, he bit away the pain, the sorrow, the horror and the fear, then mustered all his hate and delivered a blow upon an attacker. And then upon another. He roared with weakening lungs, swung with lessening limbs, and stumbled through the crowd, dying and killing, hating and fading until, at the far edge of the crowd, he saw the witch. She was still outside the town, strolling upon the plundered, ruined grounds as though wandering with a lover on a hot summer's eve.

"Aurora," he cried, and she looked over at him, wide-eyed, delighted with his audacity. The crowd parted even as they surged past, killing and maiming all before them. "I must end you," he roared, and his voice became a whisper as he stumbled towards her, swinging and missing, and then he was slipping on unsteady feet. His bowels released, and he shat his pants, pissing freely for any and all to see were they to gaze that way, and at last his body failed him completely.

Please, please, not like this.

But it was exactly like this.

He dropped to a knee as she walked to him, and suddenly, his battle axe clattered loudly to the ground, and his vision faded. He saw darkness and silence, and he saw her gaze with interest at him as he fell completely, never to rise again.

She kicked at his chest as he fell still, and then she kicked at his axe, and he was helpless to prevent her.

Then, shrugging, she left him and walked into the town, victorious, and Silas of Raven Rock died alone.

32

KAYA

*F**ailure, failure, fuken failure.***
This was the end, and Kaya could take no more. She fell to her knees at the end of the world, for she was unable to stop the ruin—unwilling to, either. She was broken, beaten, and truly lost.

She thought about her actions these last few days and believed herself a complete failure.

Belief.

She'd also believed they might hold. Believed they might even beat back the inevitable night. Believed they might slay that whore and come out grinning. But she had brought down a fine ruin upon this dreadful place. Forget belief. It had doomed them all.

She had lost her voice. In truth, she could still scream and spit and lead, but every word she spoke was empty. Had been for a time. She had tried to gather those cursed words together as though preparing for a funeral, and as once before, they never came. She was a shadow of the goddess of war she had once been.

It was Devitt who had broken her heart outright. Well, he

421

had broken whatever remained of that crust that still beat a little life into her aching limbs. Like the thief he was, in the dark of night he had slipped free and escaped the line. Escaped the town. Escaped her. Left her behind. And she, injured and broken, still stood.

Alone.

A pox upon your family, Devitt.

Fuk you.

Fuk you.

Take me with you.

With a screeching roar that travelled for miles in every direction, the gate gave way to the invaders' thousand-strong menace. As it did, her own people ate themselves. Cut and murdered each other, embracing hate over rationality, and it was a dreadful thing.

What type of leader allows comrades to turn upon each other as they did? She wondered and knew the answer.

Would you have done so, Andreas?

Not a chance.

Andreas would have seen that anger coming days ago and miles before. He would have kept those fools far apart until the end, when he alone would have harnessed their rage into something volatile and brilliant.

Andreas's Raven Rock would have held firm and won the day.

Across from her, only Rua had fought admirably. Perhaps, with no chains upon her arms, she was grateful for a little retribution.

Kaya had looked on as Silas dropped to the ground, and she had instinctively dropped with him. It was that or wait for the curs to find a ladder and come hunting her down. Silas was fierce and brave, even at the end. She did not stand with him, though. She left him to die in a wet roar.

Instead, she walked from the battle, hunched, shoulders dropped, head bowed.

The screams behind deepened as the Rock was taken in full, and the last defender was dropped, and still, she would not run. She simply walked to the tunnel, accepting her death were it to creep up behind her and rip her throat out.

I deserve this.

To her surprise, the guards still stood proud at the entrance, weapons raised, ever ready for death and carnage. They called to her as she approached, and she could only wave weakly.

"What has happened? There are no more Runners coming, though?" a guard asked. She couldn't remember his name, but at this late hour, it didn't matter. She didn't care.

"The gate has fallen. We have only moments before an army comes charging through these streets," she insisted, and they drew their blades, ready to attack, ready to throw their lives into the wind.

"Is there any more fighting up at the gate?" another guard asked.

"All are lost who sail these seas," she said, and they dropped their heads for the fallen, for their comrades, for their friends, for their families. For Raven Rock.

"What will you have us do?"

She thought them brave and honourable. They were deserving of a better leader than she. Perhaps there might still be an accord if these fiends were upon the wall, standing between the two warring factions. A defence. A line to hold.

"Get yourselves from this place. Save yourselves, for you have earned it," she instructed. It was the only pleasant order she'd given during this entire siege. And grudgingly, they did as she bade, dropping down into the tunnel and racing away through the dark, eager to escape the coming threat, leaving the Rock empty of any defence.

Only she, the broken fool, remained, and she was the last to leave. A fitting thing as well. With no lights to guide the way, she would stay as long as she needed should a straggler in need of a miracle come running around the corner. Moments passed, and no fiend or friend followed after, and Kaya thought herself a right wicked rat upon the sinking ship at the end.

She stayed longer than she should have, humming a song of sorrow to herself. It was all she could do before climbing into the tunnel herself, leaving the lid behind. Let the fiends come a-hunting her. Let them know they hadn't got everyone. It was a small victory.

Her stitches held, but she did not run. She ambled through the dark tunnel, allowing her fingers to graze the perfectly smooth surface on either side. It was as intimate a goodbye as she would allow. Above, she could hear the many hooves and feet as the invaders stomped all over her town, and her heart felt a dreary heaviness.

When she emerged from the tunnel, she slid the door closed behind her, sealing it as it did. She did not follow the well-trodden path either. She walked through the forest, following her instincts, and she felt herself coming alive as she did.

She began to walk more briskly and then broke into a jog as she came upon the near-abandoned camp. She thought of Rua and Rook, taken by surprise, and gathered her wits about her. She moved deliberately and sought out one solitary tent —the largest one of them all, in fact—and, spying it eventually, she felt her heart began to beat in excitement. Gliding in past the docile guards, confident in their own safety, she slipped inside Aurora's tent.

"Kaya," the child cried from her bindings, and Kaya's heart leapt and fell at the same moment. "Is it over? Did we win?"

"Little one," she whispered, embracing the child, knowing the value of every touch at the end of the world. "All is lost."

Aimee couldn't reciprocate the hug, for her bindings were too tight. Each limb was wrapped in chains and secured with a lock. She was laid out upon a heavy stone slab too heavy to break or move. The chains were the finest steel, unbreakable even by a heavily driven battle axe. But it was the locks that ruined Kaya's hope.

She did not recognise their construction—they were far more advanced than anything she'd ever tended to.

"I cannot break these," she whispered, and her tears fell free.

"Of course you can."

She really couldn't, and the child's faith in her was crushing.

She took her three pins from a little pouch and began to tinker with the first stubborn piece at Aimee's ankle. A dark thought, but were she to free the girl's ankles in some way, were there no further time, she could slice the girl's thumbs free of her hand and slip her out. A terrible fate for a child and a worse one for a thief. But better than the alternative.

She immediately broke a pin.

"Oh no," she moaned, pulling the metal shard free and hating it. Not even Rook would be able to accomplish such a thing, she knew, and distantly, she heard the rumble of a thousand bad things returning.

Believe.

"It's alright, Kaya," Aimee said, and she was weeping in silence.

"I will try, little one."

She fumbled and felt a turn in a tumbler; ever so gently, she eased the pin in further.

And broke it, too.

She looked around, imagining a steel bar thin enough to pry the metal and sturdy enough to last as she tended to the four different pieces, but really, she knew there was no such tool, and no time. It wasn't fair. None of it.

"Kaya, I hear them returning."

"I do, too, little one."

She went to work on that first lock again, and this time she eased it more gently than she'd ever worked a lock in her life. Her fingers did not shake, and her heart did not beat swiftly; she merely allowed her instincts to complete the task as any master lockbreaker would. The chains clinked loudly, and she felt success, felt for more, and dared to breathe as the lock began to ease itself open.

And the last pin snapped.

She stifled her scream, placed her arm over her mouth and wailed.

"I'm sorry, I'm sorry, little one," she wept, and the rumble of Riders entering the camp shook her from her stupor. Decided her fate, and Aimee's too.

"It's alright, my sister," Aimee said, and she was so brave.

"I will follow wherever you are taken; I will find a way to release you as you march."

"That is a rightly stupid idea, Kaya. Leave me—go now," Aimee said, and Kaya could only embrace her one last time, lest a Rider come through the tent flap and put her to death there and then.

"I can't leave you."

"Our people need to be warned; those who survived need a leader like you."

"I won't leave you."

"Dear Kaya, I love you with all my heart. Leave me behind, lest I scream an alarm," Aimee warned, and Kaya broke from her.

"We will meet again," Kaya pledged. It seemed a good pledge.

"No, we will not. Go now, and live well," Aimee whispered and turned from her, leaving Kaya to kiss her forehead before slipping out of the tent, out through the camp, into the green and disappearing forever.

She had intended to journey to the Deep North, but the child's words played in her mind. If ever they were to meet again, that was not the place to find her.

"Find me, little one," she whispered to the wind, and, letting one foot follow the next, turned east towards the largest bandit sanctuary. There, she could fall in among those with greater wills and stronger minds, those who deserved to lead. Kaya could watch from afar and play little part in it.

This she pledged as she trudged away from true horror.

It was a terrible pledge.

33

AURORA

Her name was Aurora, and she liked to kill. She also liked to end things on a high, like a fine tale sung by a skilled bard.

This felt like no such high. This felt like a defeat, even though she felt just marvellous about herself. Perhaps it was her new dress.

She eased the woman onto her side and undid the belt holding everything together. It was a delicate task, and she was as careful as possible. She'd already undone the buttons, so removing the dress was no difficult matter at all.

"Thank you so much for this, Rua," she whispered, but Rua said nothing. She merely stared at the wall. It was a bit of a distance away. Not a nice wall at all. Rua must have thought so, too, at the time. "Oh, and thank you for not bleeding on it either," she added, leaning close to the woman, who turned with Aurora's every careful manoeuvre.

Rua again said nothing. She did bleed, though. A few slow drops slid from her mouth; all manner of nasty things had occurred in her head when she landed on it. Or perhaps she was driven down by a heavy armoured man as he fell upon her. Whatever had happened, Aurora appreciated it.

"There we go," she said, easing the woman's bosom from the front of the dress and slipping the wonderful piece over her head.

"Bet you didn't think I'd remember, did you?"

Rua hadn't thought she would at all, and that was fine.

Stripping off her own less impressive gown, Aurora sat in the dark, enjoying the cool air on her naked skin. It was nice to be cool after such a long day in a sweaty gown. She didn't need undergarments for a night like this, and she knew her new dress would feel even better without a garment getting in its leathery way.

Perfect.

"By the way, I didn't see Kaya on my travels. Did you?" No answer. "Ah, it's a small matter. Living with such torment is probably a better fate for her. A crueller one," she suggested conspiratorially, thinking of the tunnel in the centre of the town. She fought a giggle. She thought it a wonderful thing that they had escaped as they had, and she hadn't bothered climbing down after any of the brazen brave bandits who bolted. It was a typical act on Kaya's part, fleeing like that when the end occurred.

"I think she's a bit of a bitch. What do you think?"

Rua obviously agreed but stayed silent. It was a classy move on her part, and Aurora respected her that little bit more. Aurora edged her own gown over the woman's head and pulled it down before beginning to button up her modesty.

"I'm sure you've seen the fires they lit," Aurora muttered. She could have apologised, but where did one begin to find the words? "Look, Rua, some of my kin are rightly zealous about Uden's acts, no matter what I say." Now Rua was listening. Aurora was sure she had an issue with it, but she held her cooling tongue. She was a fine comrade altogether. Aurora leaned in close and whispered, "Thankfully, there are no surviving women, but I had to allow them to burn the dead ones… I hope that's alright."

Aurora looked around at the settling town and loved it ever so, even if it had torn her army apart, challenged her soul and stirred thoughts better kept deep below.

Like deceiving a god.

"Don't be like that, Rua. I'll keep you hidden all snug in the corner, and I've ordered them to cease burning the rest of the buildings." She shrugged, looking into the dark. She could see a few buildings still burning, and thought that a fair result for both sides. "With a little luck, they'll not see you lying here at all." This part of the wall was rightly dark. It was the best she could do under the circumstances. She was certain Rua appreciated it.

"What a night, eh?"

Rua said nothing—a fair point.

They had no interest in sacking the town for wealth. That wasn't their command or their reasoning either. They had come only to kill. Leave the looting to the crows and scroungers. The town had already fallen. There was so little left to do, for she'd also forbidden the Riders from scrawling Uden's name upon any of the walls. That was out of self-preservation, in truth. She had defied the god in finishing off the town. Best not to rub her god's name in his face when she explained her actions—saying that, who knew what those Riders might do, with her back turned as she tried on a new dress?

And what a dress.

Standing up, she stretched wonderfully and edged the

dress down over her slim body; it was a rather snug and comfortable fit.

"You had good hips," she said, and Rua simply looked to the wall, where her neck held her head at a strange, alluring angle. Aurora would very much like to find her head at such an angle someday. A little more blood from her mouth, please.

"Well, it has been quite the time, dear Rua. I'm delighted I was able to see you at the end," she said before bending down and kissing the girl on the lips. She tasted the blood and felt the cooling skin, and she eased that mouth open a little more and touched her tongue to Rua's.

Bliss.

"You don't mind, do you?"

Rua didn't seem to mind.

"Because I'll stop right now if you want me to."

Rua made no effort to defy her, and she tasted her a little more.

"It's alright. There's nobody watching," Aurora insisted, and Rua must have appreciated it.

"This is just a kiss goodbye," she insisted after a time, lest Rua think it any more than that. "Just a last kiss," she said, slipping her tongue free once more, swallowing wonderfully, before suddenly standing up awkwardly as though both knew they had made a mistake.

"Just a little thing between girls is all."

She thought of Ferat and giggled. He might have liked that. Less so, if she had come upon Devitt's body and perhaps kissed him once and all.

"It is time to leave, Rua. I do hope my boys don't burn you on the way out," she said, thinking it was a fine goodbye.

She skipped away towards the front gate, her mind

already turning to greater things like bastard dissenters who dared speak against her god. She wouldn't trust it as gospel until she heard it from the mouth of her salivating god. Until then, she simply hoped for more blood and more death and the end of the world for all.

Apart from her and Uden, of course.

She looked back once more to the fine town and thought of its heroic stand. She couldn't help but wonder if she wouldn't once more face ruin upon these stoned walls, and her heart beat in excitement.

Perhaps.

She was one of the first to leave. But that was alright. They would swiftly follow. She'd already given word to her remaining generals that a march would commence long before dawn. There were a thousand miles to trudge, and she was keen to honour her god's wishes.

Back at the camp, she enjoyed regaling the weeping youth with her tales of the final battle. It was something to do as her warriors went about removing all signs of their encampment and preparing for the long march home. After so many months on the march, they knew their tasks, regardless of the fact that they'd lost so many hundreds.

After enjoying the child's misery, despite her insistence that her god would see her true potential, Aurora eventually stepped out into the early morning air and stretched wonderfully.

"You there," she called to a passing soldier with a fine enough jaw and a muscular build.

"Yes, Aurora," he said, bowing, and she was pleased he knew his place.

"Tell me dear... Ferat... what numbers do we have remaining?"

"Excuse me?"

"You are my new Ferat; do not argue." She eyed him with her godly eyes, and he squirmed. It was wonderful, and it was also something to do.

"Listen, little one," she said slowly to the larger brute, who surely must have known how things were done on the march. "You are my dear friend, Ferat… just like the last… Ferat." She took his hand and drew him alongside. "And the one before that," she insisted, and the realisation came upon him more swiftly than it had most of her previous dear friends. "… and the one before that…"

"I see," he said warily, and she was delighted. It was so much easier than taking the time to recruit a hardened general as her own. Or having to build an entire friendship from nothing, all to lose them to a careless battle axe or a wristbolt to the groin. She was a decent judge of character. She eyed him carefully.

Perfect.

She believed this Ferat looked like a right bastard with a cruel, devilish eye. Sometimes, that's all a girl needed in a best friend. It took only a little time and a little teasing, and the finer ones rose to the top.

"As… as… you wish… um… Aurora."

"Call me dear friend," she insisted, and he bowed.

"As you wish… dear friend."

She smiled and kissed him on the cheek. "Oh, I think this will be a most delightful friendship."

———

HERE ENDS THE TALE OF RAVEN ROCK.
BUT THIS WAR IS ONLY BEGINNING.

ALSO BY ROBERT J POWER

The Spark City Cycle:

Spark City, Book 1

The March of Magnus, Book 2

The Outcasts, Book 3

The Actions of Gods, Book 4

Raven Rock

———

The Dellerin Tales:

The Crimson Collection:

The Crimson Hunters, Vol I

The Lost Tales of Dellerin:

The Seven

THANK YOU FOR READING
RAVEN ROCK

Word-of-mouth is crucial for any author to succeed and honest reviews of my books help to bring them to the attention of other readers.

If you enjoyed this book, and have 2 minutes to spare, please leave an honest review on Amazon or Goodreads. Even if it's just a sentence or two it would make all the difference and would be very much appreciated.

Thank you.

ABOUT THE AUTHOR

Robert J Power is the fantasy author of the Amazon bestselling series, The Spark City Cycle and The Dellerin Tales. When not locked in a dark room with only the daunting laptop screen as a source of light, he fronts an Irish rock band, despite their many attempts to fire him.

Robert lives in Wexford, Ireland with his wife Jan, three rescue dogs and a cat that detests his very existence. Before he found a career in writing, he enjoyed various occupations such as a terrible pizza chef, a video store manager (ask your grandparents), and an irresponsible camp counsellor. Thankfully, none of them stuck.

If you wish to learn of Robert's latest releases, his feelings on the Fallout series, or just how many coffees he consumes a day before the palpitations kick in, visit his website at www.RobertJPower.com where you can join The Outcasts. You might even receive some free goodies, hopefully some writing updates, and probably a few nonsensical ramblings.

www.RobertJPower.com

ACKNOWLEDGMENTS

To Jill and Poll - for putting me in my place when I get ideas above my station. Not to mention the incredible support in all my endeavours.

To Paul and Jean – My greatest supporters from the very beginning, when really, you should have been questioning your daughter's better choices. Without doubt the best in-laws a guy could ever have.

To Bren – You keep me on my toes, get me striving for greatness, offer the best advice and the most cutting criticisms. You've earned the right to. Everyone needs a Bren in their lives. They would get so much great shit done.

To Lcass and Darian. One is a nemesis, the other is a hero. Though which one, can change from day to day. From a thousand miles away you guys are always there when I need you most. I'm lucky to call you friends. I'm luckier to hone my craft from just being around you.

To my wonderful editors Jen and Steven whose lives I no doubt make a misery for a few months every year. Thinking about it, I did it twice this year, and yet you still answer my call. The books would never be what they are without your diligence and vast patience. I would be ridiculously lost without your efforts.

And lastly, to my fans.

Thank you. You legends are the best lunatics a writer could ever ask for. Your kind words keep me going in the darkest nights and the sunniest days. This book is for all of you. You better fuken like it.

GET EXCLUSIVE CONTENT

When you join Robert J Power's Outcasts you'll get the latest news on the Spark City and Dellerin series, free books, exclusive content and new release updates.

Find out more at
RobertJPower.com